Praise for *Coming Dawn*

"A deft cat-and-mouse novel that keeps the action moving and the reader guessing."

—*Kirkus Reviews*

Praise for *Deep Sleep*

"Techno-thrillers fans will delight in military vet Konkoly's obvious expertise when it comes to the authenticity and intensity of the numerous action sequences."

—*Publishers Weekly*

"A lively, roller-coaster thriller that moves like lightning."

—*Kirkus Reviews*

"Nobody's better at spy craft, action, and intrigue than Steven Konkoly. Thrilling entertainment from the first to the last written word."

—Robert Dugoni, *New York Times* and #1 Amazon bestselling author of *The Eighth Sister*

"Steven Konkoly has blown my mind! *Deep Sleep* is an intelligent, intense, and completely unpredictable high-concept spy thriller. I'm hooked!"

—T.R. Ragan, *New York Times* bestselling author of *Her Last Day*

"Fast paced, suspenseful, and wildly creative. A modern-day masterpiece of spy fiction."

—Andrew Watts, *USA Today* bestselling author of the Firewall Spies series

"A pulse-pounding conspiracy tale in the finest traditions of Vince Flynn and Nelson DeMille . . . *Deep Sleep* is a must-read roller coaster of a thriller."

—Jason Kasper, *USA Today* bestselling author of the Shadow Strike series

"Devin Gray is the hero we need in our corner. Relentless in pursuit of truth, vindication, and saving his homeland, he is the perfect protagonist for Konkoly's newest dive into the techno-thriller world. Again Konkoly proves his mastery of the genre, drawing from real-rowed events to create a plausible and frightening glimpse into what's happening underneath our feet and behind the walls of power."

—Tom Abrahams, Emmy Award–winning journalist and author of *Sedition*

"Steven Konkoly delivers a conspiracy thriller unlike any other and proves he's at the top of his game. With a deft hand and an eye for plot intricacies, Konkoly will take you into a web of deceit that will shake you to your core and keep you turning until the very last page. The Lost Directorate has set a new bar in the world of thrillers, and Konkoly has taken his seat at the head of the table."

—Brian Shea, *Wall Street Journal* bestselling author of the Boston Crime series and coauthor of the Rachel Hatch series

"A master of action-adventure, Steven Konkoly has done it again, weaving a tale of high-stakes espionage that's ripped from today's international headlines. Plan to stay up very late reading *Deep Sleep*, as he keeps the pages turning!"

—Joseph Reid, bestselling author of the Seth Walker series

"I love a great conspiracy thriller, and Steven Konkoly has conjured one that's utterly chilling with *Deep Sleep*. From the high-stakes setup to the explosive finale, there's barely time to take a breath. Crack this one open and buckle in for one hell of a ride."

—Joe Hart, *Wall Street Journal* bestselling author of the Dominion Trilogy and *Or Else*

Previous Praise for Steven Konkoly

"Explosive action, a breakneck pace, and zippy dialogue."

—*Kirkus Reviews*

"Readers seeking a well-constructed action thriller need look no further."

—*Publishers Weekly*

"If you enjoy action thrillers that have both strong male and female characters, then this may be the series for you."

—*Mystery & Suspense Magazine*

"Exciting action scenes help propel this tale of murderous greed and corruption toward a satisfying conclusion. Readers will look forward to Decker and company's next adventure."

—*Publishers Weekly*

"Steven Konkoly's new Ryan Decker series is a triumph—an action-thriller master class in spy craft, tension, and suspense. An absolute must-read for fans of Tom Clancy, Vince Flynn, and Brad Thor."

—Blake Crouch, *New York Times* bestselling author

WIDE AWAKE

ALSO BY STEVEN KONKOLY

DEVIN GRAY SERIES

Deep Sleep
Coming Dawn

RYAN DECKER SERIES

The Rescue
The Raid
The Mountain
Skystorm

THE FRACTURED STATE SERIES

Fractured State
Rogue State

THE PERSEID COLLAPSE SERIES

The Jakarta Pandemic
The Perseid Collapse
Event Horizon
Point of Crisis
Dispatches

THE BLACK FLAGGED SERIES

Alpha
Redux
Apex
Vektor
Omega
Vindicta

THE ZULU VIRUS CHRONICLES

Hot Zone
Kill Box
Fire Storm

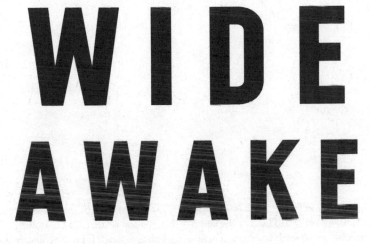

WIDE AWAKE

STEVEN KONKOLY

THOMAS & MERCER

Text copyright © 2023 by Steven Konkoly
All rights reserved.

Published by Thomas & Mercer, Seattle

www.apub.com

Amazon, the Amazon logo, and Thomas & Mercer are trademarks of Amazon.com, Inc., or its affiliates.

ISBN-13: 9781662509230 (paperback)
ISBN-13: 9781662509223 (digital)

Cover design by Rex Bonomelli
Cover image: © YS, © Aaron Foster/Getty Images;
© Sarya Asar / Alamy Stock Photo / Alamy

Printed in the United States of America

*To Kosia, Matthew, and Sophia—the heart
and soul of my writing*

PART ONE

PART ONE

CHAPTER 1

Border Patrol agent Mike Castaneda took his foot off the Chevy Tahoe's accelerator moments before entering the turn, hoping to slow the beast of a vehicle just enough to keep it from rolling off the well-worn jeep trail. *Hope* being the operative term when overdriving this two-ton hunk of metal off road. Reality being the deciding factor.

"Hang on," he said to his partner, Kelly Hazelet, who gripped the front passenger-side overhead handle like her life depended on it.

Castaneda yanked the wheel to the right, sliding into the turn. The heavy chassis leaned uncomfortably to the left for a few moments before the dirt road straightened and all four tires bit solidly into the ground. Convinced that the danger of rolling the vehicle was behind him, he gunned the engine, the Tahoe's V-8 rocketing them toward the cluster of Border Patrol trucks several hundred yards ahead, faster than any vehicle had the right to go on this kind of a ragged, unpaved road—but Castaneda didn't care. Lives hung in the balance.

The "officer down" call had gone out over the radio net several minutes ago, the senior agent present requesting "rifles." The panicked call for help had remained seared into Castaneda's head for the entire drive over.

"Two agents down! We need rifles. We're outgunned. They're all over us!"

A rare twist of coincidence and bad luck had deprived all previously responding vehicles from bringing anything more powerful than a pistol or shotgun.

Castaneda slammed on the brakes when they passed the first parked vehicle, skidding to a halt halfway down the cluster of trucks. Hazelet hit the ground before he shifted the Tahoe into park. He pressed the automatic liftgate button and opened his door, joining her as the rear liftgate slowly rose to reveal a small arsenal in the back of the SUV. Two short-barrel M4 rifles, a full-barrel M14 rifle fitted with a modest scope, two sets of body armor, and spare ammunition magazines.

They dropped into a crouch as automatic gunfire erupted nearby. They remained hunkered down long enough to determine that the bullets fired posed no immediate threat. Hazelet removed a set of keys from a pouch on her patrol belt and went to work on the rifle locks, while Castaneda yanked the body armor to the edge of the cargo compartment and checked the rifle magazine pouches on the tactical vest, verifying that they were full.

An agent wearing a dark-green Border Patrol ball cap slipped between the two nearest vehicles. He recognized the agent as Bob Porter, one of the senior section commanders. Something big must have been going down out here. Castaneda slid one of the tactical vests over his head as the agent approached.

"Thank God you're here! The next closest rifle unit is ten minutes out," said Porter. "We're in a bad way down by the riverbank."

"How bad?" said Castaneda, tightening the vest's straps.

"Two agents down. One critical," said Porter. "We can't get to them. That's the—"

A long burst of gunfire interrupted his sentence.

"Problem?" said Castaneda.

"Exactly," said Porter. "Every attempt to reach the agents has been repelled by heavy gunfire."

"Doesn't sound like rifle fire," said Castaneda.

"Submachine guns if I had to guess," said Porter. "Accurate enough to keep us back."

"Any idea what this is about?" said Castaneda.

Gunfights like this were extremely rare on the border. Most of the northbound foot traffic consisted of migrant workers having spent the last of their money on a coyote to bring them into the United States. The last thing any of them wanted was trouble. As long as they didn't cause a problem for Border Patrol agents, they'd be returned to Mexico within a week. No harm. No foul. They could try again once they saved up enough money.

Even the coyotes avoided direct conflict. They might spend a little longer in a Border Patrol detention facility but would ultimately be sent back over the border—where they'd lead another group of migrants north the same day. Opening fire on US Border Patrol agents signified something different from a standard crossing. Higher stakes for sure.

"No," said Porter, shaking his head. "One of our units spotted the group on the other side. The group was big enough to warrant bringing several vehicles over. Maybe forty migrants in total? I thought I'd keep everyone company. We stayed concealed on this side of the ridge until they reached the US side of the river. Everything went down as usual. Like it always does. Until we rolled down on them. We got halfway before the gunfire started. Evans and Ortega went down right away. They were the closest. The rest of us scrambled back up. We've been trading shots ever since."

"How many shooters?" said Hazelet, handing Castaneda a rifle.

He immediately removed a rifle magazine from his vest and inserted it in the M4 before chambering a round.

"Two that we know of," said Porter. "Located about fifty feet in front of Evans and Ortega."

"What about everyone else who crossed the river?" said Castaneda.

"About half of them have gone back across," said Porter. "The rest are scattered in the brush by the riverbank."

Hazelet joined their huddle. "I'll head west along this ridge for about a hundred yards and crawl into a position where I have a shot. You want to distract them for me?"

"They haven't been popping up long enough to take a shot," said Porter. "Just enough to keep our heads down."

"Kelly. When you're ready, I'll make a run for the two wounded agents," said Castaneda.

Hazelet, twenty years his junior, was a crack shot with the M4. Even if she didn't manage to tag both targets, she'd keep their heads down long enough for him to reach Evans and Ortega. Worst-case scenario—he could administer first aid while she kept the shooters busy. Buy everyone time for the next rifle team's arrival. With four long guns, they should be able to put a quick end to this.

He turned to Porter. "Do you have a trauma medical kit?"

"Hold on," said Porter, taking off.

Castaneda and Hazelet donned their helmets and adjusted the chin straps for a tight fit. Porter returned with an olive drab medical kit the size of a shoebox.

"This should have everything you need to stabilize Evans," said Porter.

"Let's do this," said Castaneda, before patting Hazelet's shoulder. "Shoot straight, kid."

"Run fast, old man," she said, before heading out.

A few minutes later, everyone was in position. Hazelet, lying prone in the bushes along the ridge, sighted in on the target area identified by Porter. Castaneda crouched next to Porter, directly uphill from the two downed Border Patrol agents. Porter strapped the medical kit to Castaneda's vest.

"You're good," said Porter.

Castaneda triggered his remote radio switch. "I'm ready. Tell me when."

A short burst of automatic gunfire cut through the air. A Border Patrol agent lying about thirty feet to their right quickly shimmied backward, bullets thrashing the bushes along the ridgetop above him.

"You sure about this?" said Porter.

"No. But we need to get to those agents," said Castaneda. "Ready when you are, Kelly."

"Ready on three. Two. One. Go," said Hazelet.

The bullets chased him the entire way down, starting the moment he took off. One of them glanced off his ballistic helmet before he'd even crested the ridge. Another struck his chest plate before he fully registered the helmet strike. The rest pounded the dirt around his feet or snapped inches from his face. Somehow surviving the fusillade of bullets, Castaneda slammed into the ground next to Evans and Ortega a few seconds later. He spit out a mouthful of sand and took a moment to catch his breath before bringing his rifle up to search for targets.

Downhill, a man wearing a tan ball cap nestled the stock of a submachine gun against his shoulder, aiming in Hazelet's direction. Castaneda quickly centered the ACOG sight reticle on the man's upper torso and pressed the trigger twice, the rifle's stock biting into his shoulder in rapid succession. The shooter's head jerked backward, a pinkish red mist dissipating in the light breeze behind him. Castaneda scanned the area where the shooter fell, ready to engage the second target.

"Not bad, old man," said Hazelet. "Both targets are down."

Breathing heavy, he responded, "As in permanently down?"

"What other kind of down is there?"

"There are many shades of down," said Castaneda. "Only one keeps me from getting drilled through the head."

"I can confirm they're both down for good," said Porter over the radio. "Two headshots. Nice shooting, by the way. Both of you."

"Porter. If you have anyone up there qualified in field medical trauma, send them my way. I'll leave the kit behind. I want to clear the riverbank."

"Sending a team now," said Porter.

"Kelly. You want to head down and sweep from west to east?" said Castaneda.

"Affirmative. On my way," said Hazelet.

To the west, he caught a fleeting glimpse of Hazelet heading down the ridge toward the river. She moved fast and spry, like someone twenty years younger than him would. Castaneda rose to a knee and surveyed the riverbank below him, seeing nobody. Only two bodies. Across the river, the last of the migrants had returned to Mexico, pulled out of the river by family and friends. Whoever remained below him had hidden themselves well, equally afraid of the shooters in their midst and the Border Patrol agents above them.

He turned to the two wounded agents, whom he hadn't acknowledged up to this point.

"The shooters are down. Help is on the way," he said. "I have to clear the riverbank."

Ortega nodded, visibly trembling. Evans lay on his side, unconscious, blood running down the corners of his mouth onto the sand. Three agents crested the ridge above, headed in their direction.

"Friendlies are headed down the hill," he said, before pushing himself to his feet and heading toward the river.

A few painstakingly tense minutes later, he reached the two shooters' bodies.

"Porter. This is Castaneda. We have a problem," he reported over the radio. "The shooters aren't migrants. They look very Caucasian. As in Casper the Friendly Ghost Caucasian. And that's not all. They're carrying PP-2000 submachine guns. Very fucking Russian. As in—nobody uses these but Russians. They're chambered for standard nine-millimeter parabellum rounds but can also fire a very special Russian nine-millimeter armor-piercing cartridge."

"I remember the bulletin put out on that. Very scary bullet," said Porter.

"I don't think they used those bullets, or I wouldn't be talking to you right now," said Castaneda. "We got lucky today."

"Secure the area around their bodies and don't touch anything. I'm calling in a special forensics team and notifying the FBI. Russians posing as migrants to sneak into the US is bad news."

"The worst kind of news, given what's going on in the world," said Castaneda.

CHAPTER 2

Johan Hendrick rolled his carry-on suitcase through Miami International Airport's baggage claim, headed directly for the exit. The moment he passed through the automatic doors, into the covered passenger-pickup zone, a horn sounded. A quick scan of the taxis, buses, and civilian vehicles jammed into the lower-level "arrivals" area revealed his ride. A black, late-model Range Rover parked two medians away flashed its lights repeatedly. He gave the driver a thumbs-up and cautiously negotiated the crosswalks to reach the SUV.

Miami drivers didn't seem to give a shit about pedestrian laws, even with dozens of cops around. And the absolute last thing he needed was to get tangled up in an accident—no matter how minor. There was no reason to speed up the inevitable. As it stood, his face and name would land on someone's computer screen by the end of the week. Possibly sooner. His connection to the Wegner Group would not go unnoticed. No need to plaster it on every computer screen by the end of the day. Certainly no need to try to explain away his presence in the United States to the FBI from a hospital bed. Not that it would ever get that far.

Given the nature of his true business here, the Russians would have him killed within an hour of arriving at any hospital. He was sure of it. Hendrick wasn't expendable, but he wasn't irreplaceable, either. The Russians might have to search high and low, but for the right price, they could always find another mercenary outfit willing to do their bidding. The right price being the key.

Yuri Pichugin's associate had literally made an offer he couldn't refuse. Nobody in the business turned down a payment that large, unless the proposed work went against every fiber of your being—which it didn't in this case. Hendrick had nothing against the United States as a country. He could take it or leave it. But for the kind of money the Russians had offered him, half of it paid in advance, he was more than happy to help burn America to the ground.

He tossed his suitcase into the back of the Range Rover and got in the front passenger seat, ignoring Paul Bekker's shit-eating grin until they'd cleared the airport. Bekker, the group's second-in-command, had a screw or two loose in a good way. A brilliant tactician and thoroughly competent operator, he lacked a little restraint, both socially and professionally. In other words, he could be counted on to properly shake things up on operations and uncomfortably shake you up in person.

In fact, Hendrick could barely stand to be around him for very long, a testament to the professional soldier's skills. Anyone else who acted this way around Hendrick might find themselves floating face-down in the water—or never to be found again. Bekker was an acquired taste that Hendrick tolerated like bad medicine. He knew it was good for him but wanted to spit it out nonetheless. The sooner he got out of this SUV and put Bekker to work directing the teams, the better. Unfortunately, they had a ten-hour drive ahead of them.

Hendrick preferred to use the same points of entry every time he entered a country, with the express purpose of establishing a well-worn, nonthreatening pattern for authorities. For the United States, he used Miami, Los Angeles, or Dallas, depending on where his work would eventually take him—and drove the rest of the way. He never varied from this arrangement, even if it cost him a ten-hour car ride with Bekker, his worst nightmare.

Under normal circumstances, authorities would note his arrival in the United States with little fanfare or speculation. This trip might be scrutinized a little more closely, given the tensions between Russia and the United States, but it shouldn't ultimately raise any serious alarms. Going dark on the world scene, like most of his team, would have drawn far more attention. Western law enforcement and intelligence agencies liked to keep tabs on Hendrick. Trouble tended to follow him closely. Russian-backed trouble.

"What?" said Hendrick, finally caving to Bekker's deranged glare.

"What do you mean, what?" said Bekker.

"Ten hours. Don't push me," said Hendrick.

Bekker laughed. "I'll be on my best behavior."

Hendrick avoided eye contact. "I won't even try to interpret that. How are the teams looking?"

"One of the container ships got delayed. Arrives tomorrow in the Port of Los Angeles with the rest of the California contingent and their gear. They're looking at about five days after that to take possession of the equipment. The East Coast teams are ready and waiting for orders."

"Five days is too long," said Hendrick. "Any way to speed that up?"

"Not without potentially drawing attention to the shipping container," said Bekker. "Which will draw attention to the ship—"

"And the ship's crew manifest. Yeah. Yeah," said Hendrick. "They'll have to make do with what we can acquire from one of my local contacts. It won't be the highest-end gear, but it's not like they're hitting hardened targets."

"They'll be fine," said Bekker. "They should be able to pull this off with a few knives."

"We won't have the same luxury," said Hendrick. "This is going to be the fight of our lives."

"I guessed as much, given the pay."

"Not all of us will be around to spend it," said Hendrick. "Sanderson's people may be involved."

"You mean Farrington's?"

"They'll always be General Sanderson's people to me," said Hendrick. "And don't even think of going there."

"Going where?"

"You fucking know," said Hendrick.

General Sanderson had rejected Hendrick's application to join his mercenary program back in the early 2000s, after having put him through the wringer in the foothills of the Andes Mountains. No explanation. Not even a proper goodbye. Sanderson's people had unceremoniously dropped him off in Salto, Argentina, with cash in the equivalent of several hundred US dollars and a preloaded credit card with enough to buy a first-class airline ticket back to South Africa. The rejection had consumed him for far longer than he cared to admit.

In many ways, Sanderson had done him a favor. After a few years of self-destructive behavior that nearly got him blackballed from the profession, he cleaned up his act and formed CROWBAR out of pure spite and a burning desire to prove Sanderson wrong. Within a decade CROWBAR had become one of the premier Wegner-contracted mercenary outfits in Africa.

Still, the prospect of laying Sanderson's protégé low appealed to him on every level. He'd love nothing more than to FedEx Farrington's head in a box to that smug son of a bitch.

"We haven't caught a whiff of any of them," said Bekker.

"And we won't, until we're nose to nose with them. Don't lose sight of that. They won't be the first line of defense. They'll be the last," said Hendrick. "Like I said, not all of us will get to see a final payout."

For the first time Hendrick could recall, Bekker looked slightly distraught—which was a good thing. Not only would Bekker be on his toes moving forward, but Hendrick may also have bought himself some peace and quiet for part of the ride.

CHAPTER 3

Yuri Pichugin swung his legs over the side of the rickety cot and prepared to stand. A year in confinement had honed his senses to the point where he could detect even the slightest changes within his small sphere of existence. Something about this felt different. The guard who had approached his cell moved with a purpose, his boots clicking off the concrete floor in a hurry. Whoever opened his rusty cell door within the next few seconds shared a common desire with Pichugin. The desire to spend as little time as possible down here.

The door's observation slot slid open, a pair of eyes scanning the cell.

"Remain seated," barked a voice. "Do you understand?"

Pichugin nodded. "Yes. I understand."

He'd learned long ago to answer the guards' questions promptly and clearly. They'd never beaten or abused him physically, a welcome sign that he'd retained some of his former status as one of the most feared men inside and outside of Russia, but Pichugin's day-to-day comfort in prison waxed and waned based on his own civility.

Hostility or rudeness delayed the delivery of meals or drastically reduced meal quality. The lights would flicker on and off several times during the night, or the portable metal toilet might not be emptied for a few days. His thirty-minute exercise break canceled for some asinine reason.

All minor inconveniences in the grand scheme of things—but why make an already miserable situation any less tolerable? He'd learned early on to control his temper and toe the line. On the rare occasion that he lashed out, his jailers subtly but quickly reminded him of his new station in life.

"I'm going to open this door, and you're going to step into the hallway. Don't do anything stupid," said the guard. "Understood?"

"Yes."

"Looks like this might be your lucky day. I have orders to bring you to outprocessing," said the guard. "But if you fuck with me at all, I'll see that you don't arrive. It won't be such a lucky day. Are we clear?"

He wanted to tell the guard that his release had most likely been ordered by President Putin himself, and that he had no option but to deliver him to outprocessing if he valued his life—but decided against it. Federal prison guards were the dregs of Russian society. The man may not have the reasoning capacity to mentally validate Pichugin's threat, and there was no sense in dragging this out or complicating matters.

"Yes. We are clear."

The door's main locking bolt clanged, followed by two smaller bolts. A few moments later, the heavy metal slab opened outward, squeaking on rusty hinges.

"Step into the hallway."

He did as ordered, placing his hands behind his back to make it easier for the guard to handcuff him. Pichugin kept his head down to avoid the guard's gaze, another trick he'd quickly learned upon arrival. Eye contact never ended well, even if it was accidental or entirely non-adversarial. The guards didn't seem to have the intellectual capacity to differentiate between a sneer and neutral glance, or didn't care—like mean drunks at a bar looking to pick a fight.

"No need for that," said the guard. "You're no longer a prisoner."

Pichugin looked up slowly, still suspicious of this unexpected turn of events. The guard's uniform was pressed and clean, the symbols on his uniform shirt's epaulet indicating a higher rank within the prison system. Boots polished, but not spit shined. Face closely shaved. Crops of hair poking out of his hat around the ears—not the usual buzz cut the dregs sported.

"Thank you," said Pichugin.

"Don't thank me. Thank whoever got you out of here," said the guard, stepping around him. "Stay close behind me. You have friends in high places, but this is the lowest of places—and some of the more enterprising guards can sense an opportunity when it presents itself."

"And what about you?" said Pichugin, ready to offer him a small fortune to ensure his safe arrival at outprocessing.

"I've been compensated in advance," said the guard. "Well compensated—and warned."

"What do you mean by *warned*?"

"All I'll say is that I don't plan on playing any games," said the guard. "Please. Let's move."

Pichugin trailed the guard by a few feet, as they navigated a fluorescent-lit maze of rickety metal stairs, rusty steel catwalks, and cracked linoleum hallways. For all he knew, the guard was leading him to his execution. Though he suspected that if Putin wanted him dead, the president wouldn't have gone through any trouble to keep him alive.

He'd been taken directly from the Israeli ambush on the highway south of Saint Petersburg to an undisclosed medical facility, where doctors treated his burns, and he was allowed to recover—under tight guard and strict isolation. Nothing changed with his transfer to the maximum-security prison. He'd spent the entire time in his cell, except for a daily thirty-minute walk, without the company of other prisoners.

Perhaps for his own safety, which he appreciated, but more likely to keep him incommunicado with the outside world. Pichugin still had a fortune in the real world, and the right word whispered in the right ear could get him out of here. Putin knew that to be true, regardless of the president's iron-fisted rule. But something had changed, and Pichugin was on his way to discovering whether it was for better or worse.

They reached the end of a long, caged hallway, where the guard glanced up at a CCTV camera mounted to the ceiling and held up a badge. A long buzz ensued, and the guard pushed the door inward on its protesting hinges. When it would go no farther without extra effort, he motioned for Pichugin to step inside. The moment of truth. He stepped hesitantly past the guard, watching him for any subtle movements that might suggest an imminent execution, before entering a dimly lit room, with a table in the middle—his most trusted friend sitting on the other side of it. Boris Gusev rose with a grin.

"You're alive, my friend!" said Pichugin, making his way around the table.

Gusev was more than just a friend. He'd run Pichugin's sleeper network from a secure operations center on the outskirts of Moscow until the Israelis drove a truck bomb into the facility. He'd never heard from Gusev after the explosion and had assumed the worst. His presence in this room could mean only one thing. He'd managed to salvage the remains of the sleeper program and sell it to Putin, thereby securing Pichugin's release. He bear-hugged Gusev, keeping him ensnared in his embrace long enough to whisper in his ear.

"We're back in business?" said Pichugin.

"Yes. But we shouldn't talk about it here," said Gusev.

"Where's here?"

"Novosibirsk," said Gusev.

Their backup facility was located in Novosibirsk, at the heavily fortified campus that housed the VECTOR Institute for Virology and Biotechnology.

"How far are we from—"

"Please. Let's take this conversation elsewhere."

"Okay," said Pichugin.

Gusev glanced furtively around the room, his eyes stopping on the guard—who stood just outside the thick metal door, pretending to mind his own business.

"There will be no second chances. I've been assured of this," said Gusev.

"Then we better get to work," said Pichugin.

Gusev backed up a few paces, avoiding eye contact. Pichugin's survival instinct, dulled by the year he'd spent in monotonous captivity, kicked into full gear.

"Tell it to me straight," said Pichugin.

"Fuck," muttered Gusev. "It's more of a fine-tuning job at this point. All of the wheels have been set in motion. I had no choice."

He didn't like the sound of that at all. Irrelevance was the quickest way to an early grave in this business. Gusev must have read his mind—or the look on his face.

"I refused to pull the trigger unless they released you," he said. "And put you back in charge."

Pichugin grinned despite his misgivings about the situation. "Then we better not waste the opportunity."

CHAPTER 4

Karen Thayer pushed one of the thick horizontal aluminum slats down an inch and peeked through the venetian blinds at the house across the street. Congresswoman Margaret DeSoto emerged from the shadow of the garage, pulling a suitcase to the back of the Volvo station wagon parked halfway down the driveway. Karen had been watching DeSoto and her husband slowly load the car for the past hour, presumably headed back up to her district in Maine for summer recess. Praise small miracles!

A full month of peace and quiet on Kipling Street. The town of Derwood receiving a temporary reprieve from the twenty-four-hour media coverage and nearly daily protests that followed this nasty woman and her family wherever she traveled. Ironically, Karen had nobody to blame but herself for the around-the-clock nuisance that plagued the neighborhood.

DeSoto had rented the house through an intermediary three years ago, maintaining a low profile and keeping to herself. For the first three months after they moved in, nobody in the neighborhood had any idea that public enemy number one had taken up residence among them. "DeSatan's" husband took care of the kids, rarely interacting with the neighbors, while everyone just assumed that the suit-clad woman delivered home by town car or black SUV every night, when she wasn't out of town on a business trip, was just another Beltway power broker or lawyer. She wouldn't be the first or the last suit to take up residence in a quiet suburb outside of the fray.

But one evening, while watching coverage of a protest outside the Supreme Court building on Patriot News, something clicked for Karen. The woman shaking her fist and spitting vitriol against the most consequential Supreme Court decision of the century looked a lot like the woman who lived across the street. A few days of binocular surveillance from one of her kids' upstairs bedrooms confirmed it. Margaret DeSoto, the progressive socialist who stood for everything wrong in this country, lived in their neighborhood—and nobody knew it. And not just in the neighborhood. Right across the damn street with her devil's brood!

Without thinking, Karen got on the TrueAmerica Network and started spreading the word. By six o'clock the next morning, she understood her mistake. Their normally quiet and idyllic street teemed with reporters and patriotic protesters. Her husband, Jerry, had to wait close to fifteen minutes for news vans to clear enough space for him to get out of the driveway. He wasn't pleased with her at all, but the damage was done, so they made the best of it.

Between household chores and homeschooling the kids, she'd join the small group of die-hard protesters gathered on the street, sometimes bringing the family along for some hands-on education. Things got especially heated around the last election, when counterprotesters showed up, so they kept the kids inside most of the time. But over the past several months, interest in DeSoto had somewhat fizzled on Kipling Street. The remote location, lack of any meaningful access to the representative, and Congress's shifted focus to Russia and NATO combined to normalize attention.

She was mostly glad things had simmered down, but a part of her didn't want DeSoto to have a moment's peace in life. Her own inconvenience felt like a small price to pay to make the congresswoman's life miserable.

DeSoto's family filed out of the garage toward the station wagon, each of them depositing their suitcases behind the vehicle before getting into the back seat. DeSoto's husband emerged with two duffel bags, which he dropped next to the suitcases, before kissing his wife's forehead. The two of them finished loading the family's luggage into the back, rearranging everything two or three times before finally closing the rear liftgate. The husband, her emasculated lackey, headed back into the garage, presumably to check the thermostat, check the back door—the usual final acts before departing on vacation. Were they really leaving for the entire month? Karen felt ecstatic, a burst of energy outward from within. Clearly a divine energy. Or a sign? A sign. Of course!

"Kids!" she said, directing her voice toward the kitchen.

She'd left her four perfect angels, ages five, six, seven, and eight, dining on Eggo waffles at the kitchen island. And not the whole-wheat "woke" version. Nor did they slather them in vegan butter or organic maple syrup from Maine, of all places. Their kids would grow up on Mrs. Butterworth's syrup, a perfect substitute for Aunt Jemima, which the woke mob had canceled a few years ago. They all came running into the formal living room—eager to please.

"Mrs. DeSatan and her pack of demons are leaving for the month!" she said. "Why don't you give them a nice farewell. Just make sure to stay on our yard. Don't go into the street or they might run you over and say it's your fault."

The kids took off in a ruckus of chants and cheers, each of them randomly grabbing the dozen or so signs Karen had made for them. The words didn't matter when it came to kids. Just the fact that they were out there exercising their First Amendment right against an agent of Satan was all that mattered. The kids had gathered with their signs at the edge of the street by the time DeSoto's husband emerged from the garage. He paused next to the front driver's-side door and shook his head before getting inside the station wagon and shutting the door.

Karen raised the shade behind the living room couch and removed her cell phone from her back pocket, thinking about how proud her parents would be if they could witness this moment. She'd missed the perfect opportunity to FaceTime and show them how brave their

21

grandchildren were. But all was not lost. She quickly navigated to Facebook and tapped "Live Video," keeping the phone aimed at her children.

The scene was perfect. DeSoto's stupid, angry face visible through the windshield. Her husband looking equally as disgruntled and disturbed. It didn't take much to "own" these people. They pretty much just owned themselves day in and day out. All it took was a few kids with poster-board signs. Talk about fragile. The Volvo eased out of the driveway, turning as it entered the street. Her kids chased the station wagon as it straightened out on Kipling Street, staying on the grass as they walked to the edge of the yard.

"Here's my kids owning the—"

The Volvo and her children disappeared, the picture window directly in front of her exploding inward. Karen inexplicably remained upright, her glass-shredded hands still aiming her phone toward the street. A few moments later, when the dust and debris from the blast cleared, she was left with an image that the entire world would witness within the hour. A completely gutted, flaming Volvo station wagon chassis, rolling to a stop against the bumper of a parked local news channel van—four bloodied, pajama-clad bodies strewn across the grass in the foreground.

CHAPTER 5

Karl Berg shot up from his desk, having seen enough to make his case to Audra Bauer. The convergence of events couldn't be ignored any longer. Especially considering the elevated level of "chatter" the NSA-DEVTEK team's signal-snooping algorithms had picked up over the past week. The chatter itself hadn't risen to a level of concern, but combined with the reports he'd curated from intelligence bulletins, he strongly suspected they had a serious issue on their hands.

And if there was one thing he'd learned from more than thirty years of service at the CIA, much of it spent inside this building, it was to trust his suspicion of patterns. The problem rarely jumped off the pages—or the screen, in this case—and punched you in the nose. It gently massaged your shoulders while you sat at your desk, whispering assurances in your ear. *You're reading too much into this. Do you seriously want to risk your career bringing this to your boss? I'm sure you're familiar with the fable of the boy who cried wolf. If everyone jumped at every little mixed signal, the agency would be paralyzed.*

And on and on, until the Real Time Social Media Surveillance Warning Network that "doesn't exist," according to the government, informs you that ninety-three people have been killed or wounded by multiple shooters at an ABBA cover-band concert in suburbia—ten minutes before it hit the Law Enforcement Major Incidents Warning System and twenty minutes before any news outlet reported it. Nope. Berg recognized this shoulder massage for what it was—which was why he was headed to Audra Bauer. He'd almost reached her office when Dana O'Reilly, the sole FBI agent assigned to the Joint DEEP SLEEP Task Force, stepped in front of Bauer's door, blocking him with a feigned smile.

"Dana," he said.

"Karl," she replied. "Headed to the boss's office?"

"What makes you think that?"

"I don't know," she said. "Maybe the 'oh shit' look on your face."

"Just checking in."

"Uh-huh," she said, nodding. "What pushed you over the edge? The DeSoto car bombing or the two Russians snuffed out by Border Patrol?"

O'Reilly didn't miss a beat, which was why he'd personally requested her presence on the task force.

"Actually, the arrival of Johan Hendrick in Miami—compounded by several facial-recognition hits on key members of his mercenary team in the DC area—tipped the scales," he said.

"Johan Hendrick, the founder of CROWBAR?"

"The same. We have an assassination team in town."

"We do," said O'Reilly. "But there's always an assassination team or two in town. Right?"

"Of course," said Berg. "It's DC."

"Do you need me in there to help you convince her that this is different?"

"I don't think it'll be necessary," said Berg. "The evidence speaks for itself. But don't stray too far. Just in case."

"You know where to find me," she said, before heading back to her office.

Berg chuckled. "Hey. Dana?"

She stopped and looked over her shoulder. "Yes?"

"Thank you for this."

"For what?"

"Being a good sport about all of this," said Berg. "Your presence here, while somewhat unorthodox, is highly appreciated. By me at least. I know this isn't a choice assignment for you—"

"What makes you say that?"

"I don't know," said Berg, shrugging. "I just figured—"

"You figured wrong, good sir," said O'Reilly. "Not only do I get paid extra for being here, but we've made a measurable difference over the past year. Rooting out the remains of an extensive, long-dormant sleeper network sure as hell beats the shit out of what I was doing for Ryan Sharpe before all our paths crossed again. And I say that having nothing against Ryan Sharpe. He's top-notch in my book."

"He's top-notch in all of our books, and he knows a good agent when he sees one," said Berg. "Hey. Let's grab some coffee after this. My treat."

"The benefits of being banished to Langley never end," said O'Reilly.

"Funny," said Berg, before knocking on Audra Bauer's door.

"Come in," said Bauer.

Berg opened the door and stepped inside. "Hope I'm not interrupting anything."

"Since when?" she said.

"Am I that transparent?"

"Only ninety-five percent of the time," said Bauer. "Shut the door and grab a seat. Looks like we have a possible problem on our hands."

"There goes my song-and-dance routine," said Berg.

"It's just too much for us to ignore when combined like this," said Bauer. "The elevated chatter is one thing—this is another. I've notified all the direct players. MINERVA. DEVTEK. The Senate select committee investigating DEEP SLEEP. They've been put on notice that we may be looking at another undiscovered sleeper-network activation or some kind of short-sighted, less-than-discreet revenge sanction against the US."

"Nothing about DEEP SLEEP was short sighted," said Berg. "Whatever they're up to right now has been in the works for a long time. Probably from the beginning."

"I hope you're wrong," she said.

"Me too," said Berg. "But it's better safe than sorry. We all learned a painful lesson ignoring Helen Gray."

"Not as painful as it could have been," said Bauer. "More like— should have been. We can't afford to make another mistake in this arena. The Russians have been awfully quiet in the light of the massive embarrassment we caused them on the world stage."

"Not to mention the economic fallout," said Berg. "Which economists think has cost Putin close to half of his two-hundred-billion-dollar net worth. Not a loss he's likely to take in stride."

"And then there's the upcoming election," said Bauer. "His iron-fisted control has taken a severe hit according to our analysts. He'll very likely still squeak through and win the election, but that kind of erosion of power will cost him even more of his net worth. His value is almost entirely built on his ability to enrich others. If that power founders, so does his value. And with nearly all his money outside of Russia locked down and unavailable to him, he's at the mercy of the next president."

"The next president won't let him run loose for very long," said Berg. "Which is why I'm very worried. Whatever they have planned for us is all or nothing. He's at the end of his rope."

Bauer's desk phone rang, startling Berg. That was his frame of mind right now. Highly anxious. As much as he wanted to downplay this gut-feeling paranoia, he couldn't shake it. Something was in the works, and they needed to get ahead of it—if that was even possible at this point. She answered the call, putting it on speaker.

"Audra Bauer. You're on speaker with Karl Berg in the room."

"Perfect. Karl needs to hear this," said a familiar voice. "We got your data packet and concur with your assessment. But there's more.

Fucking way more. Can you assemble the entire task force for a video call? We're kind of freaking out over here."

Bauer nodded at Karl, giving him permission to take over.

"Devin. This is Karl. We're sort of freaking out here, too, which is why we sent you the data packet," said Berg, lying about being a part of the data packet transfer. "But when you say there's more, what are you talking about?"

"The DeSoto car bombing wasn't a car bombing," said Devin. "It was a drone attack."

"Wait. This was reported as —" started Berg.

Bauer cut him off. "Devin. We'll be ready in ten minutes."

"Thank you, ma'am," said Devin, pausing for a few moments before continuing. "Have you notified Senator Steele's select committee?"

"Yes. They received the same data packet and assessment. But I can't include them in the video call," said Bauer. "Lawyers on both sides agree that direct planning or coordination between the Intelligence Community and Congress is a slippery slope. A bad idea, essentially. We'll provide them with a transcript of the call within an hour of its completion."

"Understood," said Devin Gray.

"Devin?" said Berg.

"Yes?"

"Please follow protocol on this. Don't reach out to Marnie until Steele's office officially receives the transcript," said Berg. "Things have slowed down here to the point where we may have to justify our continued existence. Let's not give the red-tape-spreading bean counters a reason to shut us down."

"Copy. See you in a few," said Devin, before leaving the call.

Bauer chuckled. "He's probably on the phone with Marnie right now."

"Yeah. And I don't blame him," said Berg. "I'll rally the troops."

"I'll take care of that," said Bauer. "Get with O'Reilly and ask her to contact the agent in charge of the investigation into the car bombing—ASAP. My gut tells me they've probably reached the same conclusion as Devin by this point, but they're dotting their *i*'s and crossing their *t*'s before passing something that scary up the chain of command."

"The implications are truly frightening," said Berg.

"More than frightening," said Bauer. "Game changing."

CHAPTER 6

Devin Gray took a deep breath before nodding at Brendan Shea, who clicked his laptop's computer mouse a few times to connect their conference room, deep within MINERVA's headquarters, with the joint task force housed even deeper within Langley. A few moments later, Karl Berg, Audra Bauer, Dana O'Reilly, and a small collection of DEVTEK and NSA faces appeared on the screen. Bauer nodded before kicking off the meeting.

"It sounds like this meeting comes as no surprise to any of us," said Bauer. "Simply put, the likelihood of recent events being a coincidence is nearly nonexistent. We're looking at the start of something. The first big question is—What are we looking at? The second is—How do we stop it before it gets going?"

"If we're not already too late," said Devin. "Do you mind if I share our thoughts? Brendan and I have been brainstorming this for two days straight."

"The floor is yours," said Bauer.

"Before I start," said Devin. "Special Agent O'Reilly. Did you manage to glean any new information from the FBI investigation into the DeSoto killing?"

"Yes," said O'Reilly. "This is obviously for our eyes and ears only right now. Understood?"

Everyone signaled their understanding through a series of nods and muttered *yeses*.

"The lead investigator told me that DeSoto's Volvo station wagon was hit by an explosive drone. They're still analyzing the pieces and explosive residue, but the initial blast pattern conforms with what the military calls a loitering munition—or, in plain speak, a kamikaze drone."

"Jesus," said Berg. "This is a worst-case scenario."

"Let's not jump to any conclusions yet," said Bauer. "It may be a one-off."

"Razorblade 800 series?" said Devin.

"They haven't determined the model or payload of the munition," said O'Reilly.

"Why do you think it's a Razorblade?" said Bauer.

"It's impossible to say for sure until the FBI finishes their analysis, but Brendan and I have watched hundreds of Ukrainian-uploaded drone-attack videos out of the Donbas region, and they look the same. The US has supplied Ukraine with hundreds of these drones. Both the 400 and 800 series. The explosive power of the DeSoto bombing very closely resembles the 800 series."

"Could it be a Russian drone?" said Berg. "Something smuggled into the country?"

"We've scoured the web for Russian videos of their KYB drone—and the explosive profile doesn't match. The KYB payload is about seven pounds of high explosives. The Razorblade 800 series utilizes the equivalent of an anti-armor warhead, like the Javelin missile. Around twenty pounds."

"I know I'm probably going to regret asking this question, but how can you tell the difference between the effects of a Razorblade 800 and KYB on a civilian vehicle?" said Berg.

Shea answered the question, having done most of the research and legwork into drones over the past twenty-four hours.

"By the adjacent collateral damage and the impact crater left behind on the street. Normally, an 800 series would be used against an armored vehicle, even a tank. The 800 series warhead is modeled after an anti-armor warhead, like the kind used in a Javelin missile. Enough to penetrate the top armor, which is normally the weakest on any armored vehicle. This results in a mission kill. If the target isn't destroyed outright, enough of the tank's turret or armored vehicle's troop compartment is wrecked to send it back for critical repairs."

"They used this against a Volvo station wagon?" said one of DEVTEK's software people.

"Yeah. And when you hit a civilian car with an 800 series, you basically vaporize the guts of the car. Plus, there's no armor to slow down the explosion, so you get a crater in the street underneath the vehicle—leaving nothing but a burned-out chassis behind, like we saw here. The KYB isn't an anti-armor drone munition. It's more of a multipurpose platform. Antipersonnel. Anti–lightly armored vehicle or structure. The KYB would have gutted DeSoto's Volvo, but it wouldn't have left a crater in the road. And it wouldn't have killed the four kids across the street."

"Overkill," said O'Reilly.

"Big-time," said Shea. "They could have killed DeSoto and her family with a 400 series, which means whoever did this either *only* has access to the 800 series Razorblade, or they wanted to send a message. Or both."

"A gruesome message," said Berg.

"Which we need to decipher, immediately. So where do we go from here?" said Bauer. "The floor is still yours, Devin."

"We need to get in touch with AeroDrone, the maker of the Razorblade, and the team in the Department of Defense responsible for shipping the drones to Ukraine," said Devin, "to figure out if we're looking at a few Razorblades captured by the Russians on the battlefield in Donbas and shipped here, or if an entire shipment has been somehow diverted into Russian hands. MINERVA will initiate a Title 93 National Security Inquiry at AeroDrone."

A Title 93 NSI gave MINERVA, empowered by Bauer's DEEP SLEEP Task Force, the right to engage any public or private corporation, business entity, or "individual business interest" in a sweeping personnel investigation, with the express purpose of uncovering potential foreign sleeper agents. Failure to immediately comply—*immediately* defined as three business days—could result in a suspension of any government-contracted or affiliated work. The definition of *work* applied ultraliberally.

Companies with no direct ties to the government were pressured in different, but equally effective, ways. The first threatened tactic being to go public with their refusal to comply. To date, no business or individual had resisted full cooperation. Nobody wanted to be viewed by their consumers as complicit in Russian spying.

"I'll sign it and get it back to you as soon as I receive it," said Bauer. "We need to hit the ground running on this. What else?"

"We should probably talk about adopting an enhanced security posture," said Devin. "We have a Wegner-affiliated, South African death squad on US soil, Russians sneaking over the border, and kamikaze drones killing Russian-unfriendly politicians. It's not hard to imagine that this task force will be targeted at some point."

"There's really no mechanism for that," said Bauer. "Other than individual caution."

"MINERVA can provide countersurveillance," said Shea. "Assuming there's some wiggle room in the task force budget."

"There is. And if it's not enough to cover everyone directly involved with the task force, I'll wrangle it out of the agency later," said Bauer.

"We can also provide a little bit of direct protection, but that's not our area of expertise," said Shea.

"I'll reach out to Richard Farrington," said Berg, "and see if we can add a little more muscle on the protection side—until we get a better handle on what we're facing."

"Special Agent O'Reilly?" said Devin.

"Please call me Dana," she said.

"Sorry. Dana. Any more word from Border Patrol on the two Russians popped at the border?"

She shook her head. "No. I submitted the information request that you gave me and haven't received a reply."

"What were you looking for, Devin?" said Bauer.

"This may sound strange," said Devin. "But I was looking for a detailed description of their physical attributes. Stuff like dental work, pictures of the palms of their hands and the bottoms of their feet."

"Why?" said Berg.

"It all goes back to the drones," said Devin. "If the Russians have somehow managed to get their hands on more than a few Razorblades, if they've somehow diverted a large shipment meant for Ukraine with the help of a sleeper inside AeroDrone, they're going to need drone operators. Lots of them. And not just any drone operator. They'll need to find operators willing to kill American citizens and train them on the Razorblade system. My guess is they had to recruit them in Russia, train them extensively, and sneak them into the US."

"So you're looking for tech-savvy Russians, who probably came from middle-class families," said Berg, nodding in approval. "Soft hands suggesting no real hard labor in their life. Same with their feet. No calluses, corns, or signs of prolonged marches suggesting military service. Decent dental care. Nothing special, but not the usual abject neglect. Not bad, Devin. If you ever want to cross over to the dark side, I think we can find you a place at Langley."

"I'll keep it in mind," said Devin.

"Devin isn't going anywhere," said Shea. "We'll see to that."

"It's not always about the money," said Berg, jokingly.

"Not always. But in this case," said Devin. "Maybe."

They all had a quick laugh before O'Reilly brought them back into focus.

"I'll get on the phone as soon as we're done here," she said.

"Thank you," said Devin. "I hope I'm wrong. I hope these guys' hands and feet resemble battle-hardened GRU Spetsnaz. I'd rather we have a few hundred ground agitators in our midst than a few hundred Razorblade-trained drone operators."

"A few hundred?" said one of the DEVTEK representatives.

"For every one Russian we randomly catch entering the US, we have to assume a lot more got through," said Devin. "Don't forget to factor in the Canadian border and the coastlines, arguably easier entry points. We have to assume that they've planted a small army of some type in the US. If the two guys killed by Border Patrol look more like potential drone operators than Spetsnaz operatives, I think it's fair to assume we have a drone problem on our hands."

"Cheery assessment as always," said Berg.

"What can we do about Hendrick and his mercenaries?" said Bauer.

"I passed everything we have to Ryan Sharpe," said O'Reilly. "He submitted a surveillance package request, but it's been met with some resistance."

"Can't he just authorize a surveillance task force?" said Berg.

"Yes," said O'Reilly, pausing for a few moments. "But he made the erroneous assumption that his request would be rubber-stamped. He didn't want to sidestep his new boss, who is a little more cautious when it comes to these things."

"God. I miss Fred Carroll," said Berg. "He should have been director."

"He should have taken better care of himself," said O'Reilly. "The stroke fairy doesn't care how good you are at your job."

"What are we looking at in terms of getting the surveillance package approved?" said Bauer.

"Warrant applications. Legal review," said O'Reilly. "Director Davitt is a real stickler for procedure, and he hates the CIA, NSA, or any agency not under his direct purview. Particularly any agency operating within the US, which he considers to be his exclusive domain."

"So he's not a big fan of the DEEP SLEEP Task Force," said Bauer.

"No. But he's not politically or institutionally stupid enough to fuck with us directly," said O'Reilly.

"Then we don't bother with Davitt anymore," said Devin. "We do this mostly outside of the FBI. No offense, Dana."

"None taken. I agree wholeheartedly," she said. "This is too abstract and fluid for the FBI."

"Then we're more or less on our own for now," said Devin.

"For now," said Berg. "Let's focus on providing countersurveillance services and limited physical security to the task force through MINERVA, while I explore options to expand on that security via trusted and reliable allies. Once we lock down our own security situations, we can look for ways to start tracking Hendrick's crew. It's the best we can do under the circumstances—given our official charter. The task force was empowered to hunt down any remaining Russian sleepers, not tackle an entirely new mess. All we can do is raise the alarm, and hope someone listens—while putting our own off-the-books plan into motion."

"Business as usual," said Bauer.

"Unfortunately," said Berg. "Devin. Can you reach out to Senator Steele's office through Marnie and see if they might be able to nudge the new FBI director in the direction of assisting our task force? All we'd be asking for is some help finding and tracking a known Russian-affiliated assassination team. Nothing big."

Devin laughed. "Yep. Just a small ask. I'll get in touch immediately. My guess is that Senator Steele has some pull at the DOJ. Not to mention that she probably won't be too thrilled to learn that the same Russians might have access to the kind of kamikaze drones that can take out an armored SUV—like the kind she's driven around in."

"Make sure you highlight that last point," said Berg. "Nothing motivates like a little self-interest."

"Any last comments or observations?" said Bauer.

Nothing.

"Stay available," said Bauer. "But most importantly, stay safe."

A few moments later, the screen went blank. Shea confirmed that the audio and video had been cut before speaking.

"They had no idea how bad the drone situation could be," said Shea.

Devin shook his head. "No. They didn't, which doesn't surprise me. Given Berg's background, which I can only assume is the same for Bauer—they tend to focus exclusively on the ground assets. In this case, their attention would have been drawn to Hendrick and his team, plus the Russians at the border—but only in the context of possible street-level saboteurs. It's the way they've been taught to think, and for them, hostile assets are walking, talking, stabbing, poisoning, or shooting their way through missions and objectives. We're looking at something entirely different here. More of a hybrid approach. If I had to guess, I'd say DeSoto was both a practice run and a warning."

"A warning about what, though?" said Shea.

"Maybe a warning to back off?" said Devin. "I don't know. Maybe DeSoto was up to something behind the scenes that scared the Russians. She's not on the joint congressional committee, but she's one of the more vocal members of Congress when it comes to halting Russian aggression."

"She's also a very polarizing figure. Ultraprogressive. Influential. Social media savvy," said Shea. "Maybe there's more to this than a warning or practice run. Look at the news. The response from the Left has been measured enough, but tensions are building. If I were going to try and ignite a civil conflict, DeSoto's assassination would have been at the top of my list."

"Fuck. Don't even say that," said Devin. "I hadn't thought of it that way—but it does make the most sense. Why else would they be doing this? Go big or go home, right?"

"Exactly," said Shea. "And if Russia is somehow back in the business of internally fucking with America, they're not going to tiptoe around this time. They're going to hammer us, from multiple angles, using whatever they have left. And whoever they managed to sneak into the country within the last few weeks. Or months. They'll look to create the kind of chaos they're famous for."

"I really wish you didn't make so much sense," said Devin.

"Tell that to my wife," said Shea. "Speaking of ball and chains, figuratively and not literally—you better call Marnie."

"Good qualifier," said Devin. "I'd hate to see you swimming back to shore on Saturday."

Shea looked conflicted. "Do you really think a weekend sail is still in order—given the circumstances?"

"I can't think of a safer place than out on the bay," said Devin. "But I hear you. We'll have to give it some thought."

CHAPTER 7

Marnie Young stared at her cell phone for a few seconds, torn between one of several DEEP SLEEP committee memos she needed to finalize for Senator Steele and a call from Devin. Part of her said that the call could wait. They'd have plenty of time tonight, over takeout from the Thai place down the street, to discuss the day's events. After sweeping their town house for bugs—a nightly ritual Devin insisted upon, despite all the hidden tell-tales that he left behind to determine whether anyone had broken in to install listening devices. Not to mention the cameras and microphones, both obvious and hidden, which she insisted he deactivate the moment he got home.

She understood his paranoia and did her best to tolerate it. Given what Devin's mother had unveiled and they had unraveled over the past year, a big part of her thought she should just embrace it as a part of life. But at some point, for this to truly work between her and Devin, he had to let go. They couldn't live like their every movement, conversation, or facial expression might be under scrutiny. How could anyone live like that?

Marnie had fallen in love with Devin long before they reunited at his mother's wake, and Devin had confessed the same not long ago. The two of them had never stopped thinking about each other, regardless of where their careers had taken them. They'd moved into a downtown Annapolis town house shortly after thwarting Russia's plans to invade Estonia, with the intention of eloping in the early fall—and celebrating their marriage with family and friends a month later somewhere on the Chesapeake Bay. *Somewhere* being the operative term. Devin didn't want to announce the location until they'd eloped, which was still a few months away.

Secrecy over every aspect of their life had consumed him. Maybe he was right, given their line of work, and the circumstances surrounding Congresswoman DeSoto's murder. But she couldn't live like this forever. Or a decade. Or even another year. They had to find a better balance, sooner than later. MINERVA was basically spook central for the CIA's DEEP SLEEP Task Force, and her position as special congressional committee cochair investigating DEEP SLEEP put her right in the thick of the administrative side of the conspiracy. She could do another year of this. Maybe. Before they had to make some kind of switch to a normal life.

Marnie answered her phone. "Hey, babe. What's up?"

"What's the committee's read on the DeSoto bombing?"

Time for a reset.

"Oh. My morning's going well. Busy with some reports for the senator," she said. "What about you? How is your day going?"

"Point taken. Sorry," said Devin. "It's just that we've come across some information that changes the game, more or less, and I'm a little agitated."

"No. It's my bad. You've been incommunicado at MINERVA for thirtysomething hours straight," she said. "I should have guessed something big was up."

"It's not your bad. I should have called earlier," said Devin. "It's just been hectic. So . . . about the DeSoto bombing? Sorry. We're operating under a time crunch."

"Understood. It's uh . . . complicated," said Marnie. "Which I'm sure comes as no surprise to you."

"No surprise at all."

"Most of the committee wants to believe she was targeted for her pro-NATO stance, but she's only one voice of many. And only one vote. Some are thinking it's an intimidation tactic," she said. "Which is reverberating through the committee. It's had a chilling effect."

"I don't doubt it," said Devin. "Targeted assassinations tend to do that. How is Senator Steele reacting?"

"Outwardly unfazed. Defiant. Her usual approach to threats," said Marnie.

"Good for her," said Devin. "But behind the scenes?"

"She's enhanced security for the committee and her staff," said Marnie. "I'm allowed to drive myself home tonight, but moving forward, I'll be picked up and dropped off by an armored SUV."

Devin's silence unnerved her.

"What?" she said.

"I'm just glad to hear they're taking this seriously," he said.

"Whatever," she said. "What's really up?"

"I just got off a teleconference with the CIA task force, which included input from the FBI investigation into the DeSoto killing," said Devin. "And the assessment has changed rather drastically."

"How drastically?"

"The FBI hasn't confirmed it yet, but DeSoto's Volvo was hit by an 800 series Razorblade kamikaze drone."

"What? No," said Marnie. "That can't be right."

"That's why I've been gone for the past day and a half. Brendan and I have watched every video posted online that features these loitering munitions."

"The Razorblade's an American drone," she said.

"Correct," said Devin. "Which is why we're very concerned. Either the Russians captured a few in eastern Ukraine, or one of their undiscovered sleepers diverted several hundred to the Russians—to be used against targets here. Brendan and I are headed over to AeroDrone's headquarters in Arlington to start digging into their employees and shipment manifests."

"Sounds like our weekend plans are off," said Marnie.

They'd planned a Saturday sail on the Chesapeake with Brendan Shea and his wife, Nancy. Ten a.m.–ish departure. Light lunch from the cooler and a cocktail or two on the water, before returning for buckets of Old Bay–seasoned crabs, french fries, and ice-cold beer at Cantler's upon return—whenever they'd had enough of the summer sun.

Devin's mother's sailboat, *Sadie*, had become a regular part of their life over the past year. They'd taken sailing lessons together toward the end of last summer, while Frank, the boatyard's owner, refurbished the boat. When *Sadie* was finally seaworthy, by early fall, they'd put their newly acquired skills to the test for a month or so, until the weather stopped cooperating and the air turned cold. Every sail on the bay had challenged their relationship in some way, unexpected twists and turns bringing out the best, but mostly the worst, of them.

Each time they returned to the marina after a day or weekend out on the water, Frank met them dockside with a seasoned, skeptical eye. By the end of their first, abbreviated season on the water, he unceremoniously declared, out of nowhere during a walk down the pier, that "they would make it." According to Frank, if a couple is still holding hands at the end of their first day out on the water, they're in good shape. If they're still holding hands at the end of a sailing season—they're good until the end of time. Marnie felt the same way.

"I don't see any reason to call Saturday off," said Devin.

"You're not worried about getting hit by a kamikaze drone out on the bay?"

"Not really," said Devin. "If they wanted to take us out that badly—they would have used them already. My guess is that they either don't have enough to spare, or they do, and they have other plans for them."

"Cheery thought," said Marnie.

"I'm far more concerned with the South African murder squad on US soil," said Devin. "Which is why I called."

"You didn't call to see how I was doing?" said Marnie, feigning dismay.

"I love you, and would have gotten to that eventually," said Devin. "But I kind of need a favor."

"Uh-huh. Related to Johan Hendrick?"

"Yes. I'm afraid he's come between us, my love," said Devin.

"Oh brother," said Marnie, laughing. "What do you need?"

"The FBI hasn't responded to the task force's request for resources to track Hendrick. Apparently FBI Director Bryan Davitt isn't a fan of the CIA, but he is a fan of bureaucratic stalling—a bad combination considering the task force's request. Is there any way you might be able to convince Senator Steele to nudge her DOJ and FBI allies to expedite the process? The sooner the FBI starts babysitting Hendrick and his crew, the better. I'm sure they don't want a repeat of last year's Baltimore fiasco."

"None of us do," said Marnie, remembering how they had barely escaped an attack that nearly leveled half a city block. "I'll get together with her chief of staff and see what we can do. How many mercenaries is the task force tracking?"

"Thirteen. Which means more like thirty. On top of the Russians that are probably sneaking over the border and entering our ports as we speak," said Devin.

"Any more information on the two Russians killed at the border in Texas?"

"No. Dana O'Reilly is reaching out to Border Patrol to ask some specific questions that I gave her," said Devin.

"Specific questions?"

"Without going into the details again, I'm concerned that those Russians may have been drone operators. I hope I'm wrong, and they were just Russian GRU saboteurs."

"I can't tell if that's a joke or not," said Marnie.

"It's not," said Devin.

"Shit," said Marnie, immediately understanding what he meant.

Russian ground agents were bad enough, but if Putin was assembling an army of drone operators in the United States, the implications were staggering. The consequences unthinkable.

"I'll press the case," said Marnie. "Are you sure you don't want to reconsider Saturday's plans?"

"We'll be fine," said Devin. "If the threat assessment changes between now and then, we'll cancel Saturday—and take Farrington up on his offer to use his safe house in Anacostia. We can move your parents and my dad there at a moment's notice."

"I wish we could move them there now, as a precaution," said Marnie.

"I agree," said Devin. "We're opening a line to Farrington and his crew on my end. Let me see what I can arrange. For all of us."

"Damn it," she hissed. "Do you really think something big is going down—again? I thought we delivered a kill shot last year."

"That's what we all thought," said Devin. "But all signs right now suggest we were wrong. Or at the very least, we underestimated the Russians' ability and willingness to strike again."

"Fucking Russians," said Marnie.

"My thoughts exactly," said Devin. "Now I know how my mother felt for most of her life."

"Right," said Marnie, not sure what to add to Devin's statement about his mother, so she went with a subject shift. "I'll be home tonight around seven. Do you think you'll be able to break free tonight?"

"Yeah. I'll be home around the same time. Maybe closer to eight," said Devin. "Do you want me to pick up food on the way home?"

"Thai food, please," said Marnie. "The usual."

"Will do," said Devin. "I'll let you know if anything big comes up today."

"Same here," said Marnie. "Love you."

"Love you, too," said Devin, before the call ended.

Marnie took a deep breath and massaged both of her temples. This was going to be a long day. She picked up her office phone and pressed the button that directly connected her with Julie Ragan's phone.

"What are we looking at?" said Senator Steele's chief of staff.

"Worse than we thought," said Marnie. "Can you wrangle Senator Steele for about ten minutes? Devin's task force needs her help."

"I can give you five minutes," said Ragan. "Starting in like thirty seconds."

"That's plenty. Thank you," said Marnie, before disconnecting the call.

She got up from her desk, which was jammed into a narrow doorless and windowless space half the size of a typical home's powder room—and made her way down the hallway toward the senator's inner sanctum. The offices increased in size as she drew closer, their occupants glancing up at her with a thinly veiled disdain.

Marnie's sudden addition to Senator Steele's staff last year had ruffled a few feathers in the office, particularly since she had an unusual amount of access to the senator for such a junior staff member. Steele was one of the more approachable lawmakers on the hill, but Marnie's role as direct liaison between the DEEP SLEEP special committee and the CIA's DEEP SLEEP joint task force put her in contact with Steele or her chief of staff multiple times a day.

To make matters even more uncomfortable for her, most of the staff in the senator's office had no idea why the newest member of the team had the kind of access that had taken some of them over a decade of service to the senator to achieve. The special committee's existence was still classified top secret. Only Marnie, Julie Ragan, Deputy Chief of Staff Mark Esperanza, and the senator knew of its existence. Since working on the special committee was her only responsibility for now, even if someone warmed up to her in the office, she couldn't talk about her work.

The final straw alienating her from the rest of the staff was the common bond she shared with Julie Ragan, who was a former Navy

F-18 pilot. Since Marnie served as a former Marine helicopter pilot, it was fair to assume that most of the office thought she'd been hired on Ragan's recommendation because of their common background— which was partly true.

Kerry Burke, the senator's communications director, got up from her desk and rushed into the hallway to intervene as Marnie approached Senator Steele's closed conference room door.

"The senator is—"

"Waiting for me," said Marnie, opening the door without knocking.

Her attitude didn't always help the situation, either, thought Marnie, before closing the door behind her.

CHAPTER 8

Devin followed Brendan Shea into the glass-encased conference room, where they took a seat at a long Scandinavian-style, teak conference table and waited silently for several minutes—until a small delegation of six AeroDrone employees arrived and took seats on the other side of the table. The glass walls surrounding them turned opaque with the press of a remote-control button, which one of their hosts produced from a concealed table drawer in front of his seat.

There was no need for introductions. AeroDrone brought the same six people every time. Danny Mohr, chief operating officer; Wendy Piret, chief legal counsel; Ron Williams, human resources; Dmitry Anastas, head of cybersecurity; Kathy Stull, chief Department of Defense liaison; and a project engineer who rarely said a word, Mike Seeberger. Devin suspected few of them would have anything to say today. The legal implications of an 800 series Razorblade having been used in the DeSoto attack were staggering. The survival of the company could be at stake.

The looks on their faces ranged from unreadably neutral to vaguely disinterested. In other words, nobody was happy to see them. Which was generally understandable given the power vested in MINERVA by the US Intelligence Community's Title 93 charter. They had the authority to turn a business inside out looking for foreign sleeper agents. In reality that wasn't how MINERVA operated. Working in tandem with DEVTEK cybersecurity specialists, they conducted discreet, top-to-bottom personnel sweeps, which included digital file reviews and in-person interviews.

The real anxiety for a company centered on the stigma of MINERVA was rooting out a sleeper. If they identified a foreign agent's presence, past or present, the company was required to notify all their customers of the breach, whether it directly affected the customer or not. This kind of disclosure tended to have a chilling effect on future government contracts. Companies had permanently gone out of business because of these disclosures.

Discovering a sleeper agent was a bittersweet moment for the MINERVA team. For smaller businesses, it often meant the death of the company, and the loss of dozens, if not hundreds, of jobs. Nobody welcomed them with open arms. Today was no exception. Danny Mohr shrugged.

"What's up?" he said dourly, immediately setting the tone for the meeting.

"How do you want it?" said Shea.

"Right between the eyes," said Mohr.

Shea glanced at Devin and nodded.

"We strongly suspect that an 800 series Razorblade was used against Congresswoman DeSoto," said Devin.

None of the AeroDrone people blinked or stirred for several moments, until Mohr turned his head toward Wendy Piret and made a subtle head motion. Piret quietly sighed before nodding back at Mohr, who put both of his elbows on the table and rubbed his chin with his hands. Devin felt like he was watching a prearranged theatrical production. Shea started drumming his fingers on the table. Ticktock. Shea's timing was impeccable as always. His fingers drew all their gazes.

"We're looking into it," said Mohr. "We agree that the explosive profile and fragmentation pattern appear similar to the effects of an 800 series Razorblade."

"Can you better define *looking into it?*" said Shea. "And I'm not trying to be an asshole. I'm trying to be expedient. We're tracking a few very likely related national security concerns. This is our task force's top priority. Bottom line? We need to know if a shipment of your drones has been somehow misappropriated or if we're looking at a few drones captured in Donbas and shipped to the US."

"Understood. We're already deeply exploring the first scenario," said Mohr, frowning. "But it's a complicated situation. We used to supply the Department of Defense with the Razorblade drones, and they sent them to Ukraine and a few dozen other US allies. However, over the past few months, the DOD has asked us to ship directly to the Ukraine Defense Ministry."

"I guess that's understandable," said Devin. "Cuts out the middle-man. Who pays for the drones?"

"The Department of Defense," said Mohr. "But like you said, bypassing DOD red tape puts the drones in Ukrainian hands almost a month faster. It's a win-win for everyone."

"Should make your chain of custody easier to follow, too," said Shea.

"Exactly," said Mohr. "We fly the shipments direct to Ukraine, with multiple AeroDrone safeguards in place. From the factory to delivery in Lviv, each shipment is watched nonstop by a four-person AeroDrone team. They have all been involved in previous DOD-supplied ship-ments, so they'd know if something smelled fishy on the receiving end. No anomalies have been reported."

"But you're starting there," said Devin. "Because it represents the greatest liability for AeroDrone."

"Precisely," said Mohr. "If we have a sleeper who somehow diverted kamikaze drones to the Russians right under our noses, that's the end of AeroDrone. If the DOD has a sleeper in their midst, we can survive the fallout."

"I don't fault your thinking," said Shea. "But given the circum-stances, we'll have to embed a full team inside AeroDrone. MINERVA and DEVTEK. The whole nine yards. Sorry."

"No need to apologize," said Mohr. "We vetted the entire com-pany with your help several months ago, and fully implemented your protocols. My money is on this being an isolated attack using a drone stolen from the battlefield in Donbas, but better safe than sorry. What can we do from our end with the DOD?"

"I think you should have Ms. Stull start applying some pressure to the DOD team responsible for coordinating the delivery of your drones to the Ukrainians," said Devin. "We'll be working that from our end, too. It sounds like it's very unlikely that the shipments were initially delivered into the wrong hands, but the road from Lviv to the battlefront in Donbas is a long one. If a shipment disappeared on that road, we might need the DOD to contact their Ukrainian counterparts down the line."

"How many drones have you delivered to Ukraine over the past year?" said Shea. "Ballpark figure."

Mohr glanced at Piret, who reluctantly nodded. "Close to four thousand, split sixty-forty between the 400 and 800 series."

"That's a lot of drones," said Devin.

"They have a lot of targets," said Mohr.

"I don't doubt it," said Devin. "Have you delivered any to the Baltics?"

Once again, Piret acquiesced with a curt nod.

"No. But we keep a DOD-approved, ready shipment of two hundred 800 series Razorblades in our main production facility, to be sent at a moment's notice," said Mohr. "In case Russia decides to take another swing for the fences up north."

"If you visited the Razorblade production facility right now, would you be able to lay eyes on that shipment and verify that it still contained two hundred drones?" said Devin.

"I personally made the trip to Texas yesterday," said Mohr. "I had our people open the packed shipment crates and count the pieces. All two hundred are accounted for. We're being proactive about this."

"I don't doubt it. We'll see you Monday morning, with our entire investigative team, and help you dig as deep as necessary to get to the bottom of this. Hopefully it's a one-off thing. A few drones captured by the Russians from a Ukrainian drone team," said Shea.

"Fingers crossed," said Devin. "For everyone's sake."

"I suggest you spend the weekend looking into every shipment delivered directly by AeroDrone to Ukraine," said Shea. "Grill the team assigned to watch over the shipments for any irregularities, no matter how trivial they may have seemed at the time. Start building an extensive list of contacts in the DOD and Ukrainian Defense Ministry—anyone that has anything to do with arranging and supplying these drones to Ukraine. Reach out to them immediately. Who handled the drone training for the Ukrainians?"

"The Department of Defense, supported by a few of our technical advisers," said Mohr. "Training was conducted near the Ukraine border, in Poland."

"Talk to your technical advisers and have them reach out to these DOD trainers. The trainers will have contacts in the Ukrainian Army. From the actual drone operators to the field commanders that decide how and where to employ. They need to get in touch with these people and press the importance of this issue. They're looking for anything that might indicate a missing shipment," said Shea. "Maybe one of the field commanders had an unexplainable delivery delay? Or the count came up short? Even the smallest detail might lead us in the right direction."

"We'll get started right away," said Mohr. "Nine o'clock on Monday?"

"Perfect," said Shea, turning to Devin. "Anything else you can think of?"

"No. We'll hit the ground running on Monday," he said.

"I'll walk you out," said Mohr.

"Do you need me to accompany you?" said Piret.

"I'll be fine," said Mohr.

AeroDrone's chief legal counsel didn't look happy to let him out of her sight—in their company. Nobody said a word until the elevator door closed, ensuring some semblance of privacy for Mohr.

"What does your gut tell you about this?" said Mohr.

Devin glanced at Shea, who nodded.

"The Russians are up to something bigger than a single assassination. There's more that you're not seeing," said Devin.

"The border incident?" said Mohr.

"Among other things," said Devin.

"We're looking at too many Russian-connected coincidences for the DeSoto killing to be an isolated attack, which is why we're coming down hard on AeroDrone," said Shea. "A couple hundred of your drones in the wrong hands spells disaster."

"Yeah. That would be a nightmare," said Mohr. "I'll make sure everyone takes this deadly serious. We'll work all weekend, day and night, to get as far along as possible before you arrive on Monday morning. The last thing any of us wants is for our drones to be used against US citizens on US soil, or anywhere."

"AeroDrone has been a critical and reliable Department of Defense provider for decades. You've turned the tide of battles and saved countless lives with your technology," said Shea. "The last thing we want is to rock that foundation, but we have to figure out how one of your drones was used to kill a member of Congress—and figure out if this is the end or just the beginning of the mayhem."

"Jesus," muttered Mohr. "We've been so careful. This is just unbelievable."

Mohr looked shaken, and not in his usual *How does this impact the company?* sort of way. The man appeared genuinely devastated on a personal level, the poker face he presented in the conference room apparently displayed for everyone present, not just Devin and Shea. The elevator door opened, revealing the three-story, glass-and-steel-beam modernist-styled lobby they'd traversed less than a half hour ago. Shea patted his shoulder.

"We'll see you Monday morning," said Shea.

"Yep. Monday," said Mohr.

Devin shook the chief operating officer's hand before they both stepped off the elevator. They didn't say a word to each other until they were back at MINERVA, located just a few miles south of AeroDrone's world headquarters in Arlington, Virginia. Shea drove his SUV into the MINERVA parking garage and proceeded to the bottom level, where he pulled into a fluorescent-lit, two-vehicle-deep metal shipping container in the center of the vehicleless parking area.

A rolling metal bay door slammed shut behind them the moment their rear bumper cleared the entrance. Shea stopped the vehicle in the middle of the bay and killed the ignition, leaving his remote key fob in one of the cup holders. They got out, leaving their doors open, and made their way to the rectangular outline of an exit door embedded in the wall directly in front of the SUV. Devin shook his head as Shea rolled his eyes.

Unsurprisingly, MINERVA took corporate espionage seriously—but almost to the point of the ridiculous, hence the requirement to "sanitize" after meeting with clients. Especially clients with hundreds of millions of dollars, or potentially billions, on the line under MINERVA's Title 93 authority. The "Scrub Tank," their current location, had been installed a few weeks after MINERVA had been made an integral part of the US Intelligence Community's DEEP SLEEP Task Force.

The overall process was interesting, to say the least. Motion detectors had surveilled the entire garage since the ground-level door opened, scanning for drones that may have either followed the vehicle back or micro-drones that detached from the vehicle upon arrival. The last thing they needed was a garbanzo bean–size micro-drone flitting around inside MINERVA and reporting their every move to one of the companies under investigation.

Vehicles returning from meetings entered the Scrub Tank, where a team of countersurveillance gurus sanitized the vehicle of electronic surveillance devices. Once "scrubbed," the vehicle would be returned to the employee's assigned parking space. Of course, the vehicle wasn't the only subject of the countersurveillance team's scrutiny. A voice echoed through the metal container, followed by a mechanical clang.

"Step inside the locker, please."

Shea and Devin proceeded through the rectangular metal hatch that had slowly swung open in front of them. They removed their clothes and footwear, down to their underwear and undershirts, and hung everything on the hooks embedded in individual upright cubbies. They left their shoes and socks on the floor in front of the cubbies.

Two men entered a few moments later and spent the next several minutes examining their outfits and personal effects by hand and by electronic wands, before clearing them to dress and proceed to the next station. Protocol stated that they wait until they had passed through the final checkpoint before discussing anything related to any of their clients.

The final checkpoint consisted of an airport-styled millimeter-wave scanner, which was rumored to be several times more sensitive than what the TSA used. Supposedly, they were safe. Fortunately, they passed through the Scrub Tank far less frequently than airport scanners. Most of the companies they investigated didn't warrant such an intrusive scan. AeroDrone was different, due to their primary products Drones.

Once they cleared the circular time-portal-like millimeter-wave scanner, Devin and Shea immediately went to work on the most pressing issue ahead of them.

"Are we still on for tomorrow?" said Shea.

"It might be our last chance to kick back for a while," said Devin. "Ten a.m. departure?"

"Sounds like a plan," said Shea. "What do you need me to bring?"

"Just Nancy," said Devin. "Unless you have any drink or food requirements."

"Nope. We'll drink or eat anything," said Shea.

"Then we'll see you around ten," said Devin, before glancing at his watch. "Still a few hours to burn."

"Get out of here," said Shea. "There's nothing else for us to do at this point. I plan on heading home as soon as my car is cleared."

"Are you sure?" said Devin. "I'm happy to keep digging."

"I'm sure," said Shea. "It's in AeroDrone's hands for now. We start earning our paycheck on Monday."

PART TWO

CHAPTER 9

Devin pulled the dark-blue Sunbrella cover snugly into place over the mainsail and zipped the two connecting ends around the aluminum mast before he made his way back toward the cockpit. Marnie had minded the helm while he struck the mainsail, keeping the boat as steady as possible. Not a big challenge today. The only thing she had to watch out for was a wake stirred up by an inconsiderate motorboat driver.

This morning's light breeze, a hopeful sign as they pulled away from the dock, unceremoniously died by noon, leaving them at the mercy of the late June sun— and the mid-Atlantic region's infamous humidity. Devin wasn't sure which was worse, but he was certain that the combination of the two made for a hard day on the water. The water as flat as glass, they turned south and motored along at a few knots, creating enough artificial breeze to keep them from sweating through their shirts. But not enough to stop the beads of sweat from building on his face. He stepped down into the cockpit, under the shade of the bimini, and used the bottom of his shirt to wipe the latest sheen clear.

"Sorry about the heat," said Devin, taking a seat. "We can turn back anytime and cool off in Cantler's. There's no shame in it. This isn't an endurance contest."

Nancy, Shea's wife, piped up immediately. "I'm totally fine. This is Maryland in the summer, and we're out on the water. It's a gorgeously hot day."

They all laughed.

"I'm stealing that," said Marnie, her attention focused ahead of the boat. "But seriously. This heat warrants a redo, regardless of whether we head back early or not. It's usually not this brutal. The maritime forecast had the usual winds out of the south to southwest at around three to four knots. Enough to putter along and stay cool."

"It's really not that bad. The cold drinks are keeping me alive," said Shea.

"Or numbing you to the heat," said Devin.

"Could be that, too," said Shea, reaching for the cooler bungee-corded to the helm stand. "Speaking of which. Can I refresh anyone's drinks?"

"I'm good for now," said Marnie. "Someone has to drive."

"I'll take a tall boy," said Devin. "One of the hazy IPAs."

"They're all hazies," said Shea.

"What can I say?" said Devin, taking the ice-cold can Shea had fished out of the cooler for him. "I'm partial to New England IPAs."

"Honey?" said Shea, glancing at his wife.

"A pinot refresh would be nice," said Nancy, before finishing the remaining sip left in her plastic cup and handing it to her husband.

"The pinot is in the built-in cooler next to the sink," said Marnie. "Just down the ladder. You may as well bring up the bottle. I think we made enough room in the cooler up here to fit it in."

Shea gave the cup back to his wife and headed below. "Be right back."

Devin cracked open his can and took a quick swig before glancing past Marnie at a bowrider in the distance. The boat had essentially remained in the same spot, relative to the sailboat, for the past hour. Not exactly suspicious behavior on a day like today. The bay was packed with boats, from fishing skiffs to luxury cruising motorboats, and many of them were pointed south—cruising lazily along. Just something to keep an eye on.

"What's up?" said Marnie. "You got that look on your face."

"It's nothing," said Devin.

"Always on the lookout," said Nancy. "Brendan's the same way. When we go to a restaurant, I just tell him to take a minute to get it out of his system. Scan the guests. Watch the servers. Then knock it off."

Marnie laughed, shaking her head. "Sounds familiar."

"I'm not that bad," said Devin.

"You might be worse," she said. "I think I'll try Nancy's strategy the next time we're out."

"How is Nancy trying to corrupt you?" said Shea, suddenly appearing in the hatchway leading into the main cabin.

"She was just explaining how she gives you a minute to settle your countersurveillance mind when you're out at a restaurant," said Marnie.

"Oh. It never really settles. I just pretend so she'll still go out in public with me," said Shea.

They all had a good laugh at Shea's confession, while he refreshed his wife's glass. He nestled the bottle in the cooler and sat down next to his wife.

"What got you talking about countersurveillance?" said Shea.

"I caught Devin eyeballing a boat," said Marnie.

"It's not like I was trying to hide it."

"The Yamaha bowrider at our five o'clock?" said Shea.

"See?" said Nancy.

Marnie started to turn her head.

"Don't look," said Devin. "Ninety-nine percent chance it's nothing. But if it's something, we don't want to give them a heads-up that we're alerted to their presence."

"If you have a pair of binoculars, I should be able to glass them from inside the cabin without them seeing me," said Shea.

"I don't think we—" started Devin.

"I'm not going to be able to relax until one of you takes a look," said Marnie. "The binoculars are in the cabinet under the chart table."

"I got it," said Devin. "I started this."

Shea opened his beer. "No argument from me."

Devin climbed down the short ladder and retrieved the binoculars from the navigation station. He stood on the portside settee, as deep inside the cabin as possible. Even if the occupants of the bowrider had a pair of binoculars pointed right back at the sailboat, they'd never see him. The contrast between the dark cabin and bright exterior would keep him concealed. He raised the binoculars and peered through the opening that led up to the cockpit. He was aligned perfectly to see over the stern of the sailboat. Unfortunately, the Sheas were blocking his view.

"Marnie. Can you turn us about five degrees to port?"

"Helm, aye!" said Marnie. "Coming to port!"

Smart-ass. The view through the hatch slowly drifted, bringing the distant motorboat into view. Devin adjusted the focus and watched the bowrider for a good half minute, not seeing anything particularly worrisome. He got down from the settee and made his way back up into the cockpit, placing the binoculars on top of the cooler.

"Well?" said Marnie and Shea at the same time.

"Four guys out fishing and drinking from what I can tell. None of them paying any unusual attention to the sailboat," said Devin. "Still. Could be anything."

"That's reassuring," said Marnie.

"If they didn't raise your hackles, I think we can relax," said Shea, before opening the backpack lying on the cushion next to him to briefly expose the metal grip of a holstered pistol. "And it's not like we're helpless."

"There's a stainless-steel Mossberg shotgun down below that shares your sentiment," said Devin.

Not to mention the compact Sig Sauer pistol on his right hip— concealed under his short-sleeved, bright-red Hawaiian-themed shirt.

"Oh brother," said Marnie.

"Oh brother is right," said Nancy, before raising her cup. "Cheers, everyone. Thank you for a wonderful day on the water."

"Thank you for joining us," said Marnie. "I just wish it wasn't 'melt your sunglasses to your face' hot out here."

Shea placed his ice-cold beer can against his face. "Life could be worse."

"To first world problems," said Devin, clinking the Sheas' drinks with his can.

Shea started to lift his can toward the cup of ice water Marnie held in her hand, but Devin stopped him.

"The ancient Greeks used to toast the newly dead with water. It was a tribute to the river that took them to the afterlife," said Devin. "Toasting someone alive with water was considered bad luck, particularly if you're on the water. I'm pretty sure the US Navy forbids it."

"The squids are superstitious like that," said Marnie.

"Well. We wouldn't want a misfortune to befall us," said Shea. "Marnie. Can I get you something less risky to drink?"

"I'm okay for now," said Marnie.

"I can steer for a while if you'd like to chill with a beverage less likely to offend the gods," said Devin.

"In that case," said Marnie, stepping aside. "I stand relieved."

She gave him a quick peck on the lips as she slid by him to take a seat on the cushions directly across from the Sheas. Devin handed her his beer. The Coast Guard aggressively patrolled the more crowded waters of the upper Chesapeake Bay, in what seemed like a futile attempt to reduce the number of boating accidents per season. Excessive speed and alcohol being the most lethal combination out on the water.

Speed wasn't an issue with a sailboat, but open alcohol containers drew the Coast Guard's attention, regardless of the vessel's maximum capable speed. They played it safer than most on the bay. No drinking at the helm, and two at most for the entire outing. She took a long drink and nodded her approval.

"Wow. This is ridiculously good," said Marnie. "Like orange juice."

"Paul came through with another delivery," said Devin. "Their juiciest hazy IPA."

"To say it's drinkable would be an understatement," said Shea.

"Have you come across any alcohol you wouldn't consider drinkable?" said his wife.

"No. What's your point?" said Shea.

They all had a good laugh, while Devin resisted every urge imaginable to look over his shoulder at the Yamaha bowrider a few hundred yards behind them. Nothing about the men on the boat suggested a problem, but he couldn't shake the general feeling of unease slowly smothering him. Maybe he should be looking skyward for drones? A quick glance at the sky was allowed, right?

"Any seagulls up there?" said Shea.

He looked down and met his colleague's glance, which suggested he chill out. Easier said than done. Devin eased the wheel to the left, swinging them gently to port, with the intention of seeing how the bowrider reacted. Shea raised an eyebrow, subtly shaking his head. Devin just shrugged. Old habits die hard, and in their line of business, kept you from dying even harder.

CHAPTER 10

Felix Orlov wiped the sweat from his face onto the sleeve of a light-blue polo shirt he'd purchased at a Target store in Annapolis less than three hours ago. Everything his crew wore right now, from top to bottom, had been acquired in a panic-induced shopping spree after receiving orders at 8:23 to report to a marina in Eastport by 10:00 a.m., dressed like respectable boat owners.

That had been the most difficult part. Switching out of the body-odor-laden, raggedy-ass clothes his team of dregs, murderers, and scum had been "released" in. Orlov and twelve other Russians had been ripped from their mildewy, un-air-conditioned cells—somewhere in the swamp-infested American South—and flown by private jet to Baltimore/Washington International Airport in the middle of the night.

Upon landing, they were given keys to a few rooms in a nearby hourly rate motel, enough cash to stuff their faces at the Denny's across the street, and the keys to three rental cars that would be delivered to the motel "when their mission crystalized." Basically, they had been freed from a most uncertain purgatory, on the presumed condition that they successfully execute one more mission for Yuri Pichugin, to earn their freedom. Or, at the very least, not to be sent back to their cells in the middle of fucking nowhere.

A fair deal, given that Devin Gray and his associates had outmaneuvered the mercenaries placed under Orlov's command three times last year. What was the American saying? Three strikes and you're out. In Russian mercenary circles it was more like—one strike and you're dead. The fact that he had been kept alive was testament to his previously unblemished record of work on behalf of Yuri Pichugin. Either that or his benefactor needed bodies to throw at a problem. A distinct possibility that had obviously crossed a few of his prison mates' minds.

Two members of the team decided in the middle of breakfast to take their own chances. They wolfed down half of their food and got up together, walking out of the restaurant without saying a word to Orlov or anyone else. Their bodies were discovered in the bathtub of one of the motel rooms after the rest of the team returned from breakfast—a single gunshot to each of their foreheads.

Fools. Orlov had no delusions about entirely breaking free and clear of Pichugin's grasp. Not for a while, at least. The oligarch's reach had proved to be unexpectedly far-reaching and surprisingly well connected. The man had the kind of reach to put him in a Russian-run prison in the middle of the United States!

Within minutes of being driven away in a police van from the Miami high-rise that Devin Gray had assaulted by helicopter, Orlov had been transferred into "federal custody." The Miami Police Department van transporting him to the police station downtown had been stopped a few blocks away from the high-rise by a rough-looking team of ATF agents, their leader stating that they had taken control of the high-rise investigation due to the automatic weapons and explosives found in the building.

The police officers offered little protest in the face of the heavily armed team of federal agents, releasing him into their custody without even calling their sergeant to question or report the transfer request. Maybe they took one look at the rogues' gallery slowly circling the van and accurately assessed the situation—choosing to survive their shift instead of dying in a hail of bullets. Orlov couldn't blame them. He would have done the same.

His captors, a hastily assembled team of Russian Mafia–affiliated contractors, informed him a few minutes after the transfer that he'd been rescued by Pichugin, after which they promptly pulled a black hood over his head and bound his wrists and ankles. At some point several hours later, he was given a sedative. Orlov woke from the drug-induced slumber in his new home, a six-by-eight-foot rusty jail cell with a dull stainless-steel toilet, a brownish-yellow-stained sink, and a metal bedframe topped with a thin foam mattress. If Pichugin had the kind of power and reach to run his own prison inside of the United States, Orlov stood little to no chance of ever escaping the man's grasp.

No. He'd have to work his way up the ladder again, until he'd redeemed himself in Pichugin's eyes. Then—and only then—would he be able to negotiate a departure from Pichugin's employ. If that was what he wanted. At this point in his mercenary career, where the hell else could he go?

Earning a top contractor slot again within the Wegner Group might be the pinnacle of whatever career he could salvage at this point. It was either that or work security at a Black Sea resort on the Russian coast— at a quarter of his previous pay. Not an option. Not after he'd enjoyed the perks of being on top for close to a decade. Whatever Pichugin wanted from him today, he planned to deliver. Orlov didn't care if it cost everyone on his team, including himself.

This would be his last chance at whatever redemption lay ahead of him—and he planned to make the most of it. Orlov eased the throttle into neutral; his plan was to drop back a few hundred yards, maybe farther, before matching the sailboat's speed. The subtle maneuver would hopefully disarm any suspicion that Devin or his colleague had developed over the past hour. Not that it really mattered.

Orlov had enough manpower and firepower at his disposal to take out Devin Gray within a moment's notice. His coconspirators, Marnie Young and Brendan Shea, were the icing on the cake, so to speak. The kind of sweet icing that Yuri Pichugin might decide would warrant Orlov's promotion out of purgatory. Then again, his minders must know who's on the boat. Everything about this morning had been planned to the finest detail. From the three boats provided to his crew at the Eastport dock, to the weapons already stowed on board, to the communications gear passed along to each boat to ensure a coordinated attack against Devin Gray when given the order. He was just a pawn in whatever move Pichugin planned to make this morning. A hit man delivered to his target's location and handed a loaded gun.

CHAPTER 11

Karl Berg jolted awake in his chair. Eyes wide and body rigid. His right hand nearly tipping his one-third-full coffee mug onto his keyboard. He shook his head and rubbed his eyes. *Why the hell was he here on a Saturday?* Oh yeah. Because he was a paranoid mothereffer who had nothing better to do. A bad combination given the reports that had reached the DEEP SLEEP Task Force's desk over the past week.

A flurry of activity in his peripheral vision shifted Berg's attention to the task force's main floor. The other paranoid em-effer with nothing better to do was headed in his direction—in a hurry. Dana O'Reilly looked as serious as he'd ever seen her, which prompted him to sit up and check his computer. Shit! The DC Joint Regional Intelligence Center's Facial Recognition Division had just sent a priority message.

Felix Orlov, the Wegner Group–affiliated mercenary involved in every attack against Devin Gray to this point, had been spotted on an early-morning train leaving Washington, DC's L'Enfant Plaza, headed east on the Orange Line, toward Annapolis. Confidence ninety-eight percent. There was no doubt that Orlov was headed in Devin Gray's direction, the mercenary's presence cementing all Berg's fears. The Russians were back in business in the United States—and they fully intended to remove any possible obstacles to their new plan. He picked up his phone, seeing the same warnings. O'Reilly burst into his office a few moments later, holding up her phone.

"We need to trigger CITADEL protocols—now," she said.

She was right. Orlov's presence in the greater DC area officially tipped the scales. The risk of an attack against members of the task force was high. Activating the CITADEL protocol would compress the entire East Coast task force into BASTION EAST, one of several secure facilities (SFACs) in the United States used to support and potentially house the president of the United States during national emergencies.

Berg, Devin Gray, and many of their DEEP SLEEP allies had spent several hours at this facility last year, assembling the foundation of a plan that would eventually stop Yuri Pichugin's attack against Estonia in its tracks. The facility had been made available to them again by Senator Margaret Steele, as an absolute last-ditch backup plan. Initiating CITADEL carried some risk. If this turned out to be a false alarm, they risked losing the privilege of using the site.

He didn't think this was an overreaction. Far too many unnervingly lethal factors had materialized in the past few days to leave anyone on the task force exposed any longer. The use of the facility today might represent the difference between life and death for many members of the task force—and the difference between success and failure in stopping Pichugin's latest attack against the United States. Better safe than sorry.

He tapped a seemingly innocuous app on his phone and entered a six-digit passcode before selecting CITADEL-ATTACK PROBABLE from a short array of options. The emergency alert system, created by Anish Gupta, sent repeated text messages and voice mail calls to every phone or device registered by members of the task force—relaying Berg's warning. Within moments, everyone should be on high alert for a possible attack.

Key members of the task force would be instructed to report to any of three locations in the Washington, DC–Baltimore area, where they would be met and taken to the CITADEL by a Department of Homeland Security Protective Detail. CIA officers would be instructed to remain at their current locations, where they would be met by CIA protective agents, who would bring them to one of the three locations. On top of that, he had some contract muscle watching over Devin, Marnie, and their families. Berg hoped none of it would be necessary.

"I'll call Audra to give her a heads-up," said O'Reilly. "Who else?"

"I got everyone else here," said Berg. "Can you cover the West Coast?"

"Should I call Devin's sister, Kari, directly or get in touch with Decker first?" said O'Reilly.

"Decker first. I kind of put a thing or two into play over the past few days—out of an abundance of caution. He'll need to get in touch with the people he has watching over them," said Berg. "Then call Kari and tell her to stay put until she's contacted by Decker's people. She'll recognize them. And make sure she keeps her dad from freaking out. He should be in the apartment. He's sleeping on her pull-out sofa. Don't ask me how I know that."

"You're CIA. I just assumed that you knew everything," said O'Reilly.

"I wish," said Berg, dialing Devin Gray's satellite phone. "Get moving on those West Coast calls."

"On it," she said, starting to leave—before pausing in the doorway. "Do you want me in or out of here?"

"Grab your shit and get over here," said Berg. "It's you and me saving the world right now."

CHAPTER 12

Audra Bauer's phone vibrated and audibly pinged at the same time. *Now what?* She checked the screen. CITADEL. Holy shit. The doorbell rang a few moments after she read the brief contents of the DEEP SLEEP Task Force's update. They'd have to be extremely cautious if Pichugin's people were posing as cops or federal agents. Her husband walked into the kitchen, holding his phone.

"Someone's at the door," he started. "Could be our extraction team."

She didn't think so. Not that quickly. Audra put her index finger to her mouth before showing him her phone. David read the alert, muttering a few obscenities.

"I'll be right back," he said.

David vanished for several seconds before reappearing with his cherished Benelli semiautomatic, pistol-grip shotgun. They huddled together, out of sight of the front door.

"I see badges," said Audra, checking the Ring app on her phone. "But I don't see how a response team could have gotten here that quickly. The CITADEL alert hit the network just seconds ago."

From what she understood about the CITADEL contingency plan, a four-person tactical team would be sent from Langley to escort them to their assigned rally point, before transporting them to BASTION EAST. Since it could take them up to fifteen minutes to arrive, the nearest available police units would be dispatched immediately, under the highest Department of Homeland Security threat protocols, to guard them until the tactical unit arrived. The two men at their front door weren't holding their badges out, but they were plainly visible on their belts. Even the police wouldn't get here this quickly. Something didn't add up.

"Will any of Farrington's people show up?" said David. "They're the only people I'd trust right now."

"No," said Audra. "Karl said they're spread out thin—covering the people who don't qualify for government protection."

"Call Karl and ask him if he can verify whether we have a legitimate team at our door or not," said David.

She navigated to Karl's number, but another Ring app update took over her phone before she could dial his number. David glanced at her and raised an eyebrow. The backyard patio's motion detector had been triggered. Audra and David clicked on the alert at the same time. Four heavily armed figures, dressed in civilian clothes overlayed with tactical gear, moved in a tight column toward the family room slider.

"This is a hit team," said David.

"Yep," said Audra.

"Get in the bedroom, lock the door, and call 911. Then call Karl Berg," said David, flipping the shotgun's selector switch to fire.

Audra drew the compact Sig Sauer pistol from the holster on her right thigh. She'd already chambered a round, so there was nothing left to do. The pistol didn't have a safety to disengage.

"You know me better than that," she said.

"Yes. I. Do," said David. "Let's work the problem one threat axis at a time. Front door first."

"Yep," said Audra. "After I call 911. For all we know, the CIA protective agents have been neutralized."

She dialed 911 and reported armed intruders before the operator could ask a follow-up question. Audra returned the phone to her pocket—the call still live—before the two of them advanced down the hallway to the front door—where David checked the Ring app on his phone again. The team on the front porch hadn't drawn their weapons, which cast a shadow of doubt on their plan. What if the team moving across their backyard was the hit team, but the two standing at their door were legitimately part of the CIA protective detail?

"Hold on," she said, sliding the pistol behind her back. "Stay out of sight, just to the left of the door. If I draw my gun, unload on them."

"Got it," said David, crouching to the left of the door with the shotgun pointing ahead of him.

Audra took a deep breath and opened the front door.

"Yes?" she said, her fingers tightening around the pistol behind her back.

"We need you to come with us," said the man on the left, his English sounding very forced and deliberate. "You're in danger. We have an armored SUV waiting."

"Are you the CIA protective detail?" she said, pointing at the man on the right.

She'd guessed that the first person to speak, the man on the left, had been chosen because he was better versed in hiding his native accent. She'd directed her question to the other man for a reason. To potentially shake things up. To draw a more candid response—or accent.

"Yeees," he said, the vowel sounding long and hard, instead of short and soft. Very South African.

The man next to him immediately realized the mistake and started to reach back along his right thigh—presumably to draw his pistol. Audra pointed her compact Sig Sauer at the man and pressed the trigger, its nine-millimeter gunshots drowned out by the repeated twelve-gauge blasts from her husband's Benelli shotgun.

The two South African mercenaries convulsed and staggered backward several feet—their torsos and heads blasted apart by David's shotgun—before unceremoniously crumpling to the brick-paver walkway in a shower of blood and brains. Glass shattered somewhere behind them in the house. She checked her phone.

"Family room," she said, pistol raised, already moving down the front hallway, toward the kitchen.

"Hold up," hissed her husband, reloading the shotgun from a green nylon bag slung over his shoulder. "We move together."

She stopped in place and listened, the sound of quietly crackling glass reaching her ears. They were already moving across the broken glass in the family room. Where the fuck was the real protective detail?

"Maybe we should hole up in the garage," Audra whispered to David, nodding at the door to their left. "Wait for the protective detail. I'll call Karl and check on their status."

Her husband glanced at the door to the garage and squinted, apparently giving her suggestion some serious thought. His head snapped toward the kitchen a moment later, the shotgun nestling even tighter against his shoulder—its business end aimed down the front hallway, toward the back of the house.

"It would buy us some time," said David, crouching next to the door. "I'll cover you. Disable the garage door so they can't open it with some kind of universal remote."

The only problem with using the garage as a safe refuge was that they couldn't lock the door. The lock was located inside the house. On top of that, the door swung into the house. At best, they could tip the garage refrigerator across the doorway, making it difficult for the team to physically enter the space. The team would have to crawl under or over the refrigerator, exposing themselves to gunfire. All they had to do was delay the murder squad long enough for the CIA protective agents or the police to arrive.

Audra slipped behind him and opened the door to the garage, before quickly moving inside and proceeding to the emergency release cord located between their two vehicles. She got halfway down the side of the closest car before the door slammed shut behind her, the doorknob clicking and dead bolt snapping into place.

"David!" she said. "Open that door and get your ass in here!"

"Too late for that," he said through the door. "I love you."

"Open the fucking—"

A vicious gun battle erupted inside the house. A deep shotgun blast or two, followed by muffled screams and a volley of sharper-sounding automatic fire. She grabbed the doorknob and twisted to no avail. Irrationally, Audra shouldered the door, forgetting that they'd reinforced the dead bolt a year or so ago. It didn't budge. She pounded on the door, the back-and-forth gunfight continuing for another half minute or so—until the shotgun finally fell silent. She raised her fist to hit the door again but thought better of it. No reason to make this easy for them.

Audra backed up and crouched behind the hood of their Land Rover, the vehicle closest to the door. She leaned out in front of the bumper and watched the doorknob closely. Several seconds later, the knob moved ever so slightly. She fired two bullets a few inches to the right of the doorframe, next to the knob, before sending three more about a foot and a half higher.

Seemingly endless gunfire immediately followed her last shot, repeatedly thumping into the opposite side of the Land Rover's engine compartment and hood. A quick look at the door, after the gun went quiet, told her everything she needed to know. The incoming bullet holes formed a tight, inward-splintered pattern on the left side of the door. They'd stacked up on both sides, and she'd taken down the one crouched to the right.

With that in mind, Audra shifted her attention to the left side, methodically firing in a horizontal spread starting three feet back from the doorframe and moving toward the door—all of the bullets placed no higher than a foot above the bottom of the door. Four shots into her deliberate pattern, a male voice squealed obscenities on the other side of the door, followed by a hard thump. Audra ducked behind the hood, knowing what would come next.

A sustained burst of automatic fire tore through the door, flattening the Land Rover's front tires and shattering its passenger-side windows.

The moment it ended, Audra leaned a few inches past the bumper and sighted in on the newest batch of holes punched through the door. She locked eyes with someone through one of the larger holes, the opposing eye widening moments before she emptied the rest of her magazine through the hole. Three bullets—followed by complete silence. Then sirens.

Audra reloaded her pistol and kept it pointed at the door, while retrieving the phone in her back pocket. She clicked on the CITADEL alert notification, which brought her to the main app interface. After entering her passcode, she clicked the WILDFIRE tab and typed a quick message.

Attacked at home by South African mercenaries.

CHAPTER 13

"How are we looking?" said Orlov.

He'd allowed Devin Gray's sailboat to drift several hundred yards farther away than he'd originally planned. Gray had eased the sailboat to port on a new course about fifteen minutes earlier, after spending the past hour headed south by southwest. Nothing dramatic, but not something Orlov could afford to ignore.

Gray either suspected a tail or had conducted a random countersurveillance maneuver. Regardless of Gray's intentions, Orlov had decided to play it safe and maintain his current heading, letting their prey meander down the bowrider's port side. As long as they didn't lose sight of Gray's boat, he could close the distance necessary to accomplish the mission in under a minute. Gray's sailboat was effectively dead in the water compared to the twenty-one-foot Yamaha jetboat that carried Orlov's team.

"No change," said Sergei, a man of few words and even fewer brain cells.

And Sergei was one of the smarter members of the dream team Pichugin had put at his disposal this morning. If things didn't go right today, Orlov would blow his own brains out on the spot instead of facing whatever fate awaited him next. Failure meant the end of the line for Orlov—on his terms. Not Pichugin's.

The satellite phone in the cup holder buzzed, and all four heads on board the boat turned in unison. Orlov snatched the phone and read the text, which included both the six-digit authentication code he'd been given at the dock followed by the words GREEN LIGHT. NO SURVIVORS. Pretty self-explanatory. He turned the wheel left and opened the throttle.

"This is it. Keep the weapons out of sight until I give the order to fire," said Orlov, before triggering the satellite phone's push-to-talk button. "Boats two and three. Start your inbound runs. Approach from the south, and do not fire on the target unless I give you permission. This *should* be over by the time you get here. If not, we'll need to coordinate our gunfire so we don't catch each other in a cross fire."

Orlov had cherry-picked the better operatives from the overall group and placed them on his boat. He kept the other boats well out of sight, but within easy striking distance. They'd reach the scene in about a minute—thirty to forty seconds after the deed was done—assuming Devin Gray and his friends hadn't brought a belt-fed machine gun or a grenade launcher on their little sailing trip. He grinned at his joke, even chuckled a little bit, before quickly remembering what had happened the last time he underestimated Gray's crew. Orlov's face went deadpan as the Yamaha raced toward its target at close to thirty knots.

CHAPTER 14

Every phone on the sailboat activated at the same time, emitting the kind of shrill alarms one might expect from a National Weather Service tornado warning. Shea had his phone out first.

"CITADEL," he said.

"Any additional information?" said Devin, scanning the water around them.

"Felix Orlov was spotted at L'Enfant Plaza, headed east on the Orange Line," said Shea.

"East on the Orange Line from L'Enfant puts Orlov heading toward Annapolis," said Marnie.

"What time?" said Devin.

"JRIC FRD hit at eight thirty-two this morning," said Shea.

"And we're just getting this now?" said Devin. "That doesn't make any sense."

"I'm just reading the alert," said Shea.

"Marnie. Bring up the shotgun bag," said Devin. "I'll take us to the nearest marina. Berg can arrange transport from there. We should be fine."

"Hon. You should head down below, too," said Shea. "And stay there until we get to the marina."

"Are we in danger?" said Nancy.

"It's possible," said Shea, before giving her a quick kiss.

"Just stay low if we run into trouble," said Devin. "You'll be below the waterline. Marnie. Show her where to go."

"Yep," said Marnie, grabbing Nancy's hand and escorting her into the cabin below.

Shea opened the backpack next to him and slid the holstered pistol with two spare magazines onto his lap. Devin unbuttoned his shirt, still looking for threats on the water. So far, so—not good. Shit. They had a fast mover inbound, heading straight for their bow. Still a good thirty to forty seconds out.

"Speedboat headed our way," said Devin. "Hurry up with that shotgun!"

"I'm hurrying!" said Marnie.

While Shea readied his weapon for action, Devin tucked the right side of his shirt into his shorts, exposing his concealed pistol. His cell phone rang a few moments later. He yanked the phone out of his pocket and checked the screen. Karl Berg. Devin answered the call.

"Can't talk right now. I have an inbound threat."

"What? How is that even—how inbound?" said Berg.

"As in I need to hang up right now," said Devin.

"Okay. Okay. I just wanted to tell you that you have friendlies in the area," said Berg. "Farrington's crew has a boat out there. I wasn't taking any chances this weekend. They'll fire off a flare before approaching. Don't pull the Coast Guard into this. That'll just confuse things."

Devin disconnected the call and jammed the phone back into his shorts, just as Marnie burst through the hatchway. She tossed a long black nylon bag on the portside cockpit cushion and started unzipping it.

"You have about twenty seconds," said Devin, pushing the throttle forward. "Nancy! Lie flat on the deck. Do not get up until we tell you it's safe. Got it?"

"Got it!" she yelled from inside the cabin.

Shea leaned out of the starboard side of the cockpit, pistol in hand.

"What's the plan?" he said.

"Buy us some time," said Devin. "Berg has people on the water. Farrington's crew."

"I meant very specifically—what's the plan?" said Shea. "They can run circles around us. We won't be here when Farrington's people arrive."

"They haven't slowed down yet, so I'm guessing they're going to slow down and turn at the last second—come alongside for a long burst of gunfire. Probably just circle around the cockpit after that, picking off any survivors," said Devin.

"That's their plan," said Shea. "What's your plan?"

Marnie racked the shotgun, chambering a shell. She nodded at Devin and crouched behind the cabin's portside windbreak.

"My plan is to fuck up their plan," said Devin. "Get ready to unload on whatever side of the boat I call out. Stay low and keep shooting. We need to put that boat out of commission. I'm sure it's not alone."

Their phones buzzed and screeched simultaneously. Shea quickly checked his phone before stuffing it back in his pocket.

"Let me guess," said Devin. "WILDFIRE?"

"Audra Bauer was attacked at her house by South African mercenaries," said Shea.

"This is about to get ugly," said Marnie.

"That's an understatement," said Devin, before increasing the sailboat's speed to full throttle—a whopping six knots.

He ducked as low as possible behind the helm console while still maintaining a full view of the approaching speedboat. Two men with long guns sat in the Yamaha's bow, ready for action. A third stood behind the driver. Any second now. There! The three men quickly moved to the starboard side of the bowrider. Before the driver could cut to port and set up a lethal starboard-to-starboard passage, Devin yanked the wheel starboard, turning the sailboat directly in front of the oncoming speedboat.

CHAPTER 15

Felix Orlov smelled redemption as he pulled back on the throttle to slow the speedboat for its final approach. They'd be alongside in a matter of moments, gunning down Devin Gray, Marnie Young, and Brendan Shea, three of Pichugin's highest-priority targets. His handler didn't care what they did with Shea's wife as long as he personally confirmed that the other three were dead.

Orlov thought about throwing her to the wolves if she survived the initial volley, to buy a little loyalty from the men, who would likely end up being part of his future crew—but they wouldn't have the time to enjoy the spoils. Gunshots traveled far and loud across water, and the US Coast Guard was out in full force today, looking for drunk boaters. They needed to be speeding away from here in less than a minute to avoid an unforgivable complication.

His hands tensed on the wheel. All it would take now was a simple adjustment to port and—what the fuck! Devin Gray's sailboat had turned directly in front of his boat, leaving Orlov no choice but to spin the wheel hard in the opposite direction he'd intended to avoid a head-on collision. To make matters worse, Orlov instinctively reversed the throttle to halt all forward momentum—effectively reversing his good fortune. The next few seconds passed in a blur.

The boat pitched violently to the right before coming to an abrupt stop, throwing all three of his shooters to the opposite side of the boat—before knocking them to their knees. Two of the three AK-12K compact assault rifles carried by his team splashed into the water between the two boats, headed for the bottom of the bay, as a fusillade of bullets and buckshot from the sailboat's cockpit hammered his men without warning.

In the bow compartment just feet in front of him, two heads snapped back instantly, the contents of their skulls splattering the tan cushions behind them and slapping against the windshield inches from Orlov's face. He turned to locate Sergei, the operative stationed just behind him in the cockpit, only to watch him flip over the side of the boat—the top half of his head missing. Orlov didn't hesitate. He jammed the throttle forward and threw himself over the starboard side of the bowrider, barely managing to grab one of the handles along the side of the boat's aft swim platform before it raced by.

He held on until the speedboat finally picked up enough speed to toss him away like a rag doll. Fortunately, he'd traveled a few hundred yards away from the sailboat before finally losing his grip. He took a deep breath and ducked under the water, frantically removing his shoes. Once he'd ditched the cheap loafers, Orlov flipped on his back and started frog kicking away from the sailboat, keeping his eye on the ever-resourceful Devin Gray. The guy had nine fucking lives! Maybe more.

But Orlov could still salvage the day. He still had two boats and seven more shooters at his disposal. A small army that should arrive at any moment. The only problem was that he had no way to talk to them. His satellite phone was in a cup holder, speeding away from him at forty knots.

Actually, he had more than just that one problem. The scum he'd put in the other boats weren't exactly awe inspiring—on any level. He'd purposefully kept them out of the initial attack for that very reason. Only a few of them had spent any meaningful time in the past on a boat, and even those few seemed to have trouble grasping the absolute basics of boating terminology required for the kind of close coordination he'd need to employ to maneuver three boats at once.

Upon leaving the dock in Eastport, Orlov was happy enough that they could steer the boat out of the marina! Now his future, and probably his life, depended on their entirely debatable competence—which was about to be put to the test. He spotted two boats speeding in from the south, placing a mental bet with himself that they'd cruise right by the sailboat, chasing down the uncrewed speedboat.

They might be dumb as rocks, but they knew how to track a GPS target. And the only GPS target inputted into their phones right now was the satellite phone speeding at forty-plus knots. He'd tried to make things as simple as possible for these idiots, synching his satellite phone's location with their phones and GPS units so they could converge on the target after his handpicked team had finished the job. So much for that. All he could do now was try to wave them down as they sped by. Assuming they didn't run him over.

CHAPTER 16

Marnie racked the shotgun's slide and pressed the trigger, the twelve-gauge double-aught buckshot striking the man in the chest—knocking his corpse clean over the side of the speedboat. He was already deader than dead from one of her previous shots, which had removed most of his head, but she was on autopilot.

Her only mission when the speedboat pulled alongside, frantically communicated to her by Devin at the last possible moment, was to put as much buckshot into the aft-compartment shooter as possible. And that was exactly what she did. Marnie fired and racked the shotgun, repeatedly, until the man was gone, oblivious to what was happening on the bow of the speedboat.

She turned her attention to the boat's driver moments after her target flew overboard—and pressed the trigger. Click. She'd emptied the six shells she'd chosen to load before the speedboat pulled alongside. The shotgun's magazine could hold eight, with an additional shell in the chamber, but Marnie had chosen expediency over maximum capacity. A decision she now regretted.

Before she could reload another shell or alert the others, the driver threw himself overboard, the boat racing forward at maximum throttle—taking Felix Orlov with it. Marnie had recognized his face right before he vanished over the side.

"That's Orlov!" she said.

"Where?" said Devin.

"He just went over the side!"

Devin and Shea quickly reloaded their pistols and fired at the man clinging to the back of the speedboat. At first the bullets splashed to the immediate left and right of Orlov, a few snapping off the back of the boat, but as the distance increased, the splashes fell shorter and shorter—until the two shooters gave up. Devin took control of the helm and pointed the sailboat toward the western shore of the bay.

"Should we go after him?" said Marnie, thumbing shell after shell from her pockets into the shotgun's tubular magazine. "Finish him off? He can't hold on to that boat forever."

Devin appeared to give it a few moments' thought before shaking his head.

"No. We need to put as much distance as possible between ourselves and Orlov," said Devin, taking out his cell phone. "He'll have a backup team nearby. He always does. We need to link up with Farrington's people before Orlov gets a second chance at us. He won't make the same mistake twice."

"They'll sit about a hundred feet away and pound us with those AKs," said Shea, before turning his attention to the hatch leading into the cabin. "Nance. How are you doing down there?"

"I'm fine," she said. "Is everyone else okay?"

"We're all good," said Shea.

"Is it safe to come up?"

"Stay put for now," said Shea, swapping pistol magazines. "There could be more of them out there."

"There," said Devin, nodding to his left.

Two speedboats raced toward them from the south, kicking up plumes of water behind them.

"Marnie. Can you take over? I need to make a call. Keep your guns out of sight for now. They might pass right by looking for the other speedboat."

Marnie tossed the shotgun on the cushion behind the helm and took over the wheel, while Devin fumbled with his phone. The two speedboats maintained their northerly course as the sailboat continued west—at a tenth of their speed. From what she could tell, the bowriders hadn't altered their direction in response to the sailboat's escape. They'd know in a few seconds.

Shea shifted over to join Devin on the port side of the cockpit, his pistol out of sight. Devin held his phone in one hand and a pistol in the other, nervously glancing over his shoulder at the two boats.

"Hold on. We might have more company," said Devin, putting the phone down on the cushion next to him.

The two bowriders, nearly identical to Orlov's boat, roared behind them, speeding north—their crews paying no attention to the sailboat.

"Orlov must not be able to communicate with them!" said Marnie, over the noise.

"They'll find him soon enough. Then we're screwed," said Devin, picking up his phone and yelling at whoever was on the other end.

Emily Miralles patiently listened to Devin's frantic plea for help, waiting for him to finish. There was no point to interrupting him. He was in panic mode. When he stopped talking, she proceeded.

"I need you to read me your GPS coordinates," said Miralles, ready to write the numbers down on a pad of paper in her lap. "Right now."

Several crucial seconds passed before Devin read the coordinates, which she immediately passed along to Guillermo "Gilly" Espinoza—who inputted them into the Sea Ray's navigation system.

"We're three minutes out. Almost due east of their position," said Gilly, before turning to Alex Filatov, who was behind the wheel. "Go. Go. Follow the GPS directions."

The twenty-one-foot bowrider lurched forward, pinning Miralles to one of the upright cushions in the boat's bow seating compartment, as Alex put the boat in a wide turn that eventually settled on a westerly course. They had been ghosting Gray's sailboat from about three miles away, trying to blend in with the motorboat traffic close to the eastern shoreline. Berg wanted them close enough to help, but not close enough to freak them out. Now it wasn't guaranteed they'd make it in time.

"We're about three minutes away," Miralles told Devin. "We'll be approaching from the east. Just on your current heading at max speed."

"We're making five knots," said Devin.

Jesus. Five knots. Their Sea Ray had just hit thirty-five. Gray and his friends would be sitting ducks for the Russians.

"Do whatever you can to hang in there for the next three minutes," said Miralles. "We'll pop a green flare—"

"Forget the flare," said Devin. "We have a visual on the two hostile boats. Use the element of surprise to your advantage. They won't be expecting you."

"Copy that," said Miralles. "Pass situation reports as you deem fit."

"Hopefully we'll still be alive when you get here," said Devin. "That's the situation."

"I have a feeling you'll still be around," said Miralles, ending the call.

Alex nodded at her. "What's the situation?"

"They neutralized the first boat without taking casualties, but they expended half of their ammunition. They're armed with two pistols and a shotgun. The Russians had AK-12s," said Miralles. "Two additional boats, carrying seven more Russians, just passed them, looking for the first boat, which is uncrewed and speeding north. Orlov was on the first boat. Gray doesn't think Orlov has any way to talk to the other boats."

"Jesus. The Russians really fucked things up," said Gilly.

"They'll recover quickly enough," said Alex. "Break out the hardware and get in touch with Gupta. We're gonna need a shallow beach to land the boat and some ground support. Tell him we're looking at the Normandy Beach scenario."

"What does that mean?" said Miralles.

"Just pass it along," said Alex. "He'll know what to do. He's already planned for this."

CHAPTER 17

Anish Gupta clicked his mouse to connect Miralles's call, praying that she was just checking in with a routine update. He had enough on his plate right now. Nothing critical, but a ton of moving parts.

"Make it quick," said Gupta, his attention focused on the text updates streaming in from the other teams.

"Alex said we're looking at a Normandy Beach scenario," said Miralles.

Gupta shot up in his seat. "What the fuck is going on out there?"

"I don't have time to explain, but it's seriously fucked," said Miralles. "Normandy Beach. You have our location. Make it happen."

"Copy. Working the scenario now," said Gupta. "Will text you the landing coordinates ASAP. Jesus. Is this for real? Were they attacked?"

"Yes, to both questions," said Miralles.

The call ended. Gupta paused for a moment. Shit. First things first. He typed a few lines of text into the early-warning system he'd created for the task force and pushed a second WILDFIRE alert out to everyone on the network. They needed to know that the Russians had attacked another group of principal players on the DEEP SLEEP Task Force, and that additional attacks could follow. Light a fire under everyone's asses, as Farrington would say. A call came in just moments after he hit SEND. Speak of the devil.

"Devin was attacked on the water," said Gupta. "Alex is looking for you to re-create Normandy Beach—on the Chesapeake Bay."

"Happy to oblige," said Farrington. "Any activity reported by any other teams?"

"None so far," said Gupta.

"The Russians are up to something big," said Farrington. "Expect things to get busy—fast."

"Business as usual," said Gupta, moments before receiving a call from one of their affiliate operatives in Los Angeles. "Shit. California just lit up the board. High-priority call. Hold on a second."

He switched to the 310-area-code call.

"Gupta. What's up?"

"This is Decker. We had a break-in at Kari Gray's apartment about three minutes ago. A man and a woman posing as LAPD detectives tried to get her to open her door. She ignored them and hid with her dad in the bathroom. Rip and Garza took care of it. They killed two armed operatives waiting in a parked van by the apartment complex's rear maintenance entrance, before making their way inside Kari's apartment—where they killed the other two before they could locate Kari and Mason."

"Copy. We'll be in touch," said Gupta, switching back to Farrington. "One of Hendrick's teams tried to grab Devin's dad and sister. Decker's people neutralized the threat and secured the Grays," said Gupta.

"The Russians are going after everyone," said Farrington. "Upgrade WILDFIRE to FIRESTORM. Everyone is in immediate danger."

"Got it," said Gupta, typing a few lines and sending out his system's most urgent warning.

CHAPTER 18

Felix Orlov couldn't believe his eyes. Actually—he could totally believe them. The two boats were chock-full of hired guns. Morons with one purpose in life. To shoot where you pointed—and that's it. Maybe it hadn't been the best idea to stack the primary boat with the few scattered brain cells Pichugin had made available to him. Perhaps he should have spread the gray matter out a little more evenly. Too late for that kind of speculation.

Orlov watched helplessly as the two boats sped past, about fifty yards away, nobody on either boat glancing in his direction—despite his arms waving frantically above his head. Fuck it. Let these idiots chase a dead boat. Maybe it was better this way. He had stashes of cash and counterfeit identity documents spread around the world. One of them sat buried just outside a cemetery a few hours from here, in Kinston, North Carolina. Thirty-two thousand dollars and enough documentation to get him to Southeast Asia, where he had more money and documents hidden. More than enough to reinvent himself.

"Who am I fucking kidding?" he muttered.

Orlov would have to sleep with one eye open for the rest of his life, if Pichugin suspected he had walked off the job. He removed the compact pistol he'd stuffed into a cargo pocket and pointed it skyward, firing evenly spaced shots until one of the boats finally veered off and turned in his direction. Having attracted their attention, he let the pistol sink to the bottom of the bay—to reduce the chance that these trigger-happy idiots might gun him down without investigating—and started waving with both hands again.

The bowrider slowed about twenty yards out and drifted slowly toward him, the two shooters in the bow compartment flawlessly keeping their AK-12s pointed at his head.

"It's Orlov! Get me out of the water," he said, choosing his words carefully.

The less he said, the better right now. He didn't want to give them any reason to consider abandoning the mission or just shooting him in the head and continuing the mission without him. The boat edged closer, until he could touch its fiberglass hull.

"Where are the others?" said the driver.

"In the water," said Orlov. "The boat you're chasing is empty. We had a problem."

Orlov made his way to the swim deck on the back of the boat, where the driver helped him out of the water.

"Call the other boat and have them join us," said Orlov. "The sailboat can't be too far away. We'll hit it at the same time."

"How far away are the others?" said the driver.

"Sergei and the others are dead," said Orlov, drawing three confused stares.

"But you just said—"

"I said we had a problem and that they're in the water," said Orlov. "The problem was that our targets pulled a fast one and unloaded on us unexpectedly. All three of them were dead before they hit the water."

"This was supposed to be an easy fucking job," said one of the gunmen in the bow.

"Well. It just got a little less easy. This Devin Gray fucker continues to defy the odds. But his luck has run out," said Orlov. "Get the other boat over here. We'll hit the sailboat hard from a safe distance with the AKs; then we'll get close and seal the deal. We need to be done with this in the next few minutes."

CHAPTER 19

Devin scanned the water with binoculars, waiting for the inevitable. Two plumes of water, each preceded by a speedboat carrying a firing squad. With Orlov still alive, they could expect another attack—sooner than later. On cue, two boats appeared to the southeast, kicking up the water behind them as they closed the distance in a tight formation. He did the mental math. Emily Miralles said three minutes. About a minute had elapsed. Orlov's boats would be here in less than thirty seconds. Possibly sooner.

"Shit," he muttered.

"What?" said Shea, who was seated next to him, watching for Farrington's boat.

"Two bogeys inbound," said Devin, pointing toward the distant speedboats. "Marnie. Bring us about thirty degrees to port."

The move would put the approaching threat directly aft, which would cut their angle of approach to zero, maximizing the time it would take for them to intercept the sailboat. He'd bought them a few more seconds.

"Aye, aye, Skipper," said Marnie, turning the wheel left, before settling on their new course.

"What are you thinking?" said Shea.

"I'm thinking we may have to slug it out with Orlov for a couple minutes before help arrives," said Devin.

"Jesus," said Marnie from the helm.

"He won't make the same mistake twice," said Shea.

"No. He won't," said Devin. "And we can't outshoot AK-12s. We're gonna have to get creative."

"Something tells me I don't want to hear your definition of *creative*," said Shea.

"You probably don't," said Devin. "Marnie. Any ideas?"

"Obviously, we can't let them roll up on us and blast away at the cockpit," said Marnie. "We have to turn and face them. Put as much hull material between us and those bullets as possible. Ideally, we'd do this at the last possible moment. Empty our weapons in their direction and force them to improvise. Right now, they're settling in on a strategy or two. My guess is that none of them involves us taking the initiative. It could buy us a little time."

"Sounds good to me," said Shea.

"I think it's about as good as it gets. Marnie. Stand by to turn starboard on my mark," said Devin.

"Aye. Skipper," said Marnie.

"Brendan. Make sure Nancy stays low. Orlov's crew is going to turn this boat into swiss cheese," said Devin. "Don't take long. This is about to go down."

Shea got up and poked his head through the hatch leading to the main cabin, passing along instructions to his wife.

"How are we looking?" said Marnie over her shoulder.

"Any second now," said Devin. "Brendan?"

"Yeah. Coming," said Shea.

"Marnie. Steady us on a due-east course, lock the wheel into place—then grab your shotgun," said Devin. "We're just looking to break their stride."

The maneuver wouldn't carry the same "wow" factor as their last move. The speedboats would have plenty of time to avoid a collision. Orlov's teams could turn on a dime compared to a thirty-foot cruising sailboat. But Marnie was right. It should force the Russians to change tactics, which would buy them a little more time. At this point, that

94

basically summed up their only viable survival strategy. Slow Orlov down in order to give Farrington's people a chance to intercede. A chance. And not much more than that. As soon as Shea settled into position on the port side of the cockpit, Devin patted Marnie's shoulder.

"Do it. Hard to starboard."

No smart-ass reply this time. Marnie just spun the oversize stainless-steel wheel to the right until it stopped—the sailboat heeling in the opposite direction as the rudder forced the hull into a tighter-than-usual turn. Devin held on to the nearest railing stanchion to keep from losing his balance and sliding across the cockpit. Marnie remained fixed at the helm station, her legs planted rock solid on the deck. Shea just leaned into the cushion behind him, letting the boat's motion keep him in place.

When the boat steadied on its new course, Devin assessed the situation ahead of them. The speedboats had already reacted, splitting apart to let the sailboat pass between them. Bullets snapped overhead a few seconds later, followed by hard cracks and deep thumps against the hull and cabin. He had another idea that could buy them a few more seconds.

"Get on the shotgun," said Devin. "I got the wheel."

"You sure?" she said, crouched low as the bullets started to strike the sides of the cockpit.

"Not really," said Devin, grabbing the wheel. "But yeah."

Shea's pistol barked twice. Then twice again. Things were about to get critical. Marnie slid into place opposite Shea, behind the raised cabin structure, the deep boom of her shotgun deafening in the cockpit. Devin took a knee and stayed as low as possible, keeping one hand on the wheel—the other holding his pistol. The gunfire intensified between the boats, the Russians' automatic rifles crackling as they raced down the side of the sailboat.

Devin let go of the wheel for a moment and took a two-handed grip on the pistol. He snapped off several shots at the boat racing down

Shea's side, before shifting his aim to starboard to empty the rest of his magazine at the boat slicing down Marnie's side. He had no idea if his efforts had any effect on the Russians. Devin ducked below the side of the cockpit the moment his pistol's slide locked back, the incoming fire far too concentrated to keep any part of his body exposed.

Marnie fired her shotgun one more time before taking cover. Shea remained upright and slightly exposed, reloading his pistol. Before Devin could tell him to get his ass down, two bullets punched through Shea's left shoulder, spraying Marnie with blood and knocking him flat on the cockpit deck. Marnie immediately tended to him, assessing his wounds. While she hovered over Shea, Devin risked a peek, seeing that the two speedboats had stopped just aft of the sailboat, one on each side.

When they slowed and started to turn, he understood the Russians' intention. To follow them from about fifty yards away, too far for accurate pistol or shotgun fire, but perfect for rifles. They'd pound the cockpit with automatic fire, driving them into the cabin—before closing in for a close-up machine-gunning of the hull. Possibly a grenade or two tossed on board. Devin and Marnie would be helpless to repel them. Time to buy a few more seconds. The mantra of the day.

Devin turned the wheel left as far as it would go and locked it in a hard left turn. They'd go in circles until Farrington's team arrived, preventing the Russians from drifting in place and easily shooting up the cockpit. *Easily* being the operative term. They'd still be able to do a number on the sailboat from any angle. The Catalina 30's thick fiberglass hull seriously slowed the 5.45 millimeter bullets fired by the Russians' AK-12s, but a few bullets had managed to penetrate the hull around the cockpit with enough velocity to pop through the navy-blue cushions and bring plenty of stuffing with them.

Eventually, the only survivable location on the sailboat would be the main cabin, which was mostly below the waterline and relatively safe from bullets. But once they retreated below, the Russians would be able to get even closer. Possibly even board the sailboat. He was buying them time.

"What are you doing?" said Marnie.

"Driving in circles to make it a little harder for them," said Devin.

She nodded her understanding before drawing his attention to Shea's bullet wounds.

"Both bullets are through-and-throughs," she said. "He got lucky."

"I don't feel so lucky," groaned Shea.

"Get him down below and break out the first aid kit. We have some hemostatic gauze that should stop most of the bleeding," said Devin. "I'll stay up here as long as possible. Hang in there, Brendan."

"It's just a through-and-through," said Shea, lying in an ever-spreading pool of his own blood. "Didn't you hear?"

Marnie grabbed Shea by the armpits and yanked him toward the hatchway. He grimaced and grunted as she hauled him through the opening, trying to ease him down the short stairway. Successful at getting him out of harm's way, but less successful at the "ease him down" part, judging by the volume of cursing and groaning bursting from Shea's mouth.

A string of bullets stitched across the cockpit, a few sparking off the steering wheel. The rest striking, and presumably penetrating, the top of the cabin. A quick look over the side confirmed that he'd bought them some time. The speedboats had to constantly maneuver so the shooters could keep firing at the cockpit. The motion interfered with their ability to aim, already enough of a challenge on a rocking boat. It didn't keep dozens of bullets from smacking into the hull or topside fixtures, but it kept the Russians from pounding them into oblivion. For now.

Devin took a few moments to reload his pistol with his last magazine before retrieving Shea's pistol from a blood-splattered seat cushion. Shea had managed to seat the magazine before taking two rifle bullets to the shoulder. Devin released the slide on Shea's pistol and tucked it into his shorts. His next move was to call Farrington's team.

"We're about a minute out from your last reported position," answered Miralles. "We can hear the shooting, but we don't have a visual. Too many boats out here. Can you pop a flare?"

"Hold on," said Devin, before scrambling across the cockpit to a small bench locker behind the helm station.

Bullets punctured the seat cushions on the port side, trying to find him. One of them grazed his back as he crawled across the abrasive plastic deck. It was only a matter of time now before he took a serious hit. He unlatched the locker and removed the flare gun kit, loading one of the four flares included. Devin didn't risk raising his hand. He lay flat on his back and held the flare gun against his chest, pointed upward. The twelve-gauge aerial flare departed a moment later, flying a few hundred feet into the air before igniting and continuing another hundred or more feet before reaching its maximum altitude and turning lazily back toward the water.

"Got it," said Miralles. "Get ready to transfer everyone to our boat. We have a boat landing site and vehicle extraction arranged."

Several bullets, fired from two different directions, punched through the back of the cockpit, missing him by inches.

"Copy," said Devin, pressing himself flat against the deck. "We may need some help with the transfer. We have one down."

"Understood. Thirty seconds," said Miralles.

The longest thirty seconds of his life.

CHAPTER 20

Felix Orlov decided enough was enough. They couldn't afford to keep playing games with Devin Gray. The Coast Guard would be here any minute.

"Vlad. Take us in alongside the back of the sailboat. I don't care which side," said Orlov, removing a flash bang grenade from the team's nylon weapons bag.

The driver increased the throttle, pointing them at the sailboat, which appeared to be stuck in a wide, lazy circle. Presumably on purpose. A clever strategy, but a limited one. He transmitted over the push-to-talk phone.

"Close in to about ten yards and unload on the boat. Two mags per rifle. Driver included. Just keep us out of your line of fire," said Orlov. "When you're done, I'm boarding this fucking sailboat and putting an end to this nonsense."

"Yep. Moving into position now," said Vlad.

The other boat responded immediately, veering away to give Orlov space before turning toward the sailboat and motoring at a modest speed. The three shooters on board crowded into the bow seating area, bracing their rifles against the gunwales. He patted his driver.

"Let's go," said Orlov, pulling the pin on the flash bang grenade before yelling at the two men in the bow. "Hold your fire until after I throw the grenade."

Once again, all three men on board the boat turned toward him—their eyes fixated on the grenade in his hand.

"Don't worry. It's just a flash bang," said Orlov, prodding the driver. "Let's go!"

"You might want to hang on," said the driver.

He reached for the nearest side rail with his free hand, the boat pitching forward only after the driver had visually confirmed that he'd taken a firm grip. They approached their target at a modest speed, while the shooters on the other speedboat tore the sailboat apart. Of the one hundred and eighty 5.45 millimeter bullets fired at the boat, at least two-thirds hit the mark—striking anything above the portside waterline.

The cockpit area splintered into a storm of teak and plastic fragments. Bullet holes perforated the raised sides of the cabin next to the hatch leading below. The aluminum boom extending from the main mast to the middle of the cockpit rattled from several hits, the folded sail cover sitting atop ripping open to expose the mainsail. The steering wheel twisting and fragmenting. At one point in the mayhem, a figure dove through the hatch to escape the gunfire. Perfect. They were halfway there.

"Open fire," he directed Arseny and Pavel, the two shooters on the bow of his boat. "One full mag on auto. Reload, then slow fire."

Burst after burst tore into the boat, striking the starboard side instead of the cockpit and hatchway area. Understandable because the sailboat was driving in circles. His bowrider finally crossed behind Gray's boat, just as his shooters reloaded—the driver bringing them along the aft, port side of the boat. Orlov prepared to toss the grenade at the open hatchway. His chance of landing it inside the main cabin was slim, but he didn't care.

Even a deafening explosion and flash in the cockpit should disorient Gray's compatriots enough to allow them to safely board the sailboat and finish the job. His next grenade wouldn't be a "nonlethal device." He'd toss one or both M67 fragmentation grenades in his hip pouch into the cabin, while his team sprayed the side of the boat with automatic fire. Done deal. If all went well, this would be over in less than thirty seconds, hopefully giving them time to escape whatever Coast Guard response might be inbound.

"We're coming alongside!" said Vlad, increasing the boat's speed.

A face appeared in the sailboat's hatchway, preceded by a larger-than-life stainless-steel gun barrel. Marnie Young. Orlov crouched low, the shotgun erupting a moment later—and shearing Vlad's head clean off his shoulders. Clean in that the driver's head essentially disappeared in a soupy, red shower of mush that splattered the cockpit. The driver stumbled to port and collapsed next to his seat.

Miraculously, the speedboat continued its intercept trajectory, the two men in the bow firing frantically at the shooter, who disappeared just as quickly as she appeared. Orlov rose and threw the grenade, instantly knowing that it wouldn't sail through the open hatch. He'd tossed it short and wide, landing it in the middle of the sailboat's cockpit. Should be enough to—what the fuck?

Automatic gunfire exploded from the direction of the second boat, causing Orlov to crouch as low as possible. The last time he checked, his boat was close enough to the second boat's line of fire to the sailboat to cause significant concern. When a hail of bullets didn't tear into his speedboat, Orlov took a quick peek at the other boat to figure out what would have possessed them to start shooting while he came alongside the sailboat. Another speedboat roared by the second bowrider, the two vessels furiously exchanging gunfire.

The flash bang grenade detonated a moment later, and its flash blinded one of his shooters, a forearm instantly rising to cover his eyes—rifle barrel lowering under the weight of a single-handed grip. Movement inside the sailboat, visible through the topside cabin windows, suggested the flash bang had not deterred his seemingly undeterrable opponents. He immediately reached over the bloodied driver's seat and pushed the throttle forward as far as it would go, the boat pitching forward and throwing everyone on board backward.

Small-caliber gunfire passed overhead and behind them as they sped away, the pistol bullets that would have assuredly struck a few of them—narrowly avoided. Unfortunately, the quick, life-saving maneuver didn't leave them unscathed.

The two mercenaries pitched backward and struck the front of the cockpit, the impact absorbed by seating cushions—and one of the windshield panels. Arseny, the mercenary closest to the bow, tripped over the other shooter and struck the driver's-side windshield head-first, his forehead cracking the glass in place. Orlov witnessed the head-against-glass collision at close range, having held on tight to the driver's seat after pushing the throttle. A hard, sick thud, followed by a streak of blood slowly sinking down the cracked window as the boat rocketed forward, left little doubt that he'd lost another shooter.

Once Orlov's bowrider had cleared the port side of the sailboat—and the immediate danger posed by the shooters inside the boat's cabin—he slid into the gore-soaked driver's seat and eased up on the throttle, all while scanning the water for the hostile speedboat that had intervened on Devin Gray's behalf. Farrington's people, no doubt.

Orlov didn't have to search for long. Bullets snapped past the boat, momentarily passing wide, before Farrington's shooters made the necessary adjustments for his reduced speed. Before he could react and turn the boat, bullets started to tear through the bow seating area and thunk into the front of the driver's console. A quick glance around the cracked, bloodstained windshield told him what he already knew. The hostile boat was dead ahead, speeding straight for him. He hopped down from the seat and pressed his body flat against the deck.

"Stay down!" he yelled at Pavel.

Fortunately, the mercenary obeyed and stayed low in the bow. The hostile boat roared down their starboard side at full speed, dozens of bullets puncturing the hull, obliterating the driver's console, and splintering the plastic along the bowrider's gunwales. He pushed the throttle forward again, hoping to put as much distance as possible between his boat and Farrington's skilled shooters. His mercenaries were once again hopelessly outgunned by these annoyingly omnipresent Americans.

A cloud of smoke billowed from the bow of his boat, quickly engulfing the entire vessel in a noxious haze. Anyone else might jump overboard, assuming that their boat was on the verge of exploding from an engine fire, but Orlov immediately recognized the smell. The Americans had managed to toss a smoke grenade onto his boat during their pass. Another impressive feat. The two boats must have passed each other traveling at a combined speed of more than fifty miles per hour. His first instinct was to slow down, but that would thicken the smoke in the cockpit.

"Get that smoke grenade out of here!" he said, climbing back into the driver's seat.

Several excruciatingly long seconds later, the smoke grenade sailed off the starboard bow and splashed into the water next to them, the smoke on board the boat dissipating almost immediately. He glanced over his shoulder in the direction of the sailboat, but his view was obscured by the cloud he'd left behind.

He suspected that Gray would attempt a transfer from the sailboat to the speedboat. If that happened, he'd have little to no chance of salvaging an already highly screwed operation. Orlov slowed the boat and turned the wheel, putting them in a lazy circle to port. His second boat sat a few hundred yards to the south, at least one of its occupants firing methodically in the direction of the sailboat. He searched the boat for the satellite phone, finding it under the adjacent seat.

"Luka. This is Orlov. I'm down two shooters. What's your status?" he said, keeping a close eye on the smoke.

The last thing he needed right now was a surprise attack while he wasn't looking. A few seconds passed before the other boat replied.

"Luka is dead. This is Artem. It's just me and Niko. And Niko's in bad shape. He can still shoot, but they did a fucking number on us. Came out of nowhere."

"Well. It's time we returned the favor," said Orlov. "Where's the boat now?"

"I think it pulled alongside the sailboat," said Luka. "But I can't say for sure. They popped a smoke grenade on the bow. It's covering them in a cloud."

"We have to put a stop to that," said Orlov. "Follow me in. We'll circle around the back of their boat and engage their right side. That's where they'll attempt the transfer."

"I'll be right behind you," said Luka.

"Hang on tight," said Orlov. "Position yourself on the port side."

Orlov turned the wheel hard left and increased the throttle.

CHAPTER 21

Devin Gray scanned the thinning smoke for the inbound speedboats, the deep roaring sound of their engines getting unmistakably closer.

"We need to move faster," said Devin. "They know what we're doing."

Miralles and Gilly had climbed aboard to help transfer Shea to the other boat.

"We're moving as fast as we can," said Miralles.

"Brendan is in bad shape," said Marnie. "Worse than we thought."

"I'm not saying that moving him will kill him, but it'll severely complicate our plan to get everyone to the CITADEL," said Miralles.

One look over his shoulder at Brendan Shea, whom Marnie and Gilly struggled to wrangle halfway out of the sailboat cabin, instantly validated Miralles's concern. Shea was basically deadweight, even though he wasn't anywhere close to dying. And his wife wasn't much better. Nancy had handled this insanity better than expected, but Devin could tell she was on the verge of a mental shutdown. Unsurprising given the circumstances.

She'd become verbally uncommunicative, just nodding or shaking her head when asked a question. Not a good sign. On top of that, she remained glued to Brendan's side, despite numerous, insistent suggestions that she get on board the speedboat while the team transported her husband. Glancing back and forth from the water to the hatchway, Devin felt a plan crystallize. Sort of. More like blob into place.

"Take them back down! We'll leave them in the cabin and take off. The Russians can't spare the time to check the sailboat. They'll follow us as we speed away. We'll let the Coast Guard deal with the Sheas," said Devin. "Brendan. Are you okay with that?"

"I'm fine with that," said Shea, grabbing his wife's arm and nodding emphatically. "We'll be fine."

"I'll stay with them," said Marnie. "Just in case."

"No. The Russians need to see more than just one new face on that boat. No offense, but the two of you are the real targets," said Shea.

"He's right," said Devin. "Nancy?"

She displayed Brendan's pistol and nodded. "We'll be fine."

"Back the way we came," said Marnie. Gilly grumbled as he helped her lower Shea into the cabin.

While the two of them wrestled Shea below, one of the boats broke through the smoke, a single gun blazing from its bow. Devin shifted the rifle given to him by Miralles toward the boat and pressed the trigger, sending a three-round burst in its direction. The recoil took him by surprise, pulling his shots off target. He'd expected a single shot. The brief reprieve gave the Russian shooter the moment he needed to accurately direct their fire, immediately followed by the second Russian boat—its shooter similarly accurate.

Dozens of bullets snapped directly overhead or smacked into the back of the two connected boats, forcing everyone to take cover. A deep grunt drew Devin's attention to Alex, who struggled to stay upright in the driver's seat of the adjacent speedboat—the windshield directly in front of him sprayed bright red. Miralles popped up from the back of the speedboat moments later, returning the favor and emptying an entire rifle magazine into the approaching bowriders, forcing them to veer south, behind the last remnants of the smoke screen they'd created to conceal the boat transfer.

"Marnie! Gilly! Get on the speedboat," said Devin. "We only have a few seconds!"

Gilly climbed out of the hatchway and scrambled over the cockpit railing onto the waiting speedboat, where he eased Alex out of the driver's seat. Marnie followed him over, catching the assault rifle thrown at her by Miralles. The two of them taking positions in the back of the speedboat. Devin stopped next to the hatchway and glanced down at the Sheas, who lay flat on the deck in the middle of the cabin, between the port and starboard settees.

Being the lowest inhabitable space on the sailboat, the main cabin deck area had kept them safe from the barrage of bullets that tore through the hull. The teak finish along the two sides and the internal bulkheads had been splintered.

"You good?" said Devin.

Nancy nodded, the pistol lying across one of her legs—ready for action.

"Get out of here," said Brendan. "Before it's too late."

"As soon as we're out of sight, hail the Coast Guard on Channel 16 and give them your GPS coordinates. The nav system is still operational," said Devin, pointing at the navigation table next to the galley.

"I have a feeling the Coast Guard is already on this," said Brendan.

"Call them anyway," said Devin. "See you on land."

"Ahoy, matey," said Shea. "Now beat it."

The moment Devin's two feet hit the bowrider's aft deck, the speedboat took off. Fortunately, he'd anticipated the necessary urgency of a quick departure and had grabbed the handle on the back of the front passenger seat as he landed. The smoke-obscured sailboat rapidly receded from view, and for several panicked moments, the Russians didn't punch through the hazy cloud drifting across the water.

A scene played out in his head during that short period of time—the Russians pulling alongside the sailboat and slaughtering the Sheas. When the two speedboats appeared, smoke swirling behind them, Devin felt nothing but deep relief. A short-lived emotion, as bullets started to kick up small geysers of water just feet behind the boat.

Marnie and Miralles returned fire with their rifles, forcing the speed-boats to open the distance. Interesting.

From what Devin could tell, the Russians were down to one shooter in each boat, which theoretically matched what was being sent back in their direction but didn't pan out under the circumstances. Part of it was physics. Firing along a relatively flat trajectory at an approaching target mostly eliminated the need to adjust for range. Miralles and Marnie could essentially line up their targets and fire, the only complicating factor being the lateral, back-and-forth motion of the boats. A bullet fired one moment might not connect with a boat in a turn.

The other part was skill. Previous combat engagements with Pichugin's mercenaries had clearly demonstrated that Farrington's operatives could outshoot the Russians. Marnie was a solid shooter, holding her own against the Russians, but Miralles stood head and shoulders above all of them. Which gave Devin an idea. He turned to Gilly, who had replaced Alex.

"Where are we headed?"

"Brownies Beach," said Gilly. "About six miles northwest of here. It has a very shallow beach. We'll run the boat aground, hop out, and rendezvous with Farrington. He's en route."

"Do you have the coordinates punched into the nav system?" said Devin.

A bullet struck the corner of Gilly's seat, cracking the frame and ricocheting into the side of the boat. Gilly turned the wheel to the right, moments before several bullets harmlessly snapped past them to the left. He reversed the maneuver, bringing them to port, narrowly avoiding a barrage of bullets that sliced down the starboard side.

"I'm a little busy right now!" said Gilly.

"We need you shooting. Not driving," said Devin, yelling into his ear over the engine noise and rifle cracks.

Gilly glanced at him and nodded. "I'm just following the GPS track to the point Farrington gave me."

"I got this," said Devin, grabbing the steering wheel and handing Gilly his rifle.

While they switched roles, a string of bullets stitched through the boat, somehow missing everyone. Devin dropped into the driver's seat and gently turned the wheel left to get a feel for the boat, while miraculously dodging another fusillade of bullets.

A quick look at the nav screen told him that Brownies Beach was ten minutes and fifteen seconds away. Add another minute for evasive maneuvering. Call it twelve minutes. A long time to go back and forth with high-powered rifles without taking additional casualties. He had an idea.

"Emily! Do you think our boats are evenly matched for speed?" said Devin.

"I think so!" she yelled, before firing a quick burst from her rifle. "They weren't gaining on us after we left the sailboat, but they could have been holding their distance on purpose."

"The boats look pretty similar," said Gilly. "Twenty-one footers. The only way they'd be faster is if they were twenty-five- or thirty-footers. But I don't think—"

"They're definitely not thirty-footers!" said Miralles. "They were smaller than the sailboat when they came alongside. Significantly smaller."

Devin checked the throttle, unable to move it forward. The bowrider rocketed across the calm water at thirty-nine miles per hour.

"We can't outrun them. They can't catch up. And we still have twelve minutes of this shit to go," said Devin, a trio of bullet strikes emphasizing his point. "The three of you need to force them to open the distance."

"I'm down to four mags," said Gilly.

"I'm down to three," said Miralles. "And I'm sharing with Marnie."

"Alex had a few more on him," said Gilly. "We should be good."

"Then let's burn a mag each and buy us some distance. Reload!" said Miralles, before yelling over her shoulder at Devin. "Keep us on a steady course when we start firing."

Devin gave her a thumbs-up as he maneuvered them back and forth a few times while they reloaded.

"Steady up!" said Miralles.

Devin settled on the course recommended by the navigation system that would take them directly to Brownies Beach—just as a deafening discord of gunfire erupted behind him.

CHAPTER 22

Felix Orlov swerved the boat hard left and backed off the throttle as dozens of bullets simultaneously struck the bow and water just ahead of it. The bullets chased him throughout the turn, some buzzing inches from his head. Others smacked into the speedboat's fiberglass hull. Like a popcorn bag reaching the end of its microwave cooking time, the number of hits and near misses slowed to nothing several seconds into the turn.

Astonishingly, the concentrated barrage had been materially ineffective. Orlov emerged unscathed, and from what he could tell, only a single bullet had grazed Pavel's shoulder, having no impact on his seemingly unquenchable desire to get this job done. Despite his wound, the mercenary had continued to track and fire at the Americans until the turn cut off his line of fire, before swiftly moving from the bow compartment to the aft seating area—his rifle snapping off rounds until his targets were out of practical shooting range.

Gray and his friends had once again demonstrated cunning brilliance. They'd forced his boats to back off, well out of effective rifle range, into a high-speed standoff. A standoff that could last until the boats ran out of fuel or the Coast Guard somehow intervened. Each of Orlov's boats had been equipped with extra fuel containers, which could be transferred into the tanks on the run. He had to assume Farrington's people had done the same, which meant that this chase could theoretically last for hours.

The Coast Guard would intervene long before any of the boats ran out of fuel. That would be his play if he were in the boat a few hundred yards ahead of them. Call the Coast Guard. Establish their identity and credentials. Subtly maneuver toward the safety of a heavily armed Coast Guard vessel. Game over for Orlov. Or maybe not. He had no choice but to continue his pursuit and hope for the best. The best being the death of Devin Gray, Marnie Young, and Brendan Shea. The alternative being a life on the run from Yuri Pichugin—a short life, ending in unthinkable torture.

No. He'd take his chances chasing Devin Gray, hoping someone on that boat made an unrecoverable mistake. That's all it would take. If Gray turned in the direction of a Coast Guard vessel, he could dispatch the other boat to cut the circle, closing the distance, while he stayed on their heels. Two boats gave him flexibility. Success today would rely on using the two boats to his advantage.

Several minutes later, having traveled in a northwesterly direction the entire time, Orlov concluded that Gray had a specific destination in mind. A dock or possibly a beach where he or Farrington's people thought they could hold off Orlov's boats long enough to be rescued by law enforcement or more of Farrington's mercenaries.

His money was on Farrington's mercenaries. If they had a boat on the water, they'd have a team or two on land—along with a few prearranged landing sites. Gray and company hoped to jump off the boat and drive away before he could bring his mercenaries into action on shore. Overall, it wasn't a bad plan, except that Orlov had no intention of letting it happen. At this speed, he could close the distance to a stationary boat in several seconds.

Gray's people might get halfway down a dock or up a beach before his two boats caught up and gunned them down. This was the mistake he'd been waiting for. Gray would have been better off trying to rendezvous with a Coast Guard vessel. Orlov was crazy, and failure today meant the end of his life as he knew it—but he wasn't suicidal.

He would have abandoned the mission the moment the US Coast Guard showed up. A few months of bliss—looking over your shoulder all day and sleeping with one eye open—in Thailand or Bali beat taking a dozen 7.62-millimeter bullets from a Coast Guard M240 machine gun today. It was all about delaying the inevitable. His life's philosophy for the past decade. Orlov had no delusions about his overall longevity in this career.

He could count the number of mercenaries he met in his late twenties that still breathed Earth's good air on three fingers. A five percent survival rate—at best. Orlov was part of a dying breed. His only goal at this point in his career was to survive the day. Delay the inevitable. A few minutes later, his opportunity to see tomorrow's sunrise came into stark focus. Devin Gray's boat turned due west, headed for the shoreline. Orlov turned his boat in synch with Gray's maneuver, before grabbing his phone from the mangled cup holder and calling Artem.

"This is it. They're either going to pull up to a dock or beach their boat," said Orlov. "I want everyone ready to roll. Fully armed. We push forward, killing anyone in our way. Cops. Civilians. I don't give a shit as long as we keep our targets from escaping. Expect additional resistance from Americans onshore. This is a pickup. They'll have people waiting for them."

"Copy," said Artem. "We'll follow your lead."

"This could get messy. I see a packed beach dead ahead," said Orlov. "And I don't intend to let that stand in the way of my ticket out of this whole mess."

"I feel the same way," said Artem. "So does Niko."

He liked the sound of that. The few mercenaries who had survived to this point were ready to go any distance to salvage their lives. The Americans adjusted their course again, now heading straight toward the beach—their intention clear.

"Looks like they're going for the beach," said Orlov. "Whatever you do, don't hit the sand at full speed. Throttle back all the way about fifty feet out and hang on tight. That should put you up on the sand. See you on the beach."

He pocketed the phone and turned his attention to the landing approach.

"Hold on tight and stay low when we hit the beach," said Orlov. "They'll probably throw something at us the moment we stop. Wait for my order to move."

"Got it!" said Pavel. "I think Arseny might be coming around. He's moving a little."

"Forgot about him," said Orlov. "We're less than thirty seconds out!"

Pavel lowered himself to a crouch in the bow compartment's deck, taking a firm grip on one of the handles attached to the side of the boat next to him. The Americans continued on their kamikaze path toward the crowded beach. He was curious to see how they'd handle landing with so many people on board. One of them a civilian. A housewife, nonetheless. *Nimble* wouldn't be the name of their game. More like *stumble*.

The American boat hit the beach about twenty seconds ahead of the Russians. From what he could tell, only four people hopped down onto the sand. Four wasn't right. There should be at least seven. Possibly six. Pavel had hammered the speedboat with automatic fire, hitting the driver—before they were forced to veer into the smoke by a concentrated barrage of bullets.

The four moved faster than expected, a few of them firing their rifles into the air to clear the small beach. Something was off. Had they left the Sheas back in the sailboat? It didn't matter. One way or the other, everything would be over in the next several minutes. If Gray and his people managed to escape, Orlov would be on the run for the rest of his short life.

No. He had to pull this one off, regardless of the odds. They'd hit the beach running and keep running until they caught up with the Americans. Attack them during their pickup. Whatever it took to keep them from escaping. Orlov caught some motion in his peripheral vision and glanced to the right. Artem had pulled even with his boat. The mercenary gave him a thumbs-up before putting his hand on the throttle. Artem was ready for the landing. Maybe he'd underestimated some of the mercenaries assigned to the job. Maybe they still had a chance at pulling this off.

He nodded at Artem and pulled back on the throttle, hoping he'd timed the landing right. The Americans had already vanished into the woods directly beyond the narrow beachline.

CHAPTER 23

Richard Farrington sprinted down the dirt trail, hauling a heavy-barreled HK416 assault rifle fitted with a bipod, ACOG Squad Day Optic sight, and a sixty-round drum magazine. Enrique Melendez, a.k.a. "Rico," followed closely behind, armed with a suppressed MP7 submachine gun. Both of them wore plate carriers bearing additional ammunition. More than enough for the job. Farrington's push-to-talk satellite phone chirped, followed by a voice report.

"We're off the beach—and on the trail," said Miralles. "Alex is gone. It's just me, Gilly, Devin, and Marnie. The Russians are about twenty to thirty seconds behind us."

Alex Filatov was dead? Fuck. He was one of the last surviving members of the original Russian team Farrington had put together nearly two decades ago for General Sanderson's covert operations program. Alex, a.k.a. "Sasha," had been there and done just about everything imaginable. Farrington pushed that aside and focused on the mission.

Movement ahead of them stopped Farrington in his tracks. Melendez settled in next to him, his submachine gun shouldered and pointed down the trail. Four figures ran toward them, Farrington quickly recognizing the first in the quick-moving column. Miralles. Then Marnie. Devin and Gilly bringing up the rear. All armed with rifles. Fuck. Alex really was gone.

"Em. I see you coming up the trail," said Farrington. "I'm on the trail with Rico. You should be able to see us."

"I got you," she said, breathing heavily for a moment before continuing. "The Russians have four still in the fight."

Miralles and the rest of the group reached them several seconds later, Farrington wasting no time explaining the plan. He handed Devin a key fob and satellite phone.

"Devin. Marnie. Keep going up the trail until you reach the parking lot. Click the fob to find our SUV. We're going to set up here and hit the Russians," he said. "If one of us doesn't contact you immediately after the shooting stops, get the fuck out of here."

Devin looked like he was about to say something.

"No time for questions. Just go," said Farrington.

The moment Devin and Marnie took off, he organized the ambush. They backed up about twenty feet and spread out in the woods. Farrington and Melendez on the left, lying behind the base of the thickest tree trunks directly off the trail. Em and Gilly on the opposite side, similarly arranged. The actual mechanics of the ambush had been predetermined by years of experience. No detailed explanation was necessary.

Farrington, carrying their most devastating weapon, would engage the Russians with bipod-stabilized automatic fire. Sixty rounds of 5.56-millimeter ammunition should do the trick, but if one of the Russians got lucky and avoided the initial barrage, the rest of Farrington's shooters would immediately pick them off one by one with short bursts of gunfire. The ambush should be over within a few seconds.

Farrington spotted three men sprinting up the trail, each of them carrying rifles. A closer look through the 3.5X optic attached to his rifle revealed a fourth mercenary, who had fallen at least fifty feet behind them.

"Em. Do you see the last guy coming up the trail?" said Farrington. "He's limping along. Falling farther and farther behind."

"I see him," said Miralles.

"The moment I initiate the ambush, I need you to take him down. Center mass hit will suffice. I just need him unable to pursue. We'll take care of the other three. Copy?"

"Copy," she said.

Farrington tracked the Russians as they rushed up the trail. They appeared desperate. As in last-chance desperate—the only explanation for their careless, headlong sprint across unfamiliar ground. They had to know better than to sprint up a trail after heavily armed targets, who had enough of a head start to stop and set up an ambush.

Then again, what choice did the Russian have? If his targets ran directly to the parking lot for a pickup, Orlov's team would be left in the dust. And Farrington couldn't imagine that would sit well with Yuri Pichugin. This morning's failure to take out Devin and company would represent another spectacular failure. No wonder the Russians were barreling full speed up the trail. Their lives depended on catching up with Devin Gray.

"Stand by to open fire," he said. "In three. Two. One."

Felix Orlov spotted his quarry through the trees. Just a glimpse, but they weren't out of reach. If he stopped right now and took his time, he might be able to hit one of them with his AK-12. "One of them" being the operative phrase. One wouldn't be enough for Pichugin. The Russian oligarch wanted all of them dead. Devin Gray, Marnie Young, and Brendan Shea, but the best he could do at this point was two out of three.

That should be enough for Pichugin. *Should.* But one was unlikely to suffice. And there was no guarantee that the "one" he hit from here would be one of the primary targets. Two of Farrington's people had headed up the trail with Gray and Young. He had to close the distance and engage the whole group at once at whatever extraction point Farrington's people had arranged at the last minute. It was all or nothing at this point.

"Pick up the pace! I see them!"

Luka pulled ahead of him by several feet, the younger operative's age advantage made painfully obvious. Orlov pumped his legs harder, closing the gap as he followed Luka around a short bend in the trail. Several steps after the trail straightened, the forest ahead of them exploded in a discordance of gunfire.

The younger mercenary stopped in place like he'd hit an invisible wall, at least a dozen bullets punching clean through his body at once. Orlov's momentum carried him directly into Luka's back, momentarily sparing him from the brunt of the gunfire sent in his direction. Before he could grip Luka's shirt and try to use him as a meat shield, bullets tore into Orlov's right side, spinning him ninety degrees to face Artem. He barely felt the dozens of bullets that ripped through his back, knocking him flat on his stomach and face.

The last thing he saw, before it all started to fade, was the side of Artem's face planted into the dirt a few feet away— a tight grouping of three bullet holes in the center of his face. One of his last thoughts was of relief. Relief that a lifetime of struggle was finally over. An odd thought, given how hard he'd fought over those years to stay alive.

CHAPTER 24

Karl Berg sat on the edge of his office chair, stunned by the reports filling the DEEP SLEEP Task Force ESR (Emergency Status Report) board on his computer monitor. The simultaneous, multifaceted attack against the task force had been extensive. Every key player had been attacked in the last ten minutes since the CITADEL alert had been issued, with the obvious exception of himself. Plus Special Agent Dana O'Reilly and all three members of the Langley-based DEVTEK team.

Berg had no doubt that every one of them would have been targeted if they hadn't chosen to spend a portion of their Saturday in the task force operations center, deep inside CIA headquarters. Rafael had brought the DEVTEK crew in less than an hour ago to troubleshoot the system algorithms and protocols they'd developed to find and track members of Johan Hendrick's South African mercenary team. He'd promised them margaritas and Mexican food as a reward, whenever they finished the job. Sadly, his counterparts in California hadn't been so lucky, San Francisco taking the brunt of the hits.

Jenna Paek, DEVTEK's chief technology officer and primary task force liaison, was gunned down waiting with friends to be seated for brunch in North Beach. Her private security detail, parked a half block down the street, had just pulled out of their parking space in response to the WILDFIRE alert, when the gunfire erupted. By the time they reached Paek, the SUV carrying the shooters had sped away and turned off Union Street. They reported her dead on the scene.

Anna Shipley, head of DEVTEK's cybersecurity division, had suffered a similar fate while jogging the San Francisco Bay Trail near the Presidio. A runner shot her in the back of the head right in front of her security detail. The detail was immediately taken under fire by a second shooter posing as a jogger, forcing them to take cover until the assassins had fled. They managed to hit one of the shooters in the leg before the two escaped.

The only good news to come out of San Francisco was that DEVTEK's cybersecurity defenses had managed to deflect a major attack against its servers. A server breach at DEVTEK could have proven catastrophic for the task force, since DEVTEK's proprietary algorithms were the key driver behind most of the task force's sleeper investigations. Their magical code, routed directly through the CIA, had proved instrumental in identifying positions previously held by Pichugin's sleeper network—in addition to rooting out a few that had been ordered to stay behind after last year's purge.

Reports coming in from Los Angeles had taken a more fortunate tack. Devin Gray's sister and father had been saved at the last second by Decker and Mackenzie's people. They had been spirited away to a secure safe house by the two mercenaries who had helped Gray and Berg escape Baltimore last year and ultimately take down Pichugin's Miami operation.

The East Coast situation appeared more complicated and nuanced. MINERVA's servers had been spiked by the same attack deflected by DEVTEK. Completely wiped out. Fortunately, the task force server and terminal access points had been set up in an air-gapped space separated from the company's main server room, the information passed back and forth between Langley and their Arlington headquarters building by encrypted, on-demand satellite transmission. Even then, the data was still routed through a stand-alone DEVTEK server, where it was scoured and scrubbed for malicious code before heading to Langley.

MINERVA's key task force participants had mostly escaped the attack unscathed. Devin Gray was headed to BASTION EAST, accompanied by Marnie Young and guarded by Farrington himself. Brendan Shea and his wife were on their way to an Annapolis hospital. The prognosis on his gunshot wound, from his own report, which just hit the network, was good. Berg scribbled a note on a pad next to his keyboard: *Transfer Shea and wife to SFAC?* Based on the latest network reporting, the rest of MINERVA's task force–assigned investigators hadn't been attacked.

Marnie Young's parents were on their way to a BASTION EAST rally point with Jared Hoffman and Elena Visser, even though her parents didn't have clearance to enter the secure facility. Another note: *Divert Marnie's parents to Farrington's Anacostia safe house?* The move would prevent an embarrassing hassle at the SFAC, and Farrington's network of safe houses were pristinely safe. He'd run this past Marnie, sooner than later.

That left Audra Bauer, who hadn't reported since Gupta sent out the WILDFIRE alert indicating she'd been attacked. They'd both tried to reach her several times, each call going to voice mail. O'Reilly signaled him from the task force floor, her hand signals very clearly telling him that it was time to leave. He held up a finger and gave Bauer's phone another try. Voice mail. He muttered a few choice words, just before an unfamiliar number appeared on his phone's screen.

"Audra?" he said.

A long pause ensued before a familiar, steely voice answered.

"They killed David."

"No. No," said Berg. "They didn't. They couldn't—"

"They did. And they were South African. Part of Hendrick's crew," said Bauer. "I'm on my way to the SFAC."

"Audra. You don't—"

"Yes. I. Do," she said.

"Okay. But—"

"David went down fighting these fuckers," said Bauer. "He'd want me doing the same—without skipping a beat. Are you on your way?"

"We were walking out the door," he said, giving O'Reilly a thumbs-up.

"Then I'll see you soon. And keep the consoling and apologies to a minimum. We need to focus on whatever Pichugin has thrown at us," said Bauer. "There'll be time to mourn later. Understood?"

"Understood," said Berg.

"Good," said Bauer, before ending the call.

He took a deep breath and exhaled. David was gone. Gone because he'd—they'd—downplayed the arrival of Hendrick's crew in the United States. The connection to Pichugin had been enough to upgrade the task force's general security posture, but without further developments directly or even indirectly suggesting an enhanced threat to specific task force targets, they had all agreed not to escalate. He should have insisted. But based on what? Even the border incident with the Russians had no nexus to an immediate threat against them.

And Orlov had been off the grid for close to a year. He'd disappeared from Miami, under questionable circumstances, and nobody had caught a whiff of him since—and everyone was sniffing. Like Pichugin, Orlov had vanished without a trace. Berg should have seen it for what it was. The powers pulling Pichugin's strings in Russia had taken him off the radar for a reason. So everyone would forget about them. The DEEP SLEEP Task Force never forgot, but they did become complacent, its attention focused on piecing together the inner workings and details of the sleeper plot, to unmask its last remnants and prevent any further damage to the United States and its allies. Its attention focused right where the Russians wanted it—off the bigger picture.

O'Reilly poked her head into his office. "The protective detail is standing by. Rafael and his team are ready to move. Director Sharpe has cleared one of the bureau's emergency response tactical teams for

BASTION EAST. They'll head to the site a little later and stay to keep us company. The more the merrier."

"The merrier indeed," said Berg, pausing for a few moments. "The South Africans killed Audra Bauer's husband in the attack."

"Shit," said O'Reilly. "I'm so sorry, Karl. I know you're close to them."

"Yeah. Good friends," said Berg. "The best a washed-up CIA officer like myself could hope for."

O'Reilly looked like she wanted to say something, but she kept it bottled up for now—an intentional kindness that Berg appreciated. He didn't want to think about the role he'd played in his best friend's husband's death, let alone talk about it.

"I'll be at my desk," said O'Reilly, disappearing.

"Hold on. I'm coming," said Berg, grabbing his phone and checking his pockets for his wallet and keys.

Not that he would need any of these items in the foreseeable future. Berg wouldn't be leaving BASTION EAST until Pichugin's latest threat had been neutralized.

PART THREE

PART THREE

CHAPTER 25

Devin Gray squeezed Marnie's hand, not sure whom he was reassuring—himself or Marnie. The two of them sat on a bench pressed between Miralles and Gilly—directly across from Farrington, Rico Melendez, and two heavily armed Department of Homeland Security protective agents dressed in full tactical gear. The benches faced each other, affixed to opposite sides of the vehicle. A simple lap belt holding them in place.

He checked his watch. They'd been on the road for seventy-two minutes since they'd been corralled into the blacked-out passenger compartment of a Mercedes Sprinter van. For the past ten minutes, they'd traversed rolling hills and gentle turns. A rural road that felt vaguely familiar.

But probably not. They could be in Delaware or halfway to Richmond for all he knew. Both within easy driving distance of the CITADEL rally point Farrington had chosen in Bowie, Maryland, halfway between Annapolis and Washington, DC. The rally point had been the closest to Brownies Beach, where they'd left behind a mess.

Once the van got moving, the driver's road maneuvers quickly disoriented Devin and the others. By design. The DHS team's job was twofold: keep both hostile surveillance teams and their passengers in the dark. CITADEL's location was clearly a carefully guarded secret.

Not only did they have no idea where the DHS team was taking them, but the team leader had insisted that they surrender their weapons, ammunition, and any mobile communications devices before departing. Understandable in the context of liability and legality, but unnerving given that they'd just barely survived a vicious attack by the Russians. At least the weapons were accessible from inside the van, even if they were under lock and key.

"How much longer?" said Farrington, leaning forward to address one of the DHS agents.

"A few more minutes," said the agent.

"A few more minutes like my parents would say when we drove from Boston to Disney World?" said Farrington.

"No. We're actually just a few minutes away," said the agent.

"Any chance we'll get our weapons back once inside?" said Farrington.

"I honestly don't know," said the agent. "But it's doubtful. We'll transfer them to the armory, where they'll be available—just in case."

"Who determines when *just in case* is in play?" said Devin.

"My guess is that'll be pretty obvious," said the agent. "But I can't imagine we'll have to worry about that. The location is secure. As in overkill secure. For a reason."

"I don't know," said Melendez. "We've busted into some pretty damn secure sites before."

"This one is different," said the agent.

"That's what they all thought," said Farrington, which shut the agent down.

True to their word, the van turned sharply and came to a stop a few minutes later. No sounds of idling traffic, music, or horns. Not an intersection. Only a deep hum and the occasional low-grade creaking sound of metal on metal. A rolling gate. The van crept forward, picking up speed on a road far too smooth and well maintained to be a public road.

"This is so familiar," he whispered to Marnie.

"I know where we are," she said.

"Really?" he said. "Where?"

"We've been here before," she said.

Then it hit him. Of course. In a few moments the road would transition to hard-packed gravel. Marnie squeezed his hand when the van's tires gripped the new surface. He could picture the meticulously groomed trees and shrubs lining the road for the next mile or so, eventually thinning to reveal a seemingly larger-than-life Greek Revival–style mansion.

"You called it," he whispered.

"Whispering sweet nothings again?" said Farrington.

Devin shrugged. "Guilty as charged."

"Seriously, though. What's up?"

Devin leaned across the van and whispered in his ear, figuring that their previous visit to this site might not have been as officially sanctioned as they'd all been led to believe.

"We're headed back to the estate we used last year," said Devin.

Farrington laughed as he sat back. "Fucking countersurveillance guys. It's like you have a sixth sense."

"I'm not the one that put it together," said Devin, before nodding toward Marnie.

"Women's intuition?" said Farrington.

"You're stretching," said Marnie. "It wasn't that hard to piece together."

"Good point," said Farrington.

Melendez said something to Farrington, who whispered a response. None of it audible. Melendez turned to Marnie and nodded, giving her a thumbs-up. The DHS agents shared nervous looks, probably suspecting a mutiny afoot. A minute or so later, the van stopped and backed up, presumably in front of the ten-bay garage Devin remembered from last time. After a longer-than-expected pause, the van's rear door swung open to reveal Karl Berg.

"Keep your observations to yourself," said Berg, blithely—a faux smile on his face.

Message received. Act like you've never been here before.

"Welcome to BASTION EAST. A phrase you'll never repeat again outside of this facility," said Berg. "Understood?"

Everyone nodded.

"Your weapons will be transported to the armory," said Berg. "Sorry. Rules of the house."

Devin raised his hand.

"I'll answer all questions inside," said Berg. "We should probably seek cover. Razorblades and all."

"I thought . . . ," started Devin. Marnie pinched his thigh.

Nice catch. He'd almost outed himself by referencing the drone-detection radar in the nearby carriage house. Three-hundred-and-sixty-degree coverage. Highly discerning between drones and birds. Able to classify drones based on their radar profile. Five-kilometer range.

"It can wait," said Devin.

"That's what I thought," said Berg, raising an eyebrow. "Let's get moving."

Once inside BASTION EAST, metal security gates descended over the double doors leading to the driveway. The DHS agents, carrying their weapons, took off down a spiral staircase. The moment the last agent disappeared, Marnie turned to Berg.

"My parents?"

"Safe. But we didn't bring them here," said Berg.

"Are you fucking kidding me?" said Marnie, stepping toward Berg.

"Hear me out, Marnie," said Berg, raising both of his hands. "Getting them the required security clearance for this facility would take time. Time we don't have. I told Hoffman and Visser to take them to one of Farrington's safe houses."

"Anacostia," said Farrington. "Bad neighborhood. But the safest location I have at my disposal. It has remained undisturbed for close to twenty years. It's basically a doomsday bunker, and I'm detailing Jared Hoffman and Elena Visser to watch over them. Jared has been with me from the start of this program. Visser is about as dedicated and skilled as they come. Your parents are safer at that house than they are here."

"I thought this place was some kind of top secret secure facility?" said Marnie.

"I don't know exactly what the fuck this is, but I guarantee you it's not as safe as the Anacostia house," said Farrington. "Hoffman will run a comprehensive SDR before he pulls into the property. Trust me on this."

"I trust you," said Marnie. "Thank you."

Farrington nodded at her before turning to Devin. "Your dad and sister are safe. Our California associates took them to a secure location. They had a close call, but they're fine."

"Thank you," said Devin.

"Don't thank me," said Farrington. "Thank Karl. He's the one that arranged the protection."

"I took some precautions under the circumstances," said Berg. "Senator Steele footed the bill."

"There was no bill for this," said Farrington, giving Berg a sour look.

"True. But she made the arrangements," said Berg. "You can thank her when she gets here. She's about thirty minutes out. Her security detail made a little detour to pick up Julie Ragan."

"So, what now?" said Devin.

"We set up shop here," said Berg. "The DEVTEK team is already working on a system migration."

"They weren't targeted?" said Devin.

"They were working on an update in the task force operations center. Special Agent O'Reilly was there, too," said Berg. "But two of their counterparts in San Francisco were murdered around the same time you were attacked. Paek and Shipley."

"Jesus," said Marnie.

"And DEVTEK's servers were attacked. Big-time. But they managed to prevent an intrusion," said Berg. "MINERVA wasn't so lucky. Their servers were wiped."

"What about Jones and Herrera?" said Devin, inquiring about the two other key task force members.

"They're here," said Berg.

"And Bauer?" said Devin.

"She's here. But there's something all of you need to know," said Berg. "The South Africans killed her husband trying to get to her."

"Is . . . she—" started Devin.

"Okay?" said Berg. "Not at all. But she's fully functional as the task force leader. One hundred percent focused on making these fuckers pay. And please don't bring up her husband. She specifically asked that everyone just leaves that alone for now. She doesn't want the distraction. Good?"

Everyone nodded, including Devin, even though he wasn't sure how he was going to interact with Bauer and just gloss over the fact that her husband had been murdered an hour ago.

"And one more thing. There have been some disturbing developments over the past hour. The task force wasn't the only target," said Berg.

"What do you mean?" said Farrington.

"Have any of you checked the news?" said Berg.

"DHS confiscated our phones," said Devin.

Berg hesitated for a moment before speaking.

"It's probably better if Gupta gives you all the details. He's been tracking and mapping all the attacks," said Berg.

"Attacks?" said Marnie.

"You really have no idea?" said Berg.

"No," said Farrington. "Like Devin said. We've been incommunicado since getting in the DHS van. And nobody was in the mood to listen to the radio after we left the beach."

"The mass shootings," said Berg. "Pichugin's attempt to wipe out the task force wasn't conducted in a vacuum. It was planned to coincide with a nationwide attempt to sow chaos and discord—to spark a civil war."

"How many attacks?" said Marnie.

"Fourteen, spread across the country, against this weekend's planned We Second the First marches," said Berg.

"We the what?" said Miralles.

"It's the latest protest against gun legislation," said Marnie. "A play on words, as in we're going to use the Second Amendment to ensure we don't lose the First Amendment."

"Wait? Who's losing their First Amendment rights?" said Melendez.

"Nobody," said Marnie. "It's all performative grandstanding pushed and amplified by a small group of politicians fearmongering their way to reelection."

"These attacks just made their jobs a hell of a lot easier," said Berg.

"They'll be seen as retribution for Representative DeSoto's murder," said Devin. "She was staunchly anti-gun."

"That's the most likely scenario. Let's make our way down to the situation room," said Berg. "Security doesn't want any of the task force members aboveground."

"We're not task force members," said Farrington, before glancing among his mercenaries.

"Well. If you want your weapons back, you'll need to go subterranean," said Berg, motioning to the spiral staircase used by the DHS agents. "Shall we?"

"When you put it that way," said Farrington, before heading for the stairs.

CHAPTER 26

Richard Farrington followed Berg through an open doorway flanked by two DHS agents carrying rifles and wearing full body armor, and a third just inside the room. He was glad to see that the powers that be weren't messing around. The DEEP SLEEP Task Force's work up until this point, along with their collective experience rooting out Yuri Pichugin's sleeper network, was irreplaceable in the grand scheme of things. Critical to both unraveling the damage previously done by the sleeper network and preventing any future damage to the United States.

The room they entered resembled a military tactical operations center—a massive flat-screen monitor taking up at least half of the far wall, flanked by two screens on each side. While the side screens featured various live news feeds, the center screen displayed a map of the United States, with fourteen red crosshair symbols spread across the nation. He assumed they represented the locations of each attack. Jacksonville. Nashville. Dayton. Indianapolis. Phoenix. Tucson. Oklahoma City. Richmond. Tallahassee. Milwaukee. Billings. Cheyenne. Spokane. Newport Beach. A mix of red and purple cities. This had the potential to escalate quickly, especially if Pichugin had more attacks planned.

The rest of the space featured a dozen or more computer workstations with widescreen monitors, all facing the main screen. Only seven of the stations were occupied. DEVTEK's task force liaison team, two investigative cybersecurity gurus, and the man known only as Rafael, sat together in the front of the room.

Behind them, Anish Gupta had pushed together two stations, moving back and forth between seats, typing furiously on multiple keyboards. The two MINERVA investigators sat at stations next to Gupta, taking orders from Farrington's tech wizard and typing away in response.

A lone middle-aged guy dressed in khakis and a polo shirt made his way back and forth between them all, checking over their shoulders and occasionally fielding a question. The task force's BASTION EAST contingency didn't include a full technical support team. The men and women in front of Devin represented the entire sum of the team that would occupy the operations center.

Berg pointed toward a door to the right of the screens. "The situation room is through that door. Gupta will brief us in a few minutes."

"Aren't we waiting for the senator?" said Marnie.

"Senator Steele didn't want to hold us up," said Berg. "She'll attend virtually, until she arrives. Ready?"

"Before we get comfortable," said Farrington. "Where's the armory?"

Berg laughed. "I was wondering when you'd ask. If you walk back through the door we just entered and take a right, you'll see a window-less door. Totally nondescript—with a keycard reader."

He reached into his pocket and removed a stack of off-white, non-descript keycards, handing them to Farrington.

"I've already informed Trent Wolfe, head of security, that you and your team are authorized entry to the security hub, in the event of an attack on BASTION EAST. They'll give you your weapons back and kit you up however you see fit."

"Fair enough," said Farrington.

"What about Marnie and me?" said Devin.

"Do the two of you need direct access, or would it suffice to follow one of us in?" said Berg.

"Direct access," said Devin and Marnie at the same time.

"Eventually," added Devin. "When things settle down. We have enough going on right now. If that's okay with you."

"That's fine," said Marnie. "Let's hope we never need to use it."

"Amen," said Berg. "All right. Why don't we get seated in the situation room."

BASTION EAST's situation room resembled the White House version. A long conference table spanned the room, each seat at the table featuring its own encrypted business telephone suite and built-in touch screen. A flat-screen monitor took up most of the wall at the far end of the room, behind the head of the table, and several screens adorned the walls surrounding the table. Farrington nodded at Nikolai Mazurov, a.k.a. Nick, the only member of his team already present, other than Gupta.

"Aren't you supposed to be making sure Anish doesn't get into trouble?" said Farrington, taking a seat next to him.

Mazurov had unofficially stepped into the role of keeping an eye on Gupta, since Tim Graves's death at Helen Gray's apartment. Gupta had been reluctant to recruit another electronics expert to fill the essential post. Instead, he'd been filling the gap himself, learning everything he didn't already know about mobile communications, encrypted communications systems, mapping, hijacking, and jamming these systems—everything he had relied on Graves to do while he dealt with computer hacking, programming his own surveillance and jamming code, and drone operation.

Within the span of a few months, he'd transformed into a one-man electronics warfare show. There was only one problem. Most of the team's jobs required him to work on the move. Enter Mazurov. Part bodyguard. Mostly chauffeur.

"He's in his element back there with the DEVTEK team," said Mazurov. "And I need a break. Anish can wear on your nerves."

"Really?" said Farrington, before winking.

"Speak of the devil," said Mazurov.

Gupta entered the room, leaving the door open. Rafael stepped inside a few moments later, closing it behind him.

CHAPTER 27

Marnie Young inadvertently made eye contact with Audra Bauer, who was seated across from her. Marnie nodded briefly, a gesture returned by Bauer, both the pain and resolve in her eyes clear. Berg, seated next to Bauer, caught the quick exchange, and gave Marnie a wink of approval. He looked more on edge than Bauer.

She had no idea how Bauer was managing to keep her head in the game under the circumstances. Her husband had been killed less than an hour ago by the same people the task force had been assigned to stop. Duty and revenge, she guessed—buoyed by an unbreakable sense of duty to the task force she'd led for over a year and sustained by a gut need to avenge the senseless murder of her husband.

Duty undoubtedly came first. Bauer was the consummate professional, from what Marnie could tell. Her absence at this critical moment would significantly weaken the task force. Berg could step in, but there was a reason Bauer had flown higher than him at the CIA. She was a natural leader. Berg was a thinker and an organizer—the absolute best at connecting dots and an invaluable asset to the team. But his abilities were far more potent with Bauer directing him.

It had become clear to Marnie through some of the hushed stories told by Karl Berg about working with Farrington's team in the past that the two of them had pulled off more than just a few significant triumphs at the CIA over the years. Successes that had unquestionably depended on them working hand in hand to accomplish the seemingly impossible.

Seeing this through to the end might give her the revenge she sought. To beat the Russians again and send Yuri Pichugin scrambling back to Putin with his tail between his legs might be revenge enough. *Might* being the operative term. Marnie detected a saltiness to Audra Bauer, similar to Karl Berg. Neither had operated in the field for decades, but she sensed that an old mantra held true for them both. You could take the agent out of the field, but you can never take the field out of the agent. Bauer would get her revenge, beyond the task force's scope. Marnie was sure of it. And Karl Berg would play an instrumental role.

Gupta raised a finger, which silenced the few quiet conversations in progress.

"I'm gonna make this as quick as possible," said Gupta, grabbing one of the remote controls off the conference table near the main screen. "We have a lot of work to do in a short period of time."

He pressed a few buttons, the main screen mirroring the map of the United States in the operations center.

"Beginning around 12:20 eastern standard time, coinciding with the attacks against Task Force DEEP SLEEP, fourteen We Second the First marches were taken under fire by shooters, employing a variety of weapons and tactics."

"No drones?" said Devin.

"Surprisingly not," said Gupta. "But we have a theory about that. We'll get to that a little later.

"The attacks truly ran a wide gamut, the only consistent feature reported so far is the use of military-style weapons. Mostly AR-15s, but a few other types were identified. Some AK variants along with a small variety of submachine guns. Most of the attacks involved multiple shooters. Two to three, some firing from slightly elevated positions or low rooftops. A few from cars parked along the protest route. In one of those cases, the shooters raced out of their parking space and drove through the entire crowd, killing and injuring dozens more."

"Jesus," said Marnie.

"The worst shooting happened in Indianapolis. Two shooters, mimicking the 2017 Las Vegas massacre, took positions high in the buildings on opposites sides of Monument Circle in the downtown area, and opened fire with automatic rifles. The protesters had nowhere to hide. Early estimates put the deaths in Indianapolis at over two hundred."

"Holy shit," said Farrington.

"The range from the shooters' positions to the monument in the middle of the circle was roughly two hundred and fifty feet. In Las Vegas, it was about fifteen hundred feet," said Gupta. "They turned Monument Circle into an inescapable killing ground. Some expect the death count to rise above five hundred."

"And the rest of the attacks?" said Marnie, her words coming out a few decibels over a whisper.

"Nothing less than twenty dead," said Gupta. "In Billings, a pair of sheriff's deputies got the jump on two shooters firing at the protesters from a van parked in an adjacent parking lot."

"Have any of the shooters been taken into custody?" said Devin.

"None. Shooters in two of the cities got away free and clear. Then there's the two in the van that were shot dead by the sheriff's deputies. Several more were killed by police. And we have three barricade situations, but those are most likely to end in suicide by cop or straight-up suicide. It's become very clear that the shooters have no intention of being taken into custody. There's a report out of Nashville that the police wounded one of the shooters while fleeing the scene. Her accomplice put a gun to her head and shot her on the sidewalk before turning the gun on himself."

"This is unreal," said Melendez.

"Tell them the worst part," said Berg.

"It gets worse?" said Marnie.

"Much worse," said O'Reilly, seated next to Berg.

Gupta changed the screen to display a collage of social media posts from all the major platforms, including some from the most popular right-leaning sites.

"Props to Dana for putting this together on short notice. Within minutes of the attacks, an onslaught of anti-gun and anti-right-wing posts started flooding social media. As you can see on the screen, the message was consistent," said Gupta, before reading a few of the posts and comments.

How do you feel about guns now? You're not the only one with guns.

This is the real meaning of a good guy with a gun!

Virginia Tech. Sandy Hook. Parkland. Uvalde. We haven't forgotten!

You want weapons of war on our streets? You got it!

You should have brought a bulletproof backpack to the march, like my kids bring to school!

The Second didn't save you today, did it?

DeSoto's life is worth a million of yours!

We're taking back our country!

"You get the idea," said Gupta.

"This could start a civil war," said Marnie.

"Hold that thought," said Berg, nodding for Gupta to continue.

"At the public, and we assume behind-the-scenes, request of the president of the United States, all major social media sites halted service about forty minutes after the attacks, in an attempt to stem the online vitriol that followed—which you can imagine went supernova. Unfortunately, and entirely predictably, none of the right-leaning sites halted service. As we speak, millions of right-wing Americans are openly planning revenge, which we can fairly assume involves the wide-open slaughter of the Left," said Gupta. "Based on the rhetoric going back and forth on these sites."

"Has the White House tried to explain to the American people that this is a Russian-sponsored attack?" said Miralles.

"No. They're floundering right now," said Berg. "We've tried to make contact but haven't been able to get through."

"Senator Steele can help us with that when she gets here," said Bauer.

"I'm not sure how much of a difference a presidential address will make. Each side of the political spectrum gets its news from its own sources. Those lines have been drawn for decades. And a Democrat president blaming this on Russia and asking everyone to calm down is unlikely to make an impact on right-leaning viewers. If they even tune in to watch."

"And to make matters worse—" started Gupta.

"How can it get worse?" said Marnie.

"Trust me, it gets worse," said Gupta. "In the forty or so minutes since the big social media platforms shut down, mimic sites posing as those same platforms have popped up at least three times, before being taken down—probably by the NSA. Some clever hackers in Russia figured out how to redirect the actual site domain names to masked domains of their fake sites. These sites look like carbon copies, right down to user history. People have no idea they're getting their information and arguing with strangers on a Russian website."

"The NSA needs to shut down these right-wing sites," said Devin. "Throw a little water on the fire."

"Or gasoline," said Gupta. "Shutting down their websites would only validate the reason they were marching in the first place and incite them even more. Think about what the right-wing TV pundits will say."

"The Russians really did a number on us," said Farrington.

"But no drones?" said Devin.

"Which brings us to a very rough working theory," said Berg. "Widespread drone attacks could be next, and they'll be used to target the Left—which tracks with the DeSoto attack."

"Civil war," said Marnie.

"More like one big simmering low-intensity conflict across the country," said Berg. "Personal attacks between neighbors. Vigilante checkpoints at town borders or neighborhood entrances. Armed civilian convoys driving through parts of town known to be on the other side of the political spectrum. All escalating into organized attacks against more polarizing targets. Hobby Lobby and Whole Foods stores burned to the ground. Statehouse attacks. Police stations under siege. And on and on, until the country grinds to a halt."

"We have a meeting scheduled with AeroDrone for Monday," said Devin. "I think we should push that up to immediately. We need to know if a widespread drone threat is real."

"How long do you think the Russians will wait to strike? Drones or no drones?" said Farrington. "Or is this it? Let's be honest here. The Russians didn't flip a coin to decide who they'd hit first with a wide-spread attack. This morning's attack may be all they need to push this country into a low-intensity civil war."

"It's possible," said Bauer. "But I can't imagine this is the end of it. I've studied the conditions and dynamics of internal national conflict, civil war, and political coups more extensively than I care to admit. It's kind of what we do at the CIA. In my experience, fabricated or organic internal conflicts share many similar traits, the most applicable in this case being that in the end—one group, aided by an outside player, commits a major atrocity, which leads to a reciprocal atrocity, often precipitated by the very same outside player. And on and on until it becomes self-sustaining. This has been the CIA's playbook for years. Same with Russia's. Pichugin didn't invent this game. He's following the playbook, which means there will be at least one more big attack to try and spark a self-sustaining firestorm of civil chaos.

"In this case, we're obviously looking at a fabricated internal conflict. Because the Russians have limited resources in the US, mainly a significantly dwindled number of sleepers, they can't go the slow-burn route. They don't have the luxury of lighting a thousand small fires and hoping a few of them spread into an out-of-control wildfire. They're using dynamite to ignite a civil war, and based on our meticulous task force calculations, they may have expended the bulk of their remaining sleepers on this morning's attack. Fourteen sites. Two to four shooters per site. That's pretty much the extent of what we determined might be left."

"You're talking about the GRU-planted sleepers that Pichugin somehow co-opted," said Devin. "Not part of the plan my mother uncovered."

"The boomers," said Marnie.

"It's hard to say for sure based on initial reports, but it appears many of the shooters worked in male-female pairs, and that they looked older."

"Like the sleeper cell we zapped in front of the town house in Baltimore," said Miralles.

"And the few dozen we've rolled up over the past year," said Devin.

"If they don't have any more soldiers to commit atrocities, they'll have to rely on other, equally destructive means," said Bauer.

"The drones," said Devin. "Assuming they have more."

"Correct," said Bauer. "Which is why it's paramount that you put the screws to AeroDrone. You might want to wait until Senator Steele arrives to call them. I'm sure the addition of a senator with her influence on the call might light a fire under their asses."

"I don't doubt it," said Devin.

Small strobe lights started to flash from the corners of the room, synchronized with a low-decibel chirp that seemed to come from every direction. Everyone's attention was immediately drawn to the lights, then to Berg, who bolted out of his seat.

"Security situation," said Berg. "We need to move downstairs immediately."

The door burst open, a man Marnie hadn't seen yet rushing inside.

"I'm Trent Wolfe. Head of security. I need everyone to exit the situation room and make your way through the operations center to the lobby just outside."

"What's happening?" said Berg.

Wolfe glanced around nervously before answering. "We just lost the drone-detection radar."

"Lost?" said Farrington.

"As in destroyed," said Wolfe. "Surveillance video suggests it was hit by a nearly vertical, top-down strike. Something explosive."

"Fucking Razorblades," said Devin.

Wolfe gave Devin a quizzical look, like he hadn't been read in on the full array of possible threats to the facility.

"I've diverted Senator Steele's convoy as a precaution," said Wolfe. "And I've deployed the in-house team to positions along the perimeter of the house."

"No. No. No," said Devin. "You need to bring everyone back into the building and keep them away from the windows. We could be looking at a focused kamikaze drone attack. That's why they took out the radar."

"He's right," said Berg. "Your people are sitting ducks out there. Get them inside immediately."

Wolfe raised his radio and issued the order to withdraw the security agents posted outside. Before anyone responded over the radio, a tightly spaced series of about a dozen thumps vibrated the room. The warning had gone out too late. The next transmission over the radio was a frantic voice.

"Wolfe. This is Sutherland. I just lost contact with the teams we sent outside."

"Jesus," said Wolfe. "That's everyone I have."

Marnie turned to Devin. "Out of the frying pan and into the fire."

"More like jumping into a volcano," said Devin. "This is going to get ugly."

"Uglier than the sailboat?"

"Way uglier."

CHAPTER 28

Johan Hendrick watched the drone attack unfold on his laptop from the back seat of a Range Rover parked a few hundred yards from the eastern fence line of the sprawling target estate. The grayscale thermal image showed a dozen near-simultaneous heat blooms erupt around the main building. When the blooms faded, he didn't see any heat signature movement suggesting any survivors. Or any survivors capable of putting up a fight.

The Razorblade 800 drones were overkill when it came to soft targets like personnel, but the 400 version didn't pack enough of an explosive punch to take out two targets separated by more than several feet. He'd insisted on the 800 versions out of an abundance of caution, despite his handler's reluctance to assign the more powerful versions to the mission—and his persistence had paid off.

The safe house's security detail had deployed in groups of two, efficiently locating themselves to cover all approaches and provide overlapping fields of fire. They also didn't take positions side by side. They spread out enough to avoid being taken out by a well-placed burst of machine-gun fire. What they hadn't anticipated was a coordinated, explosive drone attack, though the destruction of the drone-detection radar could have provided the security detachment's commander with enough of a hint to keep his people inside.

He studied the screen for several more seconds. Nobody exited the mansion to help the downed security officers. They'd gotten the message. *Go outside and you die.* Now to send the second message. *Shoot at his team from one of the windows or doorways—and you die.*

"BEEHIVE. This is ZULU. Send a drone against one of the windows on the ground level, along the front of the house. We're heading out."

"This is BEEHIVE. Requested strike en route."

BEEHIVE was the drone launch site and control center situated about five miles away in a forest clearing. A fancy description for two white panel vans driven into the middle of nowhere, one custom rigged with six desk stations containing a Razorblade tablet controller—all connected to the drone-control and communications system. The other van contained the drones and their tubular launchers.

Hendrick had met the drone team's commander once, for a quick inspection of the Russians' inventory—just to make sure it wasn't all bullshit. His mercenary team was good, but not that good. Without the drones, they stood little chance of taking the facility. He had no doubt it had been chosen as a fallback position by his targets for its enhanced security capabilities. He'd been hoping for something easier, like a suburban neighborhood safe house, but the cards had dealt him a highly secure government facility in the middle of a sprawling estate. He triggered the radio remote attached to his vest.

"Time to go to work."

He went from the silence of the luxury SUV to the rumble and popping sounds of six idling ATVs. The plan was to breach the reinforced fence with explosives and approach from the east, before splitting into two groups. One that would gain access to the ground floor of the mansion along its northern face. The other from the south. Hendrick had no concept of the floor plan or what might remain of the security force. He hadn't even known their target an hour ago. Pichugin's handler had passed along a data packet with the target location's coordinates and satellite photos about forty-five minutes ago, along with a few suggested positions along the perimeter to stage his attack. Due to the last-minute nature of the intelligence delivery, he assumed that

Pichugin's surveillance assets had followed some of the VIPs to the estate.

He assumed the same type of information had been passed to the drone team. Thirty-three minutes after the data packet arrived, just moments after his team arrived in their chosen staging area east of the estate, BEEHIVE called Hendrick to let him know that they'd arrived at their launch location. Twelve minutes ago. That was how fast this operation had moved along from nothing to an all-out assault. He hoped to conclude it just as quickly.

If he could get his teams inside mostly unscathed, they should be able to make quick work of the remaining security team. Even the most skilled government protective agents were no match for his mercenaries. He couldn't be certain of the numbers, but Pichugin's intelligence packet estimated the likely presence of fourteen additional protective agents, a mixed bag of CIA and DHS tactical agents, who had delivered the VIP targets to the safe house.

His only real problem would be Richard Farrington's people. Pichugin's handler somehow confirmed the presence of four, including Farrington, along with the possibility of two more, who had successfully evaded surveillance after evacuating their assigned VIPs. Six Farrington-trained operatives were cause for concern. His teams would have to tread lightly and work in groups to stay in the game.

"Teams are ready," said Bekker.

Hendrick nodded. "Let's blow the fence and get this over with."

CHAPTER 29

A single explosion above them shook the security hub. Was it possible that a team had already breached the facility? How the hell could they have escaped detection? The entire estate was rigged with motion sensors, cameras, and acoustic devices.

"Did they breach the house?" said Devin, tightening his grip on Marnie's hand.

Not that she needed his protection. More like the other way around.

"I don't think—" started Gupta, who was seated next to a security officer monitoring a wall of screens.

"Negative. Negative," said the security officer. "Looks like they crashed a drone through one of the front windows on the ground floor."

"They're sending a message," said Farrington. "Don't bother trying to defend the house from the windows or doorways."

"Jesus," said Wolfe. "If we can't keep them from entering the house, we need to lock all access to this level and call in the cavalry. We're two floors below ground. It'll take them too long to breach each level. We can have a rapid-response team here in thirty to forty minutes."

Farrington seemed to give Wolfe's suggestion some thought before shaking his head.

"What would happen if the house above us burned to the ground?" said Farrington. "As in an accelerated burn. Would we be safe here?"

Wolfe's grimace answered the question.

"Our biggest problem would be the smoke. These levels draw from intakes located either inside the house or vented directly from the sides of the house. We have emergency breathing devices, hoods, and some less-obtrusive options," said Wolfe, glancing around at everyone assembled in the hub. "But not enough to last thirty to forty minutes, even doubling up. Not with this many people."

"You said *these levels*," said Devin. "Can we go deeper? Do those draw from different vents?"

"The facility does go deeper. Much deeper. And those levels do draw from different vents. But that's all I can say, and I probably said too much," said Wolfe. "Unfortunately, I don't have access to those levels. Not under these circumstances."

"Not under these circumstances?" said Marnie. "We're gonna die down here. What the fuck kind of circumstance are you talking about?"

"An attack against the United States. Nuclear. Biological. Chemical. Whatever might require the president or elements of the president's cabinet to seek deep shelter," said Farrington. "Am I hot or cold?"

"I can't say," said Wolfe.

"We're not getting out of this by sitting on our asses and hoping for the best," said Farrington.

"Sir!" said one of the security techs. "We have a breach along the eastern fence line. Explosives used to create a ten-foot-wide gap. Confirmed by cameras."

"Put it up on the main screen," said Wolfe.

The largest screen in the room, located on the wall adjacent to the array of monitors in front of the technician, switched to display the gap blown in the fence. Smoke billowed in every direction from the explosion. A few moments later, four four-wheel ATVs raced through the gap, each carrying four heavily armed, body armor–clad mercenaries. After they had cleared the fence, two more sped through, each driven by a single, similarly equipped mercenary.

"Eighteen of Hendrick's mercenaries. They aren't fucking around," said Farrington. "The armory. Now."

"Who's Hendrick?" said Wolfe.

"A South African mercenary. The best of the best," said Farrington. "The armory, please."

"This way," said Wolfe, motioning them toward one of the doors in the back of the hub's control center. "How could they know about this place?"

"They didn't. Not until they followed a few of us here," said Farrington. "They probably picked a few of the DEVTEK or MINERVA people. Lower-profile targets. Then attacked the highest-profile targets to trigger our fail-safe protocols. If they got lucky and took out the high-profile targets, all the better. If not, now they're all conveniently located in the same place for cleanup. This whole thing was a setup. A trap. And we took the bait."

"Then what's the plan, if we can't stay down here?" said Devin, as Wolfe entered the access code to the armory.

"We let them breach the house, so they can't crash a drone through a window without killing their own people," said Farrington. "And we take them down room by room and hallway by hallway. Close-quarters combat. Most importantly, we don't let them burn the house down."

"Sounds like fun," said Devin.

"Not for you or Marnie—or anyone other than the protective agents. This is way above your pay grade. These aren't Felix Orlov–level mercenaries. They're more on our level," said Farrington. "My job is to keep you and the rest of the task force's big brains alive—so the task force lives on to stop Pichugin's next move."

"Estimated time of arrival for the ATVs is about three minutes if they approach directly," said the security tech.

"They won't," said Farrington. "They'll split up. Let's see what you have in the armory. I assume there's more than just a few extra rifles and our gear?"

"I've considered its contents overkill—until today," said Wolfe, stepping out of Farrington's way.

"I'll make myself useful here," said Berg.

"There's a sizable safe room just through the other door," said Wolfe. "With a repeat array of monitors. That's our fallback position. Feel free to make yourself comfortable inside."

"I think we will," said Berg, leading the DEVTEK and MINERVA people to the safe room door.

"I'll stay out here for now," said Bauer.

"Me too," said Gupta. "There has to be something for me to do."

Devin followed Farrington's team inside, immediately taken aback by the sheer scope and volume of the weapons and equipment lining the walls. He kept out of the way, as the dozen or so CIA and DHS protective agents crowded into the space and started examining the weapons. Some of the protective agents had arrived with nothing more than a pistol.

"Wolfe," said Farrington. "Are the interior walls on the ground and upper levels reinforced in any way?"

"No. The only modifications made to the house involved the exterior walls, door, and windows. Windows are bullet resistant. Doors are reinforced steel. And the walls have been given a half-inch layer of steel—layered over by drywall. Their only way in will be the windows or the doors."

Farrington removed what looked like a belt-fed machine gun equipped with a squat-looking optical sight from the rack and handed it to Gilly.

"Works the same as a SAW," said Farrington.

"Yep," said Gilly, already deftly sliding the machine gun's chamber back.

"Grab some ammunition drums," said Farrington, tossing the next machine gun at Miralles, who snatched it out of the air. "You good with this?"

"Check," she said, before joining Gilly to stock up on ammunition.

"Rico. Grab two of the compact 7.62-millimeter SCAR-17s and all the magazines available. Two rail-compatible thermal rifle scopes. And any smoke grenades you can find. The rest of you. Load up on more ammo if you have a rifle. If you don't have a rifle, get one. Preferably something you've trained with extensively. Stuff the magazines in your pockets. We don't have time for a proper loadout session. Then grab a ballistic helmet and body armor. Whatever's available. Just grab it. You have one minute. Form up in the lobby outside of the security hub when you're finished," said Farrington. "And ballistic shields! As many as you can find."

The armory descended into organized chaos, driving Devin and Marnie outside, where Berg, Bauer, and Gupta stood in a tight group, watching the array of screens.

"How is it looking?" said Marnie.

"Hard to say," said Berg. "It's difficult to imagine eighteen mercenaries can take this place out, but when you have kamikaze drones on your side, it kind of changes the calculus. What's going on in there? Sounds like quite the ruckus."

"Farrington has a plan—as always," said Devin. "I think I know what he has in mind."

"Well, he better move fast," said Bauer. "The best DHS can do is a fifty-minute ETA. They could be here by helicopter in under ten minutes without the drone threat. Under thirty by vehicle. But they won't approach the site without a dedicated KADD system. And the soonest they can get one of those out here is fifty minutes."

"KADD?"

"Kinetic Anti-Drone Defense vehicle," said Bauer. "It can track and shoot down drones. Apparently, it was designed for drone swarms."

"That would certainly come in handy," said Marnie.

"We're scheduled to receive one in the fourth quarter of the year," said the security technician. "This isn't the highest-priority secure facility in the grand scheme of things."

"Probably why they let us use it," said Bauer. "The good news is they can move a drone-detection radar system within range of the facility within twenty minutes, so at least we'll have better situational awareness."

"This will all be over long before any of this stuff arrives," said Devin.

"Sounds like it," said Marnie. "If Hendrick tries to burn the place down."

"He will," said Berg.

Farrington joined them a few moments later, carrying a hefty-looking rifle and an oversize scope. He made room for his haul on one of the emptier tables toward the back of the room.

"Let's talk while I set this up," said Farrington.

They huddled around him while he examined the rifle scope.

"Thermal scope. Smoke grenades," said Devin. "You're gonna blind them once they get in the house."

"I'm going to let them get inside and get comfortable for a few seconds before filling the first floor with smoke. If Hendrick is thinking clearly, he'll retreat immediately. He's smart. He's been around for a long time. You don't survive in this business if you're an idiot—or you can't attract the right kind of talent," said Farrington. "That was Orlov's problem. Smart, which got him this far. But the quality of his team had taken a serious dive over the years."

"If Hendrick retreats, won't he try to burn the place down?" said Devin.

"Yes. But we'll have shooters posted on the second floor. The windows are equipped with firing ports. Half of the bullet-resistant panes open inward," said Farrington. "If Hendrick retreats, we'll move the DHS and CIA protective agents to the windows to momentarily engage his mercenaries. Just for a few seconds. Maybe burn a rifle magazine before we pull them back into the interior rooms, where they'll be safe from a drone strike. Torn between gunfire from above and a clear threat from the ground level, Hendrick will be more focused on surviving than tossing pyrotechnics into the house. And even if he does, we'll toss them right back out. I assume the kitchen is equipped with a few oven mittens."

"What if he's not thinking clearly?" said Devin.

"Then we're in for one hell of a close-quarters gun battle on the ground floor," said Farrington. "Frankly, I prefer it. I think it's our best chance of permanently taking Hendrick off Pichugin's game board. We don't need him regrouping later, like Orlov, and biting us in the ass again. If he stays, we'll hunt his team down in the smoke with our thermal sights."

"What can we do, other than watch?" said Marnie, like she was reading Devin's thoughts.

"I need you to feed us real-time updates of what Hendrick's people are doing. If they retreat, I need to know immediately so I can put the second-floor shooters into action. If they stay?" he said, continuing after a long pause. "I need you to do your best to communicate their movement and location. Tech guy, Sutherland. What's your first name?"

"Brian."

"Brian. Wolfe said you can put a ground-floor schematic on the big screen," said Farrington. "And that you can shift all of the interior and exterior ground-floor feeds to the rest of the array."

"He's right," said Brian.

"Start working on that immediately," said Farrington.

"I'm on it," said Brian.

"The rest of you need to study that ground-floor schematic and come up with some kind of system to guide us through it in the heavy smoke and point our scopes in the right direction at the right time. The thermals can see through the smoke."

"Brian. Are the cameras inside the house thermal capable?" said Devin.

"Yes. It's a bit low grade compared to those scopes," said Brian. "But you won't have trouble picking out human targets."

"Are the schematics black and white?" said Devin.

"Yes."

"Do you have dry-erase markers?"

"In the safe room supply cabinet," said Brian.

"I see where you're going with this," said Farrington. "It won't be easy to maintain the tactical picture."

"It'll be a living nightmare trying to keep up with all of the movement," said Devin. "Make sure to have your people briefly raise a hand every now and then, so I don't mix them up with Hendrick's people."

"Every now and then?" said Farrington. "How about every ten seconds. This is going to be way harder than you think."

"I know it is," said Devin. "But what other choice do we have? You'll score a few hits with the scopes, until Hendrick coordinates a move against you."

"Then all of our lives are in your hands," said Farrington.

"In all of our hands," said Devin.

CHAPTER 30

Johan Hendrick parked a few feet from the southeast corner of the house and dismounted the ATV—leaving it in idle. His first order of business was to test the windows. He fired a single, suppressed shot from his compact HK416 into the south-facing window closest to the corner, the bullet ricocheting off the glass, leaving little more than a bluish-white blotch. Bullet resistant. No surprise there.

The other two ATVs screeched into place next to him, CHARLIE and DELTA teams hopping off the vehicles and spreading out along the south-facing side of the house.

"CHARLIE. Search for and shoot out any cameras. That same order goes for all teams inside the house," said Hendrick. "DELTA. The windows are heavy-duty bullet resistant. Prep the corner window for breach. Strip the whole window. Grab a step stool and place it under the window."

He triggered his radio. "WHISKEY, this is ZULU. Windows are bullet resistant. Pick a north-facing window near the northeast corner and prep for breach. Soften the interior with flash bangs before entry. Recommend using the MGL. Advise when ready."

WHISKEY was Bekker's call sign. ZULU was Hendrick's. MGL meant the Russian-made 6G-30 multiple-grenade launcher—a revolving barrel launcher that could pump six forty-millimeter flash bang grenades into the house within the span of fifteen seconds. He planned on firing them through any visible open doorways leading out of the breach room, saving one for the room itself.

"WHISKEY copies."

Several suppressed gunshots destroyed the cameras CHARLIE team could identify. Five on the house and two in the nearby trees. The security team inside would be able to watch their every move. The question was whether they could adequately relay that information, during a fast-moving close-quarters battle, to Farrington's advantage. Done inadequately, the flow of information could prove distracting. A potentially devastating disadvantage. While DELTA finished prepping the explosive tape around the window, he checked in with his eye in the sky.

"BEEHIVE. This is ZULU. What's your status?"

"Twelve drones up. Eleven with thirty minutes of loiter time remaining. One with a full forty."

"Keep an eye on the second-floor windows. If you see movement inside, report it to me immediately. I don't like the idea of detonating that large a warhead with my people one floor below, but it might be necessary depending on the circumstances," said Hendrick.

"We'll watch the second-floor windows, along with any perimeter escape points like the garage bays and ground-level doors."

DELTA team leader gave him a thumbs-up and started back to his team away from the window, sliding them along the side of the house toward the southeast corner.

"We're breaching. Stay in touch," said Hendrick, before motioning CHARLIE into position on the other side of the window.

While both teams settled in, stacked up along the mansion's white clapboard exterior, Hendrick retrieved the Russian-made 6G-30 grenade launcher, which had been preloaded with flash bang grenade variants. He nestled in next to CHARLIE team's leader, several feet from the window.

"WHISKEY. This is ZULU. We're set for breach," said Hendrick over the radio.

"WHISKEY is set. Ready breach on your mark."

He glanced at DELTA team leader, keeping his radio transmitting triggered. "Stand by to breach in three. Two. One. Breach."

The explosive strip outlining the window detonated simultaneously with a single loud crack, sending smoke and debris outward onto the grass. DELTA team went to work on the window a few moments later, two members of the team striking it with solid metal battering rams with flat frontal attachments to maximize the surface area impact. The window's guts, the glass and panes inside the exterior frame, popped inside the room with a single coordinated strike. The other two members of DELTA aimed their rifles inside, searching for targets to clear the way for Hendrick, who was up the moment the window disappeared.

He propped the grenade launcher's barrel against the windowsill and made a quick assessment of the room. Two doorways led out. One directly in front of the window. The other on the west-facing wall. He fired two grenades through the door in front of him and three deeper into the house through the other. Hendrick bounced the last grenade off an interior wall, sending it back into the room. Just in case someone very patient lay in one of the unobserved corners of the entry room.

Moments later, the grenades started to detonate inside, competing with low-order detonations and distant flashes from the team on the opposite side of the house. When the grenade inside the room just beyond the window exploded, he dropped the launcher and quickly climbed up the step ladder into the house. Within several seconds, his entire team was inside.

"This is ZULU. My teams are in," said Hendrick.

"WHISKEY reports the same," said Bekker. "We're ready to start the sweep."

The plan was to clear the ground floor first, followed by the second floor. Then look for the breach points leading to the belowground levels. If the lower levels couldn't be accessed within a reasonable amount of time—no more than twenty minutes—they'd burn the house to the ground and hope the fire continued all the way down to their targets. He had a combination of white phosphorus and thermite grenades.

The white phosphorus could ignite an entire room in one detonation, the small phosphorous particles burning for up to fifteen minutes. The thermite would burn at forty-five hundred degrees Fahrenheit, and should be able to melt through the floor, even if it was layered with steel, and create a hole leading to the level below them. Several strategically placed thermite grenades could open one of the burning rooms on the ground floor to the subterranean complex. It was the best he could do for his client if there was no reasonable way to get his teams into those levels to do the dirty work up close.

CHAPTER 31

The process that had sounded simple enough in theory a minute ago was about to be tested—with little to no margin for error. Hendrick's mercenaries had breached the ground floor and were moving in small teams toward the doors leading out of their original breach zones. Devin had arranged it as a one-way information-flow system, each team with its own responsibility to maintain its part of the flow.

The large screen displayed the ground-floor schematics for the mansion, the rooms and hallways labeled numerically with dry-erase marker by Bauer and Marnie. Kept true to the home's original Greek Revival architecture, the interior structure didn't appear to have been changed. It consisted of eighteen rooms of varying sizes, none too expansive; two staircases leading upstairs, a wide switchback staircase upon entering the front-door foyer, and a smaller staircase located toward the back of the house for convenience; three hallways in all, one leading straight through to the kitchen from the front door nicknamed MAIN STREET, another crisscrossing the main hallway accessing nearly all the rooms on both sides of the house, called BROADWAY. The other on the north side, branching off into exterior rooms: ROUTE 66.

They'd placed nine red Xs in each of the southern-corner rooms—rooms one and six, which represented all the hostile mercenaries in the house. Their jobs would be to take Berg and Gupta's location input, by room number, and keep the schematic updated in real time with enemy and friendly locations.

Devin's job was to translate the locations into immediately usable information for Farrington's team. He wouldn't be using room numbers. Devin would be identifying enemy movement and location using the clock positions. The security cameras' thermal imaging was the best, like Wolfe had said, but Devin could tell where Farrington's people's weapons were pointed at any given time. Right now, their weapons pointed toward the southeastern-corner rooms.

Farrington's two teams of two operatives lay inside rooms along the crisscrossing hallway, toward the middle of the house. He'd chosen them mostly because they had two doors. One leading to the hallway, another opening to the living spaces along the back of the home. Aside from personal protective gear, each team was equipped with a ballistic shield to protect them from the inevitable return fire, one MK46 light machine gun, and one SCAR 17 rifle. They also carried the preponderance of the smoke grenades found in the armory; the rest had been given to the DHS and CIA protective agents on the second floor.

The agents based on the second floor had been given three very specific missions. One. Toss three smoke grenades down each stairwell when ordered by Farrington. Two. Keep Hendrick's mercenaries from moving to the second floor. Three. Be ready at a moment's notice, if ordered, to open the windows and fire on any retreating mercenaries. Farrington had been painfully clear with the government agents that they were no match for the South African hit squad about to enter the house. No heroics. Just keep the mercenaries off the second level.

"The teams are stacking up to move out," said Gupta. "Four per door. Extras headed to two and seven."

The "extras" were presumed to be Hendrick and his second-in-command, each of them leading two teams.

"Rich. The teams are stacking up to leave their breach rooms," said Devin. "Four at each door leading out of the rooms."

"Copy," said Farrington. "All units. Execute WHITEOUT."

CHAPTER 32

A dozen or more solid metallic clangs hit Hendrick's ears in rapid succession, instinctively causing him to crouch and put up a fist, stopping them before they'd taken more than a few steps toward the adjacent room's doorway. CHARLIE's team leader held a flash bang grenade, finger inserted through the safety pin ring, moments away from tossing it inside. Hendrick shook his head, and the mercenary replaced the grenade in one of the slots on his tactical vest.

"This is ZULU. All units hold positions."

"WHISKEY holding," said Bekker. "Any idea what's going on?"

Three more metallic clangs rang out, one sounding nearby. He risked a peek around the doorframe, seeing all the way to the main entrance hallway. A familiar looking metal cylinder rolled along the deep cherry hardwood floor beyond the french doors two rooms down. Smoke grenades. The canister erupted in a billow of thick chemical smoke, which took no more than a few seconds to completely obscure his view into the hallway.

At least the french doors were closed, a prematurely hopeful thought. Smoke rapidly drifted into the room right in front of the doors, quickly filling the space. Was there another room to the far left? How many fucking rooms were there on this level? He turned to DELTA, a thick fog pouring through the door the team had stacked up on.

Farrington was trying to even the odds. But eighteen of Hendrick's exceptionally well-trained mercenaries against four to six of Farrington's people couldn't be evened out by some smoke. Not even with a dozen government protective agents backing him up. Something else was at play. Or was Farrington simply acting out of desperation?

A small part of him said to get the fuck out of the house now, before it was too late. Pichugin wasn't the most understanding client, but Hendrick could pay the Russian back for what he'd invested in the operation so far and throw in an additional job at no cost. It would set Hendrick back, but his services were in high demand. He'd be back in the black in no time.

No. There was no way he was backing out of this one. It might cost him some lives, but they'd eliminate Farrington and his people quickly, along with the government agents. Then it would be a matter of figuring out whether they could continue shooting people in the face or be forced to burn the place down. He triggered his radio—his transmission cut off by the sound of automatic gunfire and bullets splintering through the room's walls and woodwork.

Everyone in the room dropped to the floor to avoid the incoming fire, at least one of them permanently. DELTA's team leader, the closest to the door leading out of the room, had fallen on his side instead of flattening himself in place. A pool of blood started to spread underneath his head, as chunks of drywall and wood splinters covered everyone.

The gunfire lasted at least thirty seconds by his rough estimation—the rate of fire somewhere in the range of three hundred rounds per minute. Five per second punching through the walls, the pattern of holes in the walls in front and behind them suggesting the shooters were firing from a single, fixed location—low to the ground. Two could play at this game.

"All teams. This is ZULU. The gunfire is coming in low," said Hendrick. "Do a little math based on the bullet hole patterns and wait for my order to fire back in the direction of the gunfire."

"ZULU, this is WHISKEY. I have one critically wounded and one KIA."

d crawling from this point forward. They
int in making it easier for them," said
ut there?"

ad way," said the mercenary. "Botha is
all over. All we can do is bleed at this

" said Hendrick. "We'll get to you as

stion?" said Bekker, oddly breaking

house," said Hendrick. "It's too late

suggest," said Bekker. "We know
le of the house. Why don't we have
h a few drones. Soften them up a
with the drone strikes."

d directed the strike. Three of the
neously strike the ground-floor
mansion. He hadn't seen the
against the window along the
on the other side of the main
damage.

likely detonated against the
d on his single bullet test
ld be like striking a metal
ed the glass and detonated

ed drone strike in twenty

"Copy. I have one confirmed KIA. Another down hard."

One of CHARLIE team's members squeezed his leg. "Sir?"

"What is it?" he hissed, low crawling along the inner wall to align a shot with the incoming fire.

"Heyns is dead."

Hendrick glanced over his shoulder to see Heyns slumped against the front wall of the house, covered in dust and wood chips, two tiny red holes punched through his right cheek. The contents of his head on the wall just above him. He thought about retreating again—he was down four mercenaries and they'd barely gotten started—but shook off the thought just as quickly. This was the end of Farrington's reign. He didn't care what it took.

◆ ◆ ◆

Farrington patted Miralles on the shoulder, her signal to stop firing and take cover, as he sent Melendez the same brief message over the radio. Hendrick would put two and two together fast. Miralles scooted all the way behind the ballistic shield, which Farrington had kept propped up on one of its long sides—facing the southeast corner of the house. He braced the shield with two hands, one on the grip in the middle, the other in front of Miralles's head.

"Put your legs on top of mine," said Farrington. "Give them less surface area to—"

Hendrick's return fire started cracking against the front of the shield before he finished the sentence. The room around them disintegrated into a maelstrom of fragments, the drywall and wood studs holding it in place shredded by multiple rifles firing on automatic. The impact of the concentrated fusillade on the room probably closely resembled what Hendrick had experienced, except Miralles's MK46 light machine gun was equipped with a bipod, which stabilized her fire and allowed her to tightly control her gunfire.

When the shooting stopped, he ordered both teams to withdraw from the rooms and reload the MK46 LMGs. Hendrick's people would move quickly enough, even in the smoke. Farrington hoped to repeat the machine-gun trick one more time before the cat-and-mouse chases started. He needed to whittle down Hendrick's crew as much as possible from a distance.

"Talk to me, Devin," said Farrington, covering Miralles's withdrawal with the shield.

"Two mercs down in each room. Brings the total to fourteen. They're still lying flat in rooms one and six, but Hendrick is talking over his radio. I wish we could hear—" said Devin. "Shit. They're up and on the move. Rich: you have three hostiles moving together into an adjacent room that connects to BROADWAY. Four moving along the front of the house toward the front-entry foyer. Hendrick assumed to be with that group. Rico: you have four hostiles moving along the northern side of the house, into an adjacent room. That room opens onto ROUTE 66 and is a few steps from BROADWAY. The other three are moving into ROUTE 66 toward the front of the house. Rico's targets have to move west down ROUTE 66. I suggest hitting them when they reach BROADWAY."

"Call it out when they get there," said Melendez.

"Rich: set up your machine gun in front of the bathroom facing due east. I'll let you know when to start opening fire. Shoot from due east to southeast, then get the fuck out of there. You'll only have one room separating you from any of the survivors. We'll be keeping an eye on the second group moving toward the main foyer."

"Nice work," said Farrington.

"I'll pass that along," said Devin.

"WHISKEY. I recommen
can tell where we are. No p
Hendrick. "DELTA. You still
"This is Adisa. We're in a
KIA. Wessels is critical. I'm hi
point."

"Copy that. Hang in there,
soon as we secure the floor."

"Johan. May I make a sugg
radio protocol.

"We're not pulling out of the
for that."

"That's not what I was going t
Farrington's teams are on the west si
BEEHIVE hit the back windows wi
little. We can coordinate our advanc

"Fucking brilliant."

Hendrick contacted BEEHIVE an
twelve loitering drones would simulta
windows along the western face of th
damage done by the drone he'd crashe
front of the house, but the closed door
foyer showed signs of significant shrapn

The Razorblade 800's warhead had
thick bullet-resistant glass, which, bas
against one of the windows earlier, wou
surface. The warhead would have penetra
inside. Hard kill.

"ZULU. This is BEEHIVE. Coordina
seconds."

Devin studied "the board," as they had taken to calling the schematic filling the screen. Nothing had changed for the past several seconds since he'd reported the results of the last machine-gun barrage to Farrington.

The two teams moving up ROUTE 66 toward BROADWAY had pulled back halfway down the hallway, leaving two in place near the corner, presumably KIA, and dragging one with them. The three hostiles who entered BROADWAY from room seventeen had been shredded by Miralles's light machine gun. Berg and Gupta still detected some movement from one of them, but not the kind that suggested he was still in the fight. The mercenary had moved only one of his arms. Barely.

The four-mercenary team in room three had moved to the french doors leading to the main foyer, where they'd remained for several seconds. Hendrick wasn't giving up. Both surprising and unsurprising given the man's circumstances.

Surprising because he must have figured out how Farrington was anticipating his moves and ripping his mercenaries apart by now. Unsurprising, because he was cut from the same mold as Farrington's people. Apparently the words *surrender, retreat,* or *capitulate* weren't a part of their lexicon.

"Rich. No change to report. They're all sitting tight," said Devin.

"They're up to something," said Farrington.

"Once they start to move, it's over for them," said Devin.

It could be over for one of Hendrick's teams right now. If Melendez crawled through the kitchen door connected to ROUTE 66, concealed by the smoke, he'd have a straight shot down the hallway at the four mercenaries lined up along the interior wall. But Farrington didn't want to tip his hand. If Hendrick suspected the use of thermal rifle scopes, he'd be a fool not to retreat, regardless of his principles. Farrington wanted to engage them at the same time.

"Second floor. Let's refresh those smoke grenades. Three down the main staircase. I want Hendrick's teams choking on thick smoke when they make their move. Rico. Toss a few down ROUTE 66."

"Popping more smoke," said one of the DHS agents stationed on the second floor.

"Same here," said Melendez. "I just need to crawl over to the hallway door."

"How are you guys dealing with the smoke?" said Devin.

"The N95 respirators are keeping it tolerable," said Farrington.

Wolfe got up from his station, looking alarmed. "A few of the west-facing cameras near the western perimeter fence started autotracking objects low in the sky. But they lost them."

"How close would these objects have to be for the cameras to start tracking them?" said Berg.

"No more than a hundred yards," said Wolfe, before his attention was pulled back to the screen at his station. "Happened again. Halfway between the fence line and the facility."

Marnie grabbed the handheld radio on the table next to her.

"Rich. They're going to hit the back of the house with drones! Take cover!"

Farrington sprang into action the moment Marnie spoke the words *hit the back of the house.* He didn't need to hear the rest to know what Hendrick had been concocting. It was the one scenario Farrington had no control over, and the damage done to the east-facing room by Hendrick's "message" had left him feeling vulnerable when they finally pulled back to the kitchen and great room.

He leaped to his feet, yanking Miralles up by the drag handle on the top of her body armor vest, and dropping her facedown on the white-tiled floor of a large bathroom. In the few moments he knew remained, he placed his body between the kitchen-facing wall and Miralles, ballistic shield on its side at an angle, positioned to deflect shrapnel from hitting their vitals. If the shield made a difference at all. The Razorblade

800 employed a warhead similar to, but slightly smaller than, a Javelin anti-tank missile. In the fifteen-to-twenty-pound range. Pretty high up on the "blow the living fuck out of a room" scale.

Farrington lost all sense of just about everything a moment after forming that thought. The floor shook beneath him, the wall separating the bathroom from the great room blasting inward. A sharp, ungodly pain shot up his right leg from the knee. As pieces of construction timber, drywall, and wood molding settled on top of them, he risked a look over the shield. The interior wall hadn't been completely knocked out, but the scorched and shredded great room was visible to different degrees through most of it. A few small fires burned on the floor. Pillows ignited by the blast.

He tried to lift himself up but hit the tile hard after barely rising a few inches.

"Em. What's your status?" he croaked.

"Better than yours from the sound of it," said Miralles, who rolled onto her side. "Definitely better than you."

Farrington chuckled quietly, not feeling any pain in his chest, which was a good sign. Still, he barely had the energy to turn his head and look at her.

"Hendrick is on the move," he said. "Take the SCAR. Use the scope."

CHAPTER 34

Hendrick counted to three after the explosions rocked the house, just in case BEEHIVE mistimed one of the drone strikes. The last thing he needed was to take a chestful of shrapnel moving down the hallway. Through the french door's glass panes, some of which had cracked in place from the explosions, he spotted several pinkie finger–size, jagged chunks of sizzling metal partially embedded in the reinforced-steel front door a few feet away. Satisfied that the deed was done, he gave the order for all his mercenaries to start moving toward the back of the house.

He opened the french doors and slipped into the hallway, rifle leading the way. Once the remaining three members of CHARLIE had stacked up behind him, he started moving toward the flickering light of a few scattered fires ahead of him in the distance. Probably kitchen towels or place mats that had caught fire when the warheads detonated.

Hendrick picked up the pace, as the damage to the hallway walls became more and more evident the closer the fires appeared. Bekker had really come through with this idea. Up until a few minutes ago, Hendrick had essentially resigned himself to a complete mission failure. Going out in a blaze of glory the only option left on the table in front of him. Other than ordering a retreat—and leaving half of his mercs behind. He would have been better off following his gut and calling off the mission as soon as the smoke grenades had started popping off. He'd known right then and there that the rest of the mission would be a shit show of epic proportions. But now he was back in business.

"WHISKEY. Are you moving?" said Hendrick over his radio.

"Affirmative. They're heading down the back hallway to look for kitchen access," said Bekker. "Contact Kruger from this point forward. He's their team leader. I'm lying on my ass bleeding."

"Copy," said Hendrick. "Kruger. Let me know when you've located access to the kitchen. We don't need a friendly-fire incident."

"Understood, sir," said Kruger.

Hendrick listened intently for any signs of life coming from the back of the house. All he could hear at this point was the crackling of fire and the occasional crash of glass or part of the ceiling. Music to his ears.

◆ ◆ ◆

Rico Melendez lay on his stomach in a short hallway leading out of the kitchen, ears ringing and his now-helmetless head lying a foot past the edge of the doorway. Despite feeling like he'd been hit head-on by a bus, he inched his way back into the kitchen hallway before someone could put a bullet through his cranium. Once out of immediate danger, he glanced over his shoulder to assess the damage.

Gilly was gone. That much was obvious. He'd clearly tried to get to the pantry door nearby, but never made it. He lay on his side against the wall, a few feet from the door, a body-size, bloodied indentation in the drywall above his body. Most of his head beneath his helmet was missing, the ballistic shield lying in front of him cracked and punctured in several places. He'd probably held it in a protective position as he sprinted, the shield no match for the closest warhead's blast effect.

Melendez's short crawl to throw the grenades had saved his life. He hadn't been in the direct line of the shrapnel blast pattern. The compact passage between the kitchen and the northern hallway had put enough material between himself and the blast to keep him alive. All pure luck. He'd had trouble getting the safety pin out of the first smoke grenade and had spent way too long messing with it. If the pin had come out smoothly like the rest, he'd have tossed the three grenades long before the drones hit. Instead, he'd barely managed to toss the second up ROUTE 66 before all hell broke loose.

He triggered his radio and whispered, "Rich. This is Rico. You still there?"

A few seconds passed before he got a reply.

"Barely. What's your status?" said Farrington.

"I'm good," said Melendez. "Gilly's dead."

"Sorry to hear—" said Farrington.

"Sorry to bust in like this, but you have traffic moving up ROUTE 66 and MAIN STREET. Four coming from each direction, and they're moving faster than before. Neither have reached BROADWAY, but you don't have much time," said Devin.

"This is Rico. Engaging targets on ROUTE 66. That should slow all of them down."

"Copy," said Devin. "Rich. What's your status?"

"Emily is on it."

Melendez checked his rifle's thermal scope, making sure it hadn't been damaged in the explosion. A quick scan of the great room behind him through the eyepiece indicated that it worked fine. The scope immediately picked up the fires and dozens of hot spots along the walls and ceiling. He reversed his rifle grip—left hand now on the trigger and right hand gripping the handguard—before slowly creeping forward. The reversed grip would allow him to fire from the bottom of the doorframe, exposing little of his head to the shooters down the hall. He'd worked extensively on ambidextrous shooting for close to a decade now. He'd never shoot lefty as well as righty, but he'd gotten damn near close.

He took a quick peek down the hallway, the corridor completely obscured by smoke, before carefully bracing the rifle against the doorframe and settling in behind the eyepiece. Four figures, their faces glowing white in the grayscale image, moved cautiously toward him in a staggered column, their rifles aimed dead ahead—ready for immediate action. Melendez centered the scope's digital crosshairs on the first man's nose and pressed the trigger, dropping him to the floor and covering the face and torso of the second mercenary in the column with bright-white splatter.

Melendez's next shot punched through his head and marked the remaining two with thermally detectable biomatter. The remaining mercenaries started to panic fire, their shots striking high. Melendez put two bullets through each of them, focusing on the head and neck areas to avoid their body armor. He triggered his radio.

"Traffic jam on ROUTE 66 has been cleared. Four down," said Melendez.

"Nice work, Rico. You bought Rich and Emily some time. Hendrick paused at BROADWAY."

"Devin. Did you report a possible wounded merc farther down the hallway somewhere?"

"Affirmative. He'd crawled to the far end of the hallway. Was sitting up a moment ago. Now he's lying flat. Probably figured out the thermal scope," said Devin. "We'll keep an eye on him."

"I'm going to frag his ass," said Melendez. "We don't need any surprises."

"With what?" said Devin. "The armory didn't contain any frag grenades."

"I always bring a frag grenade with me on missions," said Melendez, before unzipping and digging through the pouch attached to his tactical vest.

He rose to a crouch once he found the M67 spherically shaped grenade and readied himself for the throw. In order to get it to the far end of ROUTE 66, he'd have to fully step into the hallway and throw it like a baseball.

"Fire in the hole."

CHAPTER 35

Hendrick stopped in his tracks—the gunfire markedly different from before. The shots tightly spaced, but clearly methodical. Unmistakably a different caliber: 7.62 millimeter. Definitely not panic fire. Now the smoke made sense. Farrington had thermal rifle scopes at his disposal, one of them possibly aimed at his forehead right now. Then again, why would Farrington drag out the inevitable? If the roles were reversed, Hendrick would have already drilled a hole through Farrington's head. Maybe only one member of the team survived the drone onslaught. They needed to move quickly.

"Let's go," he said, urging his team forward, before triggering his radio. "WHISKEY. Report."

"All four are down hard. Head or neck shots," said Bekker. "The shooter is using a thermal scope. That's the only explanation. I'm just lying flat for now. I might try to crawl in the original breach room."

"Just stay put. We'll take care of this," said Hendrick, reaching a hallway that crisscrossed the foyer hallway.

"Shit," said Bekker.

"What?"

"A fucking frag grenade just—"

A sharp explosion shook the house, cutting off Bekker's transmission.

"Bekker?"

No response. Two could play at that game. He halted the team for a moment, activating his radio.

"Frag grenades. Each of you hand one forward. Joubert. Stuff them in my dump pouch," said Hendrick, removing his grenade from a pouch on his vest. "We're going in full fucking throttle."

The house had gone deathly silent again. He listened intently for any signs of movement in the back of the house, as Joubert, number two in the team's tactical stack, quietly slipped all three fragmentation grenades into his pouch. As the mercenary added the third, he gently patted Hendrick on the shoulder. Time to scatter the cockroaches. He let his rifle hang by its sling and pulled the pin on the first grenade before rolling it up the hallway toward the back of the house.

"Grenade out," he whispered over the radio, and the entire team of four dropped into prone positions, hugging the wall.

◆　◆　◆

Miralles really wished Melendez had given her a little more time before engaging ROUTE 66 traffic. She understood his visceral reaction to seeing Gilly dead, but his uncoordinated decision had compromised her already critically pressing situation. Hendrick would go for broke with only one team left at his disposal, and they were headed directly for her—leaving Miralles no time to administer the combat tourniquet she'd just removed from its holder attached to her vest.

Farrington's right leg lay over his left, twisted at close to a sixty-degree angle at the knee—blood spreading rapidly under both legs. The leg was peppered with wooden shards and a few larger entry wounds. A quick check of his head and torso revealed no apparent serious injuries, the shield obviously having saved his life. All she knew for sure after the few seconds she'd spent examining him was that one of those pieces of shrapnel had nicked an artery. He was losing too much blood, too quickly.

"Emily. Rico. Hendrick's team just went flat at the intersection of BROADWAY and MAIN STREET. Possible second drone strike inbound," said Devin over the radio.

She grabbed the mostly useless shield and lay flat next to Farrington, shielding him from a possible repeat attack. A moment after she settled into position, she noticed a round object come to rest on the floor several feet away from the bathroom door. She shifted the shield to face the door as the grenade exploded.

Several fragments smacked hard against the shield, but the battered protective buffer withstood the onslaught, which had been mercifully minimized by distance and the narrow cone of fragmentation permitted by the door opening's angle. They'd be coming now. She rose into a crouch and grabbed Farrington's thermal scope–equipped battle rifle.

"I have to go," she said, before turning him onto his back and tossing the tourniquet onto his chest. "You need to use that immediately."

Farrington nodded grimly, as she took off. She approached the door to the kitchen area in a low crouch, reaching the opening as a second grenade rolled by. This one was overthrown. She scurried behind the remnants of the wall separating the bathroom from the living area and lay flat as the grenade continued farther into the eat-in kitchen—where it exploded. Time to die, mothereffers.

Miralles low-crawled, her objective to take a position at the scorched, shrapnel-riddled corner a few feet away. From there, she'd have a direct line of sight down MAIN STREET. The whole thing should be over in a matter of seconds. She reached the corner, ready to lean out and scan the smoke through the thermal sight for some heads, when a dark-green spherical ball rolled even with her at the corner. Miralles felt like she stared at the grenade for several seconds, but it was more like milliseconds. She was up and diving back into the bathroom without thinking, her legs not quite clearing the fragmentation zone when the MK67 grenade detonated.

She felt the shrapnel immediately, followed by the gut punch of landing flat on her equipment-laden vest. The worst part was that Farrington's rifle had been ripped from her grip by the doorframe as she haphazardly piled into the room. No fault of her own under the circumstances, but unfortunate. Her first instinct was to roll onto her back and draw her pistol. Then she started to come up with a plan, not that she had much to work with. They were trapped in a bathroom, where one grenade could kill them both. She still had Melendez out there, but they'd know that, too, which meant they'd be moving slowly. Or maybe they'd split up and try to distract Melendez somehow while they grenaded her room.

Her internal planning session was interrupted by a fourth grenade detonation, which cracked and dented the drywall several feet back from the corner of the bathroom and peppered the wall between the bathroom and MAIN STREET with shrapnel. Aside from a few annoying stings and zings, the grenade had little effect on them—but it gave her an idea.

"Emily. They're coming for you," said Devin. "Rico. Shift your aim to the kitchen area. I don't know how far you're willing to hang your ass out on this, but I need you to be able to hit anyone that tries to lob a grenade into the first room on the corner. You'll need to move deeper into the kitchen."

"All the way out," said Melendez. "I'm on it."

"Tell me when they're on the other side of the bathroom wall," said Miralles. "All of them."

CHAPTER 36

Hendrick got about a third of the way down the hallway, after crossing the main hallway intersection, and paused for a moment. The shooter who had taken out Bekker's group was still out there somewhere. If the shooter had been on either side of the end of the hallway ahead, he should be out of action. If not, crossing the threshold from the hallway to the back of the house could prove deadly for himself and the few mercenaries remaining.

"Does anyone have any of our breacher strip?" said Hendrick, well aware it could all be with the men lying dead in other parts of the house.

"This is Okoro. I have enough breacher strip for one door-size hole," said the last mercenary in the stack.

"How many detonators?" said Hendrick.

"A bag full," said Okoro. "Heyns had the rest of the breacher strip. I can go back for it."

"No. We'll just make two smaller holes with what we have," said Hendrick. "Head up to the front of the stack."

When Okoro nestled in next to him, he ordered Joubert forward a few feet to provide them cover from any ambitious shooters in the back of the house. The smoke had started to abate, likely from the large opening punched through the walls by the drones. He could see the damage the grenades had done to the end of the hallway and a few pieces of toppled or smashed furniture a little farther out.

Okoro and Hendrick set about unrolling the entire spool of breacher strip, to be sure they cut it evenly. Once cut, he slid one of the pieces to Selassie, who was keeping watch on the approaches from the front of the mansion, and ordered him to roll it up. Then they went to work forming a rough four-foot-by-three-foot shape about a foot above the bottom of the wall. More than enough to slip through—into the other room. They got about halfway finished before the bullets started punching through the wall in front of them at a rate twice as rapid as the automatic gunfire unleashed on them earlier.

Both Hendrick and Okoro were driven back against the other side of the hallway by a long, sustained burst of unremitting gunfire. He'd never experienced anything like it. Dozens of points of pain along his body, from top to bottom. Somehow still alive, but completely unable to move. He simply slid down the wall into a seated position and watched in a daze as Selassie and Joubert met the same fate, blood exploding from their arms, legs, and buttocks as they stumbled backward to join their colleagues against the wall. Joubert never made it, multiple bullets tearing through his head and dropping him like a sack of dirt.

When the gunfire stopped, he turned to Okoro, who had slumped to the floor—the back of his head broken open. Selassie remained upright for a moment, their eyes meeting long enough for Hendrick to watch the life leave them. He'd lost them all— seventeen of his best—to a handful of Farrington's people. He should have listened to that little voice when Farrington started filling the house with smoke. What was the saying? Woulda. Coulda. Shoulda. Well, he didn't. And here he was. Alive but dead. Waiting to bleed out, or worse.

A figure appeared at the end of the hallway, peeking around the left corner, leading with a rifle barrel. He tried to grab his rifle, which still hung across his chest from its sling, but his arms didn't respond. Same with his legs. He was fucking paralyzed. The operative limped down the hallway, briefly examining Joubert and Okoro as she approached. She. Even with the medical-grade mask, tactical goggles, and ballistic helmet covering most of her head, he could tell by the shape of her face. The woman looked Hendrick up and down and moved on to Selassie. She looked at Selassie and fired a single bullet through his head. Apparently she wasn't taking any chances. But why hadn't she fired a bullet into his head? Could she tell by looking at him that he was paralyzed?

"What's wrong with you?" she said, rifle aimed at his face.

"Paralyzed from the neck down, apparently," he said, surprised he could talk.

"That's what I thought. Your shooting arm looks fine, but you didn't make a move," she said. "You breathing okay?"

"More or less. Despite taking several hits to the chest plate."

She nodded slightly, like it all made sense.

"You have a C6 to C7 vertebrae injury. Anything higher and you'd have trouble breathing. Makes sense given the low-neck bullet entry." She pointed to a spot on her own neck, just above the collarbone. "Missed the trachea—and carotid luckily—not bleeding too bad for a bullet through the neck. The rest of you is leaking like a sieve."

"Nothing lucky about it. You guys got lucky," said Hendrick. "Where's Farrington, or did I manage the impossible and take him out?"

"Farrington has seen better days, but he'll be fine," she said. "The drone attack came as a surprise. Shouldn't have, but we were all a little preoccupied. I have to give you credit on that one."

"How many of you were there?" said Hendrick, curious in his last few moments to know what he'd been up against.

"Four," she said.

"Just four. Jesus," said Hendrick. "Please tell Rich, 'Well played,' for me. No hard feelings. It was all business."

"You can tell him yourself," she said.

"I'd prefer not to," said Hendrick. "So. Go on. Get it done."

If he had the use of his arms, he would have grabbed the barrel of her rifle and placed it against his forehead.

"That's not my call," she said.

Another figure dressed in full tactical kit with helmet appeared at the end of the hallway near the kitchen.

"You were supposed to have cleared the other rooms by now," he said.

"I found Hendrick. Alive," she said.

"What's his status?"

"Paralyzed from the neck down," she said. "He'll survive if he's immediately medevaced to a level-three trauma center."

"I'll call it in," he said. "He can fly out with Farrington."

"No. You can't do that to me," said Hendrick.

"Under normal circumstances, I would put you out of your misery," she said. "But your client, Yuri Pichugin, is responsible for the widespread mass shootings across the US today—and we suspect that's just the beginning. We may need your help getting a little closer to him."

"I don't have anything to do with that," said Hendrick, spitting blood onto one of his arms. "And I won't betray a client. Those are the rules."

"I promise you that if you survive this and cooperate, I will personally end your suffering, regardless of my orders. Deal?"

"My code is all I have left."

"Then you can be a head wheeled around a federal hospital," said the woman. "Quadriplegics can live a long time."

"That's fucking cruel," he growled.

"It's a cruel world," she said, before reporting over her radio that she was on the way to sweep the rest of the floor.

And then she was gone, and all he could think about was willing his hand to move far enough to trigger his radio—and order BEEHIVE to send every drone through the back window visible from the hallway—erasing him forever. Maybe they'd crash the last nine anyway, and he'd get lucky.

CHAPTER 37

Marnie placed a check mark on the last of Hendrick's mercenaries. Miralles had just completed her search of the southeast corner of the mansion.

"That's all of them," said Marnie.

"Second-floor teams. Immediately proceed to the elevator lobby. Use interior passageways only. We still have drones loitering above us—and they can't be recalled. Once the Russians figure out that Hendrick's team is wiped out, they'll use them on us. I recommend using the back stairwell so the drone operators can't see you through any of the windows. Proceed down ROUTE 66 to BROADWAY and take BROADWAY all the way down to the elevator lobby. Wolfe will meet you there."

"We need to move Farrington and Hendrick," said Melendez. "I don't really give a fuck about Hendrick, but his head might still be worth something."

Brutal humor, having been apprised of Hendrick's condition. She couldn't imagine what the South African was thinking right now, other than *kill me.* Given the gravity of the threat against the United States—Berg and Bauer would disappear him. Disappear him into a fully functioning dark site level-three trauma center that was probably being assembled at this moment, where they could take their time picking him apart for information. Both figuratively and literally.

"Marnie and I will be up shortly with two portable stretchers," said Devin.

"This is Rico. Emily took some shrapnel to one of her legs."

"I'm fine. I can carry a fucking stretcher," said Miralles.

"I'm not going to argue with her," said Melendez. "Just bring one more pair of hands and legs with you—in case."

Nikolai Mazurov, who had mostly served as a backup pair of eyes during the attack, got up from his seat.

"I have two hands and legs that work," he said.

"We're headed up," said Devin.

Marnie grabbed one of the portable stretchers and headed for the stairwell. The last thing they needed was for the drones to knock out power and trap them in the elevator. Mazurov grabbed the second stretcher and the neck brace. Devin stopped them at the door, handing them all masks.

"It's still pretty thick up there," he said.

With the masks in place, they ascended the concrete and metal stairwell to the lobby outside of the driveway entrance. Theoretically, they were now in danger. A drone strike to the door they'd used to enter the facility from the parking area outside of the garage would undoubtedly penetrate the reinforced steel door. The Razorblade 800 warhead was designed to penetrate a tank's top armor, which she guessed was thicker or at least designed from a composite metal stronger than these doors.

Devin led them up BROADWAY, past a long line of federal protective agents, many of whom recognized and thanked them for their radio coordination. The two groups bottlenecked about halfway to MAIN STREET, three bodies lying in their path. One of them had been turned over and shot through the head by Miralles, the mercenary's brains splattered beneath his head. The federal agents made room to let them through, and they continued their near-blind trek.

The smoke had thinned a little from before, but they still couldn't see more than ten feet in front of them. Melendez met them at the intersection of the two hallways. A quick glance up MAIN STREET revealed the damage that had been done by the drones and grenades. Magnitudes worse than the bullet holes that decorated the house. The kitchen–great room area looked like it had been hit by an artillery barrage.

"I'll take one of those," he said, grabbing the stretcher from Mazurov and heading up the hallway. "Nick. You follow me."

"As long as Emily doesn't punch me in the neck for implying that she can't carry Farrington out of here," said Mazurov.

"I already blamed it all on Devin," said Melendez, patting Devin's shoulder. "He'll get the neck punch."

"I'll neck punch all of you if you don't hurry the fuck up," said Miralles, suddenly appearing at the end of the hallway leading into the kitchen.

Melendez grabbed the neck brace from Mazurov and tossed it past Miralles. He pointed at the mercenary who had remained seated upright among his bullet-pulverized colleagues, against a blood-sprayed, bullet-hole-peppered wall. She'd seen some carnage in her days, but nothing like this. Nothing like the bodies back in the hallway, and certainly nothing like the four men here. Miralles had fired close to two hundred 5.56-millimeter bullets into each group—the results catastrophic.

"This is Hendrick. He's all yours. Won't be needing the neck brace. He's paralyzed, and we'd like to keep him that way."

"Fuck you," said Hendrick.

"The head speaks," said Melendez, taking off with Mazurov.

"Let's get this done," said Marnie, unfolding the stretcher. "The sooner we get him below, the sooner we can try to stabilize him."

"Please just kill me," said Hendrick. "Don't put me through this."

"Not my call," said Marnie, placing the stretcher on the floor in front of Hendrick's legs. "Ready to lift. I got the top. You got the legs."

"What about you?" said Hendrick, glancing at Devin.

"She's the boss." Devin shrugged, gripping his ankles.

"Nothing but women calling the shots around here," said Hendrick.

She ignored his comment and grabbed the shoulder straps of his tactical vest and shifted him sideways, until he lay flat on the floor. Marnie really wished Melendez hadn't tossed the neck brace. She was concerned about supporting his head to prevent further vascular damage in his neck. He was losing enough blood as it was.

"Slowly," she said, nodding at Devin.

Supporting his head with one hand and grabbing one of the vest straps with the other, she managed to keep his head from moving too radically during the transfer. Just as they lifted Hendrick's stretcher, Melendez and Mazurov turned the corner with Farrington. Miralles hobbled alongside them, carrying a beat-to-shit ballistic shield.

"Jesus. Didn't you get the weather alert. We're under drone-strike warning conditions," said Melendez. "Get moving!"

Both stretcher-bearer groups had gotten about a third of the way back to the elevator lobby when the warning they'd all feared hit their earpieces.

"Drone strike inbound. All directions."

"All teams copy," said Devin.

Marnie and Devin quickly lowered Hendrick and dropped to the floor beside him, leaving him exposed to BROADWAY's western wall. Devin pressed against Marnie, hoping to block her from any shrapnel that might enter the hallway from the east. A few feet behind them, Melendez and Mazurov lowered Farrington to the floor before lying down on both sides of him. Miralles placed the curved ballistic shield over Farrington's torso for added protection and lay down at their feet.

"This is all we can do. BROADWAY is as safe as it gets," said Melendez. "Middle of the house."

"It is what it—" started Marnie, her sentence interrupted by a tightly spaced series of explosions.

The drones started with the second floor, five hits that packed a frighteningly loud punch and rattled the house, but somehow didn't feel like threats. The upstairs was crowded with guest rooms, placing significantly more building material between the warhead explosions and the small group huddled on BROADWAY.

The last four blasts violently shook the floor beneath them before punching explosive fragments and pieces of the house through the hallway wall—all pretenses of safety instantly removed. The moment the drone strike ended, Wolfe informed them that two of the drones had struck the north and south wall. One each. Neither directly exposed to BROADWAY. The other two had been split between the east and west sides, fragging the hallway.

Wolfe's assessment—based on the twelve used previously against his people outside of the house, and the three used against the back of the house—was that the nine drones represented the last of what they had loitering above. The assumptions made sense unless the Russians had launched another wave. But why would they do that? Hendrick's mission had failed. Time wasn't on the Russians' side.

"Everyone report your status," said Melendez. "I'm fine, unless I'm paralyzed and can't feel my injuries. That one was for you, Hendrick."

"We know who it was for," said Miralles. "I'm fine. Rich looks fine."

"I can talk, you know," said Farrington. "I'm good."

"Maz?"

"I think I might have taken some shrapnel to my left leg and buttocks," said Mazurov. "Kind of stings."

"Doesn't look serious," said Miralles. "Someone will take care of that down in the hub. I don't stitch up ass wounds."

"Hey. This fat ass saved you from some shrapnel."

"A thank-you will have to suffice," said Miralles.

"Devin?" said Melendez.

"I'm a little beat up from a beam that came through the wall, but I'm fine."

"Good to go," said Marnie, already up on her elbows and checking Hendrick.

Looked like the mercenary got what he wanted. A jagged wound the size of a thumb collapsed his right temple but hadn't exited the other side. The shrapnel had retained enough velocity after tumbling through the walls and framing to pierce his skull, but not enough to pop out the other side.

"Hendrick is gone. Fragment to the right side of the head," said Marnie.

"Looks like the two of you picked the right side of his stretcher," said Melendez, getting up to take a look himself. "Yep. That's a brain scrambler. Fuck. I was really looking forward to working him over."

"His value was limited," said Devin. "We know he was hired by Pichugin. The most we could have gotten out of him was his handler information, and I'm guessing based on what we've seen over the past year, he's never met face-to-face with the handler. It's all done over encrypted apps on the dark web, or one-time-number sat phone calls. Once the Russian drone operators report his demise, all those sources will go dark."

"I'd love to get my hands on the drone-control center running the Razorblades, but I'm sure they're miles from here—or already long gone," said Marnie.

"Gupta will figure something out," said Farrington.

"Let's get moving. Rich is still losing blood," said Miralles. "We need to stabilize his bleeding while we wait for DHS to provide counter-drone protection. If I were the Russians, I'd keep a few more up there to catch anyone trying to rush out of here."

"Devin or Marnie. Can one of you take over for Nick?" said Melendez.

"Devin. Go ahead and take care of it," said Marnie. "I'll search Hendrick for anything useful and be right down. Even his sat phone might contain something we can use."

While the small entourage of Task Force DEEP SLEEP members made their way down the hallway toward the elevator lobby, Marnie searched Hendrick from head to toe, looking for anything useful—even removing his boots. She was shocked by the full extent of his bullet injuries, quite certain that he wouldn't have lasted more than a few more minutes. A few dozen holes, maybe more, had been punched through his legs, arms, and pelvic area.

A dozen or so more had torn through the fabric and pouches of his tactical vest, striking the ceramic chest plate protecting his vital organs. How Hendrick hadn't seen this coming after the first two machine-gun attacks remained a mystery. She'd seen the plastic explosive strip on the wall leading to the bathroom. Maybe he thought the grenades had done enough damage to Farrington's people to silence the machine guns. Then again, things had gotten so desperate on both sides that nobody was truly thinking clearly. The machine-gun solution stared everyone in the face, and it took four grenade blasts nearly killing Miralles before she figured it out.

"What a fucking day," she muttered, before heading off empty handed.

Even Hendrick's sat phone had taken a bullet that nearly split it in two.

CHAPTER 38

Karl Berg took stock of the aftermath, noting to himself that it could have been considerably worse. But he didn't dare express that sentiment, given the losses Farrington's team took today. Two seasoned operatives killed, one that Berg remembered being around from the very beginning. Alexei Filatov, a.k.a. "Sasha," had been a member of the small team that destroyed Russia's bioweapons operation at Vector Labs, in Novosibirsk, Russia. How any of them had made it out of there alive was beyond Berg. Somehow they'd defied the odds in one impossible situation after another. And today a burst of gunfire fired from a speedboat cuts him down.

Guillermo Espinoza, a.k.a. "Gilly," was a relatively new member of the crew. *Relative* meaning almost fifteen years. He'd been on-site in Texas when Rico Melendez and Jeffrey Munoz led the team that destroyed the subterranean laboratory True America had used to replicate a stolen Russian bioweapon. In the same raid, they'd killed the Russian scientist who'd delivered it to True America.

And that was just the dead. Richard Farrington was unlikely to fully recover from his leg injury. Surgeons these days could perform miracles, and Rich could blaze new records in the annals of physical-therapy success stories, but the unnatural angle of his right leg, and the grisly damage to his knee, suggested he'd never be one hundred percent again. More like seventy to eighty percent at best. And truth be told, he was already pushing retirement age. He could keep up with the youngest and the fittest, but Berg saw the strain.

Farrington's commitment to unraveling the Russian sleeper network, starting in Baltimore, quite possibly had the unintended consequence of permanently unraveling his team. At the very least, it had put a significant strain on their continued future operations. Berg didn't have a good sense of Farrington's total numbers, but he'd lost five top-tier operators to DEEP SLEEP. They'd suffered losses before, but that had been during their heyday, when retired general Terrence Sanderson had led the unit. The unit had downsized considerably since those days.

Rich nodded at him, almost like he had been reading Berg's mind.

"Don't look so forlorn, Karl," said Farrington. "We've taken bigger hits than this, and we keep coming back."

Berg headed over to Rich, where Miralles and one of the CIA protective agents with similar training worked to stop the bleeding. A shortened IV pole towered above them, a plastic bag of yellow-gold plasma flowing through a tube into his arm. Miralles said it had to do with keeping his blood pressure normal until they reached a site with blood reserves, where they'd start replacing the significant amount of blood he'd lost.

"I'm more worried about you," said Berg.

"I'm in good hands," said Farrington.

They locked eyes for a few moments, and Berg thought he could see Farrington's understanding of the long-term impact of his injury.

"We'll have you in even better hands sooner than expected," said Wolfe, who had obviously overheard the last of their conversation. "The DHS drone-detection radar is up and operational a few kilometers from here. The airspace above the estate is clear. Our designated medevac bird is willing to risk the trip without KADD coverage based on that assessment. A second bird carrying a DHS tactical response team will escort you to Walter Reed, just in case there's trouble, and they'll disembark with you to serve as your personal security detachment inside the hospital. It's an eight-person team, which will be augmented soon after your arrival."

"Thank you," said Miralles.

"There's also room on the bird for you and your other colleague," said Wolfe.

"The one shot in the ass?" said Miralles.

"I heard that," said Mazurov.

"I didn't want to put it that way," said Wolfe.

"We'll take you up on the offer," said Miralles.

"I'm fine," said Mazurov. "No need to haul me over to Walter Reed."

"All right. I'll start prepping the landing zone," said Wolfe. "Hey. If things get hectic and I don't see you off properly, thank you for what you did here. You undoubtedly saved all of our lives. I nearly killed us all by deploying my teams outside."

Farrington strained to bring himself up on an elbow. "Trent. We never made it clear to you how extensive the drone threat could be. I blame myself."

"That's very kind of you to say," said Wolfe. "But the captain goes down with the ship, and I was their captain. See you at the landing zone."

When Wolfe was gone, Berg shook his head. "Guy's being a little hard on himself."

"He just lost twenty of his people. That tends to weigh heavily on you. I know from experience," said Farrington, before immediately changing the subject. "So. Where do we go from here, Audra?"

"To start, we need a new location for the task force. Somewhere ultra-secure," said Bauer. "I honestly thought this was it, but I obviously couldn't have been more wrong."

"It would have been safe," said Berg. "But they orchestrated this whole thing. Sent the whole task force scurrying for safety and followed some of us here—with a sizable drone-strike capability and one of the best mercenary outfits money can buy waiting somewhere in the DC-Baltimore area for the location. Hendrick must have jumped through his ass to get here that quickly. Same with the drone team."

"They definitely wanted all of us gone," said Bauer. "They're up to something huge."

"But here we are," said Berg.

"Which means they'll bump up their timeline," said Bauer. "Like we forced them to do with the Estonia operation. Once they determine that we're still mostly operational, they'll speed things up."

"Then we need to get ahead of them. First things first, like Bauer said. Where do you set up shop? And before we start discussing task force locations, I'd like to go on the record and say that we are not relocating to Rich's West Virginia enclave. We don't have the time to get that rustic hellhole up and running—and it's too far away from the Beltway."

"I was going to suggest something closer," said Farrington. "Something inside DC."

"Risky," said Rafael, DEVTEK's mysterious head of all things cyber and technical within the company, despite never having been referenced by a title. "But close to the action."

"Langley?" said Marnie.

"No," said Berg, basically cutting off Bauer. "Nobody in their right mind would attack CIA headquarters, but it would be impossible to move in and out of Langley without being noticed. And it's kind of an obvious choice."

"The J. Edgar Hoover Building? FBI central," said Miralles. "That's about as secure as it gets, and this is essentially the definition of their job. Hunting down terrorists on US soil."

O'Reilly squashed that suggestion just as quickly as CIA headquarters.

"I don't disagree, Emily, but we're looking at the same issue. Coming and going—times fifty. There's only one way in and one way out, and it's right downtown. Crowded as fuck at all hours. We'd never spot the surveillance, but they'd have no trouble spotting us. Then there's the bureaucracy issue. Even with Director Sharpe's blessing, it would take the better part of the week to figure out the whole arrangement. I don't think we have that kind of time."

"We don't," said Devin. "With the task force still mostly intact, Pichugin will have no choice but to move quickly. This weekend at the latest. They'll target planned liberal protests, LGBTQ community events, prominent Democrat lawmakers, minority community centers and neighborhoods—anything that symbolizes the Left. They have to deliver a significantly stronger counterpunch to the mass shootings last week, in order to ignite a self-sustaining civil conflict. Our priority is to stop the second attack."

"We'll have to put our heads together to figure this one out," said Gupta. "Rafael and I already have some very rough ideas. We'll keep working on it, and hopefully have a plan of action by the time we reach our new task force location."

"May I continue with my suggestion for our new headquarters?" said Farrington.

"Please," said Devin.

"Marnie's parents are there right now, with Elena and Jared," said Farrington.

"The safe house in Anacostia," said Melendez.

"We'd move Marnie's parents to an equally safe location, something smaller," said Farrington. "But I think the safe house in Anacostia is perfect for us. It has more than enough room to house the task force. It's stocked with ninety days of supplies, not to mention weapons, comms gear, drones—"

"Can we not mention drones for a while," said Miralles, getting a small chuckle from the group.

"Plenty of operation space for a makeshift tactical ops center. We can move all the equipment from Langley and MINERVA to the site, after lengthy SDRs—"

"I don't think the CIA is going to let us walk out with their computers," said Bauer.

"We can transfer all the data to new rigs," said Rafael. "Everything on those computers belongs to DEVTEK and MINERVA anyway. Plus, it's all backed up and stored on a DEVTEK server farm. Our little secret."

Bauer shook her head. "I suspected as much, but you're honest players, so I never pushed the issue."

"We have the highest-speed satellite connectivity, and it's remained off the grid and undisturbed for nearly thirty years. Plus, it's literally a five-minute drive from downtown DC. Twenty—maybe thirty with traffic—to Langley."

"Who's taken care of it for all of these years?" said Devin.

"Caretaking has changed hands between operatives that could no longer operate with the team due to injuries. Usually operatives that haven't drawn much or any attention in the past. Nick has taken care of the site for the past fifteen years."

They all looked at Mazurov, who lay prone on one of the stretchers, a thick gauze pad taped to his rear.

"The site would suit our needs perfectly," said Mazurov.

"I'm all in, but are we looking at bedrooms?" said Berg. "This sounds like a doomsday bunker."

"Mostly bunk rooms," said Gupta.

"Great," said Berg.

"Jesus. Is that all you're worried about, Karl?" said Farrington.

"Possibly."

"The house has bedrooms on the upper levels. The safe house portion is in the basement. You're more than welcome to claim a bedroom, if you're okay sleeping under the constant threat of drone attack."

Berg laughed. "You haven't lost your charm."

"I don't intend to," said Farrington. "What else do we need to discuss before I'm rushed out of here? I don't know how long I'll be held captive at Walter Reed."

"Hopefully a month," said Berg.

"Funny," said Farrington. "But seriously. What else?"

"AeroDrone," said Devin. "I'll give them a call in a minute and let them know that I need an answer to my inventory question by the end of the day. Tomorrow at the latest. Unless there's any doubt that today's attack involved Razorblades."

"We freeze-framed a few of the images of the drones on their final approach, captured on video by cameras facing the house, and there's little doubt in my mind that they were Razorblades. They don't look like Russian drones, which have a swept-back wing profile. And the Chinese drones have a single, forward-mounted squared wing. The Razorblade has two very distinct squared wings, one mounted forward and the other in the back. I'd bet big money on those being Razorblades."

"Mr. Wolfe?" said Gupta.

"Call me Trent, please."

"Trent. I forgot to ask earlier, but does this site monitor the surrounding radio frequency traffic?"

"Passively. Yes," said Wolfe. "We absorb all RF traffic. But before you get too excited, none of the RF activity processed prior to the first wave of drone strikes, or during the entire ordeal, alerted our system. And our passive array, located on the roof of a barn several hundred yards to the south of the facility, remained operational throughout the attack. These drones typically operate between two point four and five point eight gigahertz. They need the higher-frequency ranges to send back real-time camera imagery used for targeting. Anything under three gigahertz is considered ultrahigh frequency, UHF. Above three is considered superhigh frequency. SHF."

"Sorry to cut you off, Trent, but I'm familiar with all of this," said Gupta.

"Hang on for a moment. Hundreds, if not thousands, of commercial items operate within the UHF spectrum. Right? Picking drone-control traffic would be near impossible. They have no reason to go into

SHF, so it's essentially a waste of time searching that traffic. But leave no stone unturned. Right?"

"I'm still not seeing—" started Gupta.

"I'm getting to the point," said Wolfe. "How much do you know about Razorblade jamming countermeasures?"

Gupta looked around sheepishly. "Not much."

"Through no fault of your own. The information is highly classified—which is why nobody heard this from me. Understood?"

Everyone nodded.

"I only know this because someone thought it might be helpful to my job as BASTION EAST's security director. It obviously didn't help me today, but I have a feeling some of you," said Wolfe, glancing at Gupta and the DEVTEK team, "might be able to take this information and make it work for your group."

"Can I take notes?" said Gupta.

"No. You may not," said Wolfe.

Rafael put a hand on Gupta's shoulder. "I think that between the four of us, we can re-create whatever our friend has to say."

Berg sure hoped so.

"In a nutshell. Upon launch, these drones follow a GPS track to their target. All passive. No RF signature. When they reach their inputted target location, two options are on the table. Continue a passive loiter pattern or start transmitting camera imagery, which requires it to go active. So, in theory, one of these drones could circle overhead without ever emitting a signal until it was ready to strike."

"That's the same with every drone," said Gupta. "Fly to target with GPS coordinates."

"Correct. Which brings us to the classified part. Once the Razorblade goes active and starts sending targeting data back to the end user—whoever is using the control tablet—now you have a chance to identify the drone's radio frequency. Especially on a mostly desolate battlefield like southeastern Ukraine. Not a lot of UHF clutter in the background. Here in Loudoun

County, though, you ain't picking out one of these drones from the sea of UHF clutter coming from every direction. Anyway. AeroDrone got smart about this really fast. If one of their drones detects RF interference, also known as jamming, they go RF silent and switch frequency. If they're in the middle of a 125-mile-per-hour dive onto a target and get jammed, they'll break engagement, go back into a circular loiter above the target—where they'll switch frequencies and reattack immediately."

"They sound unstoppable," said Devin.

"They were designed that way," said Wolfe.

"There has to be a way to stop them electronically," said Marnie. "Nothing is totally immune to jamming."

"I agree, but the classified assessment I was provided suggested otherwise," said Wolfe, before glancing at Gupta and the DEVTEK crew. "However. Where there's a will, there's a way— or something like that."

"They'll figure it out. They always do," said Berg. "What were you saying about jamming and interference? I don't seem to recall any of that."

Wolfe smiled, as the rest of the team echoed a similar sentiment.

"Nothing. At best, all I could offer investigators was my opinion that the attack here was conducted by drones similar in capability to the Razorblade," said Wolfe.

"The Russians and Chinese have kamikaze drones, too," said Berg. "Can't count those out."

Wolfe put a finger to his ear, a tell that something had been passed to him over the radio.

"Medevac is here, along with the escort helicopter," said Wolfe. "Let's get your wounded out of here."

Farrington raised his hand, like he was asking a question. Berg wasn't sure what to do, so he did what anyone might do. "Do you have a question, Rich?"

"Yes. Trent?"

"Yes?"

"What's your background prior to this job? What's your specialty?" said Farrington. "How did you end up here?"

"Master's degree in electrical engineering. Thesis on encrypted communications applications—with a focus on frequency analysis and exploitation. Ten years with the FBI as an electronics technician, which was a bit of a step down for someone with an EE master's degree, but the bureau wasn't hiring—though they were willing to make an exception in my case, or so they said. The work was fascinating, and I was running the seedier side of the Los Angeles field office communications gigs within a few years. Laser microphones. Drone surveillance. Wiretaps. Stingrays. Dirtboxes. Wireless signal intercept. All of it. Then someone somewhere decided I was overqualified for the job, and they offered, as in required I take, a position as electronics engineer, which was basically the most boring desk job you can possibly imagine. I surfed the government service listings until I came across a nebulous position that promised to be interesting. Thirty-nine years old, and here I am. The security king of classified facilities."

He sounded like the perfect replacement for Graves—not that Graves could ever truly be replaced.

"Anish?" said Farrington, raising an eyebrow.

"Yes. I agree."

"Trent. I'd like to make you an offer you can't refuse. When this whole thing blows over. We could use someone like you," said Farrington.

"It's like you're reading my mind," said Berg.

"How about this?" said Wolfe. "They're going to suspend me with pay the moment your team clears out of here. Hold me for twenty-four to forty-eight hours for debriefing—"

"See you in twenty-four to forty-eight hours. Gupta will give you a few ways to get in touch with us," said Farrington. "Welcome aboard."

"That's it?" said Wolfe.

"It's not exactly a formal operation," said Farrington.

"Pay? Benefits? Pension?" said Wolfe.

"I'll let the rest of the crew explain how it works," said Farrington. "Bottom line. We're all independent contractors."

Berg shook his head and chuckled to himself. God help this man, for he has no idea what he is truly getting involved in.

PART FOUR

PART FOUR

CHAPTER 39

Yuri Pichugin sipped a perfectly balanced and heated espresso, the beans flown in from his hometown of Saint Petersburg. One of a limited, but not unjustly restrictive, number of luxuries permitted under the work-release program secured by his most trusted associate, Boris Gusev. At least Putin hadn't been unreasonable with the conditions of his house arrest. Unfortunately, Pichugin was unsure how news of today's events in the United States would be received. Would the luxuries be cut in half? Would they remain the same? It all depended on one man's perception, viewed through the coldest and most calculating eyes Pichugin had seen in all his years.

From what he could see on the array of screens above Boris Gusev, public news reports coming out of the United States suggested a resounding success. The American Right had been attacked across the country, left-wing extremist groups taking responsibility, and the Left in general fanning the flames by agreeing that the attacks against the gun-toting Right had been long overdue.

Of course, nearly all the social media discourse, podcast clips, and supposedly live interviews originated from Pichugin's wide network of social media troll farms, its live operators trained extensively in mimicking Americans and escalating political rhetoric. Bot farms also played a significant role, each posing as tens of thousands of social media users—sharing inflammatory clips, posts, and comments across social media.

The cumulative effect of this tsunami of social media hate and discord now dominated all major media networks, not just the fake online networks run by another arm of Pichugin's disinformation and active measures operation. Local news networks had sent out reporters to interview citizens on both sides of the political spectrum, the live broadcasts often devolving into rabid shouting matches between political rivals, and in a few cases—violent confrontations. EVENT HORIZON was beginning to take shape. *Event horizon* meaning "the point of no return" for America.

What a shame it couldn't have been implemented ahead of BLACKOUT in Tallinn. The Americans would have been too distracted to unravel Pichugin's plans for the overthrow of the Estonian government. All their attention would have been focused inward. Regrettably, Helen Gray, a wild card he should have assassinated years earlier, had forced him to escalate the BLACKOUT timeline. They'd still been a few months out from having all of EVENT HORIZON's pieces in place.

He'd kept EVENT HORIZON a secret from Putin and his inner circle, wanting to present it to the president as a birthday present. He'd intended to kick off the first round of mass festivities in the United States on October 7, Putin's birthday. Little did he know just how badly things would deteriorate after Helen Gray suddenly reappeared on the scene. No sense in living in the past—for too long, anyway. He'd never fully shake the memory of falling so far from the top to so close to the bottom so quickly.

"How are we looking on the other side of the house. The task force?" said Pichugin.

Gusev swiveled in his chair, away from the three side-by-side-mounted screens at his desk.

"Do you want the good news or bad news first?" said Gusev.

"Good news. I need some good news," said Pichugin. "And probably some vodka."

Gusev got up and approached the bar cart in the corner of the converted dark mahogany library. Pichugin had purchased this beat-up mansion on the outskirts of Novosibirsk and refurbished it during the early years of stealing the sleeper network out from under the Lost Directorate, as a fallback headquarters location in case the Moscow site became untenable.

Khrushchev loyalists, known as Khrushchev's Ghosts, were particularly vengeful and dangerous during and after the fall of the Soviet Union, their predictions about the growing weakness and rot within the system they had faithfully served for decades having painfully come true. If they'd caught a single whiff of how he'd yanked the network out from under the KGB's most secretive directorate, they would have come after him with everything they had.

Wisely, Pichugin and Gusev, with the help of the late General Kuznetzov, had purged the directorate of its power players and absorbed the rest into their new enterprise. By the time the "ghosts" realized what had happened, the sleeper network they'd worked for decades to cultivate was in Pichugin's hands, and there was nothing they could do about it, except die one by one of natural or not-so-natural causes until none remained—which is exactly what happened.

When Gusev returned with two generous pours of vodka, and the bottle, which he set on the table between them, they clinked glasses and took a long sip of the warming liquid.

"The good news is that we've severely disrupted the task force. We've driven them underground again."

"Do we know where they are?" said Pichugin. "Sorry. Dumb question."

"From what our sources can tell, they did not end up at either CIA or FBI headquarters. Unfortunately, we lost track of all the vehicles that departed the estate. They ran lengthy and complicated surveillance-detection routes, in a few cases calling in additional vehicles to run interference. One of the incidents led to the shooting of two of our sleepers. By all witness accounts, there was no hesitation by the federal agents who ran the interdiction."

"So we have no idea where the task force is located right now?" said Pichugin. "How is this the good news?"

"We've bought ourselves some time," said Gusev. "Wherever they land, it'll sure as hell be a step down from their previous location, and the one they momentarily occupied today."

"How the hell did Hendrick fuck this up so badly?" said Pichugin. "The facility's entire security force was wiped out by drones. Farrington had four, maybe six, operatives inside, plus the protective agents that brought everyone to the facility. I don't get it?"

"That's still a mystery," said Gusev. "Which ties into the bad news."

Pichugin drained half of his glass. "Hit me with it."

"First and foremost. They know we're going to use drones for the next attack. All potential targets will be hardened against drone attack, which won't make a difference due to the sheer number of drones at our disposal, but you can be guaranteed that the task force will be looking for a unique way to jam or thwart the drones beyond what's already available to the government."

"I hate knowing they're still out there," said Pichugin. "We didn't get any of them?"

"We killed the CIA officer's husband and one of Farrington's people on the East Coast. Seriously wounded Brendan Shea," said Gusev. "On top of taking out Paek and Shipley out in San Francisco. But I don't think that'll slow DEVTEK down. Their server system resisted all attempts to breach it. We shut down MINERVA, but a preliminary analysis of the data taken from MINERVA reveals nothing related to the task force. We think they had it air gapped and possibly used encrypted satellite gear to communicate with the main task force at Langley."

"Fuck. We really accomplished very little on the task force side of the operation," said Pichugin. "They'll be back up and running within a day or two."

"Which means we have no choice but to launch the third phase of the EVENT HORIZON this weekend," said Gusev.

"Do we have enough time to generate that much outrage? Enough to get them out on the streets after what happened today?" said Pichugin.

"Actually. I think the compressed timeline might work in our favor," said Gusev. "Once the after-action report from the secure facility in Loudoun County starts making the rounds, citing kamikaze drones, lawmakers will go into hiding. We can use that to our advantage by testing some 'Where are the lawmakers when the country needs them?' messaging—then amplify that in conjunction with a kind of call to arms. A call to march on DC and demand the government does something to protect them. We'll smooth out the message."

"I like this," said Pichugin.

"We'll gorge protest organizers' pockets and bank accounts to give them the financial freedom to put together different events on the National Mall and surrounding areas. Charter hundreds of buses. Offer money for flights."

"Charter flights!" said Pichugin.

"We can do that, too. We'll start reserving massive blocks of rooms right downtown and in all the surrounding neighborhoods, towns, and cities."

"This quickly? It's the summer. Most of them will already be booked," said Pichugin.

"Not after I start offering significant cash incentives to free up rooms," said Gusev. "We already have a wide network of event organizers on the hook—and payroll. We'll offer massive discounts on these rooms to organizers and even bigger cash bonuses if they can fill entire blocks. Fly in a country music singer for a concert. Make this feel like an event that can't be missed. A real chance to demand action from lawmakers and the White House to immediately take action to make the streets safe again. To be heard again. Make the theme something like—we won't back down—that was like an American rally cry after 9/11. This can work."

"Could we get Tom Petty to perform it live?" said Pichugin, before breaking into a barely recognizable terrible version of Petty's "I Won't Back Down."

"Tom Petty is dead," said Gusev.

"Since when?"

"Over five years ago," said Gusev. "But we can try to put together some kind of musical entertainment that resonates. Maybe a Tom Petty tribute band. We'll explore all options."

"And we get everyone in one place and hit them with the drones. They'll blame the government. Who else has access to this kind of fire-power?" said Pichugin.

"Exactly," said Gusev.

"It'll spark a civil war. They'll burn the entire city down!"

"That's the hope," said Gusev.

Pichugin felt a wave of depression wash over him, the dark cloud of Devin Gray's task force raining on his moment of joy.

"How will we keep the American task force from stopping us?" said Pichugin.

"I've given that some thought, and I propose we split the drone-control teams into three separate locations, each armed with enough drones to counter whatever the government puts into place to protect the rally and do considerable damage. We'll reserve one smaller drone team to interdict any serious law enforcement or National Guard response. Like armored vehicles pulling up to one of the other drone-control teams or helicopters homing in on one of the other teams. Even if the task force identifies one of the team's locations, we have two backups."

"Sounds solid," said Pichugin, greedily pouring another drink. "Boris?"

"I'll pass. Too much work ahead of me," said Gusev.

"And what of our ground teams?" said Pichugin. "What do we have left?"

"After today, we have fourteen left around the country. I'm bringing them all to DC. We'll need them for various tasks. Some to serve as lookouts for the different drone-control stations. A few to create diversions. I don't know yet," said Gusev.

"Well. My life is in your hands," said Pichugin. "If this fails, I'm most certainly finished."

"You and me both," said Gusev. "Neither of us is walking out of here alive if this fails. Maybe I will take that drink. Just a small pour."

Pichugin filled his tumbler halfway before raising his glass. "To redemption."

"In the eyes of Putin. The only thing that really matters," added Gusev, before clinking Pichugin's glass.

Both glasses were empty when they slammed them down on the wooden tabletop.

CHAPTER 40

Devin stepped inside behind Marnie and took in the home's air, surprised to discover that it didn't smell stale. It actually had no smell at all. He followed Marnie and the rest of the group through a sizable, spotless galley kitchen and past an equally immaculate bathroom. No windows in either space. Mazurov, leaning on a hospital crutch, opened the door leading out of the kitchen and guided them into an undisturbed, circa early-1990s-decorated family room. Devin noted the bars on all the windows through the barely translucent curtains. He ran a finger along one of the wooden end tables. Nothing. Mazurov took his duty seriously.

"So. Here's the deal," said Mazurov, shifting uncomfortably on his crutch. "We don't use this room after dark. It's stayed dark at night for decades. The neighbors don't ask questions. No reason for them to start now. This isn't the best part of town, and a house that isn't too well maintained or overneglected draws no attention. That's how we've kept this place. Neutral. The door automatically locks an hour before sunset and doesn't open again until an hour after sunrise. I can override the locks in case of an emergency. We can use the kitchen or bathroom up here at any time because they don't have windows. That concludes the first-floor tour."

"Have there been attempted break-ins?" said Devin.

"Not for a long time, and the glass is shatter resistant. Whatever interest anyone ever had in this house has long since passed. And if anyone suddenly becomes interested again, the entire place is wired with pressure, acoustic, motion, and thermal sensors. Hidden cameras scan three hundred and sixty degrees, all day and all night. Nobody is getting near or inside this place without us knowing," said Mazurov. "Onto the second floor."

The group followed him back through the kitchen, just past the four-vehicle-deep garage, which ate into a significant portion of the first floor's space, to a tight switchback staircase. The stairs opened to a long hallway that ran from the front to the back of the house. No window at either end of the hallway.

"There's a full bath up here, plus three bedrooms. You won't find any light fixtures—for the same reason as the downstairs family room. If you're assigned to a room up here," said Mazurov, turning his head directly toward Berg, "better start eating your carrots, because the only light you'll find to guide your way comes from the streetlamp a few houses over. No lights. No glowing phones. Use your heads if you're lucky enough to draw one of these beds. The bathroom has no window, and there's a small light over the sink mirror that only activates when the door is closed. To keep you from peeing on the floor or breaking your neck in the shower."

"You should do safe house videos on the dark web's version of YouTube," said Berg, getting a few laughs from the exhausted group.

"Now to the actual safe house part of the safe house," said Mazurov. "Where most of you will be spending your time."

Once back on the ground floor, Mazurov reached into one of the kitchen cabinets and pressed a series of six numbers into a keypad Devin couldn't see. Six beeps and he closed the cabinet. Mazurov then proceeded to a door next to the staircase, which contained a thick wall of musty-smelling jackets. He swept the coats aside to reveal a heavy-duty-looking stainless door, the light on its door handle flashing green. The door opened into a similarly sized space, where Mazurov lifted a trapdoor in the floor to reveal a hidden set of stairs— a sterile bluish-white light automatically revealing the stairs and the plain white linoleum-tiled floor beneath them.

"This isn't creepy," said Sandra Perry, their MINERVA liaison.

Mazurov chuckled at the comment. "It's beyond creepy. The first time I saw this stairway, with the lights, I thought they were playing a joke on me—or I had done something really wrong somehow."

He led them below into a space that expanded the entire footprint of the house, and possibly the garage, all connected by a single hallway.

"Home for now," said Mazurov. "You'll find three small bunk rooms with two bunk beds in each room. Two bathrooms with shower stalls. Two conference room–size spaces, which in our case I'm guessing will be split between the operations side of the house and tech side. Sat phones and cell phones work down here. We're wired for that."

Folding tables and chairs sat stacked against the wall. Definitely not the luxury digs most of them were accustomed to. The two larger rooms were equipped with ceiling projectors and built-in retractable screens. One of the long sides of each room was covered with flat-screen monitors. The other with whiteboards. Wiring ports for every type of cable connection imaginable adorned the walls, at knee height. Devin was impressed. The facility was exactly what they needed. Most importantly, it was off the grid. Hidden from Pichugin's prying eyes.

"If you're interested, you can check out the armory. Nothing exotic. Rifles. A few submachine guns. Suppressors. Body armor. Ammunition. Night vision. Various grenades. The usual," said Mazurov. "We also have a fully stocked pantry and second kitchen area. We have more than enough nonperishable food to last several weeks. I'm praying that we're talking more like several days. If anyone has any kitchen skills, you might want to keep that to yourself," said Mazurov, laughing at his own joke. "Seriously, though. We'll be cooking our own food. The water is purified. I think that's it."

O'Reilly walked out of one of the bunk rooms. "This is literally like going to the mattresses. *Godfather* style."

"Pretty much," said Mazurov, taking a quick count of heads. "Sandra. You're going back to MINERVA tomorrow?"

"Whenever I reestablish our link," she said.

Rafael added to the conversation. "One of our teams is at MINERVA now making sure it meets DEVTEK standards. They had their system air gapped, which prevented the Russians from accessing their server, but Pichugin's people could still intercept their satellite uplink—if they really wanted to. Highly unlikely, but why take the chance? We're outfitting the task force part of MINERVA with our highest levels of cybersecurity."

"We highly appreciate it," said Sandra. "That'll allow us to work seamlessly from MINERVA. Frankly, I'm not sure how much we'll be able to add to the task force at this point, anyway, but we'll keep working the sleepers and see if we can shake something loose."

"Perfect. That leaves us fifteen people and fifteen beds. We have air mattresses for overflow, or if you don't want to sleep on the creepy-as-shit second floor," said Mazurov. "I have a very small office at the very end of the garage side of the hallway with camera feeds and alarm panels for all the sensors, where you'll find me most of the time. I can access the same information from anywhere with my tablet, so hopefully I can sit in on planning sessions and contribute more than a shitty tour to the task force."

Everyone had a good laugh at Mazurov's wrap-up before Berg and Bauer started putting everyone to work on the same configuration Mazurov had suggested. Devin pulled Berg aside with some news that he'd received on his secure sat phone.

"I got an update from AeroDrone just as we arrived. I didn't want to distract everyone until we got settled," said Devin.

"How many are missing?" said Berg.

"Four hundred never made it to their end users on the front lines. Minus the one they used on DeSoto and the twenty-five they used on us at the SFAC—that leaves three hundred and seventy-four Razorblades."

"On US soil. This is unbelievable," said Berg. "Did Mohr give a breakdown between models, 400s and 800s?"

"No. Jared is on his way over with Mike Seeberger, the guy that never says a word in any of our meetings. We think he's one of the key development engineers that works on the Razorblade system."

"That was nice of them," said Berg.

"Oh. I didn't give Mohr any choice," said Devin. "I showed him a few of the still images taken by Wolfe and told him we do this quietly and very efficiently, or I haul the entire Razorblade division down to FBI headquarters for a shakedown."

"And he believed you?" said Berg.

"I think he's scared out of his mind," said Devin. "Even with their full cooperation, this could spell the end of AeroDrone. My guess is they're doing a combination of two things right now. Trying to do the right thing. And trying to stay out of prison."

"Let's keep them focused on the former, but never let them forget the latter," said Berg.

"My thoughts exactly."

CHAPTER 41

Beads of perspiration formed on Audra Bauer's face, and not because she was nervous. The bunker's air-conditioning system wasn't designed to cool a room with space for eight bodies—now packed with seventeen. Marnie had invited—more like insisted—that Senator Steele and her chief of staff, Julie Ragan, attend, since it would likely be one of the most consequential meetings in the run-up to whatever showdown occurred with Pichugin's forces within the next week.

Mazurov appeared in the doorway connecting the two conference rooms with a box fan in hand. Since the vents couldn't be closed, the plan was to push cool air from the rest of the basement into the standing-room-only briefing room. The moment the fan whirred to life, at least half of those in attendance expressed some form of noticeable relief.

"Better?" said Mazurov.

"Much better," said Berg, seated between Dana O'Reilly and Marnie Young, who sat next to Senator Steele.

"I'll put one in the other doorway to draw in air from the other side," said Mazurov.

"I think we're fine now," said Senator Steele. "Thank you."

Bauer gave Mazurov a nod, which he interpreted correctly and vanished—heading back to his office to monitor the security feeds. In addition to the safe house's sensors and cameras, they'd added an additional layer of security, given the desperate measures Pichugin was likely employing to find them.

O'Reilly arranged for the six-agent SWAT detachment originally scheduled to augment the SFAC's security team to be staged within a three-minute radius, to serve as a rapid-response force in the event of an attack on the safe house. The team hadn't been given the safe house's location, for obvious reasons, but would be instantly provided with schematics, pictures—everything they'd need to respond to an incursion.

An additional twelve-agent FBI SWAT team, which remained on constant, twenty-four-hour alert at the J. Edgar Hoover Building to respond to threats to headquarters or nearby federal targets, would also be dispatched in the event of an attack on the safe house. Depending on traffic, they could be there within ten minutes.

Then there were the half dozen or so CIA Special Activities Center paramilitary operatives who took up residence in a nearby motel and took turns cruising the neighborhood and surrounding areas on foot and by car, looking for signs of trouble. They'd all reached out to her to express their regrets about the death of her husband and asked her if there was anything they could do. Channeling a near-pathological pragmatism that surprised even her, she asked them for this favor. None of them hesitated. In fact, to keep their presence low key, she had to turn down requests. Shaking that thought off, she started the briefing.

"Senator Steele. Before we get into the nitty-gritty detail of drones, were there any aspects of the briefing you were provided, prior to being driven blindfolded into a garage and hustled away into a basement, that you'd like expanded or repeated?"

"No. Marnie did a comprehensive job. Sounds like I dodged a bullet the other day—probably not the best choice of words," said Steele. "I'm very sorry for everyone's losses. From what I heard, your team took the brunt of the attack."

"We all took some hard hits that day," said Trent Wolfe. "But I do appreciate the kind words. Thank you, Senator."

"Are you a member of the team now or just helping out?" said Steele.

"Auditioning is probably the best way to describe my presence," said Wolfe.

"And Farrington?" said Steele.

"He'll be along in a few days, ma'am," said Miralles, who had been discharged from Walter Reed the night before. "He's doing fine."

"That's good to hear," said Steele, looking back up at Bauer.

She felt relieved not to have her husband mentioned specifically. She couldn't afford the mental or emotional distraction right now. She'd mourn after she killed the plot that had killed David.

"The bottom line here is that we're assuming that kamikaze drones will be used for the next attack, based on three factors—the biggest being that four hundred Razorblade drones never reached their end users in the Donbas region of Ukraine. The shipments, most of them replenishment drones and updated drone-control tablets, started to go missing two years ago. AeroDrone followed their procedures to the letter, but somewhere along the line, likely very close to the front lines, the shipments vanished—never to reach the end user."

"May I?" asked Seeberger.

"Please," said Bauer.

"From what we've gathered by talking directly, on the ground, with several of the known end users, mostly infantry officers in the field, the missing shipments started out and remained a trickle that impacted every unit along the front—but never all at the same time. And if any of the officers got vocal about it, they shortly received at least part of the replacement armaments they asked for, temporarily placating them. The complaints never reached the higher echelons. There was plenty of grumbling at the company command level, and some within the battalions, but little noise beyond that. Whoever coordinated the theft of our weapons played it smart."

"Thank you," said the senator. "I know I might be jumping the gun here, but is there any way AeroDrone can just deactivate the drones remotely with some kind of secretly embedded kill switch?"

Seeberger glanced at Bauer, who nodded.

"This is as good a place as any to jump into what we're here to discuss," said Bauer.

"To answer your question, Senator," said the engineer. "No. We don't embed a ubiquitous kill-switch device for remote deactivation. Once launched, the drone can't be recovered, but the operator can abort its attack on an acquired target and reassign it to another target. If no target is initially assigned or reassigned, the drone will fly until it runs out of power, or the operator can crash it into a safe area like a lake or open field. The warhead won't detonate unless it's in active target mode."

"How long can it stay airborne?" said Marnie.

"Unfortunately, we're talking about the 800 series, which can fly for forty minutes," said Seeberger.

"Wow. That's a long time," said Julie Ragan.

"If launched from its maximum range of twenty-five miles, it eats up twenty minutes of that flight time getting to target," said Seeberger.

"Hold on. You're saying this can be fired from twenty-five miles away?" said Steele.

"Yes, ma'am."

"So. They could literally hit the White House or Capitol Building from Gaithersburg, Maryland—with over three hundred and fifty drones?"

"Some would be shot down, but basically—yes," said Seeberger. "They could very quietly and very quickly fire a massed attack on pretty much any target of their choosing, across the country, or right here in the capital."

"I mean—short of installing an Iron Dome system around every city in America, how do we protect the American people from this kind of threat?" said Steele.

"That's what we're working on," said Bauer. "And we think we have a solution."

"Think?" said Steele.

"It'll work, ma'am," said Seeberger. "There are just a few complications that need to be worked out."

"And the plan will require the use of some strategic-level assets," said Bauer. "We're hoping you can help grease the slow-moving wheels of bureaucracy to make that happen."

"Trust me, with the prospect of a few hundred high-explosive kamikaze drones circling overhead, you may not need my influence to get the wheels turning. The problem will be slowing them down before they catch fire," said Steele. "So. What's the plan?"

"We need to get our hands on one of their drone-control tablets," said Seeberger, holding up an olive drab version. "I guarantee they've installed Russian encryption. Probably very similar to their Zala Aero version. The drones are delivered without encryptions, so each end user can use their own nation's cryptological protocols. It's also why we can't just send out a signal by satellite and shut down every Razorblade within the satellite's line of sight. Keeps the enemy from doing the same. If the frequency is jammed, it hops to a new frequency with the same encryption. That comes into play later."

"Mike. Can you compress this a little?" said Berg.

"Sure. Sorry. Bottom line? My guess is that they're all using the same encryptions and frequency-hopping protocols. We've been tasked by the government to look for exploits in the Russian KUB-E drone, Zala Aero's top export, and we've made the most progress in cracking their encryption. I have a suitcase full of tricks, figuratively speaking, to throw at one of these tablets, but unless we have hours to spend intercepting frequency traffic, I need to be able to plug directly into one of their tablets to break one quickly. I assume we won't have much time on our hands once one of the tablets is somehow acquired."

"Your assumption is correct," said Melendez. "The tablet will have to be taken by force, employing as much surprise as possible. You may be working with five minutes. Maybe a little more. It's impossible to say."

"Holy shit," said Seeberger, laughing nervously. "Five minutes? That's fucking nothing."

"Is it doable?" said Devin.

Seeberger took in a deep breath and exhaled before answering. "If everything goes right—and there won't be a second to spare on the back end. So you need to have everything in place to transmit over a wide band of UHF and SHF frequencies the moment we crack the encryption. AeroDrone can customize a signal in advance of the operation that will use the encryption to take positive control of all the drones and automatically crash them into the nearest body of water or unpopulated area."

"I'll make sure that happens," said Steele.

"One of the National Reconnaissance Office's satellite networks would give the widest coverage, if we're looking at coordinated attacks across the country, like the other day," said Seeberger.

"That's what we're anticipating, or assuming," said Bauer. "So what I'm hearing you say is that we just need to grab one of these tablets, anywhere in the country, and if everything goes right, we should be able to disable every drone deployed across the country."

"Correct," said Seeberger.

"Then the next step is determining the most logical site for their next attack, and somehow tracking down one of those tablets," said Bauer.

"Somehow tracking down?" said Gupta. "Give a little more credit where credit is due?"

Steele said to Ragan, "I like this guy." Turning back to Gupta, she said, "I remember you from a few years ago. I'm very sorry to hear about what happened to your colleague of many years. Mr. Graves, I believe?"

"Yes. Tim Graves," said Anish. "Thank you, ma'am."

"What happened to him?" said Wolfe.

"Don't worry about that," said Gupta. "Occupational hazard."

"So much loss here," said Steele. "This is like the tomb of unsung heroes. I'm going to fix that."

What an interesting statement. Bauer hoped she meant it. The sacrifices made by Farrington's people, previously led by General Sanderson, had gone entirely unacknowledged by the United States government. Pardons for crimes, some real, most completely fabricated, depending on whichever way the political winds blew at the time, had been their only reward and recognition—yet here they were. Still at it despite the shitty treatment they'd received for close to two decades.

"Anish? Can you summarize your plan to somehow get your hands on a tablet?" said Bauer.

"Funny," said Gupta. "Basically, after listening to Seeberger drone on and on, pun intended, about the frequency-hopping capability of the Razorblade system, Mr. Wolfe and I decided we can use this to our advantage to locate the drone-control station. The Razorblade system uses a tripod- or vehicle-mounted antenna. Looks to be about fifteen feet tall?"

"Roughly," said Seeberger.

"Each of the tablets sends and receives its command from a ground control unit attached to the antenna, which makes sure the right commands and information are going to the right controllers. Up to six tablets can run on one antenna," said Gupta.

"So they might need multiple antennae at the site, depending on how many drones they want in the air at one time," said Devin.

"Twelve is the maximum for one antenna," said Seeberger. "Which sounds like what they used against you the other day."

"Anyway. Moving this along. If we had something like the EA-18G Growler airborne over our target area, the Growler could passively analyze all of the RF frequencies over the area, specifically looking for encrypted frequencies. The Russians won't be the only ones using an encrypted frequency. Every business not stuck in the Dark Ages could be transmitting encrypted data. Personal users. The list goes on, but it'll significantly cut down on the amount of RF traffic that the Growler needs to process. Then the Growler jams a wide band of UHF and SHF frequencies and looks for new encrypted frequencies. It does this a few more times, until it confirms that the new frequencies all employ the same encryptions as before. Busted. The RF collection is passive and yields a compass bearing only, but after flying in a straight line, it gets a general fix of the location. Then it just flies in a high-altitude circle around the area, pinpointing the location," said Gupta. "Then Rico and his people mount up and grab us a tablet. Well. We go with Rico and the gang. Welcome to the team, Mike."

The color drained from Seeberger's face, the prospect of participating in an armed raid somehow having managed to elude his careful analysis of the technical side of the proposed mission to this point.

"Thanks?" he said.

"Don't worry, brother," said Gupta. "You will literally be the most important member of the team to keep alive, for the entire mission. You have nothing to worry about."

"That makes me feel so much better," said Seeberger, getting a laugh out of everyone—despite the fact that it looked like his statement had been completely serious.

"Sounds like our next step is identifying the most likely target," said Bauer. "Or two, just in case Pichugin has anticipated the likelihood that we'd focus on the most obvious target."

Melendez shook his head. "We don't have the assets to split into two groups."

"Mike. Is there someone on your level who could handle cracking the encryption if given one of the tablets?" said Bauer.

"Yes. A few who could do it just as easily, possibly even faster," said Seeberger. "Not that I was looking to get out of this, but I was going to recommend a name to replace me. She's better with the gear than I am. The only reason I'm here and she's not is that I'm her boss."

"I'm more concerned with the tactical side of the house," said Melendez. "We're light when it comes to operators, and we're going to need some flexibility when it comes to rules of engagement. I don't think we can count on the FBI for that. No offense, Dana."

"None taken," said O'Reilly. "There's a layer of red tape that would slow us down considerably."

Bauer had no choice but to play a hand she'd hoped to keep secret.

"What if I told you I could muster at least a dozen, possibly more, Special Operations Group types who would be more than willing to take this wherever it needs to go, however it needs to get there," she said.

"Then I'd say we could handle two sites," said Melendez. "How soon can you get them in the loop?"

"They're already keeping an eye on the house and the neighborhood," said Bauer. "I've worked with many of them for years. They all reached out to me when they heard about David. Didn't hesitate when I asked them to lend a hand."

A few long, silent seconds passed before Berg came to the rescue.

"We plan for two sites," he said, before turning to Senator Steele. "Which means two Growlers. Sounds like a big ask for the Department of Defense."

"It is, but I'll burn every favor I've collected over the years to make it happen," said Steele. "And speaking of favors. Doesn't Farrington's old boss, General Sanderson, have some pretty deep connections within the Department of Defense?"

"All retired by now, like him," said Melendez. "Not sure how useful they'd be, but I'll call Rich right away and put that bug in his ear."

Steele shook her head, a knowing smile on her face. "Retired is even better. They're all occupying high-paying, utterly useless board positions at think tanks, defense contractors, and other military-industrial-complex entities. Exactly where all of the highest-ranking colonels, generals, and admirals want to go when it's their time to retire. I'm sure the right word or two from Sanderson can seal whatever deal I propose."

"When you put it that way, I don't doubt it, ma'am," said Melendez.

Bauer wasn't entirely certain how or when they'd secured Senator Steele as a personal ally. Karl Berg was the nexus, but he'd remained tight lipped about it. The two didn't seem overly friendly, but maybe that was a ruse to conceal whatever connection they shared. However the partnership—if one could call it that—came about, Bauer was thankful for it. They stood no chance of stopping Pichugin's next attack without her influence and generous willingness to use it.

CHAPTER 42

A few hours after Senator Steele departed, Karl Berg took a call he'd sincerely hoped would never come. He listened to the proposal. More like a veiled threat, because everything sounded like a threat coming from them. When his former counterpart had finished, he asked a few questions, which were answered in vagaries, before they amicably agreed to talk again in twenty-four hours. Fuck! These people were relentless. For a reason—which he perfectly understood. You didn't survive for decades, surrounded by enemies on all sides, without taking a hard line with everyone, including your friends.

He pulled Bauer aside when she came into the kitchen to refill her coffee, and walked her into the pantry, closing the door behind them.

"This looks serious," she said.

"It is," said Berg. "The Mossad wants in."

"How the fuck—"

"I don't think they know any more than that we've had a task force dedicated to Pichugin's sleepers running for over a year—and that the task force vanished overnight after a lot of noise was made. They know something big is up. They're fishing."

"I'm not sure there's anything to give them," said Bauer. "I'm assuming they want Pichugin? After the highway mess outside of Saint Petersburg, I don't blame them for wanting another crack at the guy, but we held up our end of the bargain."

"That's what I'm guessing, but of course, my contact wouldn't spell it out directly," said Berg. "And you know they won't let this go. We handed them Pichugin on a silver platter, and they dropped the platter, but these aren't the kind of people that care who's to blame for dropping the platter. They want another one carrying the same thing."

"We don't need this right now," said Bauer. "We don't need them possibly getting in touch with their other friends in the government to poke around in our business. We have less than a week to stop a major attack, and there's no time to type out scenario papers or involve congressional committees. The only way we solve this problem is with the people we have right here, unencumbered by red tape and rules of engagement."

"I agree," said Berg. "We're past the point of reading the Joint Chiefs of Staff or National Command Authority into this. Senator Steele will have to explain some of what we're up to, but she's good at navigating her way through the bureaucracy. We just can't have the Israelis undermine us right now, even if that's not their intention."

"Do they ever do anything unintentionally?"

"No."

"I hate to bring this up, but is there any way your friend can sniff out Pichugin's location?" said Bauer. "If the answer is no, I won't ever mention it again."

Berg gave it some thought. He didn't blame Bauer for asking. Their backs were against the wall with the Mossad.

"I doubt it, since Pichugin has literally vanished since Russian Federation troops put him in a helicopter, but my friend did put us on Kuznetzov's trail. That turned out to be a game changer," said Berg.

"It did," said Bauer. "Without that name, Estonia could be in Russian hands right now."

"I'll give him a call. But please. Erase him from your memory. He's living on borrowed time as it is. Every time I ask him for a favor, I feel like I'm fast-forwarding that clock."

CHAPTER 43

Alexei Kaparov sat on the threadbare couch in his flat and stared out the window at the park below. Same scene every day. Pigeons owned the place until around ten in the morning, when the chess players and paper readers, all pensioners, chased them away to reclaim the wooden benches and stone tables. The pigeons would reconverge an hour later, slowly creeping in on the invaders, only to be partially driven back by canes, rolled-up papers, and halfhearted kicks that couldn't knock over an upright soda bottle. All slowly eating away at him, and it was only noon.

When his phone rang, he almost didn't pick it up, his hand going for the half-drained shot glass of vodka. He'd switched from tumblers to shot glasses to save himself from certain death. In fact, he'd thrown away every other glass in his apartment, except for the shot glasses, to prevent this unintentionally intentional suicide. It slowed him down just enough. And he was far too Russian to drink straight from the bottle. Shot glasses only, tumblers for the out-of-control boozers. The bottle for those who weren't kidding themselves about what they wanted. He wasn't there yet.

At the last moment, his hand gripped the phone, bringing it within inches of his face. The half-drained bottle had somewhat affected his vision. He squinted at the number, shaking his head when he recognized the Russian area code: 352. Kurgan Oblast. Kaparov knew nobody from the Kurgan Oblast, so it could be only one person. He pressed the green accept button on his phone's screen.

"To what do I owe the great pleasure of speaking to an old friend?" said Kaparov.

"What time is it there?" said Karl Berg.

"What do you mean, 'What time is it here'? What time is it there? You call to ask about the time?"

"You sound drunk," said Berg.

"What is this, an intervention? You're about five decades too late for that," said Kaparov.

The nerve of this guy, to call only when he wants something, which wasn't entirely true. He did call to check in on him from time to time. But to get on his case about drinking? It's the Russian national pastime. Along with chess—but he sucked at chess. Drinking turned out to be far easier.

"I apologize. Seriously. I'm under some ridiculous stress, and whether you believe it or not, I do consider you a good friend. I worry about you, even if I can't be there to worry about you," said Berg. "So. Why are you half a bottle in at noon on a weekday?"

"How did you know I'm half a bottle in?"

"I just know," said Berg. "More of a guess, but apparently I hit the mark."

"Yes. Well. I need a fucking break from this place," said Kaparov. "Retirement is killing me."

"A permanent or temporary break?" said Berg.

"I thought you retired," said Kaparov. "Do they still give you a bonus for recruiting foreign agents?"

"They brought me back from retirement on a year-to-year contract after last year's . . . revelation," said Berg. "I'm just asking if you'd like to take a short vacation or . . . a much longer one. I know the latter would do you good. I think the former would be in your best interest, health wise and financially. They'd set you up nicely."

"Short vacation for now," said Kaparov.

"All inclusive? Not the cheap version," said Berg, before Kaparov could say it.

"You're like a mind reader. I'd need a few weeks to mentally prepare for my first trip out of Mother Russia since my KGB days, but I'm at your disposal. I really appreciate this. A vacation like this isn't possible on my pension. Unless I were to lay off the vodka, I suppose."

"I'll book us at a place five of your pensions couldn't afford," said Berg. "Seriously. You've earned it. And always keep the other option in mind. My people would pay you twenty times your current pension, for the rest of your life."

"Very tempting. We'll see," said Kaparov. "So. What can I do for you in the meantime?"

"Have you seen any news out of the United States lately?"

"Looks like you have a civil war on your hands," said Kaparov.

"Yes. Compliments of a certain oligarch that didn't burn to a crisp outside of Saint Petersburg."

"Official reports say he was consumed by the flames," said Kaparov.

"A source on the ground watched him being pulled out of the burning SUV by Russian Spetsnaz and ferried away on a helicopter—never to be seen again."

"Same end result."

"We don't think so," said Berg. "I can't get into the details over the phone, for your safety, but we strongly suspect he's behind the attacks here, and that he's planning another—to spark a civil war, or at least cast the nation into chaos that will take months to fix, if not years. Have you heard anything that might suggest he's still around? And where he might be found? A third party is interested, and I need them off my back here at home."

"The same group that somehow bungled the job outside of Saint Petersburg?"

"The same," said Berg.

"You didn't hear this from me—I love saying that—but sources tell me that Boris Gusev miraculously survived the bombing at the Moscow facility. You know the one I'm talking about?"

"Yes. The same third party was responsible."

"That's what I figured," said Kaparov. "Anyway. The same sources tell me that he's been seen in and around Novosibirsk over the past year. That's all I know."

"Novosibirsk. I'll pass that along," said Berg. "And let me know when you're ready for this vacation."

"Sounds like you need at least a few weeks to work on your problem, which works best for me, like I said," said Kaparov. "I'll be ready when you've put the final nail in this oligarch's coffin."

"Deal," said Berg, before ending the call.

A luxury vacation sounded wonderful. The only problem he could foresee was if Karl Berg somehow died between now and then. Ha! That was his only worry. More like the booze talking. He screwed the bottle shut and put it in the freezer, before lying down on the couch for a nap. If all went well on Karl's end, he'd be lying in a hammock, enjoying a warm breeze a few weeks from now.

CHAPTER 44

Four days and they had little to show for the long hours scouring left-leaning activist forums, thousands of phone calls, and emails to known activists and organized activist groups. Just a few small-town protests of things like book bans and redistricting proposals—a dozen people at most, here and there. From what the task force could gather, the larger organizations and most of the grassroots organizers understood the volatility of the situation at hand. Events, protests, and marches had been canceled nationwide.

Not only that, obvious targets of rage and retribution were being actively encouraged to stay home over the weekend. Stay out of sight. Take down your political or social movement flags and banners. Scrape your bumper stickers clean. Go silent on social media for a while. Scrub your social media feeds of political or social justice posts. Don't discuss plans for backyard picnics, barbecues, or family gatherings. They had already anticipated the widespread retribution the task force feared.

Devin and the team took comfort in knowing this. Without well-attended public events to strike with their drones, the Russians would likely postpone the attack. State and federal lawmakers had been shuffled to undisclosed locations, along with most government targets of any significance. Pichugin could always target LGBTQ neighborhoods, minority community centers and churches, and fly drones through activists' windows—but the impact wouldn't be the same. It would undoubtedly be horrific, but it wouldn't have the same galvanizing effect as a mass-casualty event. And the longer the Russians waited, the more their chances of sparking the level of civil unrest needed to create a self-sustaining civil war slipped through their fingers.

"Anything?" said Devin, having run out of anything original to say yesterday.

"Nada," said Gupta. "And federal investigators in Milwaukee, alongside local authorities, just publicly stated that a preliminary digital forensic look into the couple that fired into the rally downtown showed some inconsistencies, which they refused to expand upon at this time. They also said that there's no record anywhere of the Keatons having ever purchased the rifles they used, visiting local gun stores, or having ever purchased a gun in the entire thirty-one years they'd lived outside of Milwaukee."

"Must have been radicalized at Whole Foods," said Hoffman. "Or one of those vegan restaurants."

"I don't think they have vegan restaurants in Milwaukee," said O'Reilly. "Kind of the land of cheese and beer."

"Never know. Those vegans are sneaky," said Hoffman.

"I'm sure the FBI will leave no stone unturned," said Devin.

"They'll move slowly with what they know about the sleeper network, so it doesn't come across as a conspiracy to the Right. Can't blame everything on Russia, right?" said Bauer. "Dana and I have spoken with Director Sharpe about how each field office should proceed. Spread out the findings. Ease the public into it."

"It's the smart play," said Marnie. "They're primed not to believe the federal government. To be frank, I think the bureau needs to hand this off to local law enforcement. Bring them up to speed, when all the evidence is assembled, and let them make the announcements."

"That's a solid idea, Marnie," said Bauer. "With any hope or luck, we might be able to defuse this thing enough to turn an all-out drone attack by Pichugin into a direct political liability for Russia. I just don't know if we have enough time to divert the train off the civil war track and onto the 'Russia is behind this' track before they launch the next attack. They could hit school sporting events in majority Democrat-held districts with the drones. Maybe we're not thinking of all the possibilities."

"Let's add schools to the roster and start making calls. Reach out to each state's secretary of education first and work your way down," said Devin. "All states. Every school district. Blue states first. Then red. Everyone deserves fair warning."

"May as well add day cares to the list," said O'Reilly. "Youth league sports like Little League baseball."

"We're gonna need to clone ourselves to get this done," said Hoffman.

"No sleep for the wicked," said Devin, before heading toward the other room. "I'll let them know where we stand."

Everyone looked the same on the tech side of the team. Exhausted and frustrated, except for Trent Wolfe. For some reason, he was smiling at his laptop. Devin didn't want to know why.

"Since we've come up with no targets worth the Russians' attention, we're shifting gears and reaching out to schools, day cares, youth league sports. Both red and blue states, starting with blue," said Devin.

"That's really grasping at straws," said Gupta.

"I know it is. But it's all we can think of at this point. Start working on state-level lists of these entities, their numbers, and emails for dissemination to the rest of the team. We'll divide it up evenly and do what we can to get the word out. It's a long shot, but maybe we can find a massive Little League tournament somewhere. First priority is to warn them and encourage them to call off the event. If they won't shut it down, then we'll determine whether it warrants deploying one of our teams."

"Don't bother," said Wolfe, still staring at his screen.

"I'm sorry. What?" said Devin.

"We've been looking in the wrong place," said Wolfe, turning his laptop to face Devin. "At the wrong side. Just for shits and giggles,

I checked out AmericaMax news. The only place you can find them anymore is on the internet. Have you seen this?"

Devin knelt next to the table and examined the live newsroom broadcast, reading the banner below the three commentators.

"JUSTICE FOR ALL" RALLY PLANNED SATURDAY ON NATIONAL MALL.

A scrolling ticker below it contained a steady stream of new details.

TENS OF THOUSANDS EXPECTED TO FLOCK TO DC TO DEMAND JUSTICE FROM LAWMAKERS AND ADMINISTRATION AFTER BRAZEN ATTACKS.

"WHERE ARE THE LAWMAKERS? HIDING IN BUNKERS?" ASKS ONE OF THE ORGANIZERS.

"WE'RE NOT LEAVING DC UNTIL JUSTICE IS SERVED," SAID A MAN WHO LOST HIS WIFE IN INDIANAPOLIS SHOOTING.

HOTELS BOOKED SOLID THROUGHOUT THE ENTIRE DC AREA. FLIGHTS FULL. HUNDREDS OF BUSES CHARTERED, MANY ALREADY ON THEIR WAY.

DC BRACES FOR ARRIVAL OF THOUSANDS OF ARMED PROTESTERS. "IF THE GOVERNMENT WON'T PROTECT US, WE'LL PROTECT OURSELVES."

NATIONAL GUARD TO BE DEPLOYED TO DC TO KEEP PROTEST PEACEFUL.

"Holy shit," said Devin. "This was staring us right in the face the whole time."

"Not really. I mean, how many of us ever watch these networks or visit their websites?"

"True. But still—excellent work," said Devin. "Can you put that up on the big screen? I'm bringing everyone over to take a look."

With the group assembled in the room, Devin nodded at Wolfe, who clicked his mouse and transferred the AmericaMax live news stream to the screen. It didn't take long for the gravity of what they were watching to sink in.

"This is all my fault," said Bauer. "I assumed the Russians would play by the old rules. Back and forth, escalating each time until the fuse is lit. But this actually makes even more sense under these circumstances. These people are primed to explode. When the drones start raining down on them, they'll instantly blame the government. Who else has that kind of firepower at their disposal? The protesters will ransack DC, taking out their fury and frustration on the only representatives of the government within sight. The National Guard, police—anyone in their path."

"And they'll be armed to the teeth. This won't be your usual riot," said Wolfe. "Everyone I've seen interviewed has said they don't care about DC laws. They're bringing guns to protect themselves, since nobody cares about protecting them. I've heard about every variation of that theme."

"JUSTICE FOR ALL rally," said Bauer. "Catchy."

"And it's catching on," said Gupta. "Just in the time it took for everyone to file into the room, I've been surfing a dozen different right-wing sites and news networks. This is going to overshadow every previous rally in DC. Buses are already on the way. Every room within thirty miles is booked or blocked off for those with JUSTICE FOR ALL discount codes, which you have to enter a lottery to receive. Flights into DC or BWI are full. Same with Philadelphia, Pittsburgh, Richmond, and Norfolk. Rental cars are gone."

"Sounds like a very organized effort," said Devin. "It's only been four days since the mass shootings."

"Too organized. And very well funded," said Berg. "Like this was the plan all along."

"It probably was," said Marnie. "Just like attacking us in broad daylight to corral us into the SFAC, where they no doubt planned to wipe out the entire task force."

"Pichugin's been sitting on this one for a while," said Bauer.

"If the FBI's preliminary digital forensics report suggests what I think it does, he's been planning this for a few years," said Devin. "Possibly as a 'get out of jail free' card in case his other operation failed? Or quite possibly to be executed at the same time, to sow maximum confusion in the US at a time of crisis in Europe."

"I guess we'll never know," said Berg. "But at least we finally have something concrete to work on. A definitive target. Everyone. Take an hour and collect your thoughts. Seriously. Clear your minds. Take a nap. Eat something. One hour from now we are going to hit the ground running, and I don't expect a single one of us will be catching a wink of sleep until this is over. Understood?"

"Does that apply to you as well?" said Bauer.

"Of course not. I have too much shit to do in the next hour," said Berg, getting a laugh out of the room. "But the rest of you. One hour."

Devin joined him in the other room as part of the task force filed by toward the kitchen—the rest of it likely vanishing for the bunk rooms. Marnie took a seat next to him, followed by Bauer, who leaned her elbows on the chair at the head of the table and put her head in her hands.

"Here are my big questions," said Devin. "They've been on my mind even before the new target revelation. What do we tell the rally organizers? Or do we not? What do we tell law enforcement or the National Guard on the scene, who will have one of two scenarios on their hands depending on our success—or failure? We've been treating this whole thing like we have the right to drag thousands of targets into the open, where they could be killed by kamikaze drones. Like bait. I know it's for the greater good, and it's the only way to put an end to Pichugin's madness, but I feel deeply conflicted. And if we fail, I'm going to feel completely to blame for thousands of deaths."

Marnie squeezed his hand. "We all feel this way. I've had the same thoughts. I just don't see any other way around it."

"I know," said Devin. "It's just brutal."

"Devin," said Berg. "Take it from me, decisions like these will always leave you feeling miserable. Even if we succeed. Just remembering that it could have gone the other way will trigger some dark thoughts. They've always haunted me, and I've racked up quite a few. Your questions are very normal and very valid. I wish I had something to say to take away the doubt and eventual dark moments, other than we're doing this for the greater good, but that's been my default 'feel good speech' for decades. Kind of lame, but there you have it."

"I don't have much to add, Devin," said Bauer. "But Pichugin isn't going to let three hundred and seventy-four Razorblades go to waste. Saturday represents our best chance at taking them all away from him at once. We'll work on what we can reveal to the National Guard, Capitol Police, and DC Metro Police over the course of the next day or so. Given the drone attack against the SFAC Saturday, the presence of a serious counter-drone capability on the National Mall shouldn't raise any alarms with the Russians, National Guard, or law enforcement."

Devin nodded. "I feel better about this already."

"No, you don't," said Berg. "But keep your game face on. Everyone looks up to you around here."

No pressure at all. Just the future of the country depending on his game face.

CHAPTER 45

Karl Berg felt good about the calls, but far from comforted by them. They had made significant progress toward putting some of the major pieces into play. Richard Farrington, who wouldn't be released from Walter Reed for a few days, at the earliest, had reached out to retired general Terrence Sanderson, who in turn had started working his aging network of former Beltway insiders.

Their influence waning by the day post-retirement, they still had enough influence to bend the right ears without drawing undue attention to the situation. Many of them had worked with—*dealt with* was probably the better term—Sanderson in the past. While his methods, and those continued by Farrington, had left most of them with permanent ulcers and frequent anxiety attacks, Sanderson's people had always come through for them.

As he sat in on the secure conversations between Farrington and his DC power broker buddies, from wherever they'd retired—still a complete mystery to everyone, even Rich—one by one they saw the logic in not turning Saturday into a security circus or trying to prevent the protesters from entering the city. If they didn't gather on the National Mall, they'd gather somewhere outside the city, with the same result. Drones raining from the sky, followed by an invasion of the Capitol by enraged, heavily armed protesters.

They even discussed keeping the National Guard out of the city, particularly the National Mall area, in case the task force's plan failed. They'd be put in an impossible situation if the drones hit the crowd.

Quickly overwhelmed and forced to choose between firing on protesters to escape or surrendering. It was finally decided that the National Guard had to be on the scene, in force. Keeping them out of sight would send the wrong message on a number of levels.

The JUSTICE FOR ALL crowd could turn their absence into a rallying cry, saying the government doesn't even care enough about us to protect us from a counterprotest or another attack. People watching the protesters gather with weapons on the National Mall would ask, Why would the government allow this? What's next? Let them take over the White House? The protesters have to be there, so they agreed that the National Guard would be informed of a possible "enhanced risk of incitement" that could highly exacerbate the crowd's volatility.

They'd recommend that the Guard be positioned in a way to more easily evacuate and avoid the crowds should an "event" beyond the scope of an already highly charged protest occur. Police units would be given the same warning. It was the best they could do without coming out and saying, "Be ready to run if a few hundred drones simultaneously hit the National Mall."

The task force still had a long way to go toward implementing Operation KILL SWITCH. The discussions that took up most of the day were just that—discussions to get the ball rolling. Each of those power brokers would now have to carefully approach the right people, with the right pitch—just to get the task force an audience. And there was no telling where it would go from there. Any one of them, anywhere down the line, could get cold feet and decide the plan was too risky. Take everything discussed and march it as high up their chain of command as possible to shut down the city. Declare martial law or something equally as useless and damaging. JUSTICE FOR ALL was going to have a massive rally Saturday no matter how the government tried to shut it down. The only question was, Where?

Berg nodded at Elena Visser, who ran gatekeeping at each door during the discussions and negotiations. Even Berg and Bauer weren't supposed to be listening in on the secretive conversations, but both Farrington and Sanderson felt it was necessary to keep them in the bigger loop. To give them a sense of where everything stood, and possibly to glean some of their combined sixty years–plus CIA experience at reading between the lines. Visser opened the door to the other conference room before making her way to the door leading to the kitchen.

Half the other room poured in within a few seconds, everyone taking seats or leaning against the walls, careful not to knock over any of the monitors.

"So? How are we looking?" said Devin.

"The wheels are turning," said Berg.

"Slowly," said Bauer. "But they're turning. Sounds like Sanderson has the right contacts to help us with the National Guard. We emphasized the need for counter-drone assets based on DeSoto's assassination and the attack on the SFAC. They said that shouldn't be a problem, particularly with a sizable National Guard presence. It can be justified as protection for law enforcement and the Guard."

"What about the Growler? This whole plan is dead in the water without that electronic warfare jet," said Marnie.

"Sanderson is having a few one-on-ones with some very-high-ranking former Department of Defense buddies," said Bauer. "He didn't mince words. It's not going to be easy to get one of these deployed over DC on such short notice, without having to explain ourselves to a lot of people."

"This is where Senator Steele earns her money," said Berg. "Once Sanderson lays the groundwork, she needs to walk this up to the president and the chairman of the Joint Chiefs of Staff. Lay it all on the line. That'll be a conversation Audra, Marnie, and I have with the senator."

"Can she get an audience with the president just like that?" said Marnie. "I know she has influence, but I've worked with her for a year, and I've never seen her pull off something like that."

"Senator Margaret Steele could get an audience with the pope if she wanted," said Berg. "She just doesn't abuse her influence like others in Congress—which is why I think she'll be able to secure a meeting quickly. That and the fact that she chairs the US Senate side of the committee investigating DEEP SLEEP."

"Should we consider a backup plan?" said Devin. "Anish. I know you can intercept signals, and Mr. Wolfe has a PhD in the subject."

"Master's degree," said Wolfe.

"I'm sure it's a PhD plus at this point in your career," said Devin. "I guess what I'm asking is—can you jam the radio frequency used to control the drones?"

"You've seen how we work. It may seem nifty, but it's small-scope stuff. If I can identify the frequency in question, yes, I can jam it, or at least render it useless enough to the users. We do this on a small scale when jamming encrypted radio networks to keep guards from communicating with each other in a building. Gives us an edge," said Gupta. "But that's after sitting on a site with limited RF transmissions for a few hours or more, identifying the radio network in question. We're talking a two-to-five-mile-diameter circle, maybe bigger—filled with hundreds of thousands of RF transmissions. We'd never find the drone frequency. It's statistically impossible. Jamming it is immaterial. Without the Growler or a similar aircraft's ability to analyze thousands of frequency transmissions in fractions of a second, there's no hope of finding drone frequency."

"Fair enough," said Devin. "Had to ask."

"Is Bernie still flying?" said Berg.

Melendez shook his head. "He retired a few years ago. His protégé took over the firm, but they specialize almost exclusively in aerial surveillance and VIP runs. Even back in the day, I don't think he ever carried any overly sophisticated EW gear on his C-123."

"That was quite the aircraft," said Miralles. "Held together by Band-Aids."

"Old Band-Aids," said Melendez.

"So. It sounds like there's nothing else we can do right now about these bigger pieces of the plan except wait until the cigars are lit and the scotch is poured in the darkest corners of DC—and hope the winds blow favorably," said Devin.

"Basically," said Bauer.

A voice from the doorway drew their attention. Normally quiet and reserved, Rafael, the senior DEVTEK cybersecurity engineer, offered some interesting advice.

"While the bigwigs were moving the bigger pieces around the board for a couple of hours, we actually made a lot of headway going over some of the smaller stuff. You know, like exactly what needs to go down once the Growler gives us a location fix."

"Sounds like trivial details," said Berg, before chuckling. "How about we convene in ten, and you can catch us up."

"Perfect," said Rafael. "I think we have a solid plan. But the plan is useless without the precise location of the drone-control station."

"Yeah. And unfortunately that's going to be one of our biggest hurdles," said Berg.

CHAPTER 46

Richard Farrington lay on his back with his right leg raised in traction by a series of wires and pulleys that looked like it could collapse at any moment. He was bored out of his mind, which was mostly his fault. In order to stay in the loop with the team, he'd requested a transfer to a SCIF-level recovery room, normally reserved for Command Authority, National Security Council, or Joint Chiefs of Staff-level patients.

He supposed he had Senator Steele to thank for the transfer, though it had left him with no contact with the outside world other than an encrypted satellite phone, which connected to a secure repeater. The only other connection to the outside world was a call button for the attending nurses and physicians. Not even a television. Something about the cable connecting to the television not being secure.

When his sat phone rang, he nearly smashed his hand on the hospital guardrail retrieving it. He recognized the number.

"Have you spoken with Berg yet?" said Sanderson.

"Not yet. I'll let them absorb it all for an hour. No point rushing them to any conclusions. I didn't sense anyone talking out of both sides of their mouth during any of the conversations. Some hesitation, sure, but they know what they're getting with you—and hopefully me."

"They do. On both accounts," said Sanderson. "The National Guard thing is a done deal. They'll be deployed in force no matter what. We'll push them again to make plans for a rapid evacuation in the face of being overrun if things go sideways with the task force's plan. Drone defenses will be in place, but nothing on the kind of level that could neutralize three hundred and seventy-four Razorblades."

"I don't think parking fifty KADD-Vs at the National Mall would be enough. Not that the US has that many in their inventory. Anyway, the Russians would kill the KADDs first, then use whatever was left on the crowd. It's not like they need more than fifty of those Razorblades to start a full-fledged riot on a scale we've never seen before."

"I'm not gonna lie to you, Rich. Part of me would like to see them get wiped out trying to burn the city down. True America was always about dismantling the government and rebuilding it in their image. Maybe it's time to finally get it out of their system, with high explosives and shrapnel."

"No. You're wrong about that, Terrence," said Farrington. "These aren't the same people. Some are, but the vast majority aren't. True America's days vanished over a decade ago when we took them down. Aside from a few anniversary-date rumblings about civil war and a few poorly attended protests, they're gone. What we're seeing now is America. Deeply divided."

"And marching on the US Capitol with weapons. Feels like a long-simmering grievance to me. True America style," said Sanderson.

"I don't agree. The Russians have been at this for decades, possibly longer. The Cold War never ended for them. They quickly adjusted and figured out how to fight it on terms we didn't understand for far too long. Hell. They even had their hands in True America. Remember Sean Walker, a key adviser to the president at the time?"

"Vaguely," said Sanderson.

"Drank himself into oblivion, but still somehow managed to shoot himself right through the left temple, his off hand. His BAC was .17 when they found him six hours after the coroner's declared time of death. An old Russian trick, but they forgot we don't drink like most Russians. They probably killed him by alcohol poisoning before they blew his brains out."

"I thought they just pushed people out of hospital windows these days," said Sanderson.

"Thanks for the reminder," said Farrington. "Anyway. All our evidence suggests a massive foreign-based disinformation and active measures campaign to bolster turnout at this protest and inflame its attendees. And it's only going to get worse. We also determined that they started stealing the drones nearly two years ago. We think whatever they have planned for Saturday was supposed to happen immediately before or after the attack against Estonia."

"Makes sense. Keep us distracted," said Sanderson. "And now they're just doing this out of spite?"

"We have no idea, which is why Senator Steele is going to recommend that NATO and its allies be placed on high alert following whatever goes down on Saturday. We don't want to tip our hand," said Farrington.

"Steele has quite a mountain to climb here. I don't see how she puts enough cards on the table to get what she wants, without tipping her whole hand. Once the president understands the full picture, how is she going to convince him to keep the city open? He'll order the National Guard to seal off the city to keep the protesters away. The last thing he needs is for America to watch a massacre unfold on the National Mall."

"Two reasons he'll consider our plan. One. The attack is inevitable. The Russians will do one of two things. They'll either hit them wherever they end up assembling on Saturday or Sunday, or they'll wait until the masses of protesters head back home. The protesters can't keep at this forever. Eventually, a second, massive rally will be organized, or several larger rallies will be scheduled across the country. Then the Russians will strike. One way or the other, at one time or another, the Russians are going to hit these people hard, and the administration will be blamed. Second reason? The optics of denying citizens their basic right to gather in their own capital. My guess is the Russian attack will happen on the same day. If the National Guard turns these people away, and they're attacked while massed outside the Capitol, the president will have a public relations nightmare on his hands."

"And I thought we ran some ass-clenching missions back in the day. This takes it to the next level," said Sanderson.

"You have no idea," said Farrington. "And I get to sit it out here. Alone. Out of the loop."

"Jesus, Rich. Are you on life support over there? IV drips?"

"No. My leg's in traction. That's about it."

"Then call Senator Steele, or whoever, and get your ass released ASAP," said Sanderson. "Or wheel yourself out of there. They can reset your leg when this is over. There's plenty of painkillers at the Anacostia safe house. The pity party is over."

Farrington started laughing.

"What's so funny?" said Sanderson.

"Sure you don't want to take a red-eye up here?" said Farrington. "This is going to be one for the books."

"My book is full," said Sanderson. "This is your chapter. Better not be the epilogue."

"Still plenty of room in the book."

"Good. I'll get you the Growler, even if it takes a trip up north to blackmail some people in person," said Sanderson.

"Always good talking with you, sir," said Farrington.

"Same here, Rich. When this little dustup is over, I'd like to have you and a few others down for some of the best steak and Malbec in the world," said Sanderson, before ending the call.

Son of a bitch went back to Argentina. The last place anyone would expect, given his history there.

CHAPTER 47

From what Marnie could tell, the small stuff came down to two main problems. The first being, How will we know the attack is imminent so we can target our efforts? The second? Once the attack is determined to be imminent, how does the task force cover twelve to seventy-five square miles of city with eighteen people? First things first. Anticipating the attack.

Presumably the Russians would wait until the crowds reached peak size before they initiated their drone massacre, but that was a significant assumption. Even a half-filled National Mall would result in thousands of casualties. More than enough to spark a riot and send shock waves of rage and calls for revenge through the ranks still arriving. But somehow that didn't feel right. The biggest impact would be to fill the National Mall and surrounding areas to capacity, and then send the drones.

Without some kind of advance warning that the attack was about to kick off, their only other option was for the Growler to jam intermittently, every few minutes, in the hours leading up to peak crowd size, and compare the RF picture, looking for the missing and new frequencies. That way they could potentially catch the drones while they were spooling up before being placed in their launcher or soon after launch. The problem with that method lay with the timing. Without a somewhat compressed time frame to stop and start jamming, it was entirely possible that the drone-control operators might become suspicious of a sophisticated effort to thwart their drones. Two to three hours of jamming wasn't going to escape their attention.

Rafael suggested a different approach. He theorized that Russian-initiated social media chatter and disinformation would increase across the board, building momentum as the time of attack approached. He even postulated that the mainstream site domains might be hijacked by alt-web domains, dragging all users into a fake disinformation stream that perfectly mimicked their platform of choice, and started to slowly feed them news stories about the "standoff" at the Capitol.

Posts across all platforms would report columns of tanks and armored personnel carriers moving into DC, advancing on the National Mall. Aircraft sorties from multiple East Coast Navy and Air Force bases spotted, the jets laden with bombs. Attack helicopters passing over suburbs, headed for DC. The Russians would whip the crowd into a panicked frenzy. Sheer terror that they were about to be engaged by the United States military, at the direct order of the president of the United States. Then the drones would start to hit the crowd.

The first significant increase in that social media traffic would be their sign to initiate KILL SWITCH and put that EA-18G Growler to work. Which was only the first part of the operation. The easy part. Getting both tactical and technical teams to the drone-control station's location was part two of their discussion.

"It sounds larger than it is," said Marnie. "We're assuming a two-to-five-mile-radius circle around the National Mall, so the drone teams can hide in a sea of radio frequencies."

"Hundreds of thousands of people live in that circle," said Melendez.

"I know," said Marnie. "My first thought was a helicopter. Even if just to land somewhere nearby, and not right on top of the target building."

Saya Huddleston, the AeroDrone development engineer that Seeberger claimed was the best, chimed in for one of the first times.

"They'll have at least one Razorblade loitering overhead to deal with immediate threats. A helicopter flying and landing nearby will definitely draw their attention."

"Good point. I suppose we need to think the same way about vehicles and moving in groups toward the target building," said Marnie.

"Definitely," said Huddleston. "Especially if the mayor, or whoever, implements some kind of daytime curfew or vehicle travel restrictions. You don't want to be the only car on the road headed toward the drone-control station."

"This is so fucked," said Hoffman. "We have fourteen tactical operators, including the CIA guys, who should be here right now."

"I can call them in off the street," said Bauer. "But I think you can kiss this place goodbye as a safe house if we bring them here. There's no way a few of them won't know where they are. They've been casually patrolling these streets since Sunday."

"Rico?" said Hoffman.

"We need them to be an integral part of this," said Melendez.

"Should we call Farrington first?" said Miralles.

"No. I need to pick him up at the hospital in an hour or so," said Melendez. "I'll explain the situation."

"He's coming here?" said Gupta.

"Yeah. Vacation's over," said Melendez. "Seriously, though. He didn't want to miss this. Supposedly he's fine, just a little traction for his leg. We'll have to carry him down and set him up on an air mattress or something. Who knows."

"He was a little more fucked up than a little traction," said Miralles.

Melendez shrugged. "He's headed our way. That's all I know."

"Seven more bodies. This place is definitely going to get crowded," said Devin.

"We might have to ease up on some of the restrictions," said Mazurov. "If we're essentially declassifying the place as a safe house."

"We'll see," said Melendez. "Anyway. What were you thinking for teams, Rafael?"

"Four teams. Two comprised of three operators, a driver sort of operator and two tech engineers. Then two teams comprised solely of three operators. I'm thinking the CIA officers, since they've worked together before," said Rafael. "We locate the teams in the four corners of a slightly shrunken square within the target circle, and when we get a geographical fix, we send everybody. No matter who's closer, at least three tactical operators will arrive on scene. They can assess the security situation and breach if it seems feasible. Engineers stay back if they're part of the first team on the scene. If possible, the arriving team waits for backup. That puts six tactical operators into action, with the engineers waiting safely behind. It's key that the engineers are not put into the line of fire. They're irreplaceable. Sorry."

"Six highly trained operators should do the trick," said Melendez. "Three would probably be enough. It's a good plan. Nice job."

"Thank you," said Rafael.

"So. Who's headed out and who's staying back?" said Melendez.

"Berg, Bauer, the DEVTEK team, and Farrington are staying back," said Rafael, before handing out sheets of paper to everyone within easy reach. "I've created a rough roster of the other four teams. Feel free to change them. I just based it on my observations since we've met."

The teams appeared well balanced, but there was only one problem. Rafael had split Devin and Marnie onto different teams. As if he'd been watching her reaction, Rafael slid next to her.

"I think it's for the best that the two of you are not watching each other's backs. You're too involved. I see the way you look at each other. It's not in the team's or either of your best interest," said Rafael. "If you don't agree, I apologize for overstepping."

She considered him for a long moment, wanting to be angry but unable to overcome the powerful sense of knowing that he was right.

"You're right," said Marnie. "I just hope he agrees."

PART FIVE

CHAPTER 48

Kolya Nikitin must have checked and rechecked the entire setup five times over the past hour, on top of the ten times he'd checked since they moved in on Thursday. But you could never be too careful. Too much was at stake to risk on a rat chewing through a wire, or one of his operators fucking around with the settings. Rumor had it that Pichugin wasn't a very forgiving man, and given the fact that he'd invested over a year of training in the drone-control team—on top of wildly generous salaries—Kolya wasn't about to screw this up over something as ridiculously simple as a loose wire connection.

The team was unique in many ways. All recent university graduates, with degrees in various technical fields, who were still looking for work months after graduation—their degrees harder to sell to prospective employers than university propaganda had promised. The lure of a two-year guaranteed contract, at a salary level four times what their colleagues were making right out of college, had proved irresistible.

Once they'd signed on the dotted line, the hammer had dropped. Harder on some than others. Kolya found the new terms of their deal exciting. Others did not. What they didn't know was that the Wegner Group owned their two-year contract, and they would all be sent to four weeks of basic training. A slap in the face that didn't sit well with many, despite the promise that they would never serve in direct combat roles. Technical roles only. A promise that meant little given that Wegner had never been mentioned at any point during the month-long recruitment process.

But true to their word, the team received basic firearms and hand-to-hand combat training, before moving to a facility in Novosibirsk, where they'd learned how to fly a variety of commercial drones, along with the latest versions of several nations' kamikaze drones. Once they'd demonstrated proficiency with the other drones, the real training had started.

Two months of intensive Razorblade simulators, culminating in live targeting flights with armed Razorblade drones. He now fully understood why the Russians on the front lines, and beyond in eastern Ukraine, feared these drones. They dropped out of the sky with no warning, their low profiles nearly undetectable while flying above.

With their training complete, they had been told to expect orders to deploy within a few weeks. Weeks turned into months, then months turned into a year—trapped in a less-than-luxurious Wegner barracks on a nondescript military-style base in Novosibirsk. Virtual training had continued, along with extra combat training and language classes. Nearly all members of the team had spoken workable English upon starting the training. By the end of the year, their language skills had improved significantly. They still sounded like Russian tourists, but blending in wasn't their job. They weren't spies.

They had a very specific job to do, which was what had brought them to this dusty, sparsely furnished two-bedroom apartment, with one of the keys given to him along with the shipment of drones four weeks ago. The other key had been for a rental house about an hour outside of Washington, DC, where they were to wait for orders and the rest of the team.

The Wegner Group was being as cautious as possible slipping them into the country. Kolya had been smuggled in aboard a cargo ship, where he had been kept out of sight until the ship pulled into Miami—where he'd climbed down into a speedboat late at night and was spirited away.

Others had been smuggled over the vast Canadian border or far-riskier Mexican border. Some had been brought in by sailboat from the Caribbean. When the last of the transits had been made or attempted, only six had been stopped, taken into custody, or turned back. A possibility they had planned for. Wegner had trained and sent ten more than needed to get the job done. Like Kolya, they weren't taking any chances, either. His sat phone rang.

"Da. Understood. We're ready," he said, before signaling for everyone to gather around him.

He glanced around at the seven men and women who had trained for this very moment for the past two years of their lives and would be rewarded handsomely upon their return to Mother Russia.

"Fifteen-minute warning," said Kolya. "Control team. Check and recheck your connections Firing team, start spooling up the first twenty-four drones. I want all the drones linked to a controller's tablet in ten minutes. Like we drilled. Two drones per controller. This is it. Firing team, hold up for a moment."

While the controllers scrambled back to their stations, Kolya brought the two team members responsible for handling and launching the drones from the roof in close.

"Keep an eye on your surroundings while you're up there," said Kolya. "Check out the streets below in between salvos. The alleys, We have friends on the street, but you're four stories higher. Also, keep an eye on the sky and your ears open for helicopters. If you detect any signs of trouble on the ground or in the air, I need to know Immediately. STATION 4 will have a drone overhead in ten minutes to provide cover. If you see more than one drone overhead, contact me right away. Got it?"

They both nodded, and Kolya dismissed them. The two sprinted out of the room, feet barely missing the snake of wires leading from the controller interface docks and through the window to the tripod-mounted antenna on the roof. He shook his head before looking around for a roll of duct tape. He couldn't take it anymore. Someone was going to trip on those wires and bring the whole system down.

CHAPTER 49

Marnie's earpiece crackled—Farrington's larger-than-life voice booming. They'd transported him back to the safe house, where he sped around in a wheelchair, making up for lost time. And possibly a bruised ego. He came across as a little more overbearing than usual.

"It's happening. Social media is blowing up with reports of armored vehicles and helicopters moving toward the National Mall. Multiple reliable news networks have reported a panic building among the protesters. Some of the more organized armed groups are rallying anyone with a weapon to the perimeter of the mall. They're preparing for war."

"We're also seeing some glitching at some of the major social media platforms. Both on their user interface and in their code. We have spiders crawling their sites, looking for anomalies. Incidences have skyrocketed over the past five minutes," said Rafael.

"In English, please," said Farrington.

"These are the first signs that someone is trying to mimic the sites. They'll shut down the original momentarily, then bring their version online. Users will have to enter their username and password again so the mimic site can match users to the mimicked accounts, but that's about it. Nobody will know the difference."

"I'm activating KILL SWITCH," said Farrington. "Out."

Miralles turned to Marnie, who was seated next to her. "Remember. You're third in the stack. You watch our six and provide backup as requested, and only when requested."

"She knows what—" started Jared Hoffman.

"Not like we do. Plus, it's not like her job is fluff. There's only three of us. Covering our back will require concentration and ever-shifting situational awareness. I didn't mean it as a dig."

"Got it," said Marnie.

"And you two," said Miralles, addressing Trent Wolfe and Saya Huddleston, their only real hope at stopping Pichugin's attack. "You do exactly what Nick, a.k.a. Mr. Mazurov, tells you. You don't take matters into your own hands. His job is to keep you alive until you can work your magic on one of those tablets. Shit might get messy. If Nick goes down, you contact us immediately for further instructions. Copy?"

"Yes, ma'am," said Wolfe.

Huddleston just nodded, the look on her face blank. The complete opposite of the affect she portrayed at the safe house. Fuck. Marnie'd seen this a hundred times before during her years in the Marine Corps. Bravado melting away in the face of "the real shit." Marnie leaned forward between the two front seats and whispered, "The AeroDrone tech could pose an issue. She looks shell-shocked."

Hoffman and Mazurov barely nodded, acknowledging her assessment. When she sat back, Miralles glanced in her direction and gave her the same nod. The last thing they needed was a babysitting job, but at least they knew ahead of time. They might need to use one of the CIA teams to pick up the slack if she became a burden.

CHAPTER 50

Devin stared at his watch. Two minutes had passed since Farrington initiated KILL SWITCH. He thought the process would work faster and that they'd already be on their way to the drone-control site. A big part of him worried that they'd made some bad assumptions. With a twenty-five-mile range, the Russians could have launched the drones from a farm field in Virginia. Then again, go too rural and the RF signals are too easy to identify and triangulate.

The United States military, if prepared, could fire a GPS-guided HIMARS rocket barrage at the field or drop several JDAMs from previously launched combat air patrols, destroying the operation before the drones got close enough for the controllers to assign targets. And with zero collateral damage. Using the city presented all kinds of obstacles to stopping the attack, from detection to elimination. You can't drop a five-hundred-pound JDAM on a three-story house without taking out half the neighborhood.

Once again. Their urban search was one big assumption—the mother of all fuckups. He just hoped that adage didn't apply to their decision.

"This is Farrington. ZAPPER THREE-THREE has four separate hits. I say again. Our Growler got four distinctly dispersed geographical hits. Looks like they're operating from four sites, which makes sense. Why put all your eggs in one basket? The good news is that they're all within a few miles of the National Mall. I guess that's bad news in a way, but they're within easy reach of our teams. The bad news is that we need to make an immediate decision. Go for one site or go for two. You should have the coordinates on your tablets already. I'd like to get some quick input from the field teams."

Devin scanned his tablet's screen. Shit! They were four blocks away from one of the identified targets: 815 Jefferson Street Northwest. Looked like a three-story apartment complex, not a stand-alone building. Another similar complex sat across the street, which they could use to engage the rooftop launch team. The drone-control team would be in one of the top-floor apartments, so they could run cables to the launchers on the roof. The two locations wouldn't be too far away from each other. Another advantage of putting someone on the rooftop across the street. They could narrow down the building search.

TAC-3, the CIA group in Capitol Heights, was the only other team in a similar situation. They were located a few blocks away from one of the targets, but they didn't have any of the engineers with them. TAC-2, Marnie's hybrid tactical-technical team, was located on the other side of the downtown area, in Forest Heights. Not terribly far from TAC-3, but at least a five-to-ten-minute drive. Probably more like five to seven minutes given the daytime curfew put into place by the mayor.

TAC-4, the other CIA crew, was the odd team out, sitting in northern Arlington. Their closest target was the same as Devin's, a ten-minute drive around the downtown area, avoiding the chaos headed into the National Mall. After giving it a few more seconds' thought, he made a decision—whether it was his to make or not.

"This is Devin. First things first. Contact our hotline at the National Counterterrorism Center and pass along those coordinates. They need to coordinate with DC Metro Police immediately to set up buffers around the drone sites."

Senator Steele had managed to secure a brief audience with the president of the United States, who'd put her in direct touch with the director of National Intelligence. She'd been scant on details regarding the series of meetings, but she'd clearly managed to earn their support of the task force's plan.

"In progress," said Bauer. "DC Metro received a heads-up about thirty minutes ago. All patrol units should be out of your way well before you arrive at any of the sites. The FBI's Critical Incident Response Group has SWAT teams from multiple field offices standing by to hit the sites once the drones are deactivated. They'll remain at a standoff distance until we give them a green light."

"Copy," said Devin. "Regarding our approach? I think we should split up and hit two sites. Maximize our chances of getting our hands on one of those tablets. TAC-3 and TAC-2 hit the Capitol Heights target simultaneously. TAC-2 is eight minutes away. TAC-1 will hit the north DC site when TAC-4 arrives. About ten minutes from now. We'll coordinate both takedowns to occur simultaneously."

"I don't agree," said Farrington. "Devin. Your group is right on top of one of the targets. You can get out of your vehicle now and start moving through the alleys. Leave Gupta and Seeberger a block or so away to wait for the all-clear sign. TAC-4 will be there soon enough. They can work off your ground intel and figure out their best approach. I see a four-story building across the street. One of the CIA officers should make their way to the rooftop. They can take down the launch team and the radar with rifle fire. TAC-3 is just a few more minutes away. They can back you up after you breach. That puts ten tactical operators on the job, plus the engineers. TAC-2 is going to take forever to get there, but if something goes sideways when you bring Gupta and Seeberger in, we'll have a backup tech team on-site in minutes."

"That's confidence inspiring," said Gupta.

"Just being realistic," said Farrington.

"Rich. This is Smith with TAC-3. How about this? TAC-2 has to drive in our general direction to get to the north DC site, so why don't we take a stab at breaching and neutralizing the Fifty-Fifth Street target?

We'll drive up fast and kick the fucking door down. They won't know what hit 'em."

"I don't like it," said Farrington. "Your closest backup will be five minutes away."

"If it goes to shit, at least we'll get some intel out of it," said Smith. "Traps. Response time of hostiles. Enough for TAC-1 and 4 to get the job done up north, with 2 backing them up when they arrive. If it works, we clean house and hand deliver some tablets to TAC-2 when they arrive."

"They could drop a drone on your head," said Farrington.

"We should be inside before they even know what's happening."

"Should," said Farrington. "My least favorite word when it comes to tactical work."

Bauer jumped into the conversation. "Kevin. You don't have to do this."

"It's our choice—if approved."

Devin rendered his verdict. "It's worth a shot. It might even draw their eye-in-the-sky attention away from the north DC target."

"Or put all sites on full alert," said Farrington.

"Or that," said Devin.

After a few long seconds, Farrington relented. "Okay. Give it a shot. Put your microphones on live feed, and keep talking, so we can get a sense of what you're up against—in case they drop a drone on your head in the middle of it all."

"Funny," said Smith. "We're moving out."

"TAC-4. Head directly to the north DC target location. Contact TAC-1 for instructions when you reach the area. TAC-2, make your way north and be ready to divert to Capitol Heights if this works."

After all stations acknowledged Farrington's orders, Devin addressed the vehicle.

"What do you all think?"

"It doesn't really matter at this point," said Melendez. "But I think that CIA team is getting ahead of itself. My prediction is that we're about to get a lot of good intel on what not to do."

"Get ready to move on our target, regardless of what happens to TAC-3," said Devin, wondering about Farrington's change of heart.

Is that why Farrington ultimately relented? To gain some intel on the target buildings? He hoped not. He sincerely hoped that Rich wouldn't throw good people's lives away like that. Then again, the team had volunteered, offering many of the same reasons. A risky gamble that at its best would lead to a quick, easy win. At its worst—intel gained at the cost of human lives. Devin wasn't sure he'd ever truly understand what made these people tick.

CHAPTER 51

Kevin Smith pounded the dashboard as their sedan sped down Fifty Fifth Street Southeast, trying to find a house number to get a sense of how they might be ordered—and coming up with nothing. No street-side mailboxes with numbers. No numbers on the curbs. Nothing discernible on the houses set back from the street by short, steeply sloped lawns. Everything blocked by trees or bushes.

The few numbers he caught vanished just as quickly at this speed. But they couldn't afford to slow down. If these fuckers had a drone loitering overhead, the clock had already started ticking. He'd have to rely on his tablet, and he fucking hated using the tablet for this kind of thing. The last thing he needed was to be staring at a screen while a life-and-death situation unfolded around them.

"Third structure on the left after Ayers Place," said Smith.

He used the word *structure* for a reason. Every building on the block was a two-story redbrick duplex with a covered porch. Another complication he hadn't anticipated. They had no idea which side of the duplex to breach. Not an unsolvable problem. Especially with a few wraps of breacher cord to create a hole between the two sides. But a bit of a time consumer and initiative waster. He hoped they picked the correct door from the start.

"Any idea which side?" said Caruso, sitting directly behind him in the rear passenger seat.

"None," said Smith.

Kendra Shale, the driver, carried most of their breaching gear. That was her specialty. They each had a few preprimed door poppers in case she was busy and they needed to open a door. Smith took one look at the tablet to be sure before sliding it into a case on the front of his right thigh.

"TAC-3 is three seconds out," he said, unbuckling the seat belt and releasing his rifle's safety. "Two. One. Exiting vehicle."

Shale pulled the car sharply left and stopped them against the curb at a forty-five-degree angle to the house to give herself some cover from the car door in case they were immediately engaged by gunfire. It would also allow Smith and Caruso to approach the house more directly, instead of running around the vehicle. Regrettably, the threat came from the opposite direction.

Gunfire erupted the moment Smith kicked open his door, an older man firing what looked like a vintage Cold War Skorpion machine pistol on fully automatic. The man stood behind the hood of a beat-up sedan parked a few spaces back, on the other side of the street. Caruso never made it out of the car on his feet, the rear passenger side of their vehicle taking the brunt of the machine pistol's magazine. The CIA officer crumpled to the street between his partially opened door and the car, his bloodied head thunking hard against the pavement.

Still inside the car, Smith braced the rifle against the doorframe and sighted in on the shooter, who scrambled to insert a new magazine into the machine pistol. One press of his rifle trigger ended that struggle, the man's head snapping backward. A second shooter appeared to Smith's left, a woman with gray hair rising to a crouch in the bed of a white pickup truck, aiming a military-style rifle in his direction. Shale's rifle boomed, and the woman disappeared, leaving nothing but a beachball-size red splotch on the back of the pickup cab's window.

He quickly made his way around to the front of the team's sedan and signaled for Shale to prep one of the doors for a breach.

"Caruso KIA. Taken under attack by two shooters located on the opposite side of the street from the house. One with an old-school Skorpion. The other with some kind of military-style rifle. Didn't get a good look. Both in their early sixties. Approaching right-side door. Building is a duplex," said Smith.

When they reached the door under the covered porch, Smith stopped Shale before she removed any of the door explosives. "Want to try and kick it in?"

"Save us some time if it works," she said, pivoting to watch the street. "You're a little heavier than I am."

Smith positioned himself in front of the door, let his rifle hang on its sling, and gave it a solid front kick—knocking it a third of the way open. The door smashed into something solid and soft on the other side, followed by a loud grunt. Shit. He'd probably just brained some old lady watching through her peephole. He pushed the door open a little farther, to find a woman on her knees, one hand on the hardwood floor—the other barely holding on to a Skorpion machine pistol.

The woman moved faster than Smith expected, given her apparent age, the two of them bringing their barrels up at nearly the same time. Hers a little slower. Smith's single bullet drilled a tiny red hole straight between her eyes, but she still managed to squeeze off a quick burst. The first bullet struck his chest plate, but the Skorpion's ridiculous rate of fire quickly pulled the rest of the burst high and to the left. He took a direct hit to his upper left arm, and the rest of the bullets splintered the partially closed door. His shoulder hurt like a mothereffer, but he didn't see any reason not to push on and try to take the house.

"Third shooter inside the house. Another Skorpion. Took a bullet to the left arm but feel fine. Thinking about continuing," he said, before turning to Shale. "Are you good with that?"

She shook her head, a hand pressed hard against her right collarbone area—blood pouring through her fingers. One of the Skorpion bullets had gone through the door and gotten lucky.

"Scratch that. Shale is hit bad," said Smith. "I'm getting her out of here."

"Kevin. This is Audra. Do not use your car. Stay under the porch cover and go around the side of the house to the alley. Keep as little sky visible above you as possible."

"Understood," said Smith, grabbing Shale as she slumped against the front of the house.

He moved her to the far-left side of the duplex's porch and broke out a hemostatic gauze pad from a pouch attached to his plate carrier. He lifted her hand and pressed the gauze firmly in place over the bullet hole just below her collarbone, before replacing her hand.

"Keep pressing," he said. "Need me to tape that in place?"

"No. Just get us the fuck out of here before they drone our asses," she said.

"Lift on three. Two—" started Smith, before heaving her onto his back in a fireman's carry.

She groaned in pain. "What the fuck happened to one?"

"You're lucky you got a two," he said. "Ready?"

"Just get moving," she said.

He jumped off the side of the porch, a five-foot drop onto grass— Shale muffling a scream when they landed. Smith hugged the redbrick wall as he approached the alley—his eyes darting skyward in every direction. Halfway to the alley, an air-crunching explosion rocked the neighborhood, debris flying into the street in front of the target building.

"Moving to the alley with Shale," said Smith. "Don't think they saw us escape, because they just hit the front of the duplex with one of their drones. These people are not fucking around."

"Kevin. This is Lozano. I have an idea," said his longtime CIA friend on TAC-4.

"Send it," said Smith.

"Toss your frag grenades onto the rooftop. Fuck up their gear," said Lozano. "Is that cool with HQ?"

Smith had forgotten about the frag grenades they'd been given from the safe house armory. Two M67s.

Farrington answered immediately. "They're dropping drones on our heads. We're dropping grenades on theirs. Go for it."

"I'll give it a shot," said Smith, looking for a concealed place to stash Shale.

He found a piece of plyboard leaning up against the adjacent duplex's garage—out of sight of the target duplex's right-side unit's windows—and laid her down next to it.

"Squeeze underneath that board for now," he said.

Smith watched the sky as she disappeared. He didn't see anything up there except for a bird or two passing by.

"Be right back," said Smith, before taking off for the target duplex's garage.

He updated the task force en route.

"In case I get zapped. Shale is hiding under a piece of graffitied plyboard lying against the southern neighbor's garage."

"Copy," said Farrington.

Smith moved along the back of the garage until he reached the corner that opened onto the back of the duplex. He quick-peeked with his rifle, finding flimsy-looking curtains drawn on the two upstairs windows. Thin curtains may as well have been a one-way mirror, facing the wrong way for Smith. The single first-floor window—presumably the kitchen window—had no curtains. Same with the small square window on the back door, opening onto a concrete stoup. He gauged the distance from the corner of the garage to the rooftop and decided he could land a grenade on it.

Keeping an eye on the windows, he removed one of the grenades from a pouch on his vest and pulled the pin before letting the safety lever spring away. Smith counted to two before rounding the corner and throwing it overhand in a high arc that cleared the edge of the rooftop. Panicked voices immediately ensued, and Smith took cover behind the garage, still peeking around the corner. A sharp explosion threw mate-rial skyward from the rooftop, a cloud of smoke and fine debris particles instantly obscuring his view of the rooftop's edge.

One of the second-floor windows parted, a face frantically search-ing the alley. When the face disappeared, he armed the second grenade and rounded the corner, hoping to put all that time spent at his kids' school fairs, dunking their least favorite teachers, to use. The grenade left his hand on a near straight trajectory, headed straight for the win-dow. Smith was so sure of it, he didn't stick around to witness his handiwork. He bolted for Shale, intending to get her out of harm's way and into the hands of the nearest EMT team. He got halfway down the face of the double garage when the grenade detonated—followed by screams and yelling.

CHAPTER 52

Devin had O'Reilly pull off Jefferson Street Northwest into a tree-shrouded alley just before Fifth Street Northwest, roughly two blocks from the Homewood Apartments—their target building. In the few chaotic minutes listening to TAC-3's desperate situation over the radio net, Devin had determined that they'd have to approach the target as inconspicuously as possible. The Russians would be on high alert, scouring every approach, from the sky and from the rooftop.

They couldn't risk slinking down alleyways wearing ammunition-laden plate carriers, ballistic helmets, and backpacks full of breaching equipment. One glimpse of their group and a fifteen-pound warhead would turn them into human spaghetti. They had to pare down to the bare minimum to break into the apartment building, then look for an easy, quick way to get the fully equipped CIA team inside.

Six friendly shooters should be more than enough to take down the drone-control team, along with the CIA shooter who would try to engage the launch team from the building across the street. One big question remained, and everything depended on the answer: When will it be safe to bring Seeberger and Gupta to the building? Or should the tactical team bolt with the tablets and bring it to the tech duo? The answer to that question depended on the answer to another.

Did each individual drone-control site run its own drone security, or did one of the four sites serve as a force protection unit for the whole operation, leaving the other three to focus on striking the National Mall? That's how he'd run the show if he oversaw the Russians, which meant that's how he had to proceed with the planning. He'd operate under the assumption that nobody was safe outside of the target building, or near any of its windows, even after they neutralized the Russians in the building.

"I've identified a route that mainly uses alleys and neighborhood cut-throughs to get to the Homewood Apartments," said Melendez. "There are a few tree-covered spots to cross Eighth Street. After that, we might have to break into a few houses to get to the back of the apartment building."

"We can't risk that," said Devin, giving a brief rundown of his thinking.

Nobody put up much of an argument—the thought of a Razorblade or two chasing them down had the appropriate chilling effect.

"Pistols only. Stuff your pockets with magazines. Radios under your shirts. One flash bang each, stuffed in your waistband. Elena will carry a backpack filled with breaching charges and Gupta's MPX. Once Melendez and Emily identify the street-level Russians, they'll continue down Jefferson Street and turn left on Ninth, eventually ducking into one of the alleys with access to the southwest corner of the apartment building. I'll be poking around the alley, trying to locate any additional security that might get in our way. Once Melendez, Dana, and I are inside, we'll make our way to the front entrance. Elena will time her trip down the street to coincide with our arrival, and take out the street security, before hauling ass inside. Then we'll figure out an approach for the CIA team. How does that sound?"

"Sounds good to me," said Melendez.

"I don't have anything better," said O'Reilly. "Elena?"

"I'd rather not be the drone bait, but if everything goes according to plan, it should get us all inside," she said.

"If we can't get to the front building entrance, we're not exposing you to the drone gods," said Devin. "You just keep walking, take a left on Ninth, and we'll bring you in the back way. I just thought we should take out the ground-level Russian security so we're not fighting two groups once we're inside."

"We could take everyone in the back way and leave a few strategically placed Claymores behind to discourage the Russians on the ground from following us," said Elena Visser, unzipping the bag in her lap to expose an olive drab antipersonnel mine.

"And blow up a family on their way in or out of the building?" said O'Reilly. "I'm not good with this plan."

"Then let's strip off this gear and make some adjustments to our appearance," said Devin.

His earpiece crackled halfway through their rapid transformation into civilians.

"All stations. ZAPPER THREE-THREE reports two dozen signals down. None of them airborne. They must have been staging them for launch. TAC-3 managed to take down the entire operation with a few well-placed grenades. The radar tower they're using seems to be the key. A grenade must have taken it down. I'm diverting TAC-2 to TAC-3's location to finish off the Russians inside and grab some tablets. Any chance of doing the same at the Homewood Apartments?"

"This is TAC-1. Negative. It's a four-story apartment complex, spread out over half a city block," said Devin. "We're about to approach the building on foot to look for a way in."

"Devin. I hate to do this, but I think our best chance of grabbing a tablet is in Capitol Heights. You're ten minutes away. We'll throw everything we have at that duplex when you get there. TAC-4 will arrive about five minutes after that, helping out if necessary."

Devin glanced at the team, all of them shrugging in resignation. The plan made sense. The Homewood Apartments represented the most complicated of the two scenarios.

"This is TAC-1. We're en route to Capitol Heights," said Devin, raising his hands in exasperation. "All right. Gear back on—and let's get moving."

"It's probably better this—"

"All stations. This is TAC-3. We just heard a series of about six explosions back in the direction of the target duplex. We're about a block away, taking cover. I think they leveled the place with drones," said Smith.

"Of course they did," said Farrington. "Fuck. I guess we do this the hard way. Devin. We're back to your plan. Keep HQ and approaching units advised of your progress. And keep in mind, they obviously know what we're up to at this point, which means we'll have to move quick when we get inside one of their drone-control stations."

"Copy that. We're moving out," said Devin, examining the tactical team.

"Dana. Tousle that hair. Roll your khakis halfway up your calf. Take some of that dirt and give your khakis, shirt, and shoes a little dirt bath. Maybe a light dusting on your face. Don't overdo it. You want to look scruffy, not filthy. Rico. Rip a hole in your jeans over the right knee. Swap shoes with Gupta. You have to ditch those operator boots."

"How do you know we're the same size?" said Gupta, from the back seat of the SUV.

"Because that's been my job for close to fifteen years. To observe everything," said Devin. "Anyone have a razor-sharp knife?"

Visser produced a nasty-looking blade in the blink of an eye.

"I should have guessed," said Devin. "There's not much we can do with Rico's Marine Corps buzz cut, so we need to cut him a few stylish lines on one side, or both. Make him look like a street punk."

"Dude. Nobody's cutting my hair," said Melendez.

"It's either that or pierced ears," said Devin. "Dana has a nice pair she'd love to loan you."

"Is this guy—" started Melendez.

"Trust me. I do this for a living. It's the little stuff that throws people off during surveillance."

"Fine," said Melendez.

"Roll up your sleeves and unbutton your shirt a few buttons. Then get yourself a very light dusting of dirt on your jeans and shoes. Dana. I want to see two eyebrow slits on your left eyebrow."

"What the fuck?" said O'Reilly. "I have a day job, you know—at the FBI."

"Not if we don't get this right," said Devin.

Visser seemed to find it amusing, until Devin looked her up and down.

"I think I blend in just fine," said Visser.

"I think you need a drastic haircut," said Devin, turning to O'Reilly. "Chop cut. Not too close. We don't want her looking like a stray dog. But enough to make her look edgy or something like that. Use spit or hair gel to create some points. A bit of a punk look."

"And what about you?" said Visser. "You look like you work on Wall Street."

Devin spit in his hands and messed up his hair before taking some of the fine dirt off the street next to the curb and lightly coating his hair and face.

"Now you just look like a Wall Street broker after a long night out with friends," said Visser.

"Follow me," said Devin.

He opened the back of the SUV and dragged a nylon duffel bag onto the strip of grass between the sidewalk and street, where he dumped the contents of the bag on the sidewalk. Mostly bulky clothing, jackets, a few pairs of pants, a few wigs and beards, several pairs of fake eyeglasses, a few pairs of shoes, fake badges, bottles of booze wrapped in paper bags, and a makeup kit. He pulled out a solid olive-green army jacket with black, red, and gold German flag logos on the shoulders and a pair of geeky-looking solid-black-framed glasses.

"Combined with the edgy hairstyle—"

"You mean chop job?"

"Same thing," said Devin. "You'll have a put-together look. Do you smoke?"

"Not in a long time," she said.

"Time to start again," he said, opening a small pouch that had fallen out with the rest of the gear. "They're prop cigarettes, like the kind used by actors. It's still smoke, but it's about a tenth as rough as real tobacco smoke. Use it as a prop on approach. The closer you can get to them while smoking, the better. It'll ease their concerns about you. If I wave you off your mission, ditch the cigarette immediately. Drop it and squash it. If they smell the herbal smoke, they'll know something is off."

"You're still a stockbroker," she said, before removing the pack and lighter inside the pouch.

"Not for long," said Devin, nodding at the team behind her. "Looks like it's your turn."

Melendez and Miralles had already gone under the razor. They looked a bit more street than before. He just hoped it would be enough. By the time they finished with Visser, Devin sported a scruffy beard with flecks of something in it. A faded Orioles ball cap with the remnants of a bird-shit stain on the brim. A threadbare flannel shirt, rolled up to his elbows to expose two full sleeves of tattoos, which were specially designed nylons. They wouldn't hold up to close scrutiny, but from twenty feet away or farther, they appeared real. If all that wasn't enough, the shoes and jeans he chose from the pile were so crusty looking, even Devin hesitated to put them on. All part of the show.

"Are we ready?" said Devin.

Everyone nodded, some flashing their gear under their improvised outfits.

He turned to Visser, who looked like she'd just slept off a night of punk rock mosh pits.

"MPX loaded? Spare mags?"

"Yep," said Visser.

"Then let's do it," said Devin. "Dana. Give Anish the keys. Be ready to roll when we say. We'll give you explicit directions. Make sure you follow them."

O'Reilly tossed Gupta the SUV's keys, and the different elements of the team did their thing. O'Reilly took off first. She'd stroll along the south side of Jefferson, passing by the target building. Melendez would follow about thirty seconds later, taking the north side of Jefferson. Hopefully the two of them would identify the Russians' street security.

Devin would begin his journey immediately, walking down Ingraham Street, one block south and parallel to Jefferson, until he reached the alley on Ingraham that led directly to the Homewood Apartments—where they would start their trash-picking ruse.

Visser would remain with Gupta and Seeberger until they broke into the building, when she would start her trip down Jefferson Street. Her mission was to neutralize the street threat and join the rest of the team inside.

CHAPTER 53

Rico Melendez turned left on Ninth Street and breathed a sigh of relief. The disguise had apparently worked. Neither of the two Russian sleepers identified by O'Reilly had given him more than a seemingly disinterested look as he passed by. He scanned the area for a third Russian but didn't spot one. Like the Capitol Heights site, the third sleeper would most likely be located inside the apartment building. But unlike the duplex, they wouldn't be right inside the entrance. They'd probably be concealed somewhere on the same floor as the drone-control station, possibly inside the same apartment. Or across the hallway from the apartment. He triggered the radio button hidden in one of his pockets.

"Elena. Confirming Dana's surveillance. One man with gray hair sitting behind the wheel of a nicely polished red Chevy Bronco. North side of Jefferson, about two car lengths east of the entrance to the apartment building. Second shooter sitting on a rocking chair on the porch of the second house past the apartment complex's western building. Brown hair. Smoking cigarettes. Fits the age bracket. Could have sworn I saw the stock of a rifle behind the chair when I walked by."

"Copy. Standing by to start my run," said Visser, her voice crystal clear in his concealed earpiece.

"Devin. How are we looking in back?" said Melendez. "Dana is waiting for me under some thick trees on Ninth."

"I think we've attracted some attention," said Devin. "Looks like a fellow dumpster diver, but he's not moving like one. Been there since we started working our way up the alley's trash bins. Now he's sorting recyclables from trash on a beat-up picnic table. Looks like busywork. I don't see a bag or anything he'd use to carry his stuff away."

"What's his precise location?" said Melendez.

"Southeast corner of the building at the end of the alley," said Devin. "There are about four industrial-size dumpsters located in that spot. The picnic table is on the east side of the alley, on a small patch of dirt."

"There's a small alley off Ninth that approaches the back of the apartment building, but there's about a twenty-five-yard stretch of pavement that doesn't offer much cover from the sky," said O'Reilly.

"Too risky. And we're perfectly covered by trees in this alley. That's probably why they put someone back here. I didn't even think of splitting up the pistol suppressors. I think the two of you have both of them," said Devin.

"We do," said Melendez.

"And I don't see any way to get you over here without attracting attention. There's not much tree cover from this alley to Ninth along Ingraham. The eye in the sky might be looking for you right now, just to make sure you moved on."

"Any way you can get in close enough to do it with a knife?"

"I've never killed anyone with a knife before," said Devin. "And I have a feeling this guy isn't going to let me get that close before sounding the alarm."

"Then we'll have to do this the hard way," said Melendez. "Break into a few homes with your fake FBI badges. Well. One of the badges will be real. That gets us close enough to the apartment building to minimize our chances of being spotted by the Razorblades. Not eliminate it. We'll let you know when we're about to eliminate the Russian in back."

"We'll keep working our way in his direction, then turn around when you give us the signal," said Devin. "That should drop his guard."

"Sounds like a plan," said Melendez. "Elena. I think it's time for you to start your run."

"I'm Oscar Mike," said Visser as she took off.

He caught a glimpse of O'Reilly lingering in the shadow of a massive tree next to the alleyway she'd mentioned. Melendez motioned for her to join him. When she reached him under the massive tree canopy, he nodded at the house next to them.

"Special Agent O'Reilly," said Melendez, pulling his fake FBI credentials out of his front pocket and flashing them. "Time to meet Special Agent Melendez."

"We look like fucking bums," she said.

"We're working undercover. The guns and badges will be enough," he said. "Follow me."

"Jesus. I can't believe we're actually—"

"TAC-1, this is HQ. You need to step it up. ZAPPER says they're launching the first wave. Twenty-four per each of the remaining sites. We're not sure how many they can control at a time from each site. But that's seventy-two warheads headed toward the National Mall. What's your status?"

"Breaking the sound barrier," said Melendez. "Out."

He ran up the steps to the house he'd identified and kicked the door in with his gun and badge held forward. The hallway was empty, but a few surprised shrieks from a room to the left let him know he wasn't alone.

"FBI! National emergency!" he yelled into the house. "Just stay out of the way and nobody will get hurt!"

He peeked into the room, holding up his fake badge. A woman his grandma's age sat on the couch between two toddlers, holding them tight.

"You got a warrant?" she said.

"Just passing through! We'll be out of your house in five seconds!" said O'Reilly, appearing next to Melendez.

"Who's gonna pay for the door you busted?" said the woman.

"I will. Personally. I promise," said Melendez, the two of them making their way to the back door.

A woman appeared behind them in the hallway, holding a baseball bat. "Does this have something to do with all those white folks in town?"

"It has everything to do with them," said O'Reilly.

"Then carry on with the good Lord's work," said the lady. "But you better fix that damn door like you promised. This neighborhood isn't safe."

Melendez gave her a thumbs-up before heading into the backyard, which was mercifully cloaked by trees. He opened the chain-link fence and sprinted across the alley to their next patch of cover, a tall row of bushes along the side of the target apartment building. Above them, two drones emerged, headed south—one leading the other by a few seconds. As they moved rapidly down the hedgerow, another pair of drones sailed south. Jesus. They didn't have any time to waste.

He pointed at a basement-level window a little farther down, close to the row of bushes. A tree from the yard behind the apartment building appeared to cover most of the distance between the hedgerow and window, the deep shadows cast on the grass confirming his assumption.

"Dana. That's our breach point. You bust in and clear the apartment. I'll take care of the rear sentry. We'll be back in less than thirty seconds."

He removed the suppressor from his pocket and screwed it onto his pistol's threaded barrel. O'Reilly broke off without saying a word and slid into place next to the ground-level window, placing her elbow against the bottom of the upper windowpane, where the lock would logically be located.

Glass shattered behind Melendez as he made a beeline for the rear alley. Subtlety wasn't part of the plan anymore. They had a drone strike to stop. He broke through a thick patch of bushes to emerge between two of the dumpsters Devin had referenced, his suppressed pistol leading the way.

The scene that unfolded in front of him defied all explanation. In all the excitement, he'd forgotten to notify Devin that he was ready to pounce on the sentry, so Devin and the FBI agent had taken matters into their own hands—in their own unique way. The two of them stood about twenty feet from the Russian sleeper, Devin holding out a brown bag containing a bottle and repeatedly offering the man a drink in slurred speech. The sleeper held a Skorpion machine pistol in his tight two-handed grip, ordering them to back off—somehow not noticing Melendez's entrance. Two rapid trigger presses ended the standoff, the Russian dropping like a sack of dirt to the crumbled asphalt.

"Grab the Skorpion and any spare ammunition," said Melendez. "Make sure to safe the weapon. Do you know how to use an old-school Skorpion?"

"I do," said Devin.

He grabbed the Skorpion off the asphalt and flipped the selector switch to safe before retrieving three additional twenty-round magazines.

"We found a way in, but we need to hurry," said Melendez. "I'm sure you heard the news."

"And saw it live," said Devin, glancing skyward. "There goes another salvo."

"No time to waste," said Melendez. "Elena is on her way. Once she's inside, we'll make our way up to the top floor. The CIA team can pull right up to the front door and run inside. We'll jam it open for them."

CHAPTER 54

Elena Visser had taken to her new look, pretending to rock out to songs she remembered from her teen and college years. Nothing too punk. One song stuck in her head as she snuffed the fake cigarette out on the tree in front of the Homewood Apartments, much to the visual dismay of the sleeper agent sitting in the Chevy Bronco. She gave him a look and shrugged, flicking her tongue a few times, which got him to look away. When he finally glanced back in her direction a few seconds later, she'd placed his head in the center of the Sig Sauer MPX's red dot sight and pressed the trigger, erasing the smug look from his face.

The short burst of gunfire spurred sleeper number two into action. The old lady moved faster than she'd anticipated. She was off the porch and firing a rifle on semiautomatic by the time Visser pivoted to engage—the woman's bullets missing wildly as she bolted across the lawn.

Visser squeezed off two longer bursts center mass, following her across the yard —most of them striking her chest or arms and knocking her to the grass. Visser didn't wait around to make a final damage assessment. She sprinted through the front gates of the Homewood Apartments and up a long courtyard to reach the entrance vestibule, which separated the west and east wings of the complex.

While pounding the sidewalk, desperate to get out of airstrike danger, two successive pneumatic hisses drew her attention skyward. She half expected to see a Razorblade drone dropping from the sky onto her head, though logically she understood she'd never hear the drone that killed her. Instead, she watched two Razorblades glide into view just beyond the edge of the east wing's rooftop, gaining speed and altitude as they headed south.

Just in case she was vaporized in the next moment, she transmitted over the radio.

"Drones launched from the east-wing rooftop. North side," she said, moments before she tumbled through the front doors.

Melendez and O'Reilly appeared from the sides and grabbed her, keeping her from spilling into the back of a couch in the small lobby. Before she could even try to catch her breath, they dragged her left, where Devin crouched next to the doorway leading into the east wing—his Skorpion aimed into a dimly lit vestibule. Once they were well clear of any windows, Melendez and O'Reilly let go of her arms.

"There's no way Anish and the AeroDrone guy will be able to make that run before the Russians drop a drone on their heads," said Visser.

"Then we'll have to bring them in through the back way. Same with the CIA team," said Melendez.

"If two cars drive up that alley, they'll get droned," said Devin. "Hell, *one* car will get droned at this point. They know we're in the building."

"I'm not talking about the alley," said Melendez, raising an eyebrow at O'Reilly.

"All right," she said, clearly not happy with the suggestion. "Start working your way up to the top floor. I'll smooth things over with our new friend on Ninth Street and bring everyone to your location. How much money do you all have on you?"

"What does that—" started Devin.

"Just cough up whatever you have," said O'Reilly. "We owe someone a new door. Melendez kicked it in."

Visser patted her pockets, removing a fake FBI badge. "This is all I have on me. Everything else is in the car."

"Write her an IOU," said Melendez.

CHAPTER 55

Lana Kozlova studied her laptop's screen, shaking her head. Something big was going down at the Brightwood Park site in north DC—right under their noses. The drone circling overhead had spotted at least two other operatives already inside the front entrance when the woman sprinted inside, after expertly taking out the site's street security. She'd considered crashing the drone into the entrance, to take them out, but they vanished just as quickly as they appeared. Apparently the Americans had learned a thing or two from the Capitol Heights raid.

"I want to know how the fuck they got inside," she yelled.

Dima Ilin, the best drone operator in the unit and her de facto second-in-command, spoke without taking his eyes off his tablet screen. He was one of the few who could effectively use two drone-control tablets at once.

"The sleeper in the alley is down," he said.

"That's a start," she said.

"But there's no entry door in back," said Ilin. "Just a loading dock door, which looks undamaged. The only way to open it without blowing a hole in it would be to open it from the inside."

"Well. They got inside somehow. Keep looking," said Kozlova. "And get more drone coverage on that building. I want us watching every exterior surface of that building simultaneously."

"I have six drones en route to the site," said Ilin.

"Good. Now send six more," said Kozlova. "We might have to take out the site if the Americans breach the drone-control room.

CONTROL says the only way they could have identified the locations of the sites was by using a very sophisticated electronics warfare aircraft. They're concerned that if a controller falls into American hands, they might be able to break the encryption and take control of the drones with this aircraft."

"We lost a third of the drone strike force by destroying the Capitol Heights site. If we take out Brightwood Park, that drops us to a third of our original drone-strike power. The anti-drone defense batteries on the National Mall might be able to handle that."

"If it comes to that, we'll reroute our own drones to the National Mall," said Kozlova. "But let's not get ahead of ourselves. A few American operatives inside the Brightwood Park site isn't the end of that location. The team there has been alerted, and they'll make the right preparations. Our mission is to make sure no more Americans get inside and that nobody currently inside gets out. Consider any vehicles approaching the front or back of the Homewood Apartments to be a potential target. Hit any vehicle that comes within twenty meters of the front gate or rear-alley entrance, from either direction."

"But, Lana. Not everyone is obeying the daytime curfew. A number of cars have passed without—"

"Nothing gets through!" said Kozlova. "Do you understand my order! We can't take the risk. In fact, now that we don't have any street-level security, hit anyone that tries to walk through the front entrance. That's probably how they got inside in the first place. Just walked right through the front door."

"This is crazy," said Ilin.

"Do you have a problem with my orders?" said Kozlova, exercising every ounce of self-restraint to keep her hand away from the pistol tucked into her rear waistband.

"No. But I think we're going to need to send more drones," said Ilin. "We could burn through what I've sent fairly quickly if we're going to swat every fly that lands near the apartment building."

She didn't appreciate the not-so-subtle dig embedded in his request but saw no benefit to potentially unraveling her best drone operator at this critical point in the mission. Kozlova would deal with him later.

"Send more drones," she said. "And watch all the nearby rooftops. The radar towers are a pathetically critical weakness."

CHAPTER 56

"Ready?" said Gupta, shifting the SUV into gear.

"Not really," said Seeberger, clinging to the oversize laptop case in his lap. "But I suppose we should get going."

Gupta eased them clear of the sedan parked in front of them before picking up speed. He ignored the stop sign and turned right onto Ingraham Street. Plenty of tree cover as far as the eye could see, but quite a few breaks in the cover, too. He wasn't sure if he should speed up to get this over with sooner or play it cool and stay close to the speed limit. What would attract a drone operator's attention more? Probably the speeding.

"Can you go any faster?" said Seeberger, as they passed Seventh Street.

"I'm trying not to draw attention," said Gupta, gently tapping the accelerator. "Just two blocks and then we take a right. We'll be in safe hands in less than a minute."

"Nothing about this is safe," said Seeberger. "These drones are fucking scary. I always thought they were a terrible idea, but every country was building them. The US had no choice but to keep up, and AeroDrone is the best at making drones. Never thought I'd be on the receiving end of one of these things—let alone one I helped design."

Gupta slowed down a little, Seeberger's words freaking him out a little.

"TAC-1. This is Gupta. We're a block and a half from the turn onto Ninth."

"Copy that. Special Agent O'Reilly is located six houses up on Ninth. She'll wave you down," said Devin.

"See you in a few," said Gupta.

◆ ◆ ◆

"Lana. I have a vehicle moving west on Ingraham," said Ilin.

Kozlova got up from her desk and kneeled next to Ilin to take a closer look.

"Where did it come from?"

"It just turned onto Ingraham from Seventh Street," said Ilin. "We didn't see it on Jefferson or farther north on Seventh. It kind of appeared out of nowhere. Probably a resident of one of the houses."

"Hit the vehicle," said Kozlova.

"There's a lot of tree cover," said Ilin. "These drones don't—"

"I don't care. Let the drone figure it out, and if the first one misses, fire another. Nothing gets close to that apartment building."

Ilin nodded while toggling the controller to lock onto the vehicle. With any luck, the Razorblade wouldn't break its lock on the target at the last second and blast through the roof of a house.

◆ ◆ ◆

A thick, leaf-covered tree branch dropped to the street about forty feet ahead of the SUV, and Gupta instinctively slammed on the brakes. A few moments later, a frighteningly familiar object landed on its side a few feet in front of the tree branch, pointing ninety degrees away from their SUV toward a vehicle parked on the south side of Ingraham. Their SUV screeched to a stop about fifteen feet from an unexploded Razorblade 800 series kamikaze drone. The moment Gupta shifted into reverse, his view through the windshield disappeared, the SUV rocked by an explosion that was thankfully not pointed in their direction. Not that they noticed a difference at first.

The windshield shattered in place, completely blocking his view—a few dozen aspirin-size holes poking through in no discernible pattern. The stinging pain in Gupta's face and shoulders told him that he had been hit by several of those penetrating fragments. The worst pain came from his right knuckle, which had been facing the windshield. A hesitant look at his hand revealed bright-white bone peeking through. His brain overrode the shock a few seconds into his self-assessment. Seeberger.

The engineer's glasses hung by the left ear, one of the lenses cracked, the other missing from the frame. Seeberger pressed his hands against his face, hyperventilating. Fuck. They had to get out of this car—which he only now realized was rolling backward. If the drone pilots had any doubts about the success of the first drone, all doubts had just been erased. *They'd missed!* He unbuckled his seat belt and bailed out of the SUV, sprinting around the front of the vehicle to reach the passenger seat.

Gupta had Seeberger and the surprisingly heavy laptop case out of the vehicle within seconds, the two of them scampering away for cover—which they found in a stone staircase cut into the steep lawn rising from the sidewalk. Gupta shoved Seeberger into the side of the concrete cutout and lay down next to him on the rickety stairs, their bodies shielded from the slowly drifting SUV. He glanced upward, relieved to see nothing but green leaves and scattered rays of light poking through. A quick look at the street dismissed that relief.

What if the next drone tumbled through the branches like the last one and ended up pointing at their little stairway? He had a direct view of the damage caused by the first drone. Its directional warhead punched through a parked car, leaving nothing but a fiery chassis on flat tires. It had even dug a sizable hole into the sloped lawn behind the sedan. Don't think about it. The chances of another drone landing in the street, right in front of their staircase, pointing directly at them—may as well be zero.

"Let me see your face," said Gupta squeamishly.

Seeberger slowly lowered his hands to reveal a few deep grazes and a badly, but not critically bleeding, right eye.

"Looks like one of the fragments hit your right lens and sprayed glass into your eye," said Gupta.

"That's about what it feels like," said Seeberger. "Glass crunching against my eyeball."

"Fuck. I'm so sorry, dude. There's nothing I can do for your eye right now. That's the bad news," said Gupta.

"What's the good news?"

"The good news is that the left lens held in place and saved your other eye," said Gupta.

"I guess that's something," said Seeberger. "Unfortunately, I can't do what I need to do without my glasses. And my other pair is back at the safe house."

"Then we have a real problem," said Gupta, triggering his radio.

The second drone hit the moment he started to transmit.

CHAPTER 57

An explosion outside sent Devin back down the stairwell and onto the first floor, where he could transmit without giving away his team's position. Gupta had just reported that they were approaching O'Reilly's transfer point. He prayed the explosion hadn't targeted Gupta. For Gupta and Seeberger's sake—and the mission's. The two were critical to KILL SWITCH's success, and Devin's team was clearing a path for them.

TAC-1 had just finished sweeping the first floor, even going as far as breaking into one of the apartments to scan the side of the building for a bundle of cables to make sure their assumption about the Russians using a top-floor apartment for the drone-control station wasn't faulty.

During the few seconds Devin was willing to stick his head out the window, he'd spotted what looked like a dozen or more cables and wires exiting the fourth window back from the front of the apartment building—on the fourth floor. He'd also noted during his short study of the building's exterior that all the floors had the same window configuration.

Since the apartment they had broken into contained one more window between number eight and the front of the building—dubbed window #7—they had to kick in the next door toward Jefferson Street to confirm the pattern Devin suspected. A terrified family cowered in the corner of their family room as Devin's team made their way through the next apartment, validating Devin's assessment. Each apartment had two east-facing windows—these being #6 and #5. The drone-control station was located one apartment over from this one, on the fourth floor. Or in simpler terms, the second door on the right, from the Jefferson Street end of the hallway.

He'd just shut the first-floor stairwell door quietly behind him when a second explosion rattled the building.

"Gupta? Come in," said Devin.

Nothing.

"Gupta. Are you okay? What's your status?"

A few seconds passed before a shaky voice answered. "Uh. We should be okay unless they plan to drop a third fucking drone on our heads. I'll explain later. I got some bad news to pass on. HQ. Are you listening in?"

"Always," said Farrington.

"Seeberger and I are alive, but the fragmentation from the first drone shattered his glasses and fucked up one of his eyes," said Gupta.

"Glad you're both okay," said Farrington, his statement almost comically perfunctory based on what came next. "Doesn't he have a backup pair?"

"Back at the safe house," said Gupta.

Farrington muttered a few choice obscenities before responding. "O'Reilly has the CIA team waiting to escort the two of you into the building. Are you sure he can't talk us through this?"

A short pause ensued. "His words. Not mine. Not a fucking chance, unless we have all day. Huddleston is our last hope."

"You hear that, TAC-2?" said Farrington.

"We're three minutes out," said Marnie. "We made up some time."

A third explosion shook the building.

"This is TAC-1. We just had another explosion outside."

"All stations. This is TAC-4. We just lost contact with Henderson. He'd just accessed the rooftop across the street," said one of the CIA operators with O'Reilly.

Another explosion shook the building, shattering the window at the end of the first-floor hallway and blasting the glass onto the carpeted floor.

"That's a fourth explosion," said Devin, sprinting toward the window. "This one was close. Right on Jefferson Street. I'm taking a quick look."

"We don't have any units on Jefferson Street," said Farrington.

"I know," said Devin, arriving at the window a few seconds later.

The scene below redefined the depravity of the adversary they faced. A scorched minivan sat in the middle of the street, almost directly in front of the east wing—smoke pouring out of its missing windows, and the four-foot-diameter twisted metal hole blasted through its roof. All its doors had been blown open, the edge of a baby seat barely visible through the thick smoke and twirling flames.

"They hit a civilian minivan passing in front of the apartment complex. They're hitting anything that approaches the front or back. TAC-2 can't drive anywhere within two blocks of this place, in any direction," said Devin.

"Is that TAC-1's commander talking, or are you more worried about someone's safety than getting the job done?" said Farrington, the implication obvious to Devin—hopefully not so obvious to everyone else. "TAC-4 breezed into O'Reilly's position from the south without a problem."

"And I'm sure the Russians are already wondering why TAC-4's SUV disappeared under the trees, never to reemerge," said Devin. "Their rules of engagement have changed. If you bring TAC-2 directly to O'Reilly's position, they'll drone that SUV like Gupta's, along with every house on the small stretch of Ninth Street. They know we found a way into that building. A blind spot. I don't think they'll hesitate to use the drones to try and plug the gap."

"Two cars have passed by since TAC-4 arrived," said O'Reilly. "I think they're just protecting the obvious access points."

"We don't have time for this. Sorry. But we just don't. Drones will start dive-bombing the National Mall in less than ten minutes. Possibly sooner."

"Can the Razorblade cameras see through smoke?" said Hoffman.

Marnie responded. "Huddleston says no."

"Then we do a moving drop-off covered by smoke," said Hoffman. "Do any of the CIA guys have smoke grenades?"

"We have two."

"Anyone else?" said Hoffman.

"Negative," said Melendez. "We stripped down to the bare minimum to get in here."

"It'll have to do. Hand them over to O'Reilly. We'll need them when we arrive," said Hoffman. "Once we execute the moving drop-off and keep the SUV rolling. Then we'll cover the Ninth Street stretch between Ingraham and Jefferson with smoke—get the Russians wasting drones on ghosts while O'Reilly gets us into the building."

"I'm bringing the CIA team up right now so they can assist TAC-1," said O'Reilly. "I'll be back down in time for your smoke-and-mirrors show."

Calling it a *smoke-and-mirrors show* was being generous, in Devin's opinion. He thought it was a terribly risky plan, but Farrington was right; they no longer had the time for anything complex, like his original approach to the apartment building. They needed to get that engineer inside safely, so she could do her job—and avoid a possible civil war. He opened the stairwell door and headed up to the second floor, to rejoin the rest of TAC-1.

CHAPTER 58

Rico Melendez gave the all-clear sign, and they gathered in the hallway outside of the third-floor stairwell. Nothing stood out on any of the floors below the top one. No busted-in doors suggesting a team waiting to spring into action and sneak up behind them. No trip wires setting off alarms upstairs. No motion sensors or cameras. And the best part? Nobody roaming the hallways.

Everybody appeared tucked safely inside their apartments, presumably waiting for the all clear from the authorities. Or maybe they had no plans to emerge until the protest had dispersed. Many of them were probably glued to the TV, watching the crowd gather on the National Mall, wondering if this was the start of a second civil war. The fewer people out of their apartments, the better. Less chance of collateral damage. Easier for them to focus on killing the Russians.

Devin's earpiece squawked. "TAC-4 is on the ground level, waiting outside the stairwell," said one of the CIA officers.

"Make your way to the third level and join us in the hallway," said Devin. "We're putting together a plan to tackle the target floor."

"On our way."

Several seconds later, the door slowly and quietly opened, depositing two serious-looking operators wearing tactical street kits. Plate carriers with armor on both sides. A chestful of stuffed magazine pouches. Individual first aid kits. Compact, suppressed assault rifles. And most importantly—backpacks stuffed with breaching explosives. They could execute the first half of the mission with the numbers they had right now. Pave the way for the engineer to finish it.

"Jesus. You guys look—"

"Undercover?" said Visser.

"That's one way to put it," said the stockier of the two CIA officers.

"Sorry about your guy on the roof," said Melendez.

"A tough break. Could have been any of us," said the other CIA guy. "To keep things simple. Just call us Black or White. I'm Black for obvious reasons."

"Easy enough," said Melendez. "Here's the situation. We know—hold on, let me stop myself right there. We see cables running out of a window on the fourth floor that we've determined, based on exploring the apartment building's layout, belong to the second apartment from the front of the building. On the right side of the hallway, if approaching from the stairwell."

"Second door from the end. On the right," said White.

"That's where the wires originate," said Melendez. "So that's where we're going to start. Apartment layouts are simple enough. We've examined three so far. The door opens to a combined living-dining area, with a kitchen toward the back. That's the window in question. Two bedrooms and a single, full bathroom are located off a short hallway from the combined living-dining space."

"They're probably set up at several stations in the combined space," said Black.

"That's what we were thinking," said Devin. "They'd need the room, and the ability to quickly coordinate with each other."

"Rooftop access?" said Black.

"That's still a big mystery," said Melendez. "We're guessing the stairwell continues to the rooftop, so that might be the softer of the two targets. Nail the radar and shut down their drone communications."

"The stairwell continued to the rooftop across the street," said White. "But Henderson had to blow it open with a breaching charge.

We can expect them to anticipate this move on our part, so the door will likely be rigged with explosives that will fill the stairwell with shrapnel if it's breached."

"And we'll be putting ourselves at risk of fighting in two directions at once," said Visser. "Above and below, with us stuck in the middle."

"We can Claymore the rooftop stairwell landing and keep that crew from sneaking up behind us. Focus all our attention on the apartment," said Black. "I took one out of the safe house armory."

"So did I," said White.

"I guess the big question is—Should we wait?" said Melendez. "You heard Farrington. The attack on the National Mall is about to go down."

"We only have five right now," said Devin. "When TAC-2 arrives, we'll have nine. I like those numbers better."

"True. But at best we'll only be able to use two of them. Hoffman and Miralles," said Melendez. "Marnie, O'Reilly, and Mazurov will have to stay clear of the action and watch over the tech team. Huddleston is our last hope. And to be honest, I was thinking of swapping Marnie into the assault team and putting Miralles with the engineer. Just in case the Russians pull something unexpected on us."

"Two more isn't exactly going to tip the scales in our favor," said Visser.

"Two of your best?" said Devin.

"One of my best, if I put Miralles on babysitting duty. Marnie may not come close to stacking up against any of our operators, but Miralles is injured. She isn't exactly playing her A game right now. Marnie knows her way around weapons and is a natural in a tactical situation like this," said Melendez.

"How exactly do I stack up?" said Devin.

"You're better than you think," said Melendez. "All I'm trying to say is that right here, right now, we pretty much have what we're going to have going into this. So why not just go into it now? Shave some time off the doomsday clock. One way or the other, we have to take this site down immediately and grab one of those tablets. TAC-2 can back us up if things get too hot. They'll be up here in less than five minutes. Unless they get blown up."

"Do you want to check in with Farrington?" said Devin.

"We don't have enough time," said Melendez. "Black. When we reach the fourth-floor landing, continue to the rooftop access and rig one of the Claymores."

"With pleasure."

CHAPTER 59

Marnie kept one hand on the door handle and the other tightly clasped around one of Saya Huddleston's hands as they rapidly approached the intersection of Ingraham Street and Ninth. Like all of them, Huddleston understood the stakes—and was terrified.

If they were going to be vaporized by a drone, it would happen the moment they reached the intersection or shortly afterward—and Huddleston knew it. She'd gone nearly catatonic a few blocks back, the thousand-yard stare and trembling hands taking over within the span of seconds. Marnie had taken her hand to try to comfort her, just enough to keep her from vapor locking at the wrong moment.

"I see O'Reilly," said Mazurov. "Sixth house down."

Hoffman triggered his radio. "This is TAC-2. O'Reilly spotted. Entering the intersection."

"Godspeed, TAC-2," replied Farrington.

"More like fingers fucking crossed," said Miralles.

They made it through the intersection alive, a consequential indication that Hoffman's plan might work. A few seconds later, when a thick canopy of leaves replaced the blue sky above them, Marnie guessed that the first part of the plan had succeeded. Whoever controlled the drones patrolling the skies over the different target sites had set kill box parameters that didn't automatically include traffic traveling up and down Ninth Street.

This allowed the Russians to scour the less-obvious approaches for any indication that something was "off." Because they knew the

Americans had somehow inserted a team into the building—right under their noses. The most dangerous part of their journey into the building was still to come.

"Slowing. Open your doors," said Mazurov, the SUV immediately decelerating.

"This isn't a good idea," whispered Huddleston, her face still staring forward through the windshield—at nothing in particular.

Marnie opened her door all the way before gripping Huddleston's other hand. The laptop case was slung across the engineer's chest, resting in her lap. She wouldn't need either hand to hold on to it. A good thing because Marnie intended to pull her out of the car using both hands. Miralles glanced at Marnie and nodded her approval before looking over her shoulder.

"Wolfe. You good?" said Miralles.

Wolfe sat on the edge of the rear cargo compartment, waiting for the green light to hop down.

"Good to go," he said.

"Exiting the vehicle in three. Two—"

"I can't do this," said Huddleston.

"One."

"I know," said Marnie, shifting her grip to the engineer's wrists and clamping down hard.

Huddleston's head swiveled in her direction, eyes wide open.

"Go! Go!" said Mazurov, before disappearing out of the driver's door.

Hoffman bailed a moment later, followed by Miralles, who tumbled to the street—cursing her injured leg. Wolfe was nowhere in sight, leaving just the two of them. Marnie knew this was going to be an ugly exit. It would have been difficult enough by herself, but attached at both wrists to another person? They'd be lucky not to sprain an ankle, break an arm, or crack a skull. But she didn't have a choice. She pulled Huddleston as far over as possible before turning to position her feet over the street passing beneath her. Fuck it. She pulled the engineer and simultaneously dropped down on the asphalt—the SUV's three-mile-per-hour forward motion doing the rest.

She tugged hard enough to get them clear of the vehicle, where they immediately plunged to the street and took an asphalt beating that was going to leave serious bruises and scrapes. Marnie cradled Huddleston's head the moment they started rolling, to keep it from hitting the street. When they came to a stop, in a tangle of limbs a few moments later, O'Reilly pulled the engineer onto her feet and started moving her toward a redbrick house with a brick-framed front porch.

"Get up and get moving," said Hoffman, running past her with a smoke grenade in each hand.

He pulled the pin on one and threw it into the front seat of the SUV before arming the second grenade and tossing it as far as he could ahead of the SUV. Mazurov dropped one in the middle of the street next to Marnie, while Miralles tossed three at various distances reaching back to the Ingraham intersection. Mazurov rolled his last grenade toward the smoke-filled car, as Marnie rose to her feet, feeling like she'd been mugged.

"You okay?" said Mazurov, pausing next to her. "That was one hell of an exit."

"Just banged up. Nothing broken from what I can tell."

"We need to go," said Mazurov, pointing at the open front door, where Hoffman stood—emphatically motioning for them to get moving.

The first drone hit while they were passing through the house. It was impossible to guess where it landed, but it was fair to say the Russians had just hit the SUV. They piled out of the back door, into a tree-covered backyard, before sprinting through an open gate and crossing a short stretch of exposed alley to reach a tall hedgerow. Hoffman stopped halfway down the thick hedge and motioned for everyone to keep going. Once Marnie had passed by, Hoffman pulled the pin on one of the two remaining smoke grenades and tossed it as far as he could down the western face of the Homewood Apartments' west wing, landing it about ten feet back from the building. He repeated the process, dropping the second another ten feet back from the first.

Before they reached the basement window used by previous teams to enter the building unobserved, two successive drone explosions rattled the ground, smoke rising beyond the row of houses along Ninth Street. The Russians were firing into the smoke under the trees, hoping for the best. Hoffman's plan wasn't as far-fetched as she'd originally thought.

Roughly a half minute later, by the time the last of them slipped through the basement window and dropped onto the two mattresses stacked on the floor below, another drone exploded—this time shaking the building. The Russians had taken Hoffman's final bait and hit the smoke trail leading to the apartment complex. Marnie just hoped they didn't start hitting the houses out of spite. The Russians didn't seem to care about collateral damage.

"TAC-2 is in the building," said Marnie. "Headed in your direction with Huddleston and Wolfe."

"TAC-1 and TAC-4 are breaching the fourth floor in a few seconds," said Melendez. "We'll have this cleaned up and ready for the tech team by the time you arrive."

"Rico," said Hoffman, hand signaling for the entire team to move out. "We'll be there in a minute."

"We don't have an extra minute. You heard HQ," said Melendez. "Assign Miralles, O'Reilly, and Mazurov to escort the tech team. You and Marnie can join the fun when you get here."

"What the fuck, Rico? I'm fine," said Miralles.

"You're still limping," said Melendez. "Hoffman and Marnie. We breach in one minute. Not a second longer."

"We're on the move," said Hoffman, the team already jogging down the hallway—following O'Reilly.

"Jared. The tech team doesn't need three babysitters," said Miralles.

"Until we fully understand the situation up there, I want three watching over our precious cargo," said Hoffman. "You can join the fray when we're one hundred percent confident that they're safe. Good enough?"

"I guess it'll have to be," said Miralles, struggling to keep up because of her limp.

"All right. We'll see you up on four after we clear it," said Hoffman, turning to O'Reilly, who was already pointing them in the direction of the west-wing stairwell.

"Take that up one floor to the ground level," said O'Reilly. "Cross the lobby connecting the two wings, and the other stairwell is just beyond the doors on the other side of the lobby."

Hoffman took off without a word, and Marnie followed, quickly coming to grips with the fact that this sixty-second sprint was just as likely to kill her as the Russians holed up on the fourth floor.

CHAPTER 60

TAC-1 and the two CIA officers had stacked up along the door leading out of the stairwell and into the fourth-floor hallway, weapons ready, when Marnie and Hoffman arrived.

"Where's the tech team?" said Devin.

"One floor below," said Marnie. "Waiting for a tablet. What's the situation up here?"

"We have a Claymore set on the rooftop access landing, so don't go up those stairs for any reason. We've cleared the floors below us. It's always possible they've stashed someone below us somehow, so always watch your back. The target room is to the left, once we're through the door. The plan is to open the door and split into two groups, using the door as a shield. The two of you and me will break off to the right and stack up against the wall, covering the primary team's back. The primary assault team will move toward the target apartment."

Hoffman nodded before triggering his radio. "Secondary team is ready."

"Breaching in three. Two. One," said Melendez, a slight pause before he pushed the door open several inches.

Nothing happened at first. No gunfire. No yelling. A few moments later, an olive drab spherical object fell from a tube at the top of the doorway, pointed into the stairwell, and landed at Melendez's feet, before rolling on the concrete stairwell floor. Black, one of the CIA officers, reached down and picked it up like it was litter, before tossing it down the stairwell. Everyone ducked, a good second or two before it detonated on the landing below.

The compressed sound waves created by the blast pounded their ears, rendering Devin temporarily unable to hear orders passed through his earpiece. He didn't have any trouble hearing the gunfire that had erupted on the fourth floor, bullets striking the door from both directions.

Melendez didn't waste any time leading his team into the fray. Black and White followed him to the left, while Visser unleashed bursts of gunfire from her MPX toward the back of the hallway—holding the thick metal fire door open as a shield for the rest of her team. Hoffman brought Marnie and Devin to the edge of the doorway before scream-ing in their ears to back up the primary team. His ears had clearly been taken out by the grenade blast as well. He tapped Visser's shoulder, and the two of them switched positions, Hoffman's compact assault rifle now hammering away at whatever targets lay beyond the door in the back of the hallway.

Devin and Marnie entered the hallway and joined the stack moving toward the target apartment. One of the Russians emptied his rifle, firing on fully automatic from behind the target apartment door, giv-ing Melendez's shooters no human target. One of the bullets clipped White's right leg, taking him to the floor. The rest of the bullets harm-lessly snapped by, rattling off the walls and floor until they struck the opposite end of the hallway.

The target door slammed shut, and the gunfire died down just as quickly as it had started—the hallway going eerily quiet. Devin glanced over his shoulder at Marnie, who was all business, her M4 rifle pointed at the target door. She gave him a quick look and a nod, indicating she was okay. Hoffman remained crouched behind the stairwell door, his rifle focused on the two bodies lying on the thresholds of two separate apartments. The Russians had infested this floor like cockroaches. His thoughts immediately went to the baby seat in the burning minivan. Who knew what they had done with the people who lived in these apartments.

Melendez turned and signaled for Marnie and Devin to shift to the other side of the hallway to better cover the doors directly ahead of Melendez. White had regained his footing somehow, leaning against the wall and hopping forward with the primary assault team. Devin moved with Marnie to the other side, and covered Melendez's progress. He extended the Skorpion's stock and pressed it into his shoulder, but the machine pistol was a spray gun at best. High rate of fire. Low accuracy. He kept it aimed at the doors farther away from Melendez's team, relying on Marnie to cover the closer doors with her rifle.

They had gotten within two doors of the target apartment when Melendez dashed across the hallway and placed a small piece of tape on the target door to block the peephole. On his way back, Devin noticed something odd about the door directly across the hallway from the target apartment. Small splinters on the carpet beneath the doorknob. He stopped and made a fist, which caught Black's attention, who reached out and tapped Melendez's shoulder. Melendez made eye contact with Devin, who motioned for him to meet him back by the stairwell.

Melendez looked annoyed, but with their ears still ringing from the stairwell grenade, there was no other choice for communicating more than the basics. They settled in next to Hoffman, but Devin insisted they go inside, and that Hoffman shut the door.

"What is it?" yelled Melendez, the moment the door closed.

"The door directly across from the target apartment is damaged. I saw splinters on the carpet beneath the doorknob," said Devin. "There's at least one shooter in there."

"Good eye," said Melendez, before activating his radio. "Everyone except for White and Hoffman back inside the stairwell. We have a small problem."

Less than a minute later, the team emerged from the stairwell with a revised plan to take down the apartment, while efficiently dealing with the Russian across the hallway.

CHAPTER 61

White volunteered to stay at the stairwell door and watch the team's back, a decision that made sense, given the fact that the best he could manage for movement at this point was to slide along the walls. Marnie applied quick hemostatic bandages to both sides of his leg from her individual first aid kit and wrapped tape around his leg to keep them in place. The bandages temporarily stemmed most of the bleeding, but judging by the amount of blood on the hallway and stairwell floor, they wouldn't hold for long. White would need real medical attention sooner than later.

Marnie rushed to catch up with the team, which had already made it halfway to the end of the hallway. Melendez approached the problem differently this time, the Russians' surprise spoiled by Devin's observation. Five members of the team hugged the target-door side of the hallway, led by Melendez, while Hoffman slid down the other side.

Melendez stopped his team just before the target door, never glancing across the hallway at Hoffman, who quickly and quietly affixed a prefused, quarter-pound block of C-4 to the middle-bottom section of the door opposite the target apartment. Hoffman withdrew several feet back with the wire attached to the plastic explosive charge, before attaching a "clacker" to the wire. Like the M57 firing device used to trigger Claymore mines by wire, the clacker in Hoffman's hands had been custom designed to trigger the detonator inserted into the C-4 putty.

Hoffman gave them a quick nod once the wire was attached, which sprang Melendez's team into action. Melendez, Black, and Visser huddled around the target door, pretending to be affixing charges, while Marnie and Devin hugged the wall next to the door. A few seconds into the ruse, they all sprinted away from the target apartment door, just moments before a long, concentrated burst of automatic gunfire perforated the door across the hall—dozens of bullets splintering the door and pounding the wall where the team had only moments ago gathered.

The burst of gunfire was cut short by Hoffman's C-4 charge, which might have been overkill under the circumstances. The blast essentially disintegrated the entire door, taking most of the doorframe with it. Whoever had been firing the machine gun through the door hadn't stood a chance.

Devin and Marnie moved toward the target apartment door to cover Hoffman, who crossed the hallway to place a similar charge on the target door. This time he tore the bottom half of the putty charge, below the fuse, and stuffed it in his pocket. They didn't want to damage any of the drone-control tablets. While Hoffman did his job, Melendez, Visser, and Black pulled breacher strip from Black's backpack and went to work creating three two-foot-by-two-foot squares at kneeling height along the wall next to the door—to create firing ports.

Marnie glanced through the blasted doorway across the hallway, while the team affixed the explosive strips to the wall. Inside, several feet back from the door, a man lay on his back on the floor, his body shredded from head to toe. An AK-style rifle lay at his bloodied feet. She looked back at Devin, who'd met her glance—after having just examined the grim scene himself. Marnie steeled herself for the breach. The Russians inside wouldn't go down without a brutal fight.

CHAPTER 62

Kolya Nikitin crouched behind an overturned table, his rifle aimed at the door. The rest of his team—four drone controllers—sat behind similarly overturned tables, furiously tapping their drone-control tablets. The process of shifting from one drone to another and assigning individual GPS targets wasn't quick work. The last time he'd checked, they had given geographical targets to about two-thirds of the hundred drones fired from the rooftop. Not good enough. He needed to hold off the Americans for as long as possible. The more drones with assigned targets, the better chance of getting through the air-defense system at the National Mall.

He had no idea what had just happened outside the apartment but assumed the worst. He'd moved the rooftop team down once they'd launched all the drones and stationed them in apartments on the far end of the hallway. He'd even placed one of his drone controllers in the apartment directly across the hall with one of the fully automatic AK-47 rifles, which had just fired on the Americans. The immediate subsequent explosion, followed by silence, suggested that the Americans had taken him out, along with the others.

Now he faced a dilemma. CONTROL had ordered him to assign the drones GPS target coordinates along the National Mall—then to destroy the tablets. But he'd been late getting his drones into the air due to a cable mix-up. Even after all the checking and double-checking. Very late. And all the drone explosions around the building had distracted his team throughout the last moments of their targeting updates.

A quick double-check of his team's work revealed that many of the coordinates they had generated would land drones on the periphery of the National Mall. The combination of his cable screwup, a constant stream of drones striking targets right outside of the apartment building, and the pressure of the Americans somehow getting into the building and bearing down on him had derailed everything.

The last thing he wanted to do was report the truth. CONTROL would hit the apartment with a dozen drones and call it good. But what other options did he have? Either way he was dead. So he decided to keep working on the drone coordinates until the Americans entered the apartment.

"If the Americans enter the apartment, destroy your tablet. One bullet into each. We can't let them fall into the Americans' hands."

"Why don't we destroy them now?" said one of his controllers.

"Because someone fucked up the connection to the radar, and we lost ten minutes," said Nikitin. "I don't want to mention names. We work on this until the last moment."

Which arrived about a second later. The door disintegrated. It didn't burst inward on its hinges like he expected. It was simply there one moment—and gone the next. Fortunately he wasn't in the direct path of the door's wooden fragments, which shredded the back of the apartment.

He fired a long burst into the doorway, the rest of the team following his lead—bullets striking the wall and doorframe around the missing door. But no silhouettes appeared in the smoke. Why wasn't his team destroying their tablets? He turned to yell at them, but something moved toward the bottom of the doorway. Nikitin fired again, bullets perforating the wall a foot above the floor next to the wall. Nothing. The remaining four drone controllers kept their rifles and submachine guns pointed at the door, waiting for the final breach. Flash bangs followed by soldiers, and his team had been trained how to minimize the effects of flash bang grenades.

He briefly considered ordering his team to destroy the tablets, but the prospect of killing some of these Americans overrode common sense. He'd give the order once things turned against them. And with any luck, they'd take out the breach team and continue uploading GPS targets. With all rational thought snuffed out by the prospect of fighting and beating the Americans, Nikitin decided to get a little more aggressive. He prepped a grenade and rolled it across the floor—through the doorway.

◆ ◆ ◆

Devin was still reeling from the fact that several bullets had punched through the wall an inch above his flattened body when a grenade rolled through the doorway and stopped in front of his face. Whoever had thrown it had done an incredible job, landing it a foot past the doorframe. It would have been poised to take out an entire breach team if an entire team had been gathered next to the door. Right now, it was just Devin and Marnie lying flat on the floor next to the door and Melendez crouched behind them with a pistol, ready to rush inside with them.

He grabbed the grenade without thinking and tossed it across the hall, pleasantly surprised to watch it sail straight through the middle of the blasted doorway opposite the target apartment. At best, he'd expected it to land on the other side of the hallway, where it would do less damage to the team.

The M67 fragmentation grenade hit the floor and detonated, blasting debris and body parts into the hallway and through the target apartment door. Under normal circumstances, he would have tossed it back into the target apartment, but their mission was to grab an undamaged tablet, and the team had agreed not to use grenades to clear the space.

"Nice throw," said Melendez, patting his shoulder, before initiating the final action to clear the room. "Breach! Breach!"

The three squares of explosive strip spaced four feet apart along the wall detonated simultaneously. Less than a second after the explosions, each shooter lying flat against the carpeted floor beneath the newly minted openings in the wall rose to their knees and started engaging targets inside the room. Hoffman, Visser, and Black fired on semiautomatic, barely pausing between each shot.

◆ ◆ ◆

Nikitin crouched farther behind his overturned desk the moment the wall exploded. The Americans had tricked them into thinking they would come through the front door. His colleagues, unfortunately, didn't have the same tactical foresight, and tried to shift their weapons from the door to the new threat. One by one, within the span of a few seconds, their heads snapped backward as they tried to fire their weapons—an aerosolized mix of brains and blood filling the air behind them. He'd lost control of the site. And the tablets. He removed the sat phone from his vest pouch and dialed CONTROL, as the Americans flooded the room.

Nikitin quickly relayed their situation—finally confessing that only about three-quarters of his drones had been assigned GPS coordinates—before the Americans kicked the phone from his hand and pinned him to the floor. Out of the corner of his eye, he watched helplessly as one of the American operatives collected four undamaged tablets and bolted out of the room. All he heard from the phone's speaker was an order to sanitize the site.

One of the Americans, a rather nondescript, almost Russian-looking man hovered over him, the barrel of his rifle pressed against his forehead.

"Sanitize it yourself, Pichugin!" he said to the phone in perfect Russian.

Then darkness.

CHAPTER 63

Miralles crouched next to Saya Huddleston, who sat cross-legged against the wall several feet from the stairwell door, her laptop open and ready to connect to one of the tablets. Mazurov stood on the other side of the engineer, covering the opposite side of the hallway with an MPX submachine gun. O'Reilly was inside the stairwell just in case the Russians had a few more surprises up their sleeves. Her earpiece crackled.

"This is Devin. Package inbound. I'm entering the stairwell with Marnie. The rest of the crew won't be far behind."

"Copy. We're right outside the third-floor stairwell door," said Miralles.

The stairwell door burst open a few moments later, disgorging Devin and Marnie—each of them carrying two drone-control tablets. They dashed to where Huddleston was seated and laid the tablets on the floor in front of her. She took a quick look at the lineup and chose the second from the right.

"First things first," said Huddleston, connecting a few wires to the tablet she'd chosen. "Take the other three tablets, use the physical toggle stick in the upper right corner of the tablet, and move the on-screen selector, which looks like a set of crosshairs, over the digital button in the lower right corner of the screen. The button should read ABORT. Press the physical button on the lower left corner of the tablet to select ABORT. A small window will pop up asking you to verify the order. Click the physical button again. That'll be three drones down."

Devin and Marnie went to work on the controllers, quickly aborting the three drones under their control. Huddleston was typing away at her laptop faster than Miralles had ever seen anyone type. Her fingers were a blur over the keyboard.

"Done," said Devin.

Without looking up from her screen or breaking pace, she passed on additional instructions for the tablet.

"Check the top left of the screen for a digital button that reads RB2. I found it on mine. That would be a second drone connected to the tablet."

"Yep. RB2 on all three," said Marnie.

"Click that button and follow the same procedure as before to abort the drone's mission," said Huddleston.

Several explosions rocked the building in rapid succession, the Russians hitting the target apartment with enough drones to wipe the room clean. Miralles hoped they hadn't lingered.

"Rico. This is Miralles. You guys out of there?"

No answer.

"Rico—"

The doors to the stairwell burst open again, depositing the rest of the team in the hallway.

"Close call. I think they blew up half the floor trying to take us out," said Melendez, heading in their direction. "How are we doing with the tablet?"

"The encryption is shit. Like most Russian encryption," said Huddleston.

"That's great news," said Melendez.

"I'm going to need a direct line of sight to the Growler to pass the signal along. I should be done in less than two minutes," said Huddleston, still typing away.

While the rest of the team formed a half circle around Huddleston, taking no chances on a Russian surprise, Visser helped the wounded CIA officer take a seat against the wall next to Miralles. The other CIA guy detached what looked like a more comprehensive medical kit from his tactical vest and tossed it to Visser, who offered it to Miralles, which made sense. She had the most advanced field medical training on the team. She took it and switched positions with Visser.

"Name?"

"White. The other guy is Black."

She glanced between the two and chuckled.

"This might hurt a little, Mr. White," said Miralles, grabbing the tape Marnie had used to secure the bloodied hemostatic gauze.

"It already hurts," said the CIA guy. "Do whatever you need to do."

Miralles ripped it free to reveal a neatly drilled bullet hole two inches above White's right kneecap. She turned the leg, finding a far messier exit wound. That was where most of the blood was coming from. While she used a pair of scissors from the kit to cut the man's pant leg at his upper thigh, Melendez removed a cell phone from one of his pockets and placed a call to Farrington. Their encrypted radios had been designed to illegally piggyback on emergency services P25 repeaters, which were having a little trouble deep inside this stone building.

"Rich. We need ZAPPER THREE-THREE due east of the building in two minutes, minimum altitude of ten thousand feet so we can get a clear line of sight over the building next to us," said Melendez, listening intently to Farrington's response. "Hold on.

"Ms. Huddleston. Do you have an exact frequency for your signal? Or a way for the Growler to identify it?"

"That's the tricky part," she said. "I need the Growler to jam all drone-control frequencies in the two point four to five point eight gigahertz range as soon as I'm done with the decryption. I kept one of the drones connected to this tablet, so the moment they jam the current drone-control frequency, I'll get the new frequency, which we'll use to transmit the KILL SWITCH code to the Growler."

"Did you catch that?" said Melendez, looking relieved by the answer. "Good. We'll be in touch shortly."

"Too much for you to retain?" said Miralles, getting a chuckle out of a few of the team members.

"Yeah. What was that gigahertz range again?" he said to Miralles.

"Two point something to something point eight," said Miralles.

"That's what I thought," said Melendez.

Miralles took a closer look at White's bullet wound and shook her head.

"I think we're looking at a tourniquet. The hemostatic gauze barely made a dent in the bleeding. We'll get an ambulance here the moment we take down the drones. No guarantees on whether you lose the leg or not if we do the tourniquet. Just being honest. It's your choice. I can keep applying the gauze."

"Do the tourniquet," said the CIA officer. "I lost a lot of blood."

Miralles removed the combat tourniquet from the kit and wrapped it around White's right leg about four inches above the exit wound—about midthigh level.

"That bad?" said Melendez, kneeling next to her.

"Bad enough," said Miralles.

"We'll prioritize his evacuation," said Melendez, before pulling Visser out of the protective circle. "Go relieve O'Reilly in the stairwell. We need her badge to open some doors."

"Got it," said Visser, taking off.

"Mazurov," said Melendez. "You're coming with me and Special Agent O'Reilly to find a nice east-facing apartment with an unobstructed view of the sky."

Miralles checked the tourniquet's initial tightness before grasping a windlass rod. "Now this is going to hurt. Ready?"

"Do it."

She twisted the rod until his exit wound stopped bleeding, then clipped the rod in place. When she looked up at White, the man grimaced in pain but managed to force a smile.

A smaller series of three explosions rocked the building just as Melendez and his team started knocking on doors. The wall on the southern side of the hallway, a few feet away from the window, exploded inward, spraying the hallway with wooden debris and metal fragments. Melendez and his team dropped flat as pieces of debris settled on top of them.

The Russians were getting desperate. If the drone had hit the window instead of the wall, the warhead would have detonated inside the hallway, likely hitting them all with shrapnel and a gut-twisting shock wave. Melendez, understanding the situation just as clearly, got up and kicked in the nearest eastern-facing apartment door, a heated exchange in Spanish with the woman inside ensuing. The two of them used slang insults Miralles hadn't heard since she had left her massive extended family behind in Boyle Heights to join the Army.

A few moments later, with Melendez and the woman still going at it, he waved the team over. They needed to get out of the hallway before the Russians popped a few more through the hallway windows.

CHAPTER 64

Major Franklin Stewart, Battery A commander, Second Battalion, 174th Air Defense Artillery Brigade of the Ohio National Guard, opened one of the top hatches of his command-and-control vehicle to witness the desperate battle over the National Mall with his own eyes. His job was done at this point. He'd stared at the screens looking for a human solution, finding no tricks that could outperform the computer system analyzing the multiple threats and prioritizing the targets for his battery's KADD-V anti-drone gun systems. There was nothing left for him to do now but watch the battle and hope his battery wasn't overwhelmed. Wishful thinking under the circumstances.

He climbed out of the hatch and took a seat on the edge facing the National Mall, his feet dangling over the side. His air-defense command-and-control center amounted to little more than a customized air-defense version of the S-788 Shelter mounted on the M1152 expanded-capacity version of the venerable Humvee. Basically, an ungainly-looking Army-green metal box with several antennae and a small radar sitting atop a pickup truck on steroids. At least that was how his wife described it—and she wasn't that far off.

But despite its utilitarian ugliness, the high-maintenance, pain-in-the-ass piece of gear had done its job so far. Nothing had gotten through but bits and pieces of drone. Unfortunately, the larger dome radar mounted to a twenty-foot portable metal tower thirty feet away and connected to his command-and-control center told him the worst was still to come. Another 136 drones were inbound, most coordinated to simultaneously strike within the span of several seconds.

No wonder his battalion commander had augmented the Battery A with every available KADD-V at her disposal. Not that it would matter. There was no way his battery, even with the additional KADD-Vs, could repel that large a drone swarm. They could have placed every KADD-V in the entire US National Guard and Army inventory on the National Mall, and it wouldn't be enough. Only a miracle could save the tens of thousands of people crowded around him.

The early birds struck first. They were either drones that hadn't been coordinated with the rest, or they had been assigned to target Battery A's KADD-Vs. He'd probably never know, because the dozen or so drones were destroyed several hundred yards from the National Mall by the KADD-V's variable time-fused, kinetic-kill projectiles. Fired from a Gatling gun–type barrel, the solid-aluminum projectiles exploded milliseconds before impact, shredding the drones with directed shrapnel.

Given the urban missions proposed for these air-defense batteries, the designers had sold the KKPs as less of a threat to civilians. He supposed they were correct. What goes up must come down, and a solid projectile was far more likely to cause collateral damage on the ground than a "ribbon" of aluminum. Of course, they made it sound like shredded aluminum foil would fall from the sky, when the reality was more like a hailstorm of quarter-ounce jagged pieces of metal.

His second-in-command, Captain Joe Souza, poked his head out of the hatch.

"Another thirty seconds and this all goes to shit," he said. "You might want to come inside."

"Fifteen-pound anti-tank warhead? I don't think it'll matter," said Stewart. "Why don't you evacuate the vehicle. There's nothing else we can do at this point."

"Everyone's committed to staying put," said Souza.

"Very well," said Stewart, swinging his legs back onto the vehicle. "Never know. Maybe they won't target us."

"I suspect they won't," said Souza. "They've already tried that and failed. The system prioritizes the survival of the air-defense units. They'll be going for the crowd with the next wave."

"These people won't know what hit them," said Stewart, the thought of the carnage he would soon witness leaving him infuriated. "Whoever's responsible for this better pay dearly."

CHAPTER 65

Huddleston suddenly stopped typing and looked up at Devin before nodding enthusiastically.

"It's done," she said. "Tell the Growler to jam the two point four to five point eight gigahertz frequency range. Just for a few seconds."

Devin glanced at Hoffman, who was already typing a quick text to Farrington. Melendez was still arguing with the woman in the kitchen, trying to convince her that they would pay for the damages. At least that was what it sounded like.

"Any moment now," said Hoffman.

Huddleston stared at the tablet, her eyes locked in place for what felt like an eternity.

"There! The frequency shifted," she said, clacking at her keyboard for a few more seconds before rushing to the window. "Four point two-eight-three gigahertz!"

She repeated the frequency for Hoffman, while Devin opened the window as far as possible and cut most of the screen away with a knife. They didn't want to open the window at any time prior to the exact moment of transmission. The Russians had already proved that they would go to any lengths to stop them, including the targeting of random apartments. Huddleston knelt in front of the window and typed a few quick commands.

"Hold this out the window," she said, handing Devin what looked like a stubby satellite phone antenna connected by a cable to her computer.

He held it out the window and Huddleston tapped her keyboard once before turning her attention to the drone-control tablet on the floor next to her. A few seconds later, she gave a thumbs-up.

"KILL SWITCH activated."

Devin glanced at the tablet screen, which had gone blank. Holy shit. They did it. The only question now was, *How many drones got through before they shut the Russians down?*

CHAPTER 66

Don Steckler had never run faster in his entire life, including his running back years at Austin College—and that was more than thirty years ago. The drones had started arriving several minutes ago in smaller waves, prompting righteous outrage from the crowd. The government couldn't keep them out of DC, so now they were going to hit them with some kind of disabling gas from the drones? That had been the consensus from everyone talking on their phones or radios, until a drone hit the steps of one of the Smithsonian museums and exploded in a fireball.

That was when all hell broke loose. Every man, woman, and child for themselves, from what he could tell—all live streaming the attack while running away. If the government planned on executing thousands of Americans exercising their First Amendment rights on the National Mall, the world would bear witness. That all sounded good until a second drone exploded a little closer to the main crowd, near the Capitol Building. Holding the phone up was slowing him down. Steckler put his phone away and started pumping his arms, racing north for Constitution Avenue, the wall of five-story stone buildings looking like good cover from the drone swarm about to hit the National Mall.

He burst through the thickest part of the crowd and pushed his way across Constitution Avenue, seeking cover at the corner of the building at the intersection of Constitution and Twelfth Street. The corner of the building was heavily shaded by trees, which left Steckler thinking that if the drone couldn't see him, it couldn't target him. At least a dozen people joined him in the tight stone enclave, all talking about how this was the government's plan all along. To corral them into one place and hit them with drones.

There was only one problem with this theory. As he crossed Constitution Avenue, he witnessed something he hadn't been able to see from his previous position, jammed in among thousands of protesters. A modified Humvee, equipped with a dome radar and a gun turret, sat in the middle of Constitution Avenue, a few hundred feet away, firing what looked like a mini gun skyward.

The gun's rate of fire was astonishing, thousands of empty ammunition casings already piled up around the vehicle. Every time it fired, it made a sharp buzz-saw sound, and it sent up at least a dozen short bursts in the time it took him to cross the six-lane road. That was what he had heard when he was packed into the crowd on the mall.

And that was exactly what didn't make any sense about the crowd's theories to Steckler, as he hid under the trees, tucked into the corner of a building. If the government's plan was to drone the protesters, why would they protect them at all? It's not like they could pretend they tried to keep the crowd safe and then blame the attack on a terrorist organization. None of what he was hearing from the people gathered around him made any sense. Not that it mattered. The Humvee's gun had gone silent. Probably out of ammo. The end was coming for thousands.

A few explosions shook the ground, direct hits on the crowd, judging from the fireballs and smoke rising from the National Mall. No more than four or five. He couldn't tell. Then it was over. He started to get up when tree branches started snapping overhead. The group immediately scattered in every direction, leaving Steckler alone against the cool stone wall—staring up into the tree. An oddly familiar gray object hit the branch above him and cartwheeled to the ground, landing in the gravel directly in front of him. He'd seen pictures and videos of these before. The United States had provided hundreds of these to the Baltic countries and Ukraine. He was staring at the business end of a

Razorblade drone, which looked surprisingly undamaged except for its twisted wings and cracked nose camera.

He considered taking out his phone and live feeding his last moments to social media. Maybe send a message of unity or just tell his family that he loved them. Instead, he decided to use his time more constructively, by very gingerly slipping away from the drone—before it exploded.

When he reached what he considered to be a safe distance, he sought out a police officer and warned the officer that a drone had fallen intact at the corner of the building. The officer told him all the drones had just fallen out of the sky, after the first few hit the crowd. The military must have used some kind of electromagnetic pulse device on them. Maybe that was why the Humvee stopped shooting. If that was true, the United States government had just tipped their hand to the world. Nobody thought it was possible to create a localized EMP device. He'd have to post about this later.

The next thing he did was call his wife, who had texted or called him a dozen times over the past few minutes. He'd turned the ringer off earlier. A huge pet peeve of hers. Now he understood why. His wife answered before his phone registered a ring.

"Are you okay?" she said.

"I'm fine. I'm fine," he said. "Had a close call, but I'm totally fine. How's everyone at home?"

"Two things before I hang up," said his wife.

"Wait. What?"

"One. We're all happy you're alive," she said, pausing long enough for him to interrupt.

"What's number two?"

"Your ass is never, and I mean never, getting near one of these rallies or protests again," she said. "Stay home and post your shit on the internet like everyone else! Love you. Now get your ass home."

"Love you too," he said to nobody—his wife had already ended the call.

Steckler opened the map app on his phone and checked the distance to the Holiday Inn at Dulles Airport, where he'd picked up a room for twenty-three dollars after the JUSTICE FOR ALL discount. Twenty-six point two miles. And he didn't suppose those JUSTICE FOR ALL buses that brought him here would be running anytime soon. Yep. His wife was right. He wasn't ever doing this shit again.

CHAPTER 67

Marnie turned to Huddleston and asked the question on everyone's mind.

"Can we still get hit by a drone right now?"

The engineer shook her head. "No. The drones are all dead. Warheads deactivated. Electric motors stopped. Navigation and targeting orders terminated. They're just falling out of the sky right now. You could take one home and put it on your mantel. It's basically an inert object at this point."

Devin squeezed her hand. "We did it."

"We did," she said. "I just hope we did it in time."

"We did," said Hoffman. "Farrington just sent a text. Four drones got through, before the KILL SWITCH signal disabled the rest. That's a hundred and thirty or so drones that didn't hit the crowd."

Marnie grabbed Huddleston, who was quietly putting her laptop and the tablet back in her laptop case and gave her a hug, nearly knocking her over.

"You. Did it," said Marnie.

"I guess so," said the engineer.

"Before we start celebrating," said Melendez. "Let's get EMS over here for White."

"Got it," said Hoffman, pulling out his phone.

"Nick. Pay the lady from the petty cash fund," said Melendez. "Unless you left that in our now-droned SUV."

"Leave you behind? Maybe. Leave money behind. Never," said Mazurov, producing a leather pouch, which he unzipped. "Two thousand?"

"I was thinking three," said the lady, suddenly speaking English. "That's a vintage door."

Melendez nodded.

"Three thousand it is," said Mazurov. "Thank you for your service today."

"Maybe three isn't enough," said the woman.

"This isn't your Sunday flea market. Three is the final offer," said Melendez.

"My flea market?" she said, her voice rising. "Do I look like a flea market shopper to you, *pinche pendejo*?"

"I don't know. Do you?" said Melendez.

Mazurov placed the cash on the kitchen counter and thanked her again, amid the yelling. When the entire team had departed the apartment, the door slammed behind them. More cursing from behind the busted door.

"What's up with you two?" said Marnie.

"Eh. We grew up in the same barrio of East LA," said Melendez. "But she's from one of the shit-talking areas."

"Yeah. You sounded calm in there," said Devin.

"She started that shit," said Melendez.

"Hey!" said Hoffman. "Nine-one-one is jammed. We need to transport White ourselves."

"What's the nearest level-one trauma center?" said Melendez.

Miralles had already done the research. "MedStar Washington Hospital Center. It's a little over a mile south."

"Where's our nearest vehicle?" said Melendez.

Black responded. "I think it's ours. We parked a few houses down from the entry house on Ninth Street. Unless the Russians droned it. I have the keys."

"All right. We all head down to Ninth Street," said Melendez. "We'll offer cash for the lady's car or just steal one off the street."

"Her name is Martha," said O'Reilly. "I got to know her while waiting for everyone to arrive."

"I have twelve grand left for Martha," said Mazurov.

"That should be enough to compensate her for the damage and for the temporary use of her car, which we'll return," said Melendez. "She deserves a medal for letting us use her house the way we did."

"Let's just hope it's still there," said O'Reilly.

"Fucking FBI. So pessimistic," said Melendez, winking at Dana before activating his radio. "Anish. You still with us?"

"We're still here," said Gupta.

"How's Seeberger doing?"

"He'll live, but he needs to get to a hospital right away," said Gupta.

"Meet us on Ninth Street, where you were originally headed," said Melendez. "We're arranging transportation to a nearby hospital for one of the CIA guys. We'll put Seeberger in the same vehicle."

"I assume it's safe?" said Gupta.

"The drones have been disabled," said Melendez. "Sorry we didn't keep you in the loop. It got a little busy up here. Like it did down there."

"Yeah. I might give up using drones after this," said Gupta.

"Let's not jump to any—" started Farrington, who had been monitoring the radio net.

"Just fucking with you, Rich! I knew the great and powerful Wizard of Oz was listening," said Gupta. "We're on our way."

The house still stood when they arrived, all its front windows shattered. The CIA team's car had also remained intact, though both of its front tires were flat. The lady who owned the home they'd used as a cut-through to the building ran out onto her porch.

"I don't know who you people are, but I just saw the wildest thing on TV. All them drones just fell from the sky. The same ones that were landing all over the street here," she said. "You guys did that, didn't you. You stopped the drones."

"Ma'am. Martha. I can't really comment on that right now," said Melendez, snatching the leather pouch from Mazurov. "But I do have one more favor to ask of you. I have twelve thousand dollars in this leather thingy. Could we borrow your car to drive our critically wounded friend to the hospital?"

"Shit. You can borrow the car for free," she said. "But I wouldn't mind taking some cash to get the house fixed."

Melendez handed her the pouch. "It's all yours. Please keep it. You played a key role in stopping those drones. But you didn't hear that from me."

She cackled for a moment before regaining her composure. "Can I tell anyone about this? Or is it top secret?"

"Just assume it's top secret," said Melendez. "If anyone asks. We busted through here. You didn't have any choice."

"Hot damn. Good enough for me," she said. "I'll drive the car around. I keep it out back."

"Ma'am. We'll drive the car around, if you show us where it is," said Marnie, grabbing Devin's hand.

"Ditching us?" said Melendez.

"For now," said Marnie, unsnapping her plate carrier and tossing it aside. "We'll stay with White until he's stable or his family arrives. No reason to drag any of you into a hospital, where questions might be asked."

"Good point," said Melendez.

"I'll go too," said O'Reilly. "A real FBI badge might come in handy. Does White carry CIA credentials?"

"Negative," said Black. "This was strictly an off-the-books deal."

"All the more reason to keep you and Farrington's people out of the hospital," said O'Reilly.

"You sure you're okay with this?" said Black. "The police will be all over you."

"We'll be fine. I have the ear of the director of the FBI," said O'Reilly. "I'm not worried."

Black laughed. "Damn. Nobody told me I was rolling with the who's who of every corner of the US government."

"Look who's talking," said Melendez. "Audra Bauer is a legend."

"She is," said Black. "Isn't she?"

"We need to get moving," said Marnie. "We can trade stories back at the safe house."

"Safe house?" said Martha. "Do I need to hide there for a while?"

"No. Nobody is coming after any of us anymore," said Marnie, hoping that was true for Devin and her—and the rest of the team.

"And there's no safe house," said Melendez, giving Martha a look.

"Oh. Of course not," she said, winking. "Never heard of such a thing."

Fifteen minutes later, they carried White into the emergency room at MedStar Washington Hospital Center, where he was wheeled away for immediate surgery.

CHAPTER 68

Yuri Pichugin grabbed his leather travel bag and headed for the bedroom door. His satchel sat in the study, preloaded with his identity and travel documents, plus all the cash he'd need to get away from this place—and live comfortably until he accessed the big money he'd long ago stashed away in various discreet banks around the world.

He wasn't going to make the same mistake as last time and delay his departure. Not even by fifteen minutes. EVENT HORIZON had failed spectacularly. Only a handful of drones had hit the crowd packed into the National Mall. The rest neutralized by Devin Gray and his frustratingly resourceful collection of mercenaries and agency misfits. There would be no third chance for Pichugin. He had to disappear now on his own terms or be disappeared. Wisely, he had already planned for this possibility.

He'd paid the gate guards a small fortune to let him depart the estate. Enough for them to drive the SUV they'd stashed near the gate to the Kazakhstan border and disappear. To live like kings, relative to what they were used to, for the rest of their lives. Assuming they didn't care what happened to their parents and siblings. Putin was notoriously spiteful when it came to betrayal. Then again, if they cared, they wouldn't have taken his money.

When he reached the bedroom door, Boris Gusev blocked his way. "What are you doing?" said Gusev.

"Getting the fuck out of here. I've already paid off several guards and made sure they were on main gate duty during EVENT HORIZON," said Pichugin. "I highly suggest you join me."

Gusev had a confused look on his face. "The soldiers guarding the complex are completely loyal to Putin. They're Interior Ministry Spetsnaz. They've probably reported your bribes."

"The MVD no longer exists. They were broken down into dozens of units that belong to the National Guard or the regular police. I've offered these soldiers more money than they'll see in an entire lifetime of service to Putin," said Pichugin. "Are you joining me or not?"

"Did you want me to join you? I don't recall receiving a prior invitation."

"That's because I didn't expect our operation to fall this badly," said Pichugin. "If just half of the drones had hit the National Mall, we could have called it a success. But five? And a handful that hit uncrowded areas? Hardly a success."

"I can't come with you," said Gusev. "But I won't stop you, either. Or raise the alarm. I'm going to sit down in the study and drink the best vodka on the shelves until they come for me. Then I'm going to blow my brains out."

"Don't drink too much, or you might pass out before they arrive," said Pichugin, instantly regretting his words.

He put a hand on Gusev's shoulder. "That was uncalled for, Boris. I apologize. We had a good run together. Made a ton of money. Made Putin happy. Unfortunately, we were dealt a shit hand with Helen Gray and her son. Everything comes to an end, I suppose. I'm sorry this is how it ended for us. Thank you for your years of faithful and brilliant service."

"It's been a wild ride. Well worth it, my friend," said Gusev.

"Last chance," said Pichugin. "Please join me."

"I can't. I'd rather it ended now than on the run," said Gusev.

Pichugin gave him a long bear hug, the two of them on the verge of tears, before he made his way to the garage. He'd have to drive himself out of here—a slightly daunting prospect. He hadn't driven a vehicle in years. He opened the slider to the wide patio surrounding the pool and headed straight for the doors that led into the five-bay garage. He was halfway across the patio when several figures converged on him from the shadows. Eight in total.

"Just taking a break! Thought I'd get some fresh air," said Pichugin. "Maybe sit in one of my cars and pretend I'm driving. It's not like I'm going anywhere."

The body armor–clad figures continued to approach him, saying nothing in response to his ramblings.

"Okay. I'll go back inside. Sorry," he said, angry with himself for taking a shortcut to the garage.

"We're here to escort you out," said one of the men. "The gate guards can't be trusted."

"And who are you?" said Pichugin.

"No friends of Putin. That's for sure," said the same man. "We need to hurry. The guards have just received orders to arrest you."

"But who the—"

His question was cut short when three soldiers burst through the wooden gate in the stone wall on the other side of the pool. One of them yelled "traitor," before the team of eight cut them down. The apparent leader of the small group approached him.

"Here's the situation. Putin is going down. You've been tapped as a possible successor," he said in unimpeachable Muscovite Russian.

"Me?"

"Yes. Your work hasn't gone unappreciated, even if it hasn't panned out."

"What's the plan?" said Pichugin.

Suppressed gunfire drew his attention to the open slider, where two soldiers dressed in tactical gear slumped to the patio. One of the team's operatives slipped inside the house.

"We drive two vehicles out of here," said the man. "I assume you've paid off the gate guards?"

"I have," said Pichugin.

"Well. If they have second thoughts, we'll take care of them," said the team leader. "I think we should head back into the house and make our way to the garage. We're sitting ducks out here."

"I agree. I'll lead the way."

Pichugin felt hopeful and confused at the same time as they made their way back into the house. This new development had caught him off guard. Putin ousted? He'd be lying if he didn't feel some satisfaction hearing that news. Not to mention the fact that his name had been thrown into the hat as a possible successor.

The team of silent operatives killed seven more of Putin's Spetsnaz before they reached the garage, more than confirming their claim that the order had gone out to take Pichugin into custody. The estate was swarming with guards, looking to score points with the big man. He wished Gusev had joined him. The thought of what they'd do to his lifelong friend and business partner made him sick.

The operative who had slipped away while they stood on the patio rejoined them, entering the garage from the door that led to the house.

"Gusev is dead," he said.

Poor Gusev. Putin's beasts had gotten to him first. If only he had listened and joined him! Two Range Rovers departed the garage a few moments later, the lead SUV loaded with five of the eight operatives sent to rescue him. They effortlessly gunned down two soldiers who tried to block the driveway moments after leaving the house, the convoy reaching the gate less than a minute later, where the men he'd bribed happily waved him through. He waved back before they turned left, headed for a private airfield roughly eight miles away, where a Hawker Beechcraft 400 awaited him. He was pretty sure that the jet could accommodate himself and the entire extraction team.

"I have a Hawker Beechcraft 400 waiting for us at an airstrip I had cleared and paved a few years ago," said Pichugin. "It's a little rough, but it's out of the way. Unless you have other plans or a better plane."

"We don't have a better plane," said the team leader.

"But you have other plans? Better plans?" said Pichugin.

"Much better," he said, glancing over his shoulder and nodding. "A one-way trip to Israel."

Darkness in the form of an opaque hood shrouded Pichugin's head, his hands zip-tied within seconds. Several repeated punches to the groin effectively stopped any resistance he might have offered. He'd been out-maneuvered across the board. Nothing remained for him at this point but to pray for death—a wish that was unlikely to be granted. Especially not by the Israelis. Not after Haifa.

CHAPTER 69

A few hours after carrying White and Seeberger through MedStar Washington Hospital Center's emergency room doors, they learned that the trauma surgery team had managed to save White's leg. For now. The blood loss to his lower leg had been severe, so there was no future guarantee. Devin called Farrington and passed along the good news, making sure to credit Miralles's emergency first aid with not only saving White's life, but possibly saving his leg. His wife arrived a few minutes later and was escorted upstairs by the police, after Devin and Marnie briefly introduced themselves.

The good news was quickly followed by bad news. The eye surgeons had not been able to save Seeberger's right eye. The damage caused by the fragmented glass had shredded his eyeball beyond repair. Devin and Marnie slipped out of the ER, while O'Reilly continued to wrangle with the police, who had relentlessly questioned all of them about White's tactical gear and the weapons found in Martha's car. O'Reilly sent them a text a few minutes later.

Smart call. DC is still locked down. Recommend you walk east on Michigan Ave toward University Heights. Find a restaurant or cafe. Text me the location and I'll send an FBI car to pick you up. They'll get you close, but not too close to your destination.

About thirty minutes later, a black SUV, driven by a lone FBI agent, picked them up in front of a Starbucks. The agent had been ordered to drive them across the Anacostia River to Fairlawn, where they walked the rest of the way to the safe house. Dead tired, they staggered down the narrow stairs into the standing-room-only subterranean operations center, which reeked of coffee and body odor. They were the last to arrive, and it was clear that the debriefing had started without them.

"Sorry for starting without you," said Bauer. "We'll have an in-depth debrief tomorrow at task force headquarters. I just wanted to pass along what I know to everyone who won't be at that briefing, while making sure everyone implicitly understood the delicate and highly classified nature of their participation in this operation—which never happened. And I'm sure Rich would like us out of his hair."

"You're more than welcome to stay as long as you wish," said Farrington from his wheelchair.

"I'll pass on the extended stay," said Berg. "The sooner I get out of here, the quicker I get this smell out of my nose."

Farrington laughed. "It's a little ripe down here."

"A little?" said Gupta.

"Hey," said Black, cutting into the conversation. "Thank you for running interference at the hospital. White's wife really appreciated seeing a few friendly faces when she arrived. The police put her through the wringer outside the ER."

"They put us all through the wringer," said Marnie. "We figured we'd stick around to make sure they let her in to see her husband. O'Reilly's the real hero. She's still there getting worked over by the police."

"More like working *them* over," said Devin, getting a laugh from the group.

"Well. It's highly appreciated," said Audra Bauer. "I owe White and the rest of the Special Activities Center officers a debt I can't repay. Same with the rest of you."

"We all feel the same way—about everyone who took part in today's operation," said Farrington. "This was a true team effort. Like the good ole days. Actually—this might have topped them all. We had noncombatants working side by side with shooters to solve what I thought might be an unsolvable problem."

"You didn't have faith in us?" said Gupta. "You left that out of your earlier briefing."

"I had faith that if it was solvable, this was the only group that could solve it," said Farrington.

"Sounds the same," said Gupta.

"I never meant to imply—"

"Ahhh! Just busting your chops, Rich," said Gupta.

"One of these days, Anish. I swear," said Farrington, shaking his head. "Trent. Are you by any chance looking for a new job?"

BASTION EAST's head of security took his time answering. "Ask me again in a few days."

"Smart answer," said Farrington.

Bauer took over from there. "Devin. Marnie. Like I said. We'll go over this in depth tomorrow and the next few days—probably longer— but for now, the latest casualty count on the National Mall put the number of dead at four hundred and thirty-nine. They're still working on the number of wounded. And we've confirmed that only four drones from the final salvo directly struck the crowd."

"I still can't believe that," said Devin.

"By our estimation," said Bauer. "The team's work prevented another ninety to a hundred drones from hitting the crowd. The KADD-Vs were nearly out of ammunition by the time the swarm hit. That's roughly ten thousand lives saved."

"And a civil war averted. Hopefully," said Berg. "It's too early to say for sure, but at least today's attack hasn't immediately been spun as a government plot. Yet."

"*Yet* being the operative term," said Farrington.

"We also learned that the FBI captured a few Russians at the sites in Alexandria and Marlow Heights," said Bauer.

"That's gonna sting in Moscow," said Marnie.

"It will once the State Department gets involved," said Bauer, before turning to Farrington. "I think that's it."

"We've covered the highlights that matter," said Farrington.

"Very well," said Bauer. "I'll let you get on with the business of covertly moving people out of here."

"I think we'll be retiring this location shortly—due to recent activity—but I would still greatly appreciate it if everyone continued to take the same security measures," said Farrington. "If the police busted down our door tonight or tomorrow, I don't think even Senator Steele could save us."

"After what you did for your country today," said Bauer, "I think you'd be surprised by what the senator could arrange."

"If it's not a problem, we'll crash upstairs tonight," said Devin. "I don't think either of us has it in us to try to make our way back to Annapolis."

"It's better that you don't," said Bauer. "The task force will provide secure lodging for a few weeks, until we're certain that the threat from Pichugin and Russia has passed. We'll arrange that tomorrow."

"The room is still yours," said Farrington. "Get yourselves cleaned up and join us for a celebratory drink a little later."

"Sounds like a plan," said Devin.

A few hours later, after a few too many celebratory bourbons in the safe house bunker, they finally collapsed in one of the upstairs bedrooms. Marnie leaned her head on Devin's shoulder, the two of them holding hands. He'd nearly drifted off when Marnie hit him with a question. And not just any question.

"So. What's next?" said Marnie.

"A few weeks of take-out food and hiding in a hotel," said Devin.

"I'm not talking about the next few weeks."

He knew exactly what she was talking about. The unexpected attack had shattered his confidence in the status quo, though he strongly suspected that this was the end of it. Pichugin's final gasp for air. After today, they should be safe from further attack. But still, the events of the past week had left him feeling destabilized and unsure of the future. Not their future as a couple. That felt as solid as before, if not more solid. But having your life ripped out from under you for a second time in a year left a few mental scars. Devin would always be looking over his shoulder, and he strongly suspected Marnie felt the same way. They could discuss that later, after stabilizing a few of the foundations under them.

"I know," said Devin. "I was thinking more along the lines of a new sailboat. Finalizing our wedding plans. Not in that particular order."

He wanted to add, *explore the possibility of new identities and a new life in another country,* but decided that was a discussion for later—if neither of them truly felt safe here anymore.

"The wedding plans sound like a good starting point," she said.

"Probably less complicated than a new sailboat," said Devin.

"Way less complicated, and we could invite our new friends, now that we're practically family," said Marnie. "I mean, seriously—What do these people do in their spare time?"

"They probably don't attend weddings," said Devin.

"Or ever get invited to weddings," said Marnie.

"I suppose we could add some tables to the original plan," said Devin. "But they'll remain empty. This group likes to hide in the shadows. And from what Karl told me, anytime they step into the light for too long, they get burned. Badly. They have a long history—and an even longer list of enemies."

"Well. It's the thought that counts, so we'll invite them anyway," said Marnie.

"Karl might show up," said Devin. "Maybe Bauer."

"Are we really having a conversation about which of our new friends might show up for our wedding?" said Marnie.

"Yes. We're that tired," said Devin.

"Maybe we shouldn't be making big decisions in our current state of exhaustion," she said.

"We're still getting married," he said, kissing her forehead.

"I suppose we should just call it good right there," she said. "For now."

He hugged her tightly. They would be just fine when the dust finally settled. Things might look a little different. They might have jobs unrelated to their current work. They might be living on the West Coast. Or Costa Rica. No matter what shape their lives took, as long as the two of them were together, everything would work out. He had zero doubts about that.

The two of them could endure anything after what they'd been through over the past year. Not to mention the fact that they survived most of a sailing season together. Frank, the marina owner who fixed up his mother's boat, told them that a relationship that survives a sailing season will endure forever. So forever it would be.

EPILOGUE

A crisp fall breeze cut through the procession as they followed the horse-drawn funeral coach transporting David Bauer's casket to its final resting place in Arlington National Cemetery. Devin held Marnie's hand as they walked several steps behind the main entourage, comprising immediate family.

Audra Bauer was flanked by the Bauers' only child—an elegantly poised woman in her early thirties, who looked like the spitting image of Bauer—and David Bauer's mother. David's father had passed away a few years ago. His three siblings, two middle-aged sisters and a brother, made up the rest of the group.

Karl Berg had joined Marnie and Devin for the long walk, their small group preceding a sizable contingent of David's longtime friends from his West Point and Ranger Battalion days. Nearly all of Bauer's closest friends worked for secretive teams within the CIA or other highly sensitive organizations, government and private, inside the Beltway—and couldn't risk being photographed at the service. Karl appeared to be the only attendee on Bauer's side who wasn't family. A lonely life in so many ways. Devin's mother was a testament to it.

Devin took in the endless sea of white gravestones surrounding them. The meticulously arranged lines of simple, upright stone markers a dizzying sight if you stared for too long. This would be his second Arlington burial service in the past year. Most people never attended one. His mother was buried somewhere out there, in this vast field of sacrifice.

"Will you visit your mother's grave site after the ceremony?" said Berg, as if he could read his mind.

Devin nodded. "I've only been out to visit her once since the burial."

"Mind if I join you?" said Berg. "I can always visit another time if the two of you would prefer the privacy."

"We don't mind at all," said Devin. "If you don't mind walking back to the welcome center with us to get directions. I don't think I could get us within a thousand feet of her grave site without some help."

"The cemetery is six hundred and thirty-nine acres," said Berg. "I don't think I could find my way back to the welcome center without help."

"There's just one other condition," said Devin. "A question, actually."

Marnie gave him a skeptical look.

"Name it," said Berg.

He leaned toward Berg and whispered, "What happened to Pichugin?"

Devin understood the need for the CIA to keep Pichugin's fate a closely guarded secret, but after everything they'd been through, he felt like the agency owed him some closure. At first Berg didn't react to the question. A few seconds later, the CIA officer cracked a thin smile.

"Nobody really knows. It's almost like he walked into the Dead Sea and was never seen again," said Berg.

It was enough of a hint for Devin. Pichugin was in the right hands. There would be no trial or prisoner exchange. The Israelis would extract every piece of information inside the Russian mobster's head regarding his operations and relationship with Putin, before discarding his empty husk. Devin could live with that.

"Do you really think it's over?" said Marnie.

"I do," said Berg. "I wouldn't be taking some time off if I didn't."

"Anything good planned?" said Devin.

"I think so. If my liver survives," said Berg. "I'm meeting up with an old friend. What about you two?"

"A long overdue honeymoon," said Marnie.

"I thought the wedding was next spring?" said Berg.

"It still is," said Devin. "But we eloped a few days after the agency gave us the all clear to return home."

"In case the Russians weren't done with us," said Marnie. "You know. So we had clearly defined survivor benefits . . . that kind of stuff."

"I'm sure true love had nothing to do with it," said Berg.

"It might have been a factor," said Devin, squeezing Marnie's hand.

They walked the rest of the way in silence, the solemn procession weighing heavier as they approached the grave site.

The ceremony didn't vary from his mother's. Every move precise and practiced. Every order barked by the funeral detail's officer in charge instantly obeyed. He closed his eyes at one point and found himself transported back several months. Nothing about the ceremony felt rushed, but just like his mother's—it was seemingly over in the blink of an eye. The first of three volleys of gunfire snapped him out of his reverie.

Following "Taps," the solemn bugle call played at the end of the funeral, the casket detail carefully folded the flag into the traditional tri-corner shape representing the hat worn by America's Revolutionary War patriots and passed it to the officer in charge, who then offered it to Audra Bauer. Devin silently mouthed the words that followed, their significance forever etched in his memory.

"On behalf of the president of the United States, the United States Army, and a grateful nation, please accept this flag as a symbol of our appreciation for your loved one's honorable and faithful service."

ABOUT THE AUTHOR

Photo © 2022 Bellomo Studios

Steven Konkoly is a *Wall Street Journal* and *USA Today* bestselling author, a graduate of the US Naval Academy, and a veteran of several regular and elite US Navy and Marine Corps units. He has brought his in-depth military experience to bear in his fiction, which includes *Coming Dawn* and *Deep Sleep* in the Devin Gray series; *The Rescue, The Raid, The Mountain,* and *Skystorm* in the Ryan Decker series; the speculative postapocalyptic thrillers *The Jakarta Pandemic* and *The Perseid Collapse*; the Fractured State series; the Black Flagged series; and the Zulu Virus Chronicles. Konkoly lives in central Indiana with his family. For more information, visit www.stevenkonkoly.com.